Michael Jecks gave up a career in the computer industry to concentrate on writing and the study of medieval history, especially that of Devon and Cornwall. He is a regular speaker at library and literary events, was the Chairman of the Crime Writers' Association in 2004, and judges awards for the CWA and other literary groups.

All his novels featuring Sir Baldwin Furnshill and Bailiff Simon Puttock are available from Headline.

Michael lives with his wife, children and dogs in northern Dartmoor.

Acclaim for Michael Jecks's previous mysteries:

'This fascinating portrayal of medieval life and the corruption of the Church will not disappoint. With convincing characters whose treacherous acts perfectly combine with a devilishly masterful plot, Jecks transports readers back to this wicked world with ease' *Good Book Guide*

'A torturous and exciting plot . . . The construction of the story and the sense of period are excellent' *Shots*

'Captivating . . . If you care for a well-researched visit to medieval England, don't pass this series' *Historical Novels Review*

'Michael Jecks has a way of dipping into the past and giving it the immediacy of a present-day newspaper article . . . He writes . . . with such convincing charm that you expect to walk round a corner in Tavistock and meet some of the characters' *Oxford Times*

'Jecks' knowledge of medieval history is impressive and is used here to great effect' *Crime Time*

The Templar, the Queen
and Her Lover

Michael Jecks

headline

First published in 2007
by HEADLINE PUBLISHING GROUP

First published in paperback in 2008
by HEADLINE PUBLISHING GROUP

1

Cataloguing in Publication Data is available from the British Library

ISBN 978 0 7553 3284 7

Typeset in Times by Avon DataSet Ltd,
Bidford-on-Avon, Warwickshire

Printed and bound in Great Britain by Clays Ltd, St Ives plc

Headline's policy is to use papers that are natural, renewable and
recyclable products and made from wood grown in sustainable forests.
The logging and manufacturing processes are expected to conform to the
environmental regulations of the country of origin.

HEADLINE PUBLISHING GROUP
An Hachette Livre UK Company
338 Euston Road
London NW1 3BH

www.headline.co.uk
www.hachettelivre.co.uk

This book is for
the Old Fogies again.

With loads of love to both.

Cast of Characters

Sir Baldwin de Furnshill   Keeper of the King's Peace in Crediton, and recently Member of Parliament, he is known as an astute man and shrewd investigator. Because he was a Knight Templar, he has a hatred of injustice and persecution.

Simon Puttock   Baldwin's friend, Simon was a bailiff at Lydford where he gained a reputation for honesty and fairness.

Edward II   The feckless king of England, Edward has gone down in history as one of our most brutal, sly, and devious kings. His reign was appalling, noted for the disasters, natural and otherwise, which dogged the realm.

Isabella   The daughter of the French king, Philip IV, Isabella was married to King Edward II. Theirs was not a happy marriage.

Sir Hugh le Despenser   King Edward II's lover for many years, Despenser was known for his persecution of his enemies, and his avarice. In an age of brutality he was noted for his greed, his cruelty and the dedicated pursuit of his own interests at the expense of all others.

Roger Mortimer   Once the King of England's most trusted general, Mortimer's feud with Despenser led to his split with King Edward. Arrested resisting the King, Mortimer was imprisoned in the Tower, but made a glorious escape and fled to France.

Lord John Cromwell   When the King decided to send his wife on the fateful embassy to France, he set Lord John the task of guarding her on the dangerous roads. Lord John was given four knights to help him in his task. In addition to Sir Baldwin, there were:

Sir John de Sapy   A household knight of the King, who until recently had been outlawed for supporting Earl Thomas of Lancaster during his rebellion;

Sir Peter de Lymesey   Another household knight who had been outlawed;

Sir Charles of Lancaster   A third knight who originally appeared in *The Templar's Penance*.

Joan of Bar   Queen Isabella clearly needed ladies-in-waiting during her journey, and the King allocated Joan, his niece, as well as:

Alice de Toeni   The Dowager Countess of Warwick.

Alicia   The Queen's most trusted lady-in-

	waiting. Isabella insisted on having her with her during her travels.
Richard Blaket	A man-at-arms and lover of Alicia. The Queen trusts him more than all her other guards.
Peter of Oxford	The Queen's personal chaplain.
Charles IV	King of France, Charles was a wily, shrewd and very competent king. He was also the brother of Queen Isabella.
Thomas d'Anjou	The Pope's representative at the court of King Charles IV.
Pierre d'Artois	The Comte d'Artois who took the title on the death of his father, Sieur Pierre is now a respected adviser to the French king.
Blanche de Burgundy	Originally the King of France's wife when he was only a prince, she was discovered in an adulterous affair and imprisoned at the Château Gaillard in Normandy.
Enguerrand de Foix	The Comte de Foix, this knight rules a large area in the south of France.
Robert de Chatillon	Squire to the Comte de Foix, he is a loyal servant.
Ricard de Bromley	Leader of the small band of Queen's Men, musicians commanded to accompany her on her journey.
Robert d'Artois	Father to Comte Pierre, Comte Robert died while leading a charge against the Fleming rebels in Courtrai in 1302.

Philip de Cambrai	A naker player within Ricard's band.
Janin	The vielle player.
Adam	The trumpeter.
Peter Waferer	A man in the King's service, he yet played with Ricard's band when free.
Jack of Ireland	Irish, he was a bodhran player who inveigled his way into the band.
Père Pierre Clergue	A priest from the south of France where he had been clerk to the Inquisition and the local bishop.
Jean de Pamiers	Originally from the south, Jean has recently been appointed to the garrison of the Château Gaillard.
Arnaud	A royal executioner, Arnaud learned his trade as a local executioner in Pamiers.
Le Vieux	Once a man-at-arms in the service of the King, he is now the leader of the men who make up the garrison of the Château Gaillard.

Northern France, 1325

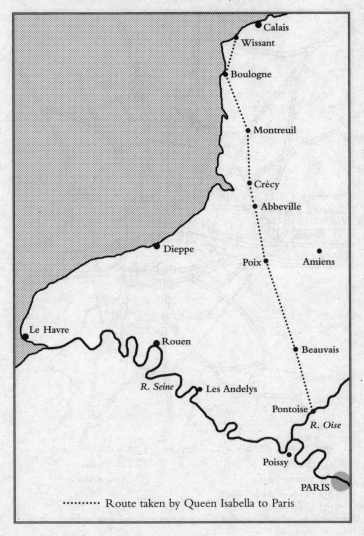

Calais
Wissant
Boulogne
Montreuil
Crécy
Abbeville
Dieppe
Poix
Amiens
Le Havre
Rouen
Beauvais
R. Seine
Les Andelys
Pontoise
R. Oise
Poissy
PARIS

•••••••• Route taken by Queen Isabella to Paris

Paris, 1325

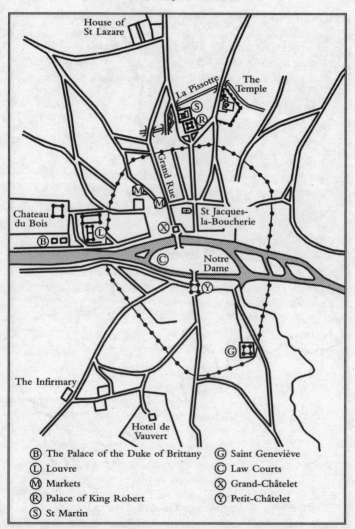

B — The Palace of the Duke of Brittany
L — Louvre
M — Markets
R — Palace of King Robert
S — St Martin
G — Saint Geneviève
C — Law Courts
X — Grand-Châtelet
Y — Petit-Châtelet

Glossary

Alaunt
An ancient type of hunting dog, strong but fast, with a broad, short head. Perhaps originally a form of mastiff, the alaunt was used to bring down or hold prey until the huntsmen could kill it.

Bastide
Provençal word that meant a fortified town.

Bataelge
Basic formation of French knighthood, riding en masse.

Bayle
The French term for a bailiff.

Bidaut
Lightly armed mercenaries from the south of France and northern Spain.

Bodhran
The common Celtic and Irish drum, formed of a circular wooden frame about twenty-four inches in diameter, with a good goatskin stretched over it. Still very popular today, its familiar timbre is recognisable in all forms of Irish music.

Calefactory
A room in which a strong fire burned through the winter months so that chilled monks could warm themselves.

Cithar
Old term for an instrument that was hit with hammers like a zither.

Citole
A four-stringed, plucked instrument, a little like a guitar.

Comptroller
This is an archaic spelling, but one

which has always been in use by the British royal families. Generally, the comptroller was the man who had command of the money for the household he served. William de Bouden was the Queen's trusted clerk up until the time her household was disbanded, and he was reinstalled for the embassy to France.

Escuier   French term for a squire – a man-at-arms who supported a knight, and could, if he displayed the right skills and chivalry, hope to be granted the spurs of a knight.

Fiddle   More of a tenor instrument than a *rebec* (below).

Gittern   Four-stringed instrument, probably for strumming like a guitar.

Kennel   The gutter in the middle of the road, into which all forms of noisome waste might be hurled in the hope that the next rains would remove them.

Nakers   Kettledrums, usually worn about the waist.

Paterae   Shields and other decorative devices of wood set into a ceiling.

Psaltery   Stringed instrument plucked with a quill plectrum.

Rebec   A fiddle with a higher note.

Rosin   Used by fiddlers and hurdy-gurdy players on their strings to increase the friction of the bow on the string. Made from distilling turpentine.

Sumpter horse   Pack horse, general horse used for transport.

Tabor	Small drum, cylindrical in shape.
Vielle	Old form of hurdy-gurdy.

Author's Note

This is a great digression from my usual Dartmoor, English-based stories, and perhaps I should say a few words about what led me to have my friends Simon and Baldwin thrown into the heart of European politics.

As those who have followed the careers of my two characters will already know, I try to base all their adventures in solid historical fact. Thus many of the stories I have written have been based upon actual murders and felonies in Devon in the early 1300s. At the same time I have attempted to capture the essence of the way people lived, and how they were affected by the degenerating national politics over this period.

Making use of people living in 'real time', for want of another phrase, has its own problems. It does mean that one must be cautious that one book doesn't start before the predecessor ended, for example. It is also important that the larger themes of political incidents are treated fairly. Those matters which would not have been brought to the attention of rural folk hundreds of miles away can happily be ignored.

However, in these times, the King made regular use of messengers across his own country and over Europe, who could all travel thirty to thirty-five miles each day. That means that even Devon would only have been a week or so behind events in London. We know that monasteries, cathedrals and other religious foundations had extensive networks of communications connecting them too. If anyone should doubt the ability of medieval man to maintain efficient lines of communication, one need only consider the fact that throughout the Middle Ages it was possible to buy fresh sea fish anywhere in England. Bearing in mind the trouble that would be involved in moving fish from the coast to places in the Midlands, it is clear that people were capable of moving swiftly when necessity demanded. And with them would come news – some of it accurate!

In the year 1325, the most important aspect of politics, internal or international, was the treaty to be signed with the French. There had been continual haggling over the precise rights of the French king compared with the feudal duties of the English king for those lands and provinces which happened to be situated in French territory. The initial disputes had been over Normandy and other parts of the great Angevin empire. By 1325, though, most of these had already been lost by the English, partly because of their own incompetence, partly due to superior French policy-making. Having the greatest and best-equipped force of men and cavalry in Christendom was no doubt something of an advantage at the time. It is astonishing to consider that when the English entered the Hundred Years War a dozen years later, the rest of the world looked in amazement at this upstart little nation trying to sting the massed ranks of French chivalry. Nobody seriously believed that the English could achieve much – and that is as true for the English as for anyone else. The English thought they were participating in some small-scale *chevauchées*, raids in search of booty, in effect.

When they defeated the French host with tactics refined over years of battling with the Scots, it was a shock to the whole of Europe. It shouldn't have been such a surprise, though. The British had a small but experienced army which was used to fighting on foot, just as the men of Morgarten had been, and those at the 'Battle of the Golden Spurs' at

Courtrai. At both battles groups of supposedly ignorant and incompetent peasants had destroyed more powerful French armies.

But in 1325 the conflict, the truce, and the negotiations between the English and the French were crucial to the whole period. Not only because they were to set the stamp on the subsequent suspicion and dislike that existed between English and French in the run-up to the Hundred Years War, which itself polluted relations between the two countries right up until the Franco-Prussian wars of the later 1800s, but because at the time this difficult and protracted parley itself helped Mortimer and Isabella plot their invasion, and gave them a ready source of supporters – the British who had been exiled under the reign of the deplorable Despenser.

So I am afraid poor Baldwin and Simon, the long-suffering companions, have been thrust into the limelight for this story. They have been cast into France for their sins, and now must live perilously amid the great forces at work to start a fresh war.

Some may be surprised by the account of the troubles of the unfortunate Lady Blanche, once princess bride to the man who was to become Charles IV. Sadly the story is all true.

The affair of the silken purses has been covered in another book[1], so I shall not go into detail here. Suffice to say that two royal princesses were shown to be carrying on adulterous affairs with a pair of brothers. The men were killed, rather horribly, and the women locked up in 1314.

Marguerite, the older of the two, was thought to be more responsible, and was thrown into a freezing cell in the Château Gaillard. She survived a short while, but the cold and poor diet put paid to her in a matter of months.

---

[1] *The Death Ship of Dartmouth*

The second was Blanche, wife of Charles. She too was thrown into a dungeon at the château.

It is said that she was made pregnant by her gaoler, and gave birth to a child in 1323. A little while before that, while she was pregnant, her marriage had at last been annulled, and in 1325 (I think – the sources grow a little vague over precise details) she was allowed to move to the convent abbey of Maubisson. Here she survived only one more year, dying perhaps because of the damage done to her constitution over the previous eleven years of incarceration.

So – was her gaoler her enthusiastic lover? Did she welcome the attentions of any man, no matter how lowly? Or was there a plot set in train by the French king or his courtiers to have her proved adulterous so that the Pope would be forced to annul the marriage? Could someone else have had a similar desire to see the marriage annulled?

I do not know the truth. However, it is all too easy to sit in judgement after some seven hundred years and take the 21st-century view. What would it be? Well, first that it was shocking that these two women should have been so appallingly treated for their sexual misdemeanours. Second, that clearly the poor woman in the cell would never have courted the attentions of a mere castle gaoler.

And yet . . .

These people lived in a different era. The two princesses were guilty not merely of betraying their own husbands. That was unforgivable enough. But they had committed a vastly worse crime: they had risked the bloodline of the kings of France. So heinous was their offence that it may have helped kill off the reigning king, Philip IV. Then, because of the women's behaviour, their existing children had to be rejected by their fathers (presuming, of course, that the princes involved *were* the genetic fathers, which was the concern and doubt).

By a sad twist of fate, the princes concerned all proved to be short-lived. By 1328, all had died, and there were no male heirs. The Capetian line had died out. That led to the election of the first of the Valois kings of France, which itself contributed to the Hundred Years War, because the English had a claim to the French throne through Isabella. However, the French refused to consider her and her descendants' claims. It was not surprising. Edward probably thought of himself as a Frenchman, but all the French thought him English. They would not have him.

So the adultery of these women was to have far-reaching consequences for hundreds of thousands in the coming century. Perhaps if they had remained obedient and chaste, European history would have followed a different course. It is an interesting speculation.

Michael Jecks
Northern Dartmoor
April 2007

Prologue

Candlemas
In the eighteenth year of the reign of King Edward II [1]

Alehouse in Southwark

Sir John de Sapy looked up as the door opened, anticipation lightening a face that had been full of trouble.

The last years had been unspeakable. Christ's blood, but a man was hard pushed to survive just now. Even friends of the mightiest in the land could be brought to destruction, the realm was so stretched with treachery and mistrust.

He had been a knight in the King's household until seven years ago, but then, when Lancaster was in the ascendant, he had switched allegiance and joined the Earl. Except the Earl had successfully squandered all his advantages, and ended up being executed by the King his cousin after raising a rebellion.

'The arse,' Sapy muttered.

There were few things more surely calculated to irritate Sir John than a man who promised much and then died leaving him in trouble – and he had been in trouble ever since the damned fool had gone and got himself killed. Sir John had been declared an outlaw, had had all his livings stolen from him by the King's men, and now he was without funds, family

---

[1] Saturday 2 February 1325

or prospects. The only hope he had was that his brother, Sir Robert, who was still in the King's household, might be able to help him to return to favour.

The door opened again, and for the second time he looked up eagerly, but there were two men hooded and cloaked in the doorway, not one, and he turned bitterly back to his wine. Robert wouldn't come. He knew it, really. He'd hoped and prayed that his brother would forgive him his foolishness in trusting that churl's hog, Earl Thomas, but how could he? To forgive John would be to open himself to the accusation of harbouring a traitor. In the years since the battle of Boroughbridge, which saw the final destruction of Earl Thomas's host, hundreds of knights and barons up and down the kingdom had been taken and summarily executed, many of them for minor offences committed on behalf of the Earl. For a man who supported one of the Earl's followers, and aided him in hiding, the punishment would be worse.

No, this was pointless. He was wasting his time. His sodding brother could hang himself. John wouldn't sit here all night like some beggar seeking alms. If his brother wasn't going to help him, he'd find someone who would. There were barons in France who'd welcome the strong arm and ruthlessness Sir John exhibited.

He was setting his hands on the table to push himself up when a hand fell on his shoulder. 'Brother, stay there.'

'Robert?' Sir John was torn between irritation at the lateness of his brother's arrival, and immense relief that he had come at last. It made him feel less alone. 'Who's this?'

'This is someone who's going to assist you, I think,' Sir Robert said. 'Meet Father Pierre Clergue. He would like your help.'

'My help?'

'Yes, *mon sieur*. Your help in seeking a heretic!'

Sunday, Quinquagesima[1]

Château Gaillard, Les Andelys, Normandy

The cell was tiny. Like a coffin. And she was sure that, were she not rescued from this hideous half-life soon, it would become her tomb. A woman of only eight or nine and twenty years, she had already lived long enough. The idea of death was not so dreadful. It would rescue her from this living horror.

Sometimes she dreamed that she had been to visit this fortress before she had fallen from grace; perhaps she had even stayed here once, although not down here in the filth and the cold. No – then she had been installed in a great chamber in a lofty tower that stood high overhead. But if it were true and not some dream that had been sent to torment her, then it was so long ago it might have been a different life. In those days, she dreamed, she had had servants of her own, maids, rich clothing, and an entire household to see to her needs. She had been pampered, beautiful – royal.

As a princess, she had lived in great towers and palaces. There had been wonderful food to eat, jewels to decorate her fingers and throat, carriages drawn by the finest horses. Her clothing was all crimson and velvet lined with fur, shot through with golden threads, and when she retired to her chamber she could fall on to a bed that had been made for her, the sheets smooth and soft, the mattress filled with down, while quilts were settled over her to keep the chill away. All who heard her would submit to her slightest whim. Men desired her; women loved her.

When she fell from grace, Blanche de Burgundy might as well have died.

In many ways she had.

---

[1] Sunday 17 February 1325

The Cardinal's Hat, Lombard Street, London

'Oh, shite!'

Ricard de Bromley ducked as the jug flew past his head and smashed against the lathes behind him. There was a burst of wild laughter from the front room of the tavern, and he glanced at his companions quickly.

'What now?'

Adam Trumpeter was in no doubt. 'We get out of here. There's no point trying to play to them in there. Listen to them!'

Janin, a tall skinny man in his late twenties who wore his long, greasy dark hair in a thin queue tied with a thong, peered round the doorway with his amiable face fixed into a look of nervousness. 'I don't think we'd be welcomed.'

'Welcomed?' Adam was an older man by fifteen years, barrel-chested and with a belly like a sea-going cog's massive rounded prow. Under his hood, he scowled, his leathery features lined and wrinkled like an old alaunt's. 'They're likely to rip our arms off and beat us with the soggy ends.'

Ricard set his jaw and sneaked another look. 'They said they'd pay us twelve pennies each,' he said mournfully, his moustache drooping as though to signal his disconsolation.

At the mention of money, it was Peter the Waferer who pulled the group together, as usual. He was always the one who kept an eye on the finances and mediated between fights. 'I'm not giving up on twelve pennies for any number of rowdies,' he declared. He took up his tabor, settling a small cudgel on his wrist, bound there by a strip of leather. 'If they want to stop me, they can try.'

He marched in, his arrogance settling the noise inside almost as soon as he pushed in with his tabor in one hand, a recorder in the other. A dexterous man, he could play the two simultaneously. With his tabor, which was one of those smaller ones which a man could carry with ease, he made a daunting figure, standing there blocking the doorway. With the unconcern of a man who knew that his master would be greatly displeased were he to be harmed, Peter strode to the farther side of the room and placed his tabor on the floor so that the royal insignia could be clearly read on his breast. Alone of the band, he was a genuine servant to the King.

The others looked at each other for a moment. Ricard shrugged, then picked up his gittern. 'Can't let him get all the money.'

Adam wore a look of resignation on his greying features. 'Don't say I didn't warn you,' he said as he hefted his trumpet.

Last to make his way in was Janin. He tossed his head and sent his long ponytail over his shoulder. Then he squared his narrow shoulders and followed them inside.

Queen's chamber, Thorney Island

Queen Isabella rose from her prayers and nodded to Peter, her chaplain, before walking from the chapel and making her way to her chamber.

The weather was foul today. As she glanced out through the tall lancet windows, she could see the rain slashing down into the turgid waters of the Thames, making the river froth and boil. Certainly not the weather to be going abroad today.

Abroad. *There* was a word imbued with many meanings. To a peasant it could mean any foreign place – a vill some twenty miles away or a different kingdom. To her it could mean walking in the garden, perhaps riding with her hounds, or even travelling to her favourite manors – Eltham or Castle Acre. In truth, she would be happy anywhere just now. If she could only go away, escape this highly decorated prison that was the palace of Westminster.

When she had first come here, she'd been delighted by it after staying in the Tower of London for a while. That was a fortress, constructed to keep the London mob subdued, and had the creature comforts of a stable, as far as she was concerned. This palace at Westminster was different; this was built with comfort in mind.

King Edward I, her husband's father, had constructed the Queen's chambers and decorated them to meet Queen Eleanor's stringent tastes. Even the other rooms were magnificent. She had heard tell of the King's Painted Chamber when she was still living in France, a mere child. All knew of the wonderful paintings that covered the walls of that massive bedchamber.

In truth, the palace here was one of the most marvellous she had ever seen. As daughter of a French king, Isabella could admit to herself that this place was as glorious as any fortress owned by her brother the king of France. And yet now it was repellent to her: it was nothing more than a gilded cage in which she might sing or flutter, but from which she could not break free.

She might die here.

Louvre, Paris

As he walked along the great corridors, Roger Mortimer was reminded constantly of how low he had sunk, simply by looking at the expressions of the men all about him.

There had been times when the idea of coming here would have been so inconceivable that it would have been laughable. Only three or four years ago he would have deemed such a suggestion to be ridiculous. Ridiculous! The word was a poor tool for him. It could not convey the depth of feeling he had now, walking behind these squires, hoping to meet with the King.

He hadn't been here long. When he first fled England, escaping from the Tower under sentence of death for plotting treason, he had made his way to Normandy. There he'd been able to live for a while without being troubled by his new enemy – England's king, Edward II, Mortimer's old friend. Men were sent to seek him in Wales and Ireland, both countries Roger knew well, and as the days dragged into weeks the King and Despenser both grew distraught.

Mortimer's concerns were focused on his children, and his dear Joan. When he escaped, King Edward had immediately set to persecute any of his friends, allies or family who were within reach of his hand. Roger had heard that Joan had been taken from her home and installed in a royal castle in Yorkshire, and all the men of her household had been removed and made destitute. Most of his children had fared still worse – his sons thrown into prison, his daughters incarcerated in secure priories, with less money to live on than a criminal in the Tower.

But there was good fortune. First, he was still alive, and so were they. Then Geoffrey, his third son, had been in France at the time of his escape, and so had avoided the fate of his siblings. He was the sole heir to Joan's mother, who had owned some of the de Lusignan lands, and had very opportunely expired just before Mortimer's escape, so through Geoffrey Roger had access to money while he was in France. Then again, the French could see the advantage in pulling the tail of the English king while they could. Which was good – but Mortimer had no illusions about the longevity of their interest in him. Once the matter of the Guyenne duchy lands was settled, his usefulness would be over, and his life worth little once more.

His heart's desire was revenge upon the King and Despenser, and to see his wife and children released from their incarceration. How he could manage that, though, was the matter which tormented him just now. He had already attempted to assassinate Despenser and the King by the use of magic, but the sorcerer involved had been betrayed, apparently, by his own assistant, and there appeared to be no other means of settling the score. Rack his brains though he might, there seemed nothing to be done.

The guards halted and opened the door, and Roger Mortimer entered the long hall of the Louvre, bowing instantly at the sight of the King.

Like his father, Charles IV was known as 'the Fair' already. It was curious to think that the kings of both France and England should be singularly tall, well formed and handsome, but perhaps it was simply proof of God's approval of them both. At his side was a watchful falconer, while nearby was his most trusted adviser, François de Tours.

'Lord Mortimer. I am grateful that you could come to see me at such short notice.'

'It is an honour to be summoned, my lord. How may I serve you?'

The King had been studying the cold-eyed killer on his gauntleted wrist, but now he passed the creature back to the falconer and pulled off the thick leather glove. 'I am sure I will find a way,' he said drily. 'However, for now, I wish to speak of other matters. You have been most useful to me recently. Your presence has been invaluable in my negotiations with King Edward. However, soon you may become an embarrassment. You will leave Paris.'

'Where would you have me go?'

'You do not question my command?'

'My king, you are master of your realm. If you tell me I must leave your side, I will obey.'

'A shame that more of my men do not show the excellent good manners you hold in such abundance,' the King commented. He beckoned a servant, who hurried over with a jug and goblet. The man bowed low as he held out the poured wine. King Charles took it and sipped. 'Yes. In a little while I think that the Queen my sister will come to negotiate the truce in Guyenne. It would be difficult were you to be here still when that happened.'

Mortimer said nothing. His failed assassination attempt would make his appearance in court rather troublesome. That much was obvious.

'There is another matter, though,' the King said. 'The Queen, I believe, has been generous towards your good lady?'

The simple mention of his Joan was enough to bring a lump to Mortimer's breast. His lovely Joan, thrown into a prison for something that was nothing to do with her. She was innocent, as innocent as his daughters. And they'd all been imprisoned because the King would only listen to the sly insinuations of that son of a whore, Despenser. 'Your sister has been most kind, your highness. She has interceded on my wife's behalf, I know. I only hope that Joan realises how much she should thank her highness. Without the Queen's aid, I do not know what would have become of her.'

'Perhaps she feels a certain guilt for all that she has caused to happen to other wedded couples,' the King said with an edge to his voice.

Chapter One

Lombard Street

Gradually, Ricard de Bromley became aware of his surroundings as a fine drizzle fell on his bearded face. He grunted to himself, and then groaned more loudly as he tried to climb to his feet. 'Not our best one, boys,' he muttered.

Beside him was Janin, his body curled into a ball about his vielle. Will prodded at him with a finger. 'Jan? Are you dead?'

'How's my . . . ?'

'It's fine. Get up.'

There were some memories of the evening before. Ricard could distinctly recall certain moments – the arrival of a massive jug of ale, leathern pots provided for the musicians; a great bull of a man standing and singing a song so filthy, so bawdy, that Ricard had immediately tried to consign it to his memory for use in another venue; the first little fight between some young apprentices in a corner as they tried to force their way into the tavern and were repulsed; the woman who wandered over and sat on his knee, intimating that she would be happy to relieve him of some of his money by relieving him. God, yes! She'd the body of a practised whore, and her

---

[1] Monday 18 February 1325

smile was as lewd as that of any Winchester Goose, but her accent was odd. Not English, certainly. Called . . . called Thomassia, that was it! She sounded more like one of the wenches from Guyenne; her husband . . . Shit, her husband was there. Guy . . .

Feeling jaw, belly, and breast, Ricard was glad to be unable to discern any apparent harm. The man had been angry, but had not started anything. Even so, that was the point at which his memory of the evening became unclear. And now the only damage appeared to be his head. That bastard son of a hog who brewed the ale in the Cardinal's Hat must have mixed something in with his hops.

Belching, he watched Janin roll over and lie still again, a beatific smile spreading over his face. 'Wake me when it's time to get up.'

'It is now, and your vielle is underneath you. You'll break it.'

'Shite! Shite! Shite! The strings'll be buggered!'

Janin's sudden urgent scrabbling to rise to his feet was enough to make Ricard grin to himself again. He gazed about him, trying to remember how he had come to this closed yard, and where his companions could have got to. The sunlight, grey though it was, was enough to make him wince. There was a man who had led them here, wasn't there? Someone from the tavern?

The woman had been foreign. Not happy talking English, from what he could tell. She'd said she was a cook, hadn't she? Ah, yes. That was it: she'd been a cook's maid in a castle, lost her job there when the kitchen staff were all thrown out, and came over here to London. Bloody foreigners coming over and making all the men regret being already married – she had one hell of a body on her, though. He could remember that! Lips that could suck the sap from an oak tree, thighs that'd crush a walnut, bubbies like bladders . . . . Ah! Yes!

He wondered sadly how his evening had ended. She wasn't here now, that was for certain. Suddenly his hand clapped over his purse, but he could breathe easily. It had not been emptied.

'Where are we?' Janin asked plaintively.

'Good question. We *were* at the Cardinal's Hat, which is just off Lombard Street, but this doesn't look like it.'

Janin nodded, gazing about him. 'When did we leave the place?'

'If I could remember that, I might remember when we came here,' Ricard growled.

'There was that woman,' Janin remembered. 'Her husband turned up.'

'Yeah, but he didn't hit me,' Ricard said absently.

'Only because the other fellow knocked him down.'

'Which fellow?'

'The one behind him. He called the man some name or other and felled him.'

'Hmm. Good. I think.' Suddenly he felt nervous. 'Let's get going, eh? We have a job to do.'

But Janin had the tail of an idea now, and he was refusing to let it go. 'That was it, wasn't it? You had that wench on your lap, her old man tried to hit you, and someone else hit *him*, so we drank some more until those bravos appeared.'

'There are times when talking to you gives me a headache,' Ricard said. He pulled some timber aside from a pile at one wall, glancing behind to see whether the others were hiding.

'What was the man's name?'

'Hmm?'

Hearing a rumbling, Ricard peered up towards a low doorway. The door, like the rest of the yard here, was partially hidden by trash that had heaped up before it, and he had to clear some of it, sweeping it away with his boot, before he could peer inside.

There, snuggled together, he saw Philip and Adam. A loud snoring seemed to imply that Peter was behind them. As his eyes grew accustomed, he saw that there was a pair of boots near Adam's head. Carefully cradled in Adam's arms was his trumpet.

It gave him a pleasing idea. He took hold of his horn, and licked his lips, then drew a deep breath before blowing a blast that would have served, so he felt, as the last trump.

Adam's eyes shot wide and he sat up, looking more like a corpse than ever; Philip tried to sit up, but his greater height caused his head to slam into the upper lintel of the low door, and his eyes snapped shut with the pain as he bent down to rest his bruised forehead in his hands. The boots disappeared from view, and Ricard was pleased to hear a complaining whine from the Waferer.

'Morning, boys!' he called with satisfaction.

'The man? What was his name?'

'Which man?'

'The one who felled the woman's old man. Didn't you know him?'

'No. Should I have?'

This was less a yard, more a grubby little alleyway, Ricard considered. Sweet Christ, but his head was bad. His belly felt as if he'd been drinking a tanner's brew of dogshit and piss – faugh, he daren't fart or belch. Both ends felt equally hazardous, damn his soul if they didn't.

There was a little mewling cry, and he frowned. It seemed to come from nearby, and he set his head on one side, peering about him. Bending, he saw a loose slat in the side of another little building – probably a hutch for a dog or a chicken, he thought, but when he peered inside the figure he could just make out was an entirely different animal.

Church of St Martin-le-Grand, London

Père Pierre Clergue was pleased when the man appeared at last. He had been growing a little anxious.

'*Mon sieur*, I am glad to see that you were successful. Please, *viens! Viens ici!*'

He watched the man halt. 'How do you know I was . . .'

'You have the . . . the *appearance* of a man who has done a great thing for the Pope and for his friends. You have done a marvellous thing, *mon sieur*.'

'It feels as if I have done a terrible thing.'

'That is so often the way of things, my friend. Now, no need to tell me more. Let us kneel and pray.'

'You will hear my confession?'

'You can tell me anything you wish, but my lips will be sealed, naturally. And I know what I asked of you, so all is well.'

'Yes. Yes, all is well. Just as you asked.'

House in Lombard Street

A door slammed behind Ricard, and he turned to see a vaguely familiar man striding towards him.

He looked older, perhaps five and forty years, and although Ricard had no idea what his name was, the face was teasingly recognisable. Probably from the night before, he told himself bleakly.

'Good morrow, friends,' the man said.

Returning his greeting, Ricard eyed him narrowly. He was dressed well in expensive cloth, with a fine hat and liripipe on his head. Ricard was certain he'd never seen him before, but the man's carriage was a little alarming. He looked like a fighter. With a rush of tingling anxiety, Ricard wondered whether his memory of the previous night was even more faulty than he had realised; whether this was the man who was married to the wench he'd fondled on his lap the previous night. No, in Christ's name, this sort of fine fellow wouldn't want to listen to them playing in a lowly tavern. He'd have commanded them to go to his house, if anything.

'Master Ricard, I am glad you are well. The weather has not been very clement, I know. Is there anything you need?'

'No. We are well, master.'

Inwardly, he was cursing, slowly and very imaginatively. The man had the graces and accent of a high-born lord. They all had the same interest in fashionable clothing, the disdainful expression, the contemptuous sneer when they spoke to men like him. And of course, the *leetle* bit of the French accent. When together, these arses only ever spoke French, as if it was something special. Well, Ricard and the others spoke English like any God-fearing Englishman should.

Still, it only proved that this man thought himself important. He had that snide, devil-take-you look in his eye that said he knew he could buy hundreds just like Ricard and his band. Well, devil take *you*, Ricard thought to himself, and may he bugger you with a thousand demons!

He had already turned back to the little hutch. Inside he had caught sight of two anxious blue eyes, and he was keen to tempt the boy or girl, whichever it may be, to come out. The walls looked weak enough; easy to pull apart, he was sure.

The man interrupted his thoughts with a pleasant smile. 'Good. Good. Now, before anything else, you will want some food, I am sure.'

'That would be welcome indeed,' Ricard said, suddenly courteous. If this fool was going to be feeding them, Ricard was prepared to be thoroughly polite. Damn silly French accent, though.

'Through here.'

Ricard led the others through a doorway into a small parlour, and from there to a tiny shop front. 'You a glover?'

'Not really. My work with skins is less . . . elevated.'

The man was denigrating his work. He had some marvellous examples of glovemaking on shelves all about the shop. Still, his eyes showed a lack of interest in discussing the matter. They glittered, almost with revulsion, Ricard thought.

There was a basket full of small loaves and some sausages. Peter, Adam and Philip fell on the food like wolves on a deer. Ricard and Janin were a little more hesitant, both feeling that hot, sweaty sensation that sometimes ale could bring the next morning.

'I would be grateful for a little help from you all,' the man said.

Ricard paused in his eating. There was something about the way he said that which made his hackles rise. 'Yes, well, you've been very generous, friend – giving us space out in your yard and breakfast and all – but we have to get back to work.'

'Oh, I know. Yes. You are the Queen's musicians, aren't you?'

Janin and Philip exchanged a look. They had all played for her once. It had been a good day, too. But a long while ago.

Ricard saw their wooden expressions. 'Oh, yes, we're called that, right enough.'

'Well, all I'd like is for you to help me to help her. That's all. Just keep an eye open for me, and when there's something that seems odd, or you feel that she might be in danger, let me know.'

Janin lifted his eyebrows. He was the one Ricard thought the brightest of them all. He'd once had a little training in Latin, and could read some things. Now he looked on the brink of being alarmed. Peter Waferer was unbothered by it all. He scooped another mouthful of sausage into the gaping maw that appeared between moustache and beard and chewed with his mouth open. Janin looked at Ricard and shook his head slightly. Not much, but it was enough to reinforce Ricard's impression. There was something in the man's tone that warned them all.

'Sorry, master, can't do that,' he said with conviction. 'We were found doing that, our lives would be forfeit.'

'But this country can be a very dangerous place. You would be doing her a service.'

'Aha.' Ricard gave a dry laugh without humour. 'Yes. For us it would become a very much more dangerous place if we tried to spy on her. So: *no*.'

'It would be a great shame if you didn't. News of your actions last night might become known.' There was something else in his tone now. It was near to rage, Ricard thought, watching him. No, couldn't be. Ricard hadn't ever seen him before, so why'd he be cross with a bunch of musicians?

He smiled broadly. 'What, doing a little show for the guests at a tavern? When's that been against the law?'

'I am sorry to say that the man whose wife you were pawing is a well-known figure, and even those who dislike him and his master recognise that there is a law against killing a glover just because you like his wife. There's a biblical reference to it, I think.'

Ricard had no rejoinder to that. His world had just fallen apart. The man had stood and walked to a little door, which he drew open. At his feet, just inside the doorway, was the body of a man. Ricard stepped forward on weakened legs and stared. The glover had been beaten to death. A short way from him was the woman from the tavern, her skirts lifted over her bared breasts, her eyes sightless. And blood. Lots of blood.

'You . . .' Ricard's clawing hands reached out to the man, but he was already a couple of paces away, and now his sword was out, and he stared down the length of it at Ricard, the point unwavering at his throat.

'You will help me and serve.'

Château Gaillard

Blanche was forced to pull the blanket about her shoulders again. It was soggy at one corner, icy to the touch, and foul with filth, but after ten years here in the cell she was uncaring. Once, she thought, she might have been revolted by the sight, the feel, the *odour*, of such a piece of material. Any man who tried to offer her a similar thing would have been whipped. So she thought, anyway. It was hard to remember. The noise of the water dripping down the walls, the scurrying of small paws, distracted her.

When first incarcerated, she was convinced that her life would soon end. Her sister-in-law had succumbed in no time. It was less than a year before poor Marguerite was dead. The happy, frivolous young woman with the cheeky smile and love of beauty had died, so Blanche felt, because of the destruction her actions had caused.

Was it true, this? Had there been such a woman as Marguerite? Was she just a figment of Blanche's imagination? A chimera, a false memory that had no basis in fact? Sometimes it seemed to her that there was no life outside these walls. There was nothing beyond the rough-hewn rock. Her life had been lived here for ever. It was easier to believe that, somehow, than to think that once she had been the wealthy, comfortable daughter-in-law of a king.

She clutched at the rosary at her waist. No. It was real. *She* was real. Marguerite had been too. They had both been brought here as punishment for their adultery, their heads shaved, their bodies stripped and clad in these rough garments. Blanche had survived a decade, submitting to all the indignities, while poor Marguerite had quickly yielded to the horror of their new situation. Her end was hastened by the news of her husband's cruelty when she was told that he had disinherited their daughter, Jeanne, in the belief that she had been fathered by another man in the course of Marguerite's adultery. That was what had killed her, as surely as a dagger, Blanche reckoned: the knowledge that her infidelity had ruined the life of her only surviving child.

So many years ago. All that time spent here in this gaol. One third of her life – a *whole third*! Two-thirds had been joyful, spent in exuberant pleasure-seeking, until that disastrous day when she and Marguerite and even little Jeanne, Blanche's sister, had been arrested for their adultery. In a wife of a prince, adultery was treason, for it compromised the royal line.

Her breast convulsed again with sobs. For the life she had lost, for the crime she had knowingly committed. For all that had happened to her – and because she could not forget the shame, the guilt, the pain, the suffering as the small ruby beads rattled through her fingers.

Chapter Two

Queen's chamber, Thorney Island

The request was brought to her by Richard Blaket, one of the guards at her cloister. At least Queen Isabella knew she could trust him. He was always enthusiastic in his service to her. In the past he had been pulled two ways, loyal to his king and to the Queen, but more recently she had seen a subtle change. It was ever since he had fallen into a passionate affair with her lady-in-waiting Alicia.

'His royal highness would be grateful if you could visit him,' Blaket said now.

'You mean my husband?'

He smiled as though she had made a witty remark. 'Of course.' But as he spoke, his eyes flitted over her shoulder to Alicia.

Isabella glanced at the ladies-in-waiting, then rose, settled her skirts, and paced slowly after him.

At least Blaket treated her with respect. Only a couple of days ago, a squire in the great hall had remained sitting when she entered. It had astonished her. The man saw her clearly, but remained on his arse!

There had been a time when no man would have dared such impudence. When she was living in France in the court of her father, Philip IV – God rest his soul! – no man would have thought to be so disrespectful to her. If he had dared, he would have learned swiftly that the royal family was quick to punish such behaviour.

But that was France. Here, she reminded herself, she was the hated symbol of a foreign power. All seemed to look on her as a spy, from what she had seen: daughter of the French royal family at a time when the French had retaken the English provinces in Guyenne. And her husband was not of a mind to protect her.

It all began with the argument over a new *bastide* which her brother sought to establish at Saint-Sardos. No permission had been sought from the English king for the construction of the little fortified town, so the local populace rose against the French officers seeking to protect the builders. There was a sharp altercation, an affray, and afterwards a French sergeant lay dead on the ground. It was just the pretext her brother needed to invade. He sent in his best general, Charles, Comte de Valois, to pacify the territory, and now King Charles occupied England's last assets in France.

The consequences for Isabella were high, because the King acted on the advice of those two reprehensible, dishonourable churls, my Lord Bishop Stapledon and Sir Hugh le Despenser. Her shameful treatment was all at their behest, yes, because Bishop Stapledon wanted her lands and mining rights, while Sir Hugh wanted to curb her authority and her influence on her husband – Sir Hugh's lover.

So her lands and privileges were confiscated by the King, her husband; her children were taken from her; her freedom was curtailed; her seal was removed to prevent her communicating with anyone unless with the King's permission; her household was disbanded and dispersed, with all her French servants arrested. She was a queen in name alone; more truly she was a prisoner, guarded at all times by Sir Hugh le Despenser's wife, like any felon in a gaol. Except a felon could expect a rope to end his confinement. She wondered what Sir Hugh planned to end *her* captivity.

'You wished to see me, my lord?' she demanded as she entered the Painted Chamber.

It was a huge room, eighty feet long and twenty-six wide, with a ceiling that rose some thirty feet overhead, studded with beautifully decorated *paterae*. On the walls were scenes from the Gospels, while the two great windows in the northern wall illuminated the chamber with a dull, gloomy light. The opulence of the gilt and silverwork was enough to take away the breath of many visitors. Today it gleamed in the light of the candles and the fire. The feeble glow from outside did little to brighten it.

King Edward II stood before the fire, his hands clasped behind his back. Isabella ignored the esquire and the two clerks at their table near the first of the windows, and marched to her husband.

He looked older, she thought. The lines had been carved deeper into the flesh at the sides of his mouth, and his cheeks looked sunken. His blue eyes were still bright and shrewd, though, and although his long face was grim, he still possessed the aura of power which had always been his mark. And the undeniable handsomeness.

'You are aware of the situation with your intolerable brother,' he began.

Isabella bridled to hear her brother denigrated in this manner, but before she could draw breath King Edward was continuing, spittle flying from his lips in his rage.

'He has sent me three ultimata. If I wish to retain my lands in France . . .' His voice was strained, as though he was close to choking, but he recovered himself and lifted his chin. 'If I wish to have them returned to me, perhaps I should say, then I will have to submit to his will. I must go to France to pay homage to him for those lands, and hope that he will later deign to let me have them back. It is *intolerable* that he should make such demands upon me, a king!'

'What has this to do with me?' Isabella asked coldly.

'Woman, I need an extension of the truce which presently exists. I cannot submit in a moment to such demands. He must be made to see that. I have to have an ambassador to whom he will listen.'

'Then send one.'

'I shall, madam, I shall,' he said coldly. There was a look of suspicion and doubt in his eye. 'I have chosen you.'

Château Gaillard

Down here deep in the rock beneath the castle's walls, not even a breath of wind could penetrate. The air was always damp, cool and noisome, even in the hottest summer.

No soughing breeze could venture here. There were times she had wished that she could have been incarcerated in a high chamber in a tower. At least there she might have the consolation of a view of fields and woods; the feel, perhaps, of sunlight on her flesh. And the smells! Smells of hay, of flowers, even of the dry, hot winds of summer. There would be consolation in the freezing gales that howled from the north and east. Just to sense the air moving over the hair of her skin would be better than this eternity of cold, moisture-laden stillness. The only smells she ever detected here were those of the sweat and foulness of her gaolers.

They could be kind, though. One had comforted her when she had heard of her husband's attempts to have her marriage to him annulled, the Pope refusing to permit it. When she had been brought here, she had scarcely been eighteen years old. The very idea that she could be thrown into a cell like this had never occurred to her. It was so far from her experience, she had never imagined that she could be forced to live in such a place. And yet, perhaps that was all part of her dream? Maybe there was nothing beyond these walls. She had been born here, perhaps, raised here in this chamber in the rock, and she had invented all the memories of dancing, feasting, loving . . . that was easier than to think that it was as a young woman she had been brought here, and she would die here. And better by far that she should not think of her child. Her child was lost to her now.

She heard the rattle of locks farther along the corridor, a shocking, startling sound that shook her from her reverie. Any disturbance here in the cells was a distraction to be welcomed, no matter what it presaged. Blanche eased herself up to a crouch, her legs and back aching, head tilted to hear the better.

A door was thrown wide, and she heard the tramping of booted feet along the stone floor, the rattle of chains, the low mutter of men's voices. And then her door was opened, and a leering, bearded face peered in at her.

'It's your time, woman. Get up!'

She rose to her feet slowly, her hands flat against the rough stone wall.

The man held out his hand, all four fingers curling back to the palm in the universal sign of beckoning, but she was as nervous and flighty as an unbroken mare.

'My child?' she asked as firmly as she could, but even her own ears told her how her voice quavered, and her hand went to her rosary for comfort. It was made of beads of ruby, a wonderful gift. The last her husband gave her before she squandered his trust . . . his love. It was the only item she had been allowed to keep when she was brought here, for her chaplain insisted that she must be permitted her beads. It was her sole possession.

'You are to be set loose from here, my lady,' the gaoler said, ignoring her. His lip curled into a grin, but there was a sadness in his face. He would miss her.

Holy Mother Mary, but she hated this man. Even more

than her husband, who had not defended her when she was left here to moulder, she hated this man.

But there was one whom she hated more even than him. More than any other person, Blanche detested the bitch who had caused her to be arrested with her sister and sister-in-law, and thrown into this cell. The woman who told the King of her suspicions about the three royal wives and had them followed until their guilt was transparent to all.

That bitch, the she-wolf, Isabella, queen of England.

Queen's chamber, Thorney Island

Back once more in her chamber, the Queen sat at a cushioned seat set into one of the tall lancet windows, and gazed out at the river.

'My lady, was there anything interesting he wanted to speak about with you?' Lady Eleanor asked after some moments.

Queen Isabella was careful to give the appearance of surprise at hearing the woman's question. 'You mean you were not already made aware of the suggestion? I am shocked, Lady Eleanor.'

It was difficult to restrain herself after so many months of living with this foul woman. At first she had tried to befriend Eleanor, the King's niece as she was, and included her in many festivities and parties. For a long time, she had never berated her for laziness or foolishness, although God alone knew how many occasions there had been which justified sharp rebukes. Eleanor had always been a welcomed guest, no matter what the hour, no matter how great the annoyance of the interruption. All that changed when she married that arch-deceiver Sir Hugh le Despenser.

When he first came into their lives, it was as a paid informer for the barons. They kept him in the King's household in order to try to curb any independent action on his part, which they all wanted after the years of Piers

Gaveston. After the latter's death at the hands of a small party of barons, Despenser had gradually become more and more essential to the King, and the King began to trust no one but him. All those who had been his most loyal servants had been forced from him. Even his greatest general, Roger Mortimer of Wigmore, had been driven into near rebellion, and had helped the Lords Marcher with their sudden attack on the Despenser territories which Sir Hugh had taken from others by force or by deception. There was nothing he coveted which he would not grab.

Poor Mortimer. He had been ousted from the King's side, then kept in the Tower until he broke out in such a spectacular fashion, riding for the coast with two allies and escaping to France. All because Despenser looked upon him as a mortal foe – Roger Mortimer's grandfather had killed Despenser's on the field at the battle of Evesham fifty or more years before.

So, just as the King had found Despenser installed within his household, so too did Queen Isabella have the Despenser's own spy in *her* household. All her maids had been replaced by Lady Eleanor's friends and accomplices. Any new lady-in-waiting had to be approved by her. And meanwhile, all the Queen's letters were perused by her before being sealed by the Queen's own seal, which Eleanor held about her neck at all times.

'Obviously the King would not discuss private matters with me,' Lady Eleanor said coolly.

The Queen's response was more tart. 'I am surprised. I had thought that your husband would have kept you informed about their business, my lady. Especially when it is so important for the realm.'

Lady Eleanor went white on hearing that. She pursed her lips angrily, but said nothing more, merely gathered up her skirts and flounced from the room.

'You defeated her there. She must grow tired of constantly

being bested by you!' Isabella's maid Alicia chuckled, rising from her stool and walking to her mistress when she saw the finger beckon. 'My lady?'

'Prepare yourself, Alicia. We are to go to France to my brother's court. I am to be the King's ambassador.'

Alicia gasped and clapped her hands, and then was still, her eyes thoughtful.

The Queen nodded. 'Yes. The King still refuses to go to pay homage to my brother. But he is king of France – it is unthinkable that my husband should evade his feudal duty. He must go at some point.'

'Yet Lady Eleanor's husband . . .'

'Hugh le Despenser will oppose my husband's journey with all the skill and persuasion he can muster, and that devil has much of both. He is as crafty and mendacious as any politician. But that may give me an opportunity he has not considered,' she added pensively.

'He means to do you harm,' Alicia said sharply.

'Harm me? What harm could he do to me in my brother's country? I shall be safer there than here in my adopted home.'

'If an unscrupulous enemy wished to harm you, he would find his task that much easier in France, my lady,' Alicia insisted.

The Queen was already looking once more out through the window at the Thames and did not answer. There was no need to. She knew it already.

Queen's cloister, Thorney Island

Alicia was cautious about how she made her way from the Queen's chamber to the door that led from the cloister to the Queen's private little garden. Crossing the sweet-smelling camomile lawn, she reached the gate at the far side. There she knocked quietly twice, then once more.

Immediately the gate opened and Blaket peered in, his face

wreathed in smiles. 'Alicia, my love, my heart, my life. Come here!'

'My!' she gasped when he had embraced her for long enough. She set her fists against his breast to push him away. 'If this is how you respond to a scant half-day's separation, I'll have to be careful not to leave you for a day.'

'You mustn't leave me for so long. That would be torture,' he said, but in his eyes there was a darkness and no flippancy.

'Not just for you.'

'Ah, you don't love me as much as I love you,' he said.

She cocked an eyebrow and set her head to one side. 'So we are into competitive lovemaking now? My lord, I love you more than you love me.'

'No, I love you most.'

'Possibly true, then. I will not get into an argument,' she said shortly, drawing away and smoothing her skirts.

'What? Is there something the matter?'

'It is said that our lady may be travelling soon.'

'And you will be going with her?'

'Don't look like that, my love,' she said softly. 'We would be back as soon as possible.'

'Would she take a guard with her?'

Alicia smiled. 'If she has any say, she will know which guard she can trust, won't she?'

It was a relief to hear her say that with that sweet smile on her pale face. He pulled her to him again and held her tight, saying nothing. He had proved himself to the Queen in the last weeks. No service had been too much for him. And now all he wanted was to remain with her when she went.

With Alicia, too, of course. She was his lovely, lively little bird. A wonderful smile, a warm, generous spirit, those bright blue-grey eyes that lit up his soul – life would be hell without her. 'Thanks to God for that. I can't let you go to France alone.'

'I scarcely think I'd be alone. Not with the Queen, her clerk, her chaplain, her honour-guard of knights and men-at-arms,' she declared archly.

'No. Of course not.'

She frowned quickly. 'How did you know it was France?'

'Eh?'

'I told you we would be travelling, but you just said "France". How did you know?'

'Do you really think there are any secrets here in the King's palace?' he asked and chuckled.

She smiled in return, giving him a hug. It was that, then, which had made his eyes anxious and black. Little surprise. Everyone knew how potentially dangerous a journey to France could be, especially now with war hanging over both nations like a cloud of brimstone.

Chapter Three

Lombard Street, City of London

'Interesting,' Janin said. 'So now we're suddenly the Queen's Men, are we? That's a snappy name for a band like us. Except we've nothing to do with her just now.'

'It's hardly the way I'd have wanted to have things go,' Adam said. He turned to the scowling Ricard. 'Why the hell did you have to start pawing that woman in the first place?'

'Shut up talking like that! You're talking daft,' Philip said. 'If she'd gone to your lap and started getting you all sweaty, you'd have done the same thing.'

'It's not the point, though, is it?' Adam demanded. He stood square to Ricard, hands on hips.

Ricard looked up from the small figure before him as though noticing him for the first time. 'No. It's not. You're right. The point is, some murderous bastard's got his fist on my jacket and he won't be likely to let go until he has all he wants.'

'We're not even anything to do with the Queen, though, Ric. What the hell are you going to do?' Peter Waferer asked plaintively.

Ricard ignored him. 'Who are you?' he asked of the boy.

'Charlie Chatty.'

'Charlie Chatty, eh? A good name,' Ricard said.

He was at a loss as to what to do with the child. If he was right, this little lad was the son of the woman who'd been murdered last night. The woman who'd died, apparently, just so that the flash git there could blackmail him and the boys into spying on the Queen. The child looked only about three years old, if that. He could walk, talk a fair bit, and judging by his bright blue eyes and sandyish hair he was healthy enough. Thanks to Christ they hadn't taken him out before the man had left the house. He had insisted on speaking to Ricard, alone, and when he had gone Ricard had made his way to the hutch. The mite had screamed at first when he pulled the side away, and shrank back at the wall as though expecting to be killed, but after being given some bread and a sweet cake he had come along with Ricard happily enough. Every so often his eyes clouded and he looked about him anxiously, but then he would glance up into Ricard's face and, God help Ricard, he appeared comforted by him. So now he had this additional little parcel of work clinging to his belt. The thought of the lad's mother's body in that foul chamber was enough to make him want to spew, so he was determined not to desert the boy, but that left him with the question of what to do with him.

'Did you hear me?' Peter demanded.

'Yes, all right? Look, you're a King's Waferer – don't you have some access to the palace? To the Queen? Could you . . .'

'Not a chance. I'd do anything to help you all, but I can't bugger about. I've got a wife, kids to look after. I can't take a gamble on my job.'

'No more he can,' Philip said heavily.

'How about one more kid?'

'Do me a favour, Ric! Look at the brat! What would my wife say, eh? She'd ask where the hell I'd got him, then kick my arse from Eastchep to West for keeping a slut on the side and bringing my bastard home with me!'

Janin watched and listened to their gloomy conversation. Their mood was grim at best. The sight of the two bodies, one ravished, both stabbed and beaten to bloody death, was enough to make any man's stomach turn. Worse to find the child there too. Of course, more to the fore of their collective minds was the fact that were they to fail in the command given to them, they would end up in a similar manner to the lad's parents: slain and thrown to the dogs.

Their host had smiled at them coldly as they gathered about him. Ricard in particular was eager to break his head. He had been attracted to that woman, and to see her destroyed so utterly was shocking. They hadn't just slashed at her, they'd beaten her about the face until she was almost unrecognisable. Janin, the most reflective of the band, was thinking carefully as they surrounded the fellow, his sword still at Ricard's neck. 'Ric – if you were going to blackmail a little mob like ours to do your will, would you go into a room with them and let them into your secret there, all alone?'

Ricard had been breathing hard and fast, his mouth closed. Gradually his face lost its bellicose flush, and he became more rational. 'Where are his men?' he had demanded.

Their host had answered. 'Outside. There are two over the road there. I can see them from here through the window. Look for yourself. If you try to harm me, they will see. If they sound the alarm, the hue and cry will be here in moments. And people will find some musicians who were very loud and rowdy last night, and tried to rape a respectable woman, a Madam Thomassia, whose husband Guy was lately a man-at-arms in France. And anyone who breaks in here to rescue me will find you here with that same man and woman, both dead. They are not fools. Two dead when you had shown such interest in them last night,' he said contemptuously. 'Oh, and they'll find me: a nobleman, who will denounce you. For those murders. Do you think you could escape the rope? Or perhaps they would think up a better way to kill you. The London mob can be most inventive.'

Ricard had glanced at Peter, who was standing at the open window staring out. He had looked back at Ricard and nodded.

The man's plan was straightforward enough. He would lose the bodies if the musicians did what they were told, but if they failed the law would soon be after them. They would never know peace again. They would become outlaw.

It was Adam who had asked the obvious question. 'What makes you think you could persuade people that we did these murders in a day, let alone a month or more?' he scoffed.

The man smiled with a sly confidence. 'The glovemaker in there was a loyal servant of Sir Hugh le Despenser. He will be sure of your guilt, and your fate will be just as certain.'

'You think you can tell him that? He'd as likely run you through. Sir Hugh le Despenser trusts no one,' Ricard scoffed.

'He doesn't trust me, no. I am no friend of his. Still, he can't hurt me.'

That had been definite enough for Ricard. Everyone in the realm knew of Sir Hugh, the avaricious friend of the King. He was ruthless and determined. Any man who harmed him or his friends must look to his back. There was little safety when Sir Hugh became your enemy. And this fellow, whoever he was, had enough poise and assurance for ten. He was not joking. Just looking at him, you knew he was telling the truth. He knew Despenser. And he had men. This was no footpad.

Now, sitting here and reflecting on that appalling meeting, it was Ricard himself who asked the question that was troubling Janin. 'If he killed the man and his wife, then he's not a friend to Despenser, is he? He said as much. A loyal Despenser man wouldn't kill another Despenser supporter, would he?'

'You think so?' Peter Waferer said, his head low. 'Despenser would kill his mother if he thought it'd win him a new manor. His men are the same. They think nothing of killing like this. No, you may be sure that he's a man of Despenser, and that we're all in danger now. Us, and my family. God! My wife! My children! How could this have happened?'

'How can this be so, though? If he was really known to Despenser,' Ricard said, 'wouldn't he have been at court? Surely you'd have seen him, Peter?'

'Hah! Do you know how many men come through the palace gates every day? It's a small city of its own, and I'm only a waferer, when all is said and done. I may wear the King's tabard, but I'm a kitchen knave, and when I'm working I don't see the faces of all the King's guests. A kitchen knave is hardly best placed to study them.'

'Well, keep your eyes open in case you do see him up there, in God's name!' Janin said, still very rattled. 'We need to know who he is.'

'I'll see what I can learn,' Peter said.

'What can *we* do?' Janin demanded. He looked to the leader of their group, then down at the lad standing in front of Ricard. He had taken up a little ball, and was rolling it experimentally over the floor, frowning intently.

Ricard sighed and shook his head. 'First, I suppose, we have to see whether we can wheedle our way into the Queen's good books. Any ideas?'

Château Gaillard

It was much later when Jean stopped dead on the steps from the curtain wall, appalled by the sound of anguish from the tower.

The scream was unsettling, but here in the château it was all too common to hear the demented shrieks of the imprisoned or condemned. The sound travelled widely about the great tower, shivering on the breeze, the only part of the prisoners that could escape the five-metre thick walls.

There was something about this cry, though, that gave him pause. He had been strolling about the upper curtain wall, keeping an eye out every so often, but scarcely worrying too much. The land about here was pacified after a hundred years of French rule. No, his duty was to keep his eyes and ears open to the risk of an escape from within the prison.

Now, even as he looked down into the main court area about the great keep, he could see the small party making their way from the stairs that led to the cells. There was a pair of guards in front, leading a tattered and thoroughly dishevelled woman. That she was one of the prisoners was known to him. He had seen her plenty of times before. With her shaved head and sackcloth tunic, she was the one whom the guards discussed with lowered voices. Someone had told him that she was a very important prisoner, but no one had elaborated on that snippet. For his part, he hardly cared who she might be. As far as he was concerned, if someone was here, it was because they had committed an offence which merited the punishment.

There was a shriek, and Jean watched, dumbfounded, as the woman tried to drag herself free of her guards, but they gripped the manacles at her wrists and yanked her back towards the gates. In the poor light down there, Jean was unclear what happened, but it appeared that she was trying to go towards the chapel. Not that she could hope to succeed. The two guards were soon hurrying from the place, the woman dragging her feet between them, turning to stare behind her, wailing pitifully. It quite ruined any remaining vestiges of calmness which Jean had enjoyed.

After the gate had been secured once more, the timbers dully thudding into their sockets in the frame, Jean moved away from the wall. It had been an unpleasant sight, that poor woman being dragged from this place of misery and incarceration. Even now he could hear someone else weeping in despair. No doubt another prisoner was mourning the loss of his freedom. As he descended the wall ladder, he was glad to leave the noise behind. And then, as he entered the outer court, he stopped.

'Sweet Mother of God,' he murmured.

Before him, sprawled at the base of the wall near the chapel, Arnaud, the executioner and torturer, was sobbing uncontrollably.

Queen's chapel, Thorney Island

Peter the Chaplain was happy that night as he polished the cross and then bent to sweep the floor.

Brought here by John Drokensford, the bishop of Bath and Wells, Peter had been given the duty of chaplain to the Queen as a means of atoning for his crimes, but now he had the feeling that his services would shortly become unnecessary. Bishop John had intimated that soon his time here would be done, and perhaps a small church could be found for him not too far from Oxford, the place of his birth. That was enough of a reward for him. He would go there, grow vegetables, keep a dog, and honour and praise God every day.

He finished his cleaning and made his way to his small chamber, where he took up a lump of cheese and slice of bread. He was chewing hungrily when a man arrived from the Queen.

'You are wanted, Chaplain.'

He swallowed and eyed the man with a passing coolness. 'I'm eating. Nothing's that urgent.'

Nor was it. He had learned that if little else in the years since he'd killed his woman's murderer.

He had run away from his church with the wife of one of his parishioners, hoping that they would be able to hide themselves somewhere – perhaps even make their way to France and find a rural refuge there. And one morning Peter woke beside his naked woman to see her husband above them with a great sword. It swept down, and she died, but Peter wrestled the weapon from him and stabbed him again and again, the blood flying in a fine spray at first, then in filthy gobbets.

Over the years he had grown to understand the depth of his own offence. Her death, her husband's, both were on his hands. They were his responsibility. And fortunately Bishop John had persuaded him that he could find peace and salvation: first by protecting another innocent woman from her husband. That was why he was here at Thorney Island – he was trying to help Bishop John look after the Queen's interests.

'It is most urgent, she said,' the messenger insisted. He looked near to tears.

In the end, the chaplain took pity on him and set his bread aside for later. Walking swiftly, he went with the man to the Queen's rooms.

Later, he returned to his own chamber and stood a moment looking all about him with an air of sadness. He felt like a traveller who was about to launch himself on a desperately dangerous journey; one from which he might never return.

He looked finally at the lump of bread still sitting on the barrel. A corner had been taken by some rodent while he had been out. Rats were everywhere, even here in the King's palace. He shrugged. After all he had just heard, he had lost his appetite anyway.

Instead of sitting and eating, he went to the long chest in the far corner of the room. Here, under his vestments, he found his sword. It was the one which he had taken from the husband to kill him. The sword he had defiled with its owner's blood.

Now he drew it and hefted it in his hands thoughtfully. Soon he might be forced to use it again.

Château Gaillard

Later, when he stopped for a cup of hot wine at the brazier in the corner tower, Jean asked le Vieux about Arnaud and that scene after the woman's departure. Le Vieux was the oldest warrior there, and easily the most experienced, which was how he had lost his left arm and his right eye. The empty socket appeared to gleam as he gazed up at Jean. 'Him? Arnaud of the glowing tongs? Forget that bordello's whelp.'

'But he was so sad to see the woman leave.'

'I would be too. There are few tarts in Les Andelys for a man like him. The torturer? Even the sluts would turn their noses up at the man who could later stamp them with the *fleur-de-lys* for doing what he wanted.'

'He was rutting that bitch?'

'Hah! You shouldn't speak of the lady like that. Not where others might hear you.'

'She was just a rich woman, wasn't she?'

'Not "just a rich woman", no. She would have been our queen, lad, and don't forget it.'

'Mother Mary's . . . And Arnaud loved her?'

The old man shrugged emphatically. 'When a man has sired a pup on a bitch, he will feel something for her, even if it's not exactly love.'

'He fathered a child on her?' Jean said, aghast.

'Aye. Poor thing died two weeks later, but it made him mad about the woman. Still is, I expect,' he added thoughtfully.

'Is that why she pulled towards the chapel?'

Le Vieux shrugged expansively. 'Perhaps. Maybe she wanted to pray for a good journey.'

'The baby wasn't buried there?'

'Buried? No, it was left out for the wild animals, I think. It was illegitimate – no priest would give it the last rites or bury it in consecrated ground.'

Chapter Four

The Temple, London

Sir John de Sapy entered the great gate that gave on to the broad court.

This was his first time here in the London Temple. Once it had been the headquarters of the most powerful and wealthy religious order in the country, but since the destruction of the Temple it had lain empty, confiscated by the King. Now the Pope had demanded that all such property should be passed on to the Hospitallers, but this area had been retained by the King – until recently.

Sir Hugh le Despenser had taken it instead.

Sir John saw the men at the doorways, and tried to control the sensation of nervous prickling at his back at the thought of all those in here who would be happy to draw steel and push it into him, were they told that he was the enemy of their master. He willed his legs to carry on none the less. He was a knight, and no one would scare him off.

There was a door in front of him, and a man opened it for him. He held Sir John's gaze as the knight approached, but Sir John was starting to become irritated by the attitude of all the watchers about the yard. He stopped, lowered his head and stared truculently at the man. Gradually the other fellow began to look uncomfortable, and finally he looked away.

Satisfied, Sir John continued. As he drew level with the man, he was ready with his hand on his dagger's hilt. If the other so much as twitched a finger, he was ready to draw his blade and kill the bastard . . . but the man gave him no cause. He entered, and the door closed behind him.

'Sir John. I am glad you could come.'

It was a small hall, with a pleasing tiled floor. There was a chimney with a fire roaring in the hearth, and by its light Sir John saw a cold-eyed man sitting on a stool. It was Sir Hugh le Despenser.

'Sir Hugh,' he said, but his throat had closed up, and the only noise that came out sounded as if he was being slowly strangled.

It was enough to bring a cynical grin to the Despenser's face. He was a man committed to his own profit and pleasure, and he ruled through a mixture of utter brutality and largesse. Those who were his friends waxed in the bright glow of his approval. Those who were not his friends waned. He liked to see men afraid. It showed that they respected his position.

'You have been of service to me, Sir John.'

'I am glad.'

'Until lately you were outlawed. That will cease immediately.'

'You can persuade the King to pardon me?'

Despenser stood and walked to a narrow table at a wall. He took up a scroll and tossed it over to him. Sir John opened it and looked at it helplessly.

'It is your pardon,' Despenser said flatly. 'And to ensure that your return to the King's household is fully appreciated, I have some legal documents you can witness for me.'

'I don't know how to thank you,' Sir John stammered.

'We shall think of a way,' Sir Hugh said. He eyed Sir John thoughtfully for a moment. 'Perhaps you could join an embassy for me. Your help was appreciated by Père Pierre. Perhaps you could go and see him. He tells me that the church of Sainte Katerine in Paris has the most wonderful Mass to celebrate Easter. Perhaps you should go and enjoy it.'

Ash Wednesday [1]

Furnshill, Devon

Sir Baldwin de Furnshill, Keeper of the King's Peace in Devon, was startled awake at the shrill scream, and was already on his feet, his hand reaching for his sword, before he realised what had woken him.

In the corner of the room, swathed in warm blankets and a cloak, sat his wife, who gazed at him with exasperation. 'Baldwin!'

'Ah – I am sorry, my love,' he declared, dropping the sword's blade back into its scabbard. Pulling a thick blanket from the bed, he threw it over his shoulders and padded across the floor to her side, kneeling with an elbow at her thigh.

'Good day, Baldwin,' he said softly to the small body in his wife's arms.

Baldwin, his son, stared back at him short-sightedly, his wizened little face comically ancient for his three and a half months.

'He still finds it hard?'

'We both do,' Jeanne responded, exhausted.

Baldwin put his hand on her shoulder. He was anxious for her. This was their second child. Richalda had been somewhat troublesome occasionally, but both had assumed that this one would be easy. They knew how to bring up a baby; they had done so once. The second time would be perfectly straightforward.

But little Baldwin was not to be so accommodating as Richalda. Where she had cooed gently when she woke, Baldwin screamed; when Richalda was hungry, she had sucked the pap with urgent enthusiasm, needing no assistance

---

[1] Wednesday 20 February 1325

– little Baldwin spent one month drinking from one breast and weeping when the other was presented, and the following month drinking from the other and ignoring the first. And he was awake at regular intervals through the night, while sleeping happily through the day. Although his father would never have confessed it to his wife, he would rather be left in charge of a wild bear without stick or steel to protect himself than be left alone for half a morning with this little boy. Love him he certainly did, but he also loathed and detested the child on occasion. The thought of being solely responsible for him filled him with dread.

'Did he in the end?' Baldwin asked, stifling a yawn.

'Yes. As soon as you jumped from your bed like a man with a rat on his backside, the poor little chit burped.'

Baldwin eyed his son sombrely. Every meal he took led to screaming, or so it seemed most of the time. It was simple enough to cure him – a series of gentle pats on the little devil's back always did the trick – but the immediate effect was shocking in the extreme. For one with such a small frame, the monster could generate a huge amount of noise.

Now, though, having woken both parents and, from the sounds behind the house, the hunting pack too, little Baldwin appeared to think that he had achieved all that could be expected of a fellow, and was breathing gently, eyes closed. Jeanne rose and carried the precious bundle to the little cot beside the bed, carefully installing him before climbing into their bed again. She patted the blanket beside her, and he returned to it, putting an arm about her.

Yes. Little Baldwin was taking his toll on her. Jeanne's hair was thinner, and her face was pale and drawn, like one suffering from a long starvation. He had seen people with that look – the women and children at Acre as the siege set in. And then, when the plagues took hold, they too gave women the same bright eyes and anxious, strained appearance. Baldwin was fearful that this son, this cause for celebration, could become a disaster for him. For losing his Jeanne would be a disaster, a catastrophe from which it would be very difficult for him to recover. He dreaded the very thought.

'Careful, husband. You will crush me!' Jeanne whispered.

He kissed her gently on her forehead, but did not let her go. Instead he sat still, arm around her shoulder, until he heard her breath grow more regular, and then remained there, watching the sun light the cracks in the timbers of his shutters.

The messenger in the King's tunic arrived not long after they had breakfasted.

Michael's Cross tavern, Westchep, London

After the service that marked the beginning of Lent, they gathered again to discuss their predicament. Only a fool would have been keen to meet again, Philip thought to himself, but as he sat waiting the others gradually drifted in.

This was a good little alehouse. It was little more than a low undercroft running alongside the road, with a wide window giving out on to the people hurrying past. Once, so Philip had heard, it had been a large building, but then about fifty years ago the church next door, St Mary-le-Bow, had lost her steeple, and it had crashed through this neighbouring property. Well, the place had to be rebuilt after that, so it was one of the newer, brighter buildings in the road.

Philip had taken a seat on the bench at the window, and he welcomed Janin, Ricard with the boy, and then Adam. The tavern had a young maid at the bar, and she smiled to see the boy. Soon Ricard had deposited him with her and joined the others.

'Not managed to lose him yet?' Adam asked.

Ricard was quiet awhile. He had an appalling sense of responsibility for the boy. Somehow he felt guilty that the lad had lost his parents. It wasn't his fault that some mangy arsehole son of a feral tom cat had killed the glover and his wife to get at Ricard . . . and yet somehow the blue eyes staring at him made him feel guilty. He held his tongue rather than try to explain.

There was no sign of Peter.

'He won't come if he's a brain,' was Janin's view. 'He has two daughters to think of.'

'Aye. Not like you, eh, old man?' Adam teased Ricard.

They all smiled at that. It was one of the jokes they were wont to hurl back and forth in their casual banter on normal days. Ricard was known to be the most prolific of them all, and had fathered seven children all told, five of them still living. But today was not a normal day, and the smiles soon dried.

'Yes, well, some of us have the strength to achieve greatness. There's nothing showy about me.'

'That's true,' Adam said, speaking into his ale.

Ricard scowled. 'Just size ain't all, is what I meant. You have to know what to do with it too, and I have plenty of skill, you see.'

'Yeah. You showed that with the wench on Sunday night,' Philip said quietly.

'Shite, you always have to bring things down to your level.'

'Yes. Well,' Janin said quickly, but not fast enough.

Philip looked up steadily. 'My level may be low, but so was killing her and her old man.'

There was a sudden silence. Then Ricard flushed angrily. 'You mean you think I did that to them?'

'Who else could have? I've been thinking about it, and that fine fellow wasn't there in the tavern, was he? But the two had been dead a while. That smell . . . they were so cold. They hadn't just died that moment.'

Janin was staring at him with a frown on his face. 'You mean to say you reckon Ric murdered them both? On Sunday night when we were that pissed we could hardly walk? Don't talk wet!'

'It couldn't have been Ricard,' Adam agreed dully. 'Look at him! When he's drunk, he sits down and giggles to himself. He never attacks people or hurts them.'

'And I didn't on Sunday night,' Ricard said.

'Not even if you were so drunk you can't remember what you did?' Philip said nastily.

'Look, if I was that drunk, I'd not have thought to wash myself afterwards. Whoever did that to them must have ended up looking like a butcher,' Ricard said sensibly. 'There's no blood on my clothes, Philip. It must have been him, whoever he was.'

'So what'll we do?' Janin said.

'I've been reckoning. I think that there're places where people would pay to hear good music and singing. We could try somewhere a little further from here. I don't know – York, or Lincoln . . .'

'*York!*' Adam burst out with horror. 'You ever spoken to a man from there? They all talk funny! Can't speak real English, and you try to make them understand what you're saying, and they all go dumb, like you're speaking Flemish or something. York!'

'Well, we can't just walk up to the Queen and say, "Look, your Maj, we're a bit hard up for money just now, and by the way, you look like you could do with a decent bit of music to cheer you up, so how about it?" can we? Talk sense!'

'I think you're mad if you reckon that wandering that far away is going to do us any good. No, I vote we stay here in London. It's a huge city – we could easily lose ourselves in it, and no one need find us again.'

'You think I'm mad? Who do you think that bastard was serving in that room when he slaughtered the man and his wife? He said he was no servant of Despenser, but if he wasn't, who is his master? And if Despenser gets to think we're involved in the death of two of his friends, do you seriously think that there's anywhere in this city which is safe for us? If you reckon there's anywhere secure from him and his bloody servants, you're more of a cretin than I thought. If you want to ignore what he wants and stay here, nice and close to his dagger, then you do that. Me, I'm going to see if I can keep my blood in my veins just a little longer.'

'If we just keep our heads down a while . . .'

'Despenser can wield a sword low enough to catch your neck no matter how much you duck or crawl! Don't be stupid! That fellow yesterday found us easily enough, didn't he? How well do you think we could hide in the city? You prepared to throw away your instruments? I know I'm not losing my gittern for anyone! But if you keep hold of your things, you'll be spotted as a musician immediately. How long'll you survive then?'

Janin asked, 'What did he tell you to do?'

'He told me to keep in touch with him. We're to listen out for any snippets that could put the Queen in a bad light, and to tell him.'

'How, though? Where was he going to be?'

'He said there'd be someone who'd come to see us. He'd have a sign to show he was genuine – a picture of a peacock. He'd show us when he needed our help.'

Philip blinked slowly. 'He'd have a picture of a peacock? What, a tapestry? Something on parchment?'

'He didn't say,' Ricard said coldly. 'I didn't suggest it to him, he suggested it to me, all right?'

'Well, I still think we should stay put. What's he going to do to us here? There are too many people around for him to threaten us in the city,' Adam declared.

'Keep thinking like that and soon you won't be thinking at all,' Philip grunted.

'Philip's right. Despenser's enemies, and those he reckons aren't helpful enough, tend to end up dead,' Ricard said. 'So that's what we have to do. Spy on the Queen, or run for it. And we can't spy on her because we aren't really her players. A little ballocks, and suddenly we're deep in the shit. So, if one of you has got a better plan, I'm listening. Otherwise we run for it.'

'I'd think that just asking might be enough.'

They all spun about on hearing Peter's voice, Janin playing a short tune to celebrate his arrival.

'What are you doing here, you silly bastard?' Ricard demanded when Peter had sat down.

'I can't just leave you all in the lurch, can I? What would you lot get up to without me helping you?'

'Bloody sight less dangerous shite,' Adam muttered into his ale once more. 'Sorry, sorry, but I can't help thinking that.'

They ignored him. It was Adam's most irritating trait, this verbal apology that was never seriously meant.

'I asked. I got.'

Ricard was shaking his head in confusion. 'What do you mean? You asked what?'

'I took your advice. I asked whether we could get a billet with the Queen. She's got no household now. Did you know that? She's lost all her servants, all her ladies, everything. So when I offered our services, they said yes. Apparently they all remember us from our last evening there.'

Ricard scowled, Janin looked away pensively, and Adam gazed into his ale. Peter was left looking from one to the other of them with a speculative suspicion. 'All right, so who did it? Ric, did you put your hand up a fine lady's skirt? Adam? Did you puke in the hallway? Janin, were you caught making poetry with a wench in there? Come on, what happened?'

'Don't you remember?' Ricard asked.

'No.'

'You don't remember drumming away happily and leering at the little strawberry blonde in the front? The one with the ever-so-tight bodice and the arse you said would be like an archer's target? The one with lips you said could suck a nail from the church door? The one with the . . .'

'Christ in chains!' Peter had the grace to colour. 'Are you sure? Me? When was that? I don't remember it at . . . But there was no trouble about it.'

Ricard and Janin exchanged a look, then Ricard gave a frown of agreement and shook his head emphatically. 'No, no. There was no trouble at all.'

'So I was bad, then?'

'I think she thought so,' Janin said. 'Still, she said you weren't all that bad. Once we found some money in your purse to replace her shirt and clean her skirts.'

Peter wasn't sure. The five of them would routinely take the piss out of each other, and it was quite possible that they were lying in their teeth . . . but he did have a vague recollection of a gorgeous little Venus with the face of an angel – and the body of a fiend bent on tempting the innocent. He could remember playing his tabor with ever-increasing vigour, then leaving it as it was impossible to play the kind of tune he wanted with such a staid, boring instrument. No, he was a master musician, so he picked up his recorder and started to play that instead. He could recall leaning against the wall, playing like the devil himself as she smiled and laughed. Her pleasure was all he needed to drive him on. It was that night he'd argued with his wife, he recalled. Be more than an argument if she ever heard about this, he reckoned.

'You are sure of this, Peter?' Ricard said. 'They'd let us back?'

Peter could not help but look down shamefacedly. 'No, I'm sure there's no problem. Not really.'

'Even if she herself thought we would be allowed back in, there's all the others. The King and she aren't friendly just now,' Janin pointed out.

'The lady I spoke to was Lady Alicia, one of the Queen's ladies-in-waiting, a blonde. She said she remembered me only too well. Actually she was a bit off at first. Then she laughed . . . You say the wench was strawberry blonde?'

'With the sort of body no angel would ever need,' Janin agreed solemnly.

'Oh. *Oh!* Christ's ballocks, I never . . . I didn't remember. Well, she didn't seem upset, anyway. She can't have been offended.'

Ricard nodded and shrugged. 'Well, she wasn't hurt or anything. You didn't rape her, you just tried to grapple. Your incapacity saved her from any danger.'

'Incap— what?' Philip stuttered.

'Well, we're in, like I said,' Peter repeated. 'She took me to see William de Bouden, the Queen's old clerk. He's in charge of the money for her now, and he's agreed. So you lot're now the Queen's Men again. Official.'

Chapter Five

Hythe, Kent

Père Pierre Clergue scowled as the wind whipped about his sparse hair, and thumped his hand upon his hat to hold it in place. He was an amiable-looking man usually, but today he was feeling disgruntled and saw no reason to hide it.

There was so much to be done, and at his time of life he really should be able to take things more easily. Perhaps secure a post in a quiet convent somewhere after his efforts for Holy Mother Church. It was nothing less than he deserved. But every so often the cardinal would use him as a messenger, and provided it was business which benefited the Church or the Pope himself, Pierre was content.

He had spent too many years in service now. From the early days when he went to Pamiers to help the Inquisition to the present – he had grown old in his harness. And now he must return to the cardinal to report on the latest matter. It was hard.

A wave broke over the sheer, and he ducked a moment too late. Well, this was his last time travelling over the sea. He would have to make that clear. He was too old for this kind of journey.

Château Gaillard

Jean had heard le Vieux tell others that this was once the castle of the mad English king, Richard, the one known as *Coeur de Lion*. He was the last of the Norman kings to show any spirit, he was. He'd go anywhere for a fight. *Sacrée Dame!* Jean had been in one battle in his life, and he had no desire ever to become embroiled in another. He had seen his brother killed at his side, spewing a thick, bloody froth as Jean stared at the crossbow bolt lodged across his breast, pinning his arm to his body; a little later his father was decapitated by a fleeing man-at-arms on horseback. On his return he learned that his wife was dead too – raped and murdered. There was nothing in war to tempt a man. Not a man like him, anyway. Those who hankered after it were mad. They saw only the possible loot. Booty was a soldier's dream. But only if you got your hands on it.

Still, that old king knew something about building a castle. This one had suffered over the years. It had taken only one year to build, from the defences set across the River Seine to the little bastions in their lakeside defences to the great fortress itself, but it had only survived as long as the authority of its builder. As soon as King Richard died, his brother King John showed himself to be less than competent at defending even this jewel. From what Jean had heard, it was the loss of this castle that guaranteed the end of English rule of Normandy.

The sun was failing now. On a whim, he climbed to the walkway of the great tower, and stared out over the river towards the west. The sky was lit with a yellow-orange series of horizontal streaks which grew darker as he watched, deepening to a crimson which licked the surface of the Seine below him with flames. And then a cloud drifted over the sun and the colours paled, and the twilight reminded him it was time he returned indoors to the fireplace.

There was no snow yet this year, but the sky was surely threatening it. It was that time of year when a sensible man was cautious about walking on the stone-paved walls, or on the timber steps that led a man from one wall to another. A castle like Château Gaillard was designed for ease of defence, not for the safety of any single individual, and a man who enjoyed life was sensible if he took some precautions. A patch of ice on the stone of a wall could all too easily send a man flying into the ditch. Only last month Jean had seen a man slip on the frosted step of a staircase. He'd fallen heavily on his elbow, which shattered, sending shards of bone through his sleeve. By some miracle, he'd lived, although the barber had taken off the remains of the limb. So now the castle was one man down, and others were forced to take on extra duties.

Jean made his way down from the great keep, nodding to the men coming up. The steps here were indoors, and he was sure-footed enough here in the dry, his armour grating and clattering as he went down the steep spirals. No, it was outside he had to be careful, as he left the mass of the donjon behind him and went to the quarters set beside it, where all the soldiers lived.

There was a thick pottage simmering over the fire, and he went to the warmth with relief, holding his hands to it until he could feel the flesh of his palms almost scorching.

Others soon joined him, men from the north, east and west walls. To the south there was the out-work, almost a separate fortress in its own right, with its own guards who had their own fires and food.

The last man in was the one they all preferred to ignore. Not a guard like them, he didn't share in the same camaraderie. They all felt it, too: the revulsion. The sight of him was enough to make Jean's stomach start to clench with disgust. Not that Arnaud was repellent to look at, nor that Jean was overly bothered by his taking advantage of the woman prisoner. That was normal – a benefit of the job, more or less. No, it was the understanding of what Arnaud did, what he could do to others, no matter what their station. Nobody was safe from him.

Only le Vieux himself appeared to be unbothered. As Arnaud entered, the old man automatically moved a little, creating a space at his side, and the two men sat together like the old campaigners they truly were, eating their food and watching their companions like warders in a gaol eyeing the prisoners. Which was, in a way, no more than the truth. They had all been rescued from different prisons.

Arnaud. Arnaud. The torturer. The mere thought was enough to make Jean feel sickly in his belly. He had saved Jean's life, perhaps, but Jean could not like him. There was no trust between them. How could Jean trust the man who had done such things?

Yes, it was Jean who was most affected by Arnaud out of all those in the chamber. After all, he knew what the torturers from the Inquisition could do to people. He'd seen it.

Thorney Island

The Queen of England was no stranger to fear now, yet the terror was closer, more poignant, the stronger her hopes of freedom grew.

Alicia was already in the hall when she returned from the second meeting with her husband. 'Your highness?'

'Yes. He has confirmed it,' Isabella said. She was still quite shocked, and as she held up the papers for Alicia to see, she saw that her hand was shaking.

'It is one thing to be told, it is another to have the papers,' Alicia said.

She read them quickly, but Isabella made no further comment about them. All that mattered was that the papers were genuine. Safe conducts for her and her party to travel to France to visit her brother and negotiate the truce for Guyenne. All there, all clear, all precise and correct. If he were to withdraw from the plan now, it would send her demented, she was sure. It was her last hope, her last opportunity of freedom. Once she had succeeded in shaking the dust of England from her feet, she would be secure once more. But she had to get away. She must not allow anyone to see how much she craved this journey, because if her husband or his lover, the dreadful Despenser, were to learn how deeply she desired it, they would realise that she had deceived them.

'My lady, you are safe!' Alicia whispered, so quietly her lips barely moved.

'And you? You are happy to have those musicians back?' Alicia nodded. 'They will suit our purpose.'

'I will have him castrated if he tries to hurt you.'

'I would do it myself if I thought he was a danger – to me or to you!' Alicia breathed. 'I've already told Richard about the man. He'll look after me.'

Isabella had learned how to dissemble and pretend to be a play-actor. She gave a fleeting grin, but then glanced at Alicia with a cold, outraged demeanour, and imperiously held out her hand for the papers. She did not so much as glance in the direction of the other women in the room.

They were all the spies of Despenser.

3rd day of Lent[1]

Alehouse at gateway to Palace Yard, Westminster
They were all nervous as they marched under the entrance gate to the great palace complex of Westminster on Thorney Island. Charlie, in Ricard's arms, buried his head in Ricard's neck. It was odd – just that little proof of the lad's sense of vulnerability was enough to make Ricard's breast swell. He felt as if he could kill dragons to protect him. And then they fell under the shadow of the gatehouse, and his courage

---

[1] Saturday 23 February 1325

cooled. The mere sight of the huge belfry at the abbey next door made him duck his own head down. There was too much money and magnificence here for them. And of course they were here to do the bidding of someone else and spy on the Queen.

'One thing I still don't understand is,' Janin had said as he scuffed his boots along the road to the palace, 'why they want us so badly. There must be some good reason why they want a motley band of brothers like us to be near the Queen.'

'Maybe that's it?' Philip said. 'They think we're so motley, no one would suspect us of any deviousness.'

'Well, naturally they'd respect our position. Perhaps it's just that. They know that a Queen's Musician is likely to be able to keep close to her, eh?' Ricard grunted.

They were no nearer an answer when they reached the alehouse inside the gateway. It was here that they were supposed to meet their companion Peter. He was to introduce them to the Queen's Comptroller, but when they gave their names to the guard at the door, they were told to wait and someone would be sent to find their companion.

'He's a musician, you say?'

The man's suspicion was not hidden, but few in these troubled times were not distrustful of strangers, and no one was more wary than a king's guard. There had been attempts to assassinate the King and his friend since Mortimer the Traitor had escaped from the Tower.

Ricard answered for them all. 'Peter Waferer – he plays the tabor. He ought to be up and about by now.'

'Wait here.'

They were forced to hang around for a long while. It was soon apparent that no one had seen Peter that morning so far, and as the sun climbed in the sky the guard quickly grew bored with their presence. He called a lad over and asked whether the musicians could be taken to the Queen's

Comptroller. Soon they were being escorted over the great yard towards the exchequer buildings, two extensions added to the massive hall built by William II more than two hundred years ago.

The main exchequer chambers were full of black-garbed clerks working on numbers, and there was a large table with a chequered cloth on it, although all the men seemed to be scrawling on parchments or in books rather than looking at the money on it. And there was a lot of money, enough to make Ricard salivate, almost. There was no sign of the man they must see, though, so they were taken out through a small door into the great hall itself. Here there were several courts hearing cases, the judges sitting in attitudes of either boredom or keen attention. They followed their guide down behind the court of Common Pleas and King's bench, past a massive marble table which was, so Ricard was told in a hushed tone, the Chancery, before being led out through the rear of the hall into a small chamber nearer the river. At last they met William de Bouden.

'Who in God's name are you lot? What's that brat doing in here?'

The bawled demand was enough to make all of them drop their heads, and their guide respectfully bowed and apologised.

'My lord, these are the musicians for the Queen. They're here to join her on her journey, if it pleases you.'

'No, it bloody doesn't. Scruffy-looking bunch of tatter-demalions! Where in hell did you find them, eh?'

The guide was sensibly silent at that question, but Ricard felt that somebody ought to speak, so he pulled off his hat respectfully and cleared his throat.

'You hawk and spit in here, man, and you'll spend the next year in the King's gaol!'

'My lord, I was only going to say that we played for the

Queen some while ago, and she remembers us. Perhaps she wanted us to join her when she rides off to wherever she's going. Where is it? York? Lincoln?'

'Bloody York? Lincoln? Christ's bones, man, she'd hardly need musicians for a local journey like that. No, she's off into danger in France, and some of us are going with her. Sweet Mother of God, though, these bastards stink! She will want nothing to do with them.'

The guide bent his head. 'Earl Edmund himself has asked that you take them. The embassy is to be as flattering to her honour as possible. The Earl respectfully asked that you find some money for them, so that she has her full dignity during her embassy. No ambassador would think of travelling so far to meet so prestigious a ruler without some form of musician, and Earl Edmund is assured that these are actually very good players.'

'Earl Edmund said that? Dear heaven! When someone with his intellect sinks to selecting musicians, there's no telling what sort of man he may find.' He curled his lip at them. 'Well, you can't put them in front of her looking and smelling like that. Take them to the wash house and see that they're made presentable. Throw away those rags of theirs, and give them some more suitable clothes. The Queen's own colours, mind. You'll all get the usual fare: food and drink with the rest of the senior servants, two tunics a year, and occasional tips when you play well. All right? The boy can't come, though.'

'He's mine!' Ricard heard himself say. Shite! Why'd I say that?

'Where's his mother? No. Don't answer that. Well, don't let the little devil steal anything. He'll get what he deserves if he does,' de Bouden said disdainfully, looking at the overawed Charlie. 'Good. Now piss off, the lot of you. As if I didn't have enough to deal with already.'

In no time, so it seemed, they were all back out in the great yard, and as their guide left them, muttering about finding them new clothing, they exchanged looks.

'Who's this Earl Edmund?' Philip demanded.

'Don't you remember anything?' Ricard said. 'He's the King's brother.'

'What's he worried about the Queen's musicians for, then?'

'Perhaps he wants her to be shown in the best light. She is his sister-in-law.'

'I don't like it,' Philip said. 'Why should he be so keen to see us go there with the Queen? I've never seen him.'

'We are to have money, clothing, food and drink,' Janin breathed.

'But we have to throw out our old clothes,' Adam muttered.

'For a guaranteed allowance of food and drink, I can live with that,' Ricard said.

'And me, I suppose,' Philip said, although he still looked doubtful.

'Where *is* Peter, though?' Janin wondered.

'He'll show up,' Ricard said. 'He always does.'

City ditch, near Ludgate

Simon Corp had known better days. He shuffled along with a stick, peering into the ditch, hoping to see something that might help pay for a little food or a mug of warmed ale. Sometimes a man could see a coin in the filth, or a small knife that had been accidentally thrown out with the rubbish that householders hurled into the ditch here. It smelled evil, both from rotting food and from the excrement with which it had been mingled, and Simon had to hold a shred of cloth over his nose to ward off the offending odour. The tanners worked all along here, and they threw much of their waste into the ditch, a repugnant combination of urine and dog's turds, just to add to the stench.

In the past he had been quite well off, and with his lad John he had hoped to start to have an easier life. Of course, it had been hard when his wife grew ill, but at least when she died she stopped being a drain on their resources. Until then, Simon and John had had to share the task of looking after her. Some women from the parish did try to help, but there was little enough anyone could do. She was dying; they all knew it.

A month ago, now. Just when the weather changed. That was when she'd gone. A rattle in her throat, that was all he'd heard. Just a rattle. Then there was the soft slump as her spirit left her, poor Joan. And she was gone.

Yes, he'd hoped that after that he and his lad would be able to keep more of the money they laboured for, but before he knew what was happening, God save him if his thick as pigshit son didn't get into a fight. Trying to steal a horse, so they said, although it wasn't proved yet. Had to wait for the justices to hear the case. But there were enough men who believed it. Well, the bastards would believe anything of anyone who was poor. A poor man is a thief, someone said in Simon's earshot. He would have attacked the speaker, except he wasn't sure who it was. His hearing was less good than it had been.

Aye, well, if there'd been money in his purse, he'd have fought the damned lot of them. They were passing unfair judgement on his boy, and any man who repeated that kind of slander was deserving of a buffet on the head, rot their souls. His little John was as good as any young lad. He was a reliable, honest fellow. Better than most of them who lied about him.

John. He was in the gaol now, just up there, over the wall inside the city. God knew what would happen to him. They said he had an evil reputation, but that wasn't the boy's fault. God knew he'd tried to get along without upsetting people, but when a fellow had nothing, and he saw the wealthy strolling past, caring not a whit for anyone else, money in their purses, rich clothes on their backs, the sort of people who never had to work, who'd never felt the cold, who hadn't experienced the way that fingers would crack in the brutal chill while one was working out in the ditches . . . people like that were all too keen to condemn a fellow just because he knocked a man on the head in desperation. It wasn't *fair*!

He prodded away with his stick, and then, heaven be praised, he saw it! A distinct gleam. It must be metal – perhaps a knife, or a jewel set in some gold? There was a clear glinting through the mud where his stick had scraped the surface.

Scrambling gingerly down the bank, he reached the spot and began to dig with his fingers in the filth. There was something there, a hard disc of some sort, and then he uncovered a drum, a tabor. At the rim there was a gleaming ring of steel which had a leather thong bound to it, trailing off into the mud. That was what he had seen. Just a metal ring from a drum. It was tempting to swear, but then he shook his head and crossed himself in pious gratitude. A drum, once cleaned, and so long as the thing hadn't lain there too long and become rotten, would be worth a few pennies. He might be able to sell it for enough to buy a loaf.

He gathered it up, and began to make his way up the slope once more, but the thong held him back. Till then he had thought that it was just trailing loose, but now he understood that it was tied to something. Giving it an experimental pull, he thought it gave slightly. He tugged harder, jerking it, then drawing it steadily, and it began to give. Further and further, until he stopped very suddenly. Gasping, he began to step backwards, but stumbled, and then, keeping his eyes firmly fixed on the mud, he scuttled up the bank and out of the ditch.

'You all right, old man?' a fellow called, seeing his discomfort.

'Sweet Jesus, come and look at this,' Simon Corp said, and then started to bellow hoarsely for the hue and cry – before pausing to puke.

Chapter Six

Château Gaillard

Jean left his companions and walked out to the walls, untying his hosen and spraying the wall until his bladder was empty, conscious only of the relief.

Finished, he settled his clothes and began to make his way back to the guard rooms, but then turned away at the last moment. There was no hurry. All the others would be in there, drinking their beer and wine, swapping the tall stories they had rehearsed so many times before. There was nothing new for them to share with each other. Jean knew them as he knew the hairs on the back of his hand. They were too familiar to be interesting: old Berengar with his untidy mop of greying hair cut to fit beneath his steel cap so that none showed, only his great red nose and enormous moustache; Guillaume, the black-haired Norman with the narrow face and close-set brown eyes that appeared so shrewd and suspicious; Pons, the fair man from the east, with the muscled shoulders and carriage of a warrior much older than his three or four and twenty years. And then there was Arnaud.

All must detest a man such as that. The torturer and killer of so many, who seemed to take pleasure in the suffering he inflicted. Everyone in the garrison had heard the gloating tone of voice he used while he described cutting off a nose or lips for some infringement. Once he had told Jean of the 'great' times he had enjoyed down in the south with the bishop, Jacques Fournier. He had been assistant to the executioner, and had himself put many men and women to the fires. Those had been great days, he had said. It had taken all Jean's self-control not to plant his fist in the man's face.

More recently his revulsion at the sight of Arnaud had grown. The men had told him that Arnaud had repeatedly raped the woman in the cell below the tower. The one who le Vieux had said would have been a queen, were it not for one crime.

Le Vieux was himself an odd man. Certainly he had seen much in his life. He was one of the oldest men Jean had ever met. Over time, he must have fought in any number of battles. Someone had told Jean that he too had been in the battle of the Golden Spurs, at Courtrai, when the rebels had all but destroyed the flower of French chivalry. The rebels had taken the spurs and war belts from the dead and used them to decorate their churches. Le Vieux had been one of the foot soldiers there, and had been back afterwards to help hunt down the guilty – all those who'd assisted the rebels to defeat the French host.

Jean liked to listen to him, though. He wouldn't talk much about his experiences in wars, but he was honest when he did – he had no false pride, only genuine satisfaction in some things he felt he had done well. He was a man who had learned honour in the course of a long and hard life. But tonight he would be sitting with Arnaud.

No, Jean did not want to re-join them. Instead, he walked up around the line of the wall of the inner *enceinte*, over the great ditch and in through the gatehouse. He climbed up on to the walls and stood there gazing at the River Seine as it wound its way past the castle and the little town of Les Andelys nearby. It was a lovely place, this. Safe, with good views all about the countryside.

There was a shout, and Jean glanced at the sky automatically to see what the time might be. It was the first watch after their lunch, of course. There was no need to check. And yet there was something that made his hackles rise. Something felt wrong. It was nothing obvious, but there was enough of a sense of danger to make him move away from the open, crouching down a little while he listened and watched.

For some while there appeared to be nothing to alarm him. No running, no men calling or blowing horns, only a strange sense that something was not well in the castle. And then he heard it: a rasping, panting breath.

It made him think of a man he had once known. That one had had not an ounce of cruelty in his heart, but he had been chased to exhaustion like a hart, and when Jean saw him, the fellow was already near to death. He stood in a little clearing, bent over, hands resting on his thighs, looking about him with desperation, so confused by the chase that he couldn't recognise his own pasture where he had been a shepherd. He died a short while later – a sword thrust ended his life.

Then Jean saw Berengar, hurtling around the wall like a mountain goat, fleeing some terrible horror. There was already blood running freely from a wound in his scalp, and his fists moved back and forth as though he was trying to punch the air from his path. He flew over the court and through the gate to the next section of the fortress, and just as Jean was wondering what he should do, whether he ought to chase Berengar and bring him back, he heard a loud laugh and saw Arnaud leaping over some rubble and haring off after Berengar, a long, bloody knife in his hand. At the sight, Jean shrank away. Arnaud must have become *insane*.

He heard the skittering sounds of little stones as the two rushed off, and he was tempted to go straight to the stables to fetch his horse, but he couldn't. He was in the service of the King, when all was said and done, and he must honour that service. So he slipped back down to the gatehouse and walked quietly back towards the guard house.

But he didn't make it inside. On the threshold, he saw

something lying in the dirt. He found his steps slowing. In the doorway there was a body. A bloody mess, a man with only red horror where his face should have been. It had been pounded with a hammer, from the look of it. Nearby there was another body. This one was still moving, and Jean recognised Guillaume. He was on his back, and the breath was rattling in his throat as he clutched at the wound in his breast as though to stop the slow pumping of the blood that came in bright, scarlet bubbles. Jean went to him and tried to ease his last moments, raising him and trying to calm him, giving him the only comfort he could, cradling his head in his lap.

Guillaume looked up at him with terror in his eyes, looking into the doorway, then up at Jean. Not for long – thankfully his misery was soon over. As soon as his body had tensed that last time, then melted, like a child going to sleep, Jean set him back on the ground.

The man lying in the doorway was not le Vieux. The poor old man must still be lying inside. If Arnaud had any sense, he would kill the experienced warrior first, and then the others. Still, the fellow could have had little enough sense to have done this in the first place. The dead man there must be Pons. His hair . . . and the jerkin he wore. It looked like Pons . . . Reluctantly, Jean entered the guard room. There at the side of the table was le Vieux, lying on the ground, blood oozing from a wound above his ear.

A clattering of stones from outside. He didn't stop to think; he couldn't carry le Vieux to safety, not with a maddened Arnaud behind him. They'd both be killed. No, he must flee.

Jean ran on light, quiet feet to the small gate that led out to the escarpment. The door was bolted with a baulk of timber, and he pulled it aside silently, then eased the door open a little, and slipped out.

And once out, he ran and ran.

City ditch, London Wall

The musicians heard about their friend's death later in the afternoon, and were soon there at the ditch just over the other side of the great wall from the Fleet Prison. The inquest was just finished when they got there, and the body was being carried away on a makeshift hurdle, four men transporting it reluctantly, one looking as though he would soon be sick from the smell. Charlie stood studying the proceedings with apparent interest.

'The poor bastard,' Ricard muttered.

'What happened to him?' Janin wondered.

There was a small crowd already thinning, but one old man showed no sign of wishing to leave the place. 'It was me found him. Poor little shite-wit. Must have been wandering out after dark to be killed like that. Probably set on by footpads.'

'He was robbed?' Ricard asked.

'They took his purse, yes,' Corp agreed mournfully. If it had been discovered at the inquest, he'd have been kicking himself for not finding it first.

'Poor Peter,' Adam said.

'A bad way to die.'

'Stabbed? Was he knocked on the head? Throttled?'

'Oh no. He was held under until he choked. They drowned him – in all that muck! Can you imagine?'

It was a short while later, as the four remaining musicians stood in a tavern just along from Temple Bar, toasting their dead friend, that the thought occurred to Janin first.

'Ricard,' he said, 'why would a man kill him like that?'

'How should I know? I'm no murderer. Maybe it was a drunk who decided he didn't like the look of Peter's face, or something. Or just a cutpurse who thought it'd be easier to kill him than rob him.'

Janin nodded slowly, but without conviction. 'If that was the case, why drown him? Hitting him over the head would be easier, or stabbing him. Why'd someone want to drown him there?'

'You tell me.'

'Someone who knew a man and his wife who are dead, I was thinking. If they wanted revenge on the men who'd killed them, and everyone was saying there were these musicians who'd been leching after the wench? Perhaps a brother or father? They may want revenge – and a death in a nastier way than a quick stab.'

Ricard gazed at him blankly for a long moment, and then longer and harder at Charlie, who was playing and giggling loudly with another small brute. He hurriedly polished off the remains of his ale. 'I think we ought to get back to the palace and stay there until we leave the country.'

West of Paris

The old cart rumbled slowly, and yet Blanche had to hurry to keep up. Her hands were fettered, a long chain leading from her wrists to the rear of it, and were she to fall, she would be dragged some way before being able to get to her feet.

Her eyes were tormented by the light still. It was so hard to see where she was going, and while the dust from the wheels plagued her, worse was the sheer pain of the brightness lancing into her eyes and making her head ache for every moment of the journey. She was so unused to the light.

Still, the anguish was worth it for the unadulterated delight of the sensation of being in the open once more. Dear Christ in heaven! To hear the birds again, to see trees and the little shoots that showed spring might not be so very far away, was so overwhelming, she spent much of the journey wondering whether she should laugh aloud, or jump and dance with pure joy. It was like being reborn.

Perhaps, given a little time, she might grow to feel that she had indeed become renewed. It would take much, though, to achieve that. To feel truly alive again she must be able to forget her past. To forget her husband the king of France, to forget their children – to forget the gaoler at Château Gaillard . . . No. She could not think of such things. Better by far to remain in the present and live for the future. That was sensible. Much more sensible.

Live for now, and pray to God.

Château Gaillard

Le Vieux groped for consciousness like a diver deep in a pool desperately striving for the surface.

He had been here sitting by the fire with a mug of beer in his hand, talking with the others. Jean had walked out earlier, said he needed a piss. All the others started telling stories. There was little else to do now that their most important prisoner was gone. Without Queen Blanche, there was little to do.

Of course! Le Vieux had been telling them about her, about her appalling conduct – adultery when married to the heir to the throne. Such depravity, such dedication to her own pleasures, had led to her arrest. She was condemned to come here, and here she should rot.

Astonishing that her husband had become king in so short a space of time. A good man. Pious, honourable, committed to his realm. Le Vieux had known him for many years, and had met him once, in Paris. His commander had introduced him. That was in the days when Charles's father had still been alive, of course. Dear Philip the Fair of blessed memory. *There* was a man!

There was a smell. Unpleasant. It reminded him of battlefields long ago.

He had told them all about the bitch, yes. And then he had told them about her spreading her legs in the gaol, how she'd given birth later. Yes, and how she'd wept when the child was taken away. Well, any mother would. But the adulterous wife of a prince of France could not keep an illegitimate child.

Arnaud had loved her, so he said. She was his best, his favourite. All the others here knew that. They'd looked away when the conversation moved in that direction. No one wanted to think about such things.

And then it was that Arnaud's impatient slapping and prodding started to wake him. 'What? Eh?'

'Vieux! Vieux! Wake up! He escaped. Look around you!'

Les Andelys, Normandy

Jean reached the town an hour before dark, and hurried up the narrow streets, heart pounding, feeling sick and faint from the horror of the castle.

'Where is the *bayle*?' he called when he saw a man. The fellow stopped dead at the sight of him, staring, and then jerked his chin towards the top of the town. Jean thanked him, and lurched off again, going cautiously on the cobbles.

It was strangely silent in the town today. Usually this would be a bustling little place, with hordes thronging the streets. Now, though, it seemed almost deserted. It was . . . *wrong*. Jean felt his legs begin to slow, and instead of rushing headlong, he began to walk more hesitantly.

There were shouts from up towards the town's square, and he bent his steps that way, wondering what was happening.

'The entire garrison has been slain,' a man was shouting. 'All dead.'

Jean stopped. He was about to breathe a sigh of relief when a cold, unpleasant certainty struck him. There was no way anyone could have got here before him. Surely Arnaud was still chasing Berengar, and even if he wasn't, he couldn't have reached here yet, could he? He was busy carving holes in Berengar's body, surely. But all the other members of the garrison were dead. Who could have come here?

Filled with trepidation, he went to the wall and sidled up towards the marketplace, keeping to the shadows and looking about him with anxiety. This made no sense.

In the market he saw the bailiff standing on a cart, haranguing the crowds who ringed him.

'I need some men to come with me to see what's happened and help to clear up. We'll need to clean the bodies and move them. Who's coming with me?'

'Not just that, Bayle. Someone'll have to read the last rites and prepare them for a vigil in the church,' a man shouted.

'We are fortunate that this man came, then,' the bailiff said. 'The castle's vicar came to tell us all about the madmen up there. He can officiate at the services.'

He beckoned a chubby father down at the wheel, and the smiling, benign fellow climbed on to the cart with him. 'This is Père Pierre Clergue of Pamiers. He will help us. Any more questions?'

Only one, Jean said under his breath. Who was this 'castle's vicar'? He'd never seen him before in his life. And he was supposed to have come from Pamiers, the place where Jean had witnessed that awful atrocity, and been arrested before being released to come here.

And then another, sickening thought struck him. It was too soon for anyone from the castle to have arrived, no matter who this man was. Yet the town had been told of the killings. That meant this man had to have been aware that the garrison *was going to be killed*.

'Christ in chains!' he groaned. He had to get away. Run! Go somewhere far away.

No. He would go to Paris and tell the King's men there what had happened. That would be best.

As soon as the menfolk of the town had made their way out and across the river to the castle, Jean himself hurried out, and took the road east and south, praying and sobbing as he went.

Chapter Seven

Château Gaillard

The castle smelled like a charnel house, Père Pierre thought as he wandered about the great court.

Once it would have been a magnificent place. The walls were all limestone, white and gleaming, but at some time in the past it had been sacked and many of the walls were in poor repair. Still, it was a place of happiness to him. It would hopefully mark the end of a long journey.

'In here, Père!'

The *sergent* had the brains of a goat, but he was reliable enough. Père Pierre climbed up and crossed the bridge from the outer fortress into the upper, main section, to where the *sergent* stood waiting. 'It's not a pretty sight, Père. Are you sure you are ready for this?'

'Oh, I think so,' the little man said with a deprecating smile. His amiable blue eyes were sad as he took in the place.

He was used to the sight of bodies. From that first journey down to the south with the madman Arnaud and the scruffy man-at-arms, the man all knew simply as le Vieux, he had been in close communion with the dead. So many over the years. He had helped dear Bishop Fournier with the Inquisition, writing down the testimony in his careful, small but neat hand, and then going with so many to hear their last words and praying with them.

Better than most, too, he knew exactly what sort of man Arnaud was. From the day when the poor woman had died, he had known. Arnaud had demanded that they leave instantly, desperate to run from that place. And later in the prisons, when he looked after the women in their cells, Pierre had felt sorry for the women as he heard them weep, sob, or scream as Arnaud left them. All had the same end, the pyre. Agnes in particular had died badly, he recalled. Arnaud had been cross with her, because she had not been nice enough to him, so he had let her death come as slowly as possible. Shameful.

So many memories, so many dead. He only hoped that today there would be just one more. The world would be a safer, better place without that one face, he thought.

He took a deep breath, and fingered his rosary, murmuring the prayers as he crossed the court towards the guard's building. Here the bodies were sprawled in undignified postures, the flies all over the sightless eyes, the gaping mouths. There were already little white clusters of eggs in the wounds. Early, he thought, for flies, but the damned things were always present.

Praying, making the sign of the cross, muttering the words that should aid the souls' passage to heaven, he made his way about the dead men. He pulled a face at the smells and sounds of buzzing, but continued on his way.

'And the others?' he asked.

'There aren't any more,' the *sergent* replied.

'There must be!' Dear God! Don't say that the madman has escaped! Pierre prayed silently. Please, not that!

Second Thursday of Lent[1]

Louvre, Paris

The work was tedious, but Cardinal Thomas d'Anjou was glad of it. He polished the gold and silver at the altar of the

---

[1] Thursday 28 February 1325

little chapel with a vigour that was entirely absent from his usual demeanour.

A taciturn man, he usually displayed little feeling, but in a church or chapel he could enjoy submitting to the service of God. It was an essential part of his life, this careful cleaning of all the paraphernalia of his religion, and he enjoyed it all the more the higher up the ladder of authority he climbed within the Church. There were some who said that he might be the next pope. Well, perhaps so, but he would not worry himself about that. He had two masters: God and the king of France. Fortunately the latter was as religious as he was himself, and service to one meant satisfying the other.

The knock at the door was an unwelcome distraction. He pursed his lips, frowning down at the jewel-encrusted cross he had been cleaning, and then sighed. 'Yes?'

Two men walked in, and he looked from one to the other. 'François?'

The older of the two, a narrow-featured man with the appearance of a hawk, with greying hair over hard, piercing brown eyes, nodded. 'I do not think you have met Père Pierre?'

'Ah, you are the father from the Comté de Foix?'

The father, a chubby man with the face and figure of a man unused to travel, bowed delightedly at being recognised. His clothing was stained and worn, with many loose threads and muddy patches. He looked, as he was, the latest in a long line of peasants, the cardinal told himself.

His face betrayed none of his disgust for the tatty fellow. Instead he looked at François enquiringly.

'It is done,' François said.

'Good. Then there are only a few loose ends remaining which need to be tied.'

Vigil of Feast of Piranus[1]

Queen's chamber, Westminster

The Queen nodded and thanked the company. All was arranged, then. She was to be leaving the next day.

At least she would not appear to be a pauper begging at her brother's door. Her worst fears had not been realised, thanks be to Christ. She would have with her a train of more than thirty people all told. True, all had been selected by her husband – or more likely Despenser – but that would scarcely matter. She had her own plans, after all. Did everyone really think her so stupid?

Perhaps they did. They could not cope with the idea that a woman might have a brain of her own. Despenser had fully surrendered to her, in so far as he had stopped attempting to have her destroyed. No, he was content for her to leave the country and achieve a diplomatic treaty with her brother, provided Despenser and the King did not have to go to France themselves. That would be too dangerous. Despenser knew full well that his life would be forfeit, were he ever to set foot on French soil. That was the price of his piracy when he had been younger, when he had overwhelmed a French craft and stolen it, killing the crew. Now he was *persona non grata* in France.

However, she still found it astonishing that the fool believed her when she pretended to have forgotten his insults, his lies, his mendacious treatment of her. He thought either that she was so dim she had not noticed, or that she was so foolish that she had forgotten and forgiven. He had himself forgotten that she was a woman of the royal house of Capet of France. She would *never* forgive an insult. *Never!*

---

[1] Monday 4 March 1325

When Queen Isabella first arrived here in England, she had been a young and naïve child, ready to do her duty by her new husband. At the time they had both been little more than pawns in the great game that was diplomacy. Neither had been given any choice in their partners. Their futures were set upon their joint path by their fathers, the kings of France and England, to cement a peace between their bickering nations. The Pope agreed, and thus the life of the seven-year-old girl had been welded to the nineteen-year-old man's at a betrothal ceremony in Paris. Her husband-to-be, Edward of Caernarvon, was not there. She was not to meet him for another five years, when he took her hand in the cathedral of Our Lady of Boulogne. Soon afterwards they left France for England.

'Your royal highness? There are some men here to meet you.'

The esquire bowed so low, for a moment she thought that he would beat his brow upon the paved floor.

That was one of the aspects of her life which was so confusing. In all her years as a child she had been treated with the respect due to a queen. It was fitting for a woman of her position in the world. But when she reached England her life had changed. As she watched the men being brought in, she could remember that time so clearly. The shame, the dishonour she felt, how demeaned she had been.

When she was wedded, her father had showered gifts on Edward, rich jewels and rings, and had sent more for Isabella as part of her dowry. She was a queen in her own right, after all. There was an agreement that when they were married, Isabella would have lands dowered to her from the king of England's French territories. But when they had been living together for a little, the twelve-year-old queen was disturbed to find none of the promised money appearing. There was nothing with which to support herself, let alone her household of knights, squires, servants . . . She was forced to resort to resentful letters to her father. And then she saw that the rings and trinkets promised to her had appeared on the person of the unlovely Piers Gaveston, her husband's 'friend'.

It made her cold with rage to learn that her husband could prefer the company of that vain, arrogant, *sneering* Gascon. He made those first few months – nay, years – miserable for her. By her husband, she was treated as a child. As his sister, perhaps. Ignored, unloved, and only occasionally summoned to royal events.

Perhaps it was understandable. Now a woman of almost thirty years, she was better able to see how a man like her husband might have viewed her. He, a grown adult of five and twenty years, she a small girl of only twelve. It was no surprise, in truth, that he would seek the companionship of others closer to him in age. After a time she had grown to appreciate this. She did not grudge her husband his affairs with other women, even when one gave birth to his bastard, and she was able to feel willing to console Edward when the lad died on his first campaign.

When the barons finally grew so disaffected with the repellent Gaveston that their rage could not be controlled, and he was slaughtered, it was to her that the king turned for sympathy and comfort. And for a while, for a little while, they were truly husband and wife, a fruitful union that gave her four children – the princes Edward and John, and then Eleanor and little Joan, her darling. In those years Isabella had felt her life was fulfilled. She had a merry companion in her king, and a contented little family.

But then the King developed a passion for this latest favourite, Sir Hugh le Despenser.

The man whom she would wish to see dead.

'Your highness, your servants.'

She smiled at her husband's men, the men whom

Despenser had selected to watch her every step of her way on the return to her homeland, and managed to fit a graceful smile of welcome to hide her revulsion.

New Palace Yard, Westminster

'So what do we do about him, then?'

Ricard looked at Adam with exasperation. 'Look, I'm not going to leave him behind with someone I don't know. Poor bratchet!'

'Be a bleeding sight poorer if he comes with us to France and dies from the food or something,' Adam said.

'He comes.'

'Fine. You thinking to use him to replace Peter?' Janin asked reasonably.

'Come on! Peter was good with the tabor, I know, but we don't need a man with a tabor to make our music.' Ricard looked down at Charlie. The child was resting in the crook of his arm as they spoke. He seemed a remarkably contented little boy. Thank God he hadn't seen his parents in that state, even though he had been scared enough of something to bolt from the house and hide in the hutch. Was it the noise of Ric and his mates turning up late at night? They hadn't been that loud, had they? But they'd all slept through the murder of the man and his wife. They'd been pretty ruined, then. And this little boy had been woken by them, probably, and sought the only safe place he knew, somewhere he played regularly, no doubt.

'It was his harp I'll miss most,' Janin was saying. 'You remember how he used to be able to get that crispness from his strings? Very good.'

'He was all right,' Ricard conceded, stung. 'But I think I can play my gittern well enough to make up for it.'

'I didn't mean . . .' Janin protested hopelessly, but there was no point apologising. Ricard was upset, but so were they all. 'I just miss him, that's all.'

'We all do,' Philip said.

'And tomorrow we're off?' Adam asked again.

'That's what the comptroller said,' Ricard acknowledged.

The day before, he had been taken to William de Bouden, the Queen's Comptroller.

'We shall be leaving in two days. Prepare your men to be in the New Palace Yard at dawn with all their instruments packed for a journey.'

'Where are we going?'

De Bouden was a square-set man for a clerk. He had a gruff manner, with steely eyes that brooked no nonsense. 'You honestly mean to say you've been walking about the palace with your ears closed? The whole place is discussing the Queen's mission to her brother. Are you deaf?'

'I just wasn't sure where in France we'd be going.'

'To see the King. But perhaps I was mistaken. Have you been to France?'

'Um. Well, no.'

'But you can read a map of the land? You know where towns are?'

'Um.' Ricard grinned helplessly.

'Then why do you want to know? You will be travelling with the Queen, that is all. And you will be careful to ensure that your other musicians are well behaved and don't misbehave on the way. We have letters of safe conduct, but they won't protect a randy stallion who tries to mount a French filly. Is that clear?'

Ricard could still remember that freezing stare, as though the man was gazing through his flesh at all his innermost desires. Someone must have told him about the way the men had behaved last time they'd played before the Queen. He could kick Peter for what he had tried. Poor bastard. 'They'll be—'

'Good. Now go! I have a thousand little matters to sort before we leave.'

Ricard shook his head now at the memory. The man had dismissed him with a wave of his hand and turned away instantly as though refusing to become concerned with any matters relating to the musicians. Hardly surprising. The fate of Ricard's motley little group was irrelevant to him. He had provisions, travel arrangements and route planning for a group of thirty to forty men and women to see to, as well as the headache of all the horses, wagons and carts which would be needed to transport the necessary victuals and other supplies to Dover or wherever they were going to sail from.

There was nothing much else for them to do just now. All their instruments were here with them, as usual. His old citole was beside him, ready to be wrapped first in a soft cloth, then in an oiled blanket to protect the strings and the wood.

He had always been inordinately proud of the device, ever since he had first seen it. It had been in a small workshop back in his home town of Bromley, and his eyes had been drawn to it immediately. The wood had a lovely sheen to it, giving the body a golden glow. It had the shape of a young woman's figure, with the broad hips at the base, with a slender waist and narrow upper section. From here the neck projected, leading to the large head in which the four keys holding the strings were inserted. He stroked the neck gently. The instrument had been with him for almost fifteen years now, and it was still his proudest possession, which was why he would never take it to a tavern like the Cardinal's Hat. Too much risk of some drunken arse trying to break it in a place like that.

Carefully setting Charlie down on the bench beside him, he picked it up and started to strum. He always found that music aided his thoughts, and just now his thoughts were black – as he knew his friends' were.

Peter the Waferer had never been a particularly close companion of his. The man was always a little over-arrogant about his position in the King's household – a man who could command an income with the kitchen staff and still earn a little more from his ability on the tabor was, so he thought, a man of some substance. He didn't make too much of it, but every so often he would make some little comment or other, and Ricard usually felt that it was directed at him. It pained him to hear it.

A man shouldn't speak ill of the dead, but Peter was, truth be told, probably the one from the band whom he would miss least. He was always thinking of his family – fair enough, true, but no good for a team like theirs. And he wasn't that essential. There were only a couple of tunes where they needed his kind of drumming.

'What's that tune?' Janin asked, eyes narrowed as he listened, his head set to one side like a hound.

Ricard hesitated. In truth, he didn't know what he was playing. Perhaps a mixture of songs he had heard or played in his life, or something he'd heard so long ago it was outside his memory. 'Call it "Peter's Tune", or "The Waferer's Biscuit",' he said with a grin.

'That'll do for me,' Philip said, tapping his knee in time to the music as Ricard began to play again.

Janin eased his hurdy-gurdy out of its leather bag and set the rosin to the wheel. Soon the three were playing, and Adam drew a grimace and reached inside his tunic, pulling out his little whistle to join in.

As usual, a small gathering formed about them as they played. Music was always a comfort to those who had little else to help them relax. A pair of young women lifted their skirts and started to dance to the music, and one carter held out his elbows to them both. They linked arms, and were soon swinging around together, laughing and shouting as they whirled about.

One man in particular was lounging near the alehouse at

the gate, Ricard saw. He watched them all for some while as they played, and then strolled towards them as the dancing fragmented, one girl giving up and tottering away breathlessly, dropping exhaustedly on to a stool.

When Ricard felt that they had played enough and exhausted that tune, he glanced over at the others, indicating it was time to end. Janin nodded back at him, Philip closed his eyes in acknowledgement, and Adam grinned, his lips still about his little whistle. After one more round of the tune they all stopped together.

There was a sudden burst of applause, and Ricard stood to take a bow. He swept off his hat, intending to hold it out for a collection, but folk saw his move and began to leave hurriedly before they could be asked to donate. All except the man Ricard had noticed. He remained, although he ignored the proffered hat.

'Very good. You lot play well together. You could do with another drummer, though.'

'We had one. He died.'

'Oh, that was your friend, was it? I heard about a man found up at the London ditch.'

'Someone killed him up there.'

'He was drowned in the shite, wasn't he? Why'd someone do something like that to a fellow?' the man wondered aloud.

Ricard didn't like this conversation. He replaced his hat on his head and turned away to put his citole back in the bag.

'Have you found anyone to replace him?' the man asked.

Ricard gazed at him. He had an odd accent. He certainly wasn't from round here, not from London – and not from Surrey or Kent, as far as he could tell. The fellow was not overly tall. He had calm grey eyes, a pleasant smile, and crows' feet that showed he was a man who enjoyed life. His grey hair was cut short in the old fashion, and he was clean-shaven. His clothes were clean, his linen shirt so spotless it was almost painful to look at. 'Why are you so interested?'

'I was thinking, if you needed another drummer, perhaps a bodhran player could come along with you?'

Ricard eyed him up and down, considering. He was about to answer when he heard a call from the hall behind him, and they were called to the Queen's presence.

Chapter Eight

Queen's chamber

Baldwin smiled as he was introduced to the other men in the chamber, but inside he was still anxious. If only he had been able, he would have remained at home with his wife and their children.

But no man could refuse the King's summons with impunity. He had demanded Baldwin should come here, so Baldwin had complied. At least he had Edgar, his sergeant from those far-off days when he had been a Knight Templar, to stay in his manor with his wife and ensure that she was safe. His son was causing him concern, though. The lad would not suckle as children should, in Baldwin's experience. Like any other rural knight, he had bred many animals, and he knew as well as any other husbandman what a young creature needed. A boy like Baldwin needed plenty of milk, and while he refused to suckle from both breasts he was not gaining as much as he ought. While Jeanne was reluctant to admit that her son was not feeding enough, she accepted that he might be able to do better, and Baldwin had instructed Edgar to enquire as to whether there was a woman in Crediton who would be willing to act as nursemaid and wet nurse to his little boy. That way, perhaps he could ensure not only that his son received adequate sustenance, but that his wife was given some time to rest and would suffer less from exhaustion.

He should be there, though. It was ridiculous that he should be drawn over to London now, with the likelihood of being sent to France to escort the Queen, when his duty meant remaining at the side of his wife.

Except no man had any duty which could take precedence over the interests of the King, of course. All were the King's subjects, and owed their lives and wealth to him.

The others here were a mixed bag, though, he thought as he studied them.

William de Bouden he knew by reputation. The shortish, thickset and glowering ginger-haired comptroller was, so far as he knew, honourable and reliable. He had been the Queen's Comptroller before, and Baldwin had heard that she was furious when he was removed from his post. However, all her friends and servants were taken away from her at the same time, so her rage at his departure was probably only an indication of her general discomfiture, rather than at this specific man's removal.

One of the King's better generals was going to lead the Queen's diplomatic party: Lord John Cromwell. Tall and dark-haired, with narrow features but bright, intelligent black eyes, he had been Lord Steward to the King's household for some while, and although he must have felt the same concern as barons like Mortimer before the supposed rebellion of the Lords Marcher three years ago, he had remained true to the King. Baldwin wondered at that. He had himself stayed constant, but the doubts had been terrible.

There were three other knights in the room being granted their brief audience with the Queen, and one was familiar: a tall, fair, handsome man with the haughty blue eyes of one who knew that the world existed to amuse and satisfy him – Sir Charles of Lancaster.

Baldwin had met him with Simon while they were travelling on pilgrimage to Santiago de Compostela, and he had been with them on their return when they had been shipwrecked off the island of Ennor. Sir Charles had been a loyal vassal of the Earl of Lancaster, but when the Earl had been killed after his ill-conceived opposition to the King, Sir Charles had been left without a master. Like so many other homeless and rootless knights, he had left the country to travel abroad, seeking fame and fortune in the only way a chivalric man could, at the point of sword or lance. But even there his attempts to gain some prestige and honour failed. Now, however, he had clearly become less a mercenary, more a respected household retainer of the King. He wore the King's own badge at his breast.

The other two, so Baldwin learned as they were introduced, were Sir John de Sapy and Sir Peter de Lymesey. Neither was known to him. Sir John was a man of middle height, with a square face and calm grey eyes, while Sir Peter was a little taller, more of Baldwin's own build, but with a strangely rectangular face and dark eyes under heavy brows. Both stood with their hands on their swords, and bowed only cursorily. At least Sir Charles bowed like a knight honouring a lady, Baldwin thought as he also bent at the waist. However, when he straightened up again, he saw that amusement in Sir Charles's eyes, and wondered whether the ostentatiousness of his reverence was purely to conceal his cynicism about the lady's position. All knew about Despenser's hold on the King.

'*Ah, Sieur Baldwin de Furnshill, n'est-ce pas?*' the Queen was saying, and Baldwin urgently bowed again, returning his attention to her.

'Your highness,' he responded, also in French. It was fortunate that he, like almost all knights, was multilingual. Every man who served the King must learn the King's first language, French, as well as the common English tongue. In Baldwin's case he must also speak some Latin for conversations with the clerks in his courts and with the men of the Church, and he had been forced to pick up some of the old language that was still so common about the west of

Devon and Cornwall. In comparison with that, the French of this lady was a great deal easier.

'You are alone here? Your friend the bailiff is not with you?'

'My lady, I came here alone, I fear.'

It was true enough. He would have given much to know that his old companion Simon Puttock was at his side. There were so many dangers he could conceive during this mission to France. It would have been comforting to know that Simon was with him.

'You should have asked him to join you, *sieur*.'

He bowed without answering. When he glanced about him, he was pleased to note that Sir John and Sir Peter were muttering quietly to each other as they looked at him. Clearly they were wondering who this stranger might be.

It was curious, he felt, that when there were so few knights up and down the country – perhaps two thousand all told – it was possible to be met at every turn by a fresh face. For his part, he was sure that he had never met these two, but that was little surprise. After all, he was a rural knight from the wilds of Devon with no interest in the goings-on at court. He spent his days seeing to his livestock, hunting, and increasingly being involved in the day-to-day affairs of the local courts, both as a Keeper of the King's Peace, and as a Justice of Gaol Delivery. That was enough to keep him busy.

More recently, and against his will, he had been elected as a representative of his county in Parliament, although he had been forced to attend only one meeting so far. When he was coming up to London more regularly he would be forced to get to know many more men like these, no doubt.

As the introductory audience finished, and Baldwin was able to leave the room, he reflected on that fact. The idea of meeting more of his peers was not comforting.

* * *

As the men left her, Queen Isabella eyed them closely. That keeper, Sir Baldwin, was known to her after the investigation he had conducted into the deaths in the palace earlier in the year, and if she didn't trust him totally, she was at least as sure as she could be that he was an honourable man.

It was the others about whom she was nervous. Her comptroller, William, was well known to her, of course. He had been with her for many years before the King removed him. Now she had demanded his return, and she felt fairly comfortable that he was loyal still. He was her man. The same could not be said for Cromwell and his other three knights. De Sapy, she thought, looked shifty – the sort who would change allegiance as the wind changed; de Lymesey she did not like. He had a directness of staring that made her feel as though he was undressing her. Not quite disrespectful enough for her to complain, but there was that sexual note in his eyes. She would not dare trust him alone. Lancaster himself she was quite certain of. He was a mercenary, and entirely untrustworthy. So, if she were to offer a bribe to de Sapy, he might be reliable enough for a while, she thought. And that was the best she could say about them.

Now the lower orders were being trooped in to her. The cooks, the clerks under de Bouden, some guards, and finally a band of musicians.

These last were a shockingly scruffy lot. Their leader was clad in a tabard with her insignia, but although the material was clean and fresh he managed somehow to make it look ancient. This man, Ricard, introduced a tubby, younger man called Adam, fair-haired and tousled; then a slender fellow with bright eyes and the manner of a sparrow; then a heavier-set drummer with lowered, suspicious eyes, and finally a tall fellow with the delightful lilt of the Irish. He bowed most graciously, and she honoured him with a smile and slight nod of her head.

His tones reminded her of Mortimer. That poor man had been successful in Ireland before he had fallen from grace. He'd been sent there to stop the ravages of the Scottish, and it was largely because of his efforts that the Gallowglasses had been thrown into the northern seas.

'Blaket, I am glad you shall join us on this,' she said to Richard.

He nodded, his eyes reflecting his pride in her words. Alicia was just behind her, and she saw his gaze go to her. But then Isabella saw how his eyes darkened as he took in the sight of the musicians.

It was enough to make her smile. The group was careful to avoid looking at Alicia, she noticed, and there was no surprise there. After the way their companion had insulted her the last time they had played in the palace, it was wonderful that they had dared to return here. But they were reliable. Not only were they competent as musicians (though not as good as some of the singers she was more used to), they were also known to her. The fact that they had behaved rather disreputably on the last occasion meant that this time they would be sure to be more cautious in their manners. She did not wish for any bad feeling to be caused by fools who were supposed to be there for entertainment just because they grew lecherous towards some French girls.

No, she was content. Blaket might be unhappy to see them – Alicia must have told him how the man had attempted to molest her – but they would serve her purposes.

'Is that boy with you?' she asked suddenly.

The leader of the musicians reddened and grunted that yes, he was a little lad whose mother was dead, and they had—

'No, that is enough. Bring him here to me.'

She studied the little fellow with a heart that felt taut and painful. 'He is a handsome little man. I like his face. He reminds me of my brother when I was a child myself.'

'Your majesty, would you mind if I brought him with me? There is no one I can leave him with in safety, and I would be anxious for him all the time.'

The Queen considered, then nodded. 'And if you have trouble arranging transport – for he will not be able to walk all the way – you have my permission to put him into one of the carts. He is very young.'

She had thanked them all for joining her on her journey, and now she watched them depart to prepare for the start.

'Well, Alicia? What do you think?'

'The musicians could do with a good clean. De Bouden promised me that he had seen them washed.'

'He lied,' Isabella said. She looked about her. Eleanor was at the far end of the room, briefing the ladies-in-waiting who would be travelling with her, and was for a moment out of earshot. 'Which was the man who tried to rape you?'

'He was not here.' Alicia smiled. 'Perhaps he was too nervous to come with them.'

'Maybe,' Richard Blaket said. He had approached them from the doorway, and now he stood gazing after the men as they left. 'He is not there. The Irishman has replaced him.'

'Good,' the Queen said. As she spoke, she saw her chaplain in the doorway and beckoned him. 'I am thankful you too will join me, Peter.'

'I am glad that my presence comforts you,' he responded. 'Although whether there can be a happy conclusion to the embassy, I doubt.'

'Let us hope that there may be,' she said.

Thorney Island

Baldwin was glad to be out of the little chamber, and as he walked along the corridor which led to the great hall and out to the palace yard before it, he was aware of Sir Charles's footsteps behind him.

'Sir Baldwin, a moment, sir.'

'It is a pleasure to see you again, Sir Charles.'

There was a laziness in Sir Charles's eye that betrayed his mood. He was amused to see how Sir Baldwin had hurried from the room. 'You are as easy in the presence of royalty, I see, as you always were in any other company.'

'I don't know that I understand you,' Baldwin said. He was reluctant to consider their last meetings on Ennor. During his time there, to his shame, he had committed adultery with a lonely woman, and the memory was still painful – especially the aftermath when he returned to England and his wife once more. 'But tell me, how is it that you are now a household knight?'

'When the last time you saw me I was a desolate renegade, you mean?' Sir Charles said sharply – and then laughed aloud at the sight of Baldwin's face. 'Don't take me too seriously, Sir Baldwin. I am permitted a sense of humour, I think.'

'There is much about you which appears to have changed,' Baldwin said.

'It is some little while since we were thrown up on the beaches of Ennor, is it not? One year and a half, and yet it could be a decade for me. We parted in Cornwall, did we not? I made my way to London, hoping that I might find some position which would be not too arduous, while not attracting too much attention from any enemies – such as men in the King's employ! But when I was discovered by one of them, to my astonishment I learned that I was not considered a dangerous enemy of the King, as I had expected, but was fully pardoned.'

'Why would that be?'

'Ah. Well, I happened upon an old friend. Do you know Sir John de Somery? He is a knight banneret in the King's household. There are few enough of them, in God's name. Time was, back in the tenth year of the King's reign, when there were some fourteen or fifteen. Now there are three. At the same time the King has reduced his knights from almost fifty to about half that.'

'I am surprised.'

'So was I. But he had so many who proved to be unreliable. Men who agreed to serve him in exchange for clothing, food and drink, and living at his expense, are fewer than those who seek money. Why, Sir John de Somery receives two hundred marks for his service, along with thirty men-at-arms. It is a better way for the King to remain armed and stable.'

'You mean that a man will be more loyal to a mark than to his oath?' Baldwin asked.

'Ach, you are one of the old breed, Sir Baldwin. Believe me, this is the way of the future. Kings cannot expect men to fight and die at their side just because of the past. A man will fight when he can see that his service will enrich him, though.'

'Not I.'

'So you have no need of money. I envy you. Me, I need a new horse. And when I find one, I shall require a good saddle for him. And a decent courser must have the best provisions. Some the King will provide, of course, but for the rest, well, perhaps I shall have to buy it myself. And now I can.'

'Tell me, though, what of your service to Thomas of Lancaster? Did that not give the King some pause for thought? Surely a man who was the loyal retainer of an enemy – for that was how the King viewed his cousin – would have been viewed askance?'

'Not today, old friend. No, you saw the man beside me in there? Sir John de Sapy? He was a member of the household six or seven years ago, but during the Lancaster rebellion he was on my side. We were companions in the Earl's host. Yet he too has been received with a welcome back into the King's fold. It helped him that he was ever a friend of Sir Hugh le Despenser, of course.'

'Oh. Any friend of Sir Hugh's is to be received with honour into the King's service, then?' Baldwin said with a sinking feeling.

'Afraid so. Personally, I dislike the man intensely, but it has to be said, he has the kingdom clenched in his fist. There is nothing that happens in the realm without his approval.'

'What of the other knight? Sir Peter?'

'Lymesey? Did you never hear of the lady in Warwickshire? Forget her name, but it was Sir Peter who took all her lands, and when she tried to have her case heard in court, he prevented it. It's the first time I've heard of an assize of novel disseisin being abandoned because a knight threatened all concerned that they'd be burned, maimed or murdered if they continued. One has to admire the determination of a man like that.'

'No,' Baldwin said with determination. 'I fear I cannot agree with you.' To himself he added that such dishonourable behaviour was the mark of a thief, not a noble.

'No matter. I refuse to argue with you, old friend. Yet you will have to respect them both, for we are all bound to protect her majesty on the way to meet the French king.'

'Tell me about this journey,' Baldwin said, glad to move the conversation away from the behaviour of other knights.

'Ah. That. Yes. It may be a challenging duty, I fear. The Queen's task is to persuade her brother to give up all the lands he's just managed to take from our king. Yet short of planning a full-scale invasion of Guyenne, there is little our Edward can do to regain them. King Charles must know he has the whip hand.'

'Yet he will surely not wish to leave his own sister with egg smeared on her face?'

Charles shrugged. 'He is a man – she is a woman who's married his enemy. What would you do?'

'She is the mother of the future king of England too,' Baldwin pointed out. 'Surely King Charles would not wish to deprive his nephew of his inheritance?'

'If he could force the boy to pay homage for them, he'd probably be glad of the chance to have the English prince bend the knee to him. But it'll be a while before the prince becomes king. He is still young, and so is his father. There is no sign of the good King Edward suffering an early death.'

'So her mission will be a challenge. What of our duties?'

'There are we knights, also Lord John, of course, and the men-at-arms. I think that we will present enough force to guarantee our safety on the way. However, it is rumoured that many, including the traitor Mortimer, could be preparing a welcome for us. That is what I fear more than anything: the attacks of our king's enemies while we are abroad.'

'I see. But as you say, we shall be a strong enough force to defend ourselves from most attacks.'

'I do so hope.'

Obesta shrugged. 'He is a man... and his woman will
obey. By them, what would she do?'

Chapter Nine

Alehouse at gateway, Thorney Island

Ricard and the others gladly agreed to the stranger's
suggestion that they might repair to the alehouse. It was
always one of their favourite meeting houses, and the weather
was growing cold, so they all trooped into the alehouse and
ordered ale, before sitting and talking.

His name, so he said, was Jack of Dublin. His story was
short enough: he had been a loyal servant of the King in his
homeland, fighting the murderous bastards from Scotland
who served under the Bruce, and when they had succeeded in
destroying the invaders Jack had returned to England to see a
little of how the world worked. There was more to life than
living in a provincial city like Dublin, he said with a smile.

'There's also more to being a musician than talking about
it,' Ricard said. 'Or impressing a queen with a bow. How
good's your playing?'

When Philip and Adam grunted their agreement, he led
them out to their cart. From it he pulled his gittern, listening
to the tune of the strings. His citole he left wrapped. It was too
valuable to him to keep wrapping and unwrapping. Better to
leave it. The gittern was a cheaper instrument, the one that he
took into taverns and alehouses. Janin had already begun to
crank the handle of his hurdy-gurdy, and now Adam started to
pipe a tune, while Philip tapped out the beat. Charlie stood
watching them all open-mouthed.

When they re-joined the Irishman, Jack set his pack on the

floor and took up a large cylinder of leather. Grinning, he untied a buckle and withdrew a large bodhran and stick. He set it on his knee, his head bent as he listened to the tune, and then nodded once and began to beat the drum. Yet he didn't use the simple rhythm of the others, but instead beat at double the pace, thundering on the skin as though he was galloping while the others ambled. And he could vary the sound by pressing on the back of the skin, so that it sounded more firm and powerful, or taut and crisp.

'You're called Jack, you say?' Ricard said as they finished.

'Yes. What do you think?'

'I think we need to talk before making a firm decision,' Ricard said, glancing at the others as he spoke.

Jack nodded and told them he would wait to hear their decision – he would be outside. He stood and walked from the room without once looking back, to Ricard's annoyance; he would have preferred even a brief sign of doubt. This man appeared to have the arrogance of a bishop.

'Well?' Philip asked.

'He can play,' Ricard admitted.

'Play? He beat the shite out of Peter's playing. I miss Peter, but God's teeth!' Adam contributed. 'I mean, I'm sorry, but I can't lie. I miss Peter, but Jack is better than Peter would ever have been. Did you see how fast his drumming was? I could hardly see the stick in his hand, it was moving so quickly.'

'Why is he suddenly here?' Philip wondered.

'Who cares? We could do with a decent drummer.'

'Meaning?'

Adam suddenly realised what he had said. 'Sorry, Philip. No offence meant; I was thinking of him compared with Peter.'

'You should remember not to speak ill of the dead,' Ricard said quickly before an argument could erupt.

'For my money, we shouldn't take him,' Janin said.

'Why?' Adam demanded. 'I mean, I'm sorry, but he's easily the best I've heard in a while, and we could do with someone who can pick up a tune that quickly.'

Janin shook his head slowly. 'I don't think it'd show much respect for our old companion if we were to replace him so soon after his death. It hardly shows much feeling for him, does it?'

'Marg would understand,' Ricard said. Margaret, Peter's widow, was sensible enough. She had a good head on her shoulders, and she would know the sort of pressures that were being exerted on them without her husband's tabor.

'Marg may, yes – but the problem is not her. It's him. Jack. Who is he? Where did he come from? He saw us playing, and suddenly appeared. Just when we lost our main drummer. That to me seems a bit too much of a coincidence.'

'Oh, come on, Janin!' Adam scoffed. 'You trying to tell me that he had some part in killing Peter to join us? Look at us! Who'd want to join in with us unless he was keen on the music? And I have never heard of a man killing a musician to join a band, have you? It's more normal to join in with some music and see if you fit – just as Jack did just now. No, I say we let him join us. We could do with him, and he's keen.'

'Janin?' Ricard asked. He was watching the hurdy-gurdy player closely.

'I'm not happy about him. He looks the part, yes, but I just have this odd feeling that he's not all he makes out to be.'

'So do I,' Philip said with a glower at Adam.

'So it's two for, two against,' Adam said.

'No,' Ricard said. 'I agree with Janin. I think we shouldn't have any new member. And I don't like the way he just appeared today, one day before we leave with the Queen's party. It seems odd, that. Just think, were something to happen, if he turned out to be an assassin or something, and tried to kill her, we'd all be taken and tortured as a matter of routine. I don't want to be crippled because we took a drummer in a hurry.'

'But he's the best I've heard!' Adam protested.

'If he's so keen to join us, he'll wait for us to get back. In any case, he may not even want to travel to France. Why should he? He'd probably be more than happy here.'

'You've already introduced him to the Queen,' Adam pointed out.

'No. He tagged along while we introduced ourselves. There's a difference,' Ricard said. But he hoped the Queen would appreciate it.

Jack the Irishman was waiting outside as they all trooped out, and eyed them briefly before his gaze settled on Ricard.

'I'm sorry,' Ricard said. 'The trouble is, you see, we're off tomorrow, and the idea of taking on someone new just now is a bit hard. When we're back, maybe? Look, tell us where we can find you, and we'll look out for you when we're back.'

'Oh, don't worry. I can find you,' Jack said, smiling. He shrugged. 'It's a pity, though. I like your music. You play with a sense of fun – there aren't many musicians can do that.'

'Aye, well. Sorry.' Ricard was suddenly uncomfortable. This man had the most penetrating gaze of anyone he'd ever met. 'Right, well, we'd best be off, then. Packing the last odds and sods.'

'Oh? I thought this was all your stuff,' Jack said, glancing pointedly at their packs. When his gaze rose to Ricard again, there was a small smile at the edges of his mouth.

'Goodbye. Godspeed, and maybe we'll see you when we're back,' Ricard said uncomfortably.

Baldwin saw the little group of musicians and a small boy crossing the yard, but thought nothing of them. He was considering Sir Charles's words and trying to find any

comfort he could. There was little enough, he had to con-
clude. He was riding to a dangerous foreign land with a lord
whose allegiance was probably to the King alone, with two
knights who were simple mercenaries who were most likely
in the pay of Sir Hugh le Despenser, an evil man whom
Baldwin had cause to despise, and with Sir Charles, who
would sell his mother, if he hadn't already done so. And all
these were with him to protect the Queen, a lady who clearly
needed all the aid Baldwin could provide, but was the
undoubted enemy of Despenser and was presently as good as
estranged from her husband. The only reason she was being
entrusted with this embassy was that her brother was the
French king.

He grunted to himself. It was not the most cheerful of
reflections, he told himself. And there was one other aspect to
this litany of woe: his position as a renegade Templar.

In his early years he had been as devout as any pilgrim, and
when he was old enough he took a ship and sailed to the Holy
Land to protect the last Christian toehold: Acre. He nearly
died there, and it was the Templars who rescued him and saved
his life. For that, as soon as he was fit again, he had willingly
given his life to the service of the Order. When the Order was
rounded up on Friday 13 October during the first year of the
King's reign, he had been away on Templar business, and
escaped the mass arrests and torture. As such, he was a
renegade, and if found he could be executed immediately.

Ach, it was little enough risk. The Templars had been
disbanded eleven years ago; the actual arrests were seven
years before that. It was very unlikely that anyone would still
be about in Paris who could recognise him. The chances were
he ran the same risk of being seen and recognised here in
London as in Paris. And if the worst came to the worst, he
could rely on the protection of his letters of safe conduct.

Yet it was true that if a priest in the Church recognised him and denounced him, those letters would become useless. Even if he were to escape arrest in France, he would no longer be safe in England. There was nowhere where the long arm of the Church could not reach him.

With that grim thought, he turned to make his way back to his room to prepare for the coming day, only to find himself confronted by a tall man with laughing dark grey eyes set in a face burned brown by the wind and sun. At first, he could only gape. Then: 'Simon! What on earth are you doing here?'

'The same as you, old friend. I've been summoned to aid you in the journey to France.'

Queen's cloister, Thorney Island

Blaket was already in the little alcove near the gate when Alicia reached it. In her arms she held a lamb's shank and a skin of good dark wine, and she proffered her gifts before allowing him to take her in his arms again.

With his face buried in her neck, he said, 'I hate to think of those musicians being near to you.'

'I could wish I hadn't told you about them,' she replied. 'It makes you so grim, my heart.'

'If anyone tries to harm you, I shall stop them,' he said firmly.

'Do not worry. The man who tried it wasn't there.'

'No?'

'Apparently he was drowned in the city ditch. De Bouden told me just now. The musicians were considering finding a man to take his place.'

He cuddled her closer, but even as he did so he grew aware of a stiffness about her body. 'What?'

'The man in the ditch – that wasn't you, was it? You didn't kill him because of what he did to me?' She stood upright, her eyes fixed on him with an immeasurable concentration. He had killed before, as she knew.

'You think I did that?'

'Did you?'

'No. It was not me,' he said.

'Good,' she said, and appeared to melt into his embrace again.

'Perhaps it'd be best if they stayed behind?' he wondered.

'Why, love, are you jealous because they can wind an instrument? Would you prefer that to me? Because you have *me*, don't you?'

He grunted and placed his hands on her backside, pulling her nearer. 'In that case, they can do what they like,' he said. 'I'm content!'

New Palace Yard, Thorney Island

It was some little while later that Ricard and the others separated for the afternoon. They each had different tasks to undertake before they left in the morning. For his part, Ricard wanted to make sure that he had provisions – smoked sausages for the journey, some dried meats, and plenty of gut for his strings. A musician never knew where he'd be able to pick up the next supply. And now he had an extra mouth to think of, he thought to himself, glancing down at the boy.

'You the musician?' a man asked.

Turning to him, Ricard found himself confronted by yet another messenger in the King's livery. 'Yes? What now?'

'You are to come with me.'

Sweet Mother of Christ, these flunkies always think that their business is so bloody vital, Ricard said to himself as he took the boy's hand and followed the man round the side of the great hall and in through a small door. He was taken through another hall, through a little door and up some stairs until he had no idea where he was inside the palace complex. The place might have been designed to confuse a body, he thought. 'Where are we going?'

'Here.'

A door was opened, and he found himself thrust inside.

'Sir William?' he said with some surprise.

William de Bouden was seated at a broad table, his fingers steepled before him. 'Ah, Ricard de Bromley. And you . . .' he added, looking pointedly at Charlie. 'Well, good day to you. Are you prepared for your departure tomorrow?'

'Well, there are one or two matters. Mostly ready, yes.'

'I have heard you were speaking to a servant. A drummer.'

'The Irishman? Yes, we made some music with him.'

'He is very good, I understand.'

'Good enough,' Ricard agreed, thinking of the rapid drumming of the bodhran. But then he frowned. What was this about? Why would de Bouden wish to speak about the Irishman when he had so many other matters to concern him, not least the safety of the Queen?

He was answered immediately. 'The Queen liked the look of the man. She knows he is respected as a drummer, and would enjoy listening to him during the journey. If you have space, you could bring him with you. Do you have too many men already?'

'Well, no, I suppose . . .'

'That is settled then. The whims of a queen are not to be lightly disregarded, man. You may go now.'

And Ricard found himself outside the door. With a perplexed, 'Well, ballocks to that!' he shook his head, wondering why de Bouden wanted the man with them. He certainly did not believe the story about the Queen asking for him. There must be another reason.

And then he remembered – he hadn't the faintest idea how to get back outside from here.

Chapter Ten

Feast of Piranus[1]

Louvre, Paris

The King of France sat back on his throne as the cardinal entered, his robes hissing as the fur trimming swept over the floor. He stopped near the King, bowing but holding the King's eye as he did so.

There was an arrogance in these men of God that no other would dare display before him, King Charles thought to himself, keeping his features devoid of all emotion. It took an effort sometimes, in God's name.

This one, Thomas d'Anjou, was one of the worst. Others would at least make some civil display as a matter of courtesy, but this one was full of piss and wind. He had few of the attributes of a diplomat, and believed that anything he said would automatically be taken as the word of God. Arrogant fool! Well, kings could be arrogant too. And Charles was not of a mind to give up his own position in the world just for a man in holy orders who wanted to pretend to have authority over him.

The cardinal looked about him at the knights and dukes surrounding the King, and King Charles gave a shrug of agreement, waving the men aside.

---

[1] Tuesday 5 March 1325

'Your highness, I bring word from your Holy Father in Christ. The Pope has asked me to communicate his thoughts to you.'

Controlling his impatience, King Charles nodded. 'Speak.'

'He believes that the present state of affairs between your kingdom and that of the King of England is a canker that affects the whole of Christianity.'

'Then he should aid me in my desire to see the king of the English become more reasonable.'

'The Holy Father would like to see the English and French burying past disputes and coming to an agreement.'

'I agree.' King Charles wondered where this could be leading.

'The Pope will be happy. There is an urgent need for a fresh crusade to wrest the Holy Land from the heathens who have overrun it. We must unite in our love of God to smite them and recover Christ's birthplace.'

A crusade! That would be a marvellous undertaking. To lead his armies across the seas to Palestine was the height of a king's aspiration. 'I would be delighted to join such an undertaking.'

'It would permit both you and the English to join together in love of God to do His will. But first there must be peace between your nations.'

'There will be peace – as soon as my brother-in-law agrees to come and pay homage for the lands he holds from me. He must come here and kneel before me and swear his allegiance.'

'Perhaps he will. But you should also make allowance for the fact that he is a king in his own right. He deserves respect. Especially if he makes the effort to come here and make his peace with you.'

'For his realm, I have no ambition. For the lands of mine which I allow him to administer and rule, I expect him to show me the same respect as any knight, any marquis, any duke. Just as he expects of his barons and earls. We are of a similar mind.'

'Perhaps another embassy would aid the negotiations?'

The King pursed his lips. 'And who would you have me send? Or do you suppose to tell me whom the English should send to me?'

'I am sure that you will have heard that the Pope has requested the English to send your sister to you. That way, you would have a friend with whom to discuss this affair.'

'It is entirely up to the English king whom he decides to send to me.'

'I know that, naturally. But, if he were to send the Queen, would you be comfortable to negotiate with her?'

'I have already indicated to the English king that I would.'

'In that case, I am pleased. Perhaps we can hope to see a successful resolution of this matter before long. And then we may hope to begin to plan for a crusade.'

King Charles nodded and the audience was over. The cardinal bowed again, this time walking backwards all the way to the door out of the hall, showing considerably more respect than he had on the way in.

In the past King Charles's father, King Philip the Fair, had been able to rely on several well-trusted advisers, but one in particular, William de Nogaret, had been especially dependable. There were few of his stature now, sadly, since his death. It was William to whom Philip had turned when he needed a pretext to expel the Jews and take over their wealth; it was the same William who had written up the accusations against the Knights Templar which had seen them persecuted, tortured, killed, and their wealth confiscated to the benefit of the Crown.

But Charles had some advisers of his own, whose loyalty was beyond doubt. He looked around him now, and beckoned François de Tours.

'What did you make of that?'

François was older than the King by a decade. He was a lean, tall, ascetic man who spent much of his time, when the King was travelling, in the Île de la Cité, the ancient palace that had grown to become the centre of all administration for the French state. Now he stood and bent respectfully at the King's side.

'He plainly wished to see how you would react to the idea of Queen Isabella's coming here to meet and treat with you in her husband's place.'

'So that means that the Pope himself already knows that the English are likely to send her, then.'

'I should think it likely.'

'And he is concerned as to how I may respond to her.'

'I would assume that would be because of her part in the affair of the Tour de Nesle, my liege.'

The mere mention of that episode was enough to make King Charles forget to maintain his equanimity. His face flushed, and he had to clench his jaw a moment to prevent his angry words from spilling out, but then he regained control, his features lost their angry colour, and he could breathe a gentle sigh.

'I have forgiven her that.'

'I was analysing the situation, your highness. If I gave offence, I—'

'No, François. You were correct to mention it. You must always feel free to advise me without fear. I cannot trust your judgement if you are anxious about raising certain matters before me.'

But it was a difficulty, as both men knew. King Charles still had no children. His father had died eleven years ago, and King Charles was the fourth king since then. He was the last in the male line of the Capetian blood. If he were to die without a son, his family would have failed.

If only that slut Marguerite de Burgundy, his brother's wife, had not been so promiscuous. The bitch took delight in all things, and her position as the wife of the future king of France gave her leeway unavailable to others. But when she was discovered in her adultery her fall was devastating. She was dead within the year – but the damage was already done. It broke his father's heart, and Philip the Fair was dead a twelvemonth later.

Blanche, Charles's wife, was found to be guilty along with Marguerite. She was taken from him and thrust into a foul dungeon to rot. She deserved her fate – they both did – because they had put cuckolds' horns on the two princes, but it was a desperate position for the royal family. Suddenly both heirs had lost their wives. And without a wife, neither could breed.

Blanche's marriage to him was not annulled for some time. At last, three years ago, it was, and immediately Charles remarried – this time the lovely Marie of Luxembourg. She conceived and bore him a son, but mother and child both died in the birth. Louis, the boy had been named. His second son. The first, poor Philip, had died aged only eight in the year his mother's marriage to Charles was annulled.

'Your highness – would you like some wine?'

'François, no. I am fine,' the King said. 'I was remembering my sons.'

'I am sure that your wife will bear you many strong and healthy boys,' François said soothingly.

'I hope so.' Jeanne d'Evreux was as beautiful as she was young. At only fifteen years old, she was perfect for producing a child. Or so he hoped.

It was odd to think that he was about to marry his third wife; that he had already fathered four children, but all were dead. He mourned them all, but he had a duty as king, and that was to leave his realm in the capable hands of a boy.

Still, it made the visit of his sister poignant. After all, if she had not denounced his first wife, Blanche would probably have whelped more boys for him. His line would be secure. Instead here he was, fighting to find a woman who could bear him his heir and save the line of Capet.

François bent a little nearer. 'There is one other matter, my liege. The Château Gaillard. The lady has been removed, and all is taken care of.'

The King looked at him with eyes that glittered with anger. '*All* is taken care of?'

There was an edge to his voice which François had never heard before, a thrilling of hatred. 'As you say, my liege. The lady, and all those who could have told the story.'

'Good. And now you will never mention that place nor her to me again.'

François nodded and walked from the room.

The cardinal was waiting outside when François arrived. 'Well?'

'He is happy that all proceeds.'

'You told him all?'

'Only about the garrison.'

'Did you tell him one man escaped?'

François said nothing, merely stared at him.

'You know it as well as I.'

'Cardinal, the man will die. Already men from Les Andelys search the roads between there and his home in the south. No matter where he goes, he will be found. And destroyed.'

'Good. A heretic like that must be removed, like a rabid dog, before he can infect other good people.'

'Never fear. He will.'

The cardinal nodded. He felt only an increasing glow within his breast. This embassy would be the culmination of so much effort, with good fortune, and then the hosts could be collected and men and arms would sail once more for the Holy Land. The king of France would command the combined forces of Christendom, and at last Jerusalem would return to the control of Christ's people.

And the man who had orchestrated all this would, perhaps, be granted the post of papal representative in God's holy city.

New Palace Yard, Thorney Island

Ricard grunted to himself, head huddled down under his hood as the rain began to fall again. 'Sweet Jesus, this bloody weather is enough to make a duck pissed off!' He pulled his cloak tighter about him and Charlie.

Janin at his side was protectively shielding the bag containing his hurdy-gurdy under his heavy cloak. 'I don't know about that, but I'm certain sure it won't do my strings any good.'

'Rain is the one catastrophe that helps none of us. We'll just have to rely on Adam's piping and our singing if we're called on to entertain the party.'

'Philip's singing?' Janin asked doubtfully.

'Hmm.' Ricard looked over at Philip. He was standing with a scowl of such ferocity, Ricard was surprised the rain had the temerity to continue to fall.

They had been up before the dawn, all ready and prepared to leave, but then when they were about to depart, although the Queen had arrived, the King had not. It seemed that he and Despenser were huddled together in the palace discussing some matters of great importance. Either that, or they were still lying abed, Ricard thought grimly.

Their new companion was a little distance away from them. He had a slight smile on his face, but then, Ricard had always heard that the land of the Irish was as wet as a vill's pond. He was probably used to it.

'What about you, Jack of Ireland? Can you sing a tune or two?'

'Me? I suppose I know a few.'

'Good. We may need you to save us from Philip's voice, then,' Ricard said.

As Philip protested his ability, Ricard narrowly studied Jack from the corner of his eye.

Janin had summed it up when Ricard told the others last night.

'Well, he can play. Perhaps it was just that – the Queen's Comptroller wanted a good musician to replace Peter.'

'And perhaps cats can fly,' Philip had said. 'Our friend Peter dies, and then this new drummer is foisted on us? Too much of a coincidence, I'd say.'

'Look, maybe you don't like him, but I think his playing is still a lot better than Peter's used to be. Sorry, I know none of us likes to admit that, but there it is. I think it's better to be honest about things.'

'Shut up, Adam,' Philip had said sharply.

'What do you say, Jack? Will you sing?' Ricard asked now.

'Ah, now you should hear my voice, Ric. I have the purest notes this side of the mountains.'

So saying, he walked away, whistling. Philip and Janin exchanged a look, and it was Janin who glanced at Ricard with a vaguely confused expression on his face. 'What do you suppose that means?'

'I reckon it means I'll be getting the bastard to sing most of the songs on the way,' Ricard said. He huddled more closely inside his cloak, feeling a drip work its way down at the back of his neck and trailing on to his shoulder. Charlie wriggled and grunted, and Ricard was tempted to snarl.

He hated hearing his name shortened.

Saturday next after the Feast of Piranus[1]

Dover

Simon Puttock was relieved to arrive at Dover, although there was a strong sense of revulsion at the thought of once more being forced to board a ship and cross the sea.

It was not an irrational fear that he held of seafaring. He had experienced all aspects of sailing, and he disliked them. Ships rolled and bucked alarmingly, he had discovered. Even when a man stood up on deck, running the risk every few minutes of a soaking, the fact that the horizon rotated about the prow made him need to heave. Any food he consumed would immediately return and have to be discharged over the side. And when all this was endured with moderate patience, the next disaster would be either an attack by pirates or a shipwreck. Having suffered all of these more or less natural calamities, Simon was not keen to explore the delights of sailing once more.

'There they are,' he said, pointing to the group nearer the harbour.

Baldwin looked where he indicated. It had been noticeable that the King and Despenser had travelled much of the way together, while the Queen and her ladies and knights had been kept towards the rear of the long column of travellers. Now, at last, the three were standing together, while Lord John Cromwell listened near the Queen's shoulder. 'Lord John is taking his duties seriously, I am glad to see.'

'He would, wouldn't he? The man is honour bound to protect her, after all.'

'I suppose so,' Baldwin said. 'But I wonder who picked him? It was unlikely to have been her Majesty.'

---

[1] Saturday 9 March 1325

'I hope it wasn't Sir Hugh le Despenser, then,' Simon muttered. Both knew how poisonous relations had grown between Sir Hugh and the Queen in recent months.

The sound of laughter came to them, and they both peered at the group.

'Is that the Queen?' Simon asked.

'I believe so,' Baldwin said. 'And she is kissing Sir Hugh!'

'I don't think I can believe what I'm seeing,' Simon said.

Queen Isabella was chuckling and exchanging pleasantries with the King's favourite, and as they watched, she rested her hand on his arm and spoke to him again. Then she was away, kissing her husband respectfully, and curtseying to him before walking off with Lord Cromwell. The King and his friend watched them as they made their way down to the harbour.

'Perhaps all is well again now,' Simon ventured. 'She is travelling in some style, after all. She must have money from the King. Maybe he's realised her value to him?'

'And maybe it was all a ruse to lull his suspicions,' Baldwin said. 'There is something else in her mind, I am sure. She loathes Sir Hugh. I am quite certain of that. The two men in the world whom she hates more than any other are him and our friend the bishop of Exeter. It is inconceivable that she could have so changed her feelings in the last weeks.'

'Well, how has she been when you have spoken to her recently? Are you sure there has been no difference?'

'Simon, you have been with me at every moment on this journey. When have you seen me with her?'

'Never?'

'No. She has been with her women at all times and has avoided being with me or any of the other knights.'

'Why should that be? Perhaps she wishes to remain alone so that she can consider what she must say to her brother?'

Baldwin looked at him. 'What is she likely to want to say?

She has advisers and clerks aplenty. The only things which they will not be privy to are the loving things which a brother and sister will say when they are meeting for the first time in some ten years or so.'

'Ten years?' Simon was quiet for a moment. 'To think of leaving your own land and not seeing it for ten years . . .' He looked at the ships in the harbour with a reluctance that bordered on terror.

'Simon, do not panic! We have among the best shipmen in the world here to take us over the sea.' Baldwin laughed. 'I do not think that it will take them very long to carry us over the little puddle that separates us from France.'

'It was not only that which worried me,' Simon said. 'It was the thought of what is waiting for us at the other side.'

Chapter Eleven

Friday before the Feast of St Edward the Martyr[1]

Poissy

Jean had reached this town on his way homewards, before realising that there was nothing for him there. Where was there anything for him to find? His old home was burned to the ground, his wife and child were dead, his father and his brother had both died in the wars trying to defend the honour of his comte – and now that he had failed in the simple task he had been set by his comte, helping to guard an old fort, there was nowhere for him to go. He was homeless, and unless he could persuade his comte that the slaughter of the guards was not his fault, he would be thrown into gaol himself.

After hurrying to Les Andelys and hearing the comments, escape to Paris had seemed the best option. He should tell someone that Arnaud had gone mad and killed all the other guards. But when he looked at himself, he realised that when he had picked up Guillaume much of the man's blood had drained on to him. Suddenly, he wondered how another would look at him, a stranger to this area, telling a wild story about someone else who went mad and butchered all the guards, while he alone survived – although smothered in the gore of the dead. It would not look good. Especially since his accent

---

[1] Friday 15 March 1325

was so different. He spoke the beautiful dialect of the Languedoc, while all the people about here had the harsh twang of Norman French. He was an outsider again, and here he must be viewed askance.

No, rather than that he would return to his lord and report to him, direct. But in so doing, he would again be open to criticism. Why had he not reported to the nearest town, sought out the King's officers and ensured that the murderer was found? Explaining that he was terrified would not serve to protect him. He had a duty to perform, and his cowardice had ensured that the criminal had escaped. There was no excuse for that.

So here he was, in a small town to the north-west of Paris, wondering what he should do to extricate himself from this mess. The more days passed, the more trouble he faced. If he had sought out his lord on the first day, perhaps he would be all right. As it was, he was now a thief himself. At the first opportunity he had stolen a fresh shirt and hosen, while his leather jack had been carefully washed in a stream to remove all the blood. So now he was condemned no matter what he tried.

At least he had a place to rest his head. The other guards had no heads to rest. And Arnaud was perhaps still on the loose.

There was one possible silver lining to the cloud, though. Perhaps, if people had found the château and all the bodies, they might think that he was one of the victims as well. They could assume that he had been slaughtered along with Guillaume, Pons and the others. Yes, that was a thought: maybe Jean had died in the eyes of the officials, and was no more. Could he be free, at last, from the taint which had been with him for so long?

Was it possible? Were the crimes of his past finally laid to rest?

Boulogne

It was mid-morning when Simon gratefully followed the suit of all the knights and climbed into the saddle once more.

Dear Christ in heaven! They'd reached France within hours of leaving England, making landfall at Wissant, and the same day the Queen had commanded that they should make their way to Boulogne and give thanks for their safe and swift journey. Well, Simon wouldn't argue with that. They had arrived in one piece, which was more than he had hoped for when they set off. Almost as soon as the ship pulled the sails up, or whatever the blasted shipmaster called it, there had been a dreadful crack and one of the sails had simply burst. One minute it was a whole sheet, the next there was this almighty report and the thing was in shreds. Apparently it happened quite often. In his post as representative of the Keeper of the Port of Dartmouth, he had heard of such things, but this was the first time he had witnessed it, and he did not enjoy it.

Still, it was the only disaster on the journey. The sailors ran up and down the lines at either side of the cog, and soon the sail was replaced, and then they were making their way quickly enough, with just a little bucking and rocking to unsettle his belly. He only had a chance to throw up four times before they reached the French shore.

As soon as they made landfall, he expected to unload the ship and set off to meet the French king's representatives, but no. Instead Queen Isabella had been determined to see the church of Our Lady in Boulogne, where she made offerings and devotions. The whole town seemed to turn out to meet her and her entourage, and all thirty or so were invited in and given a royal welcome, lodging and food. There the party remained for five days, with no one showing the slightest inclination to get a move on, other than Simon and Baldwin.

It was not until the sixth day that they received the order to gather up their belongings and leave the town. At last they would make their way to meet the king of France's representatives.

Simon was unhappy. 'Baldwin, you're perfectly comfortable here, aren't you? But the people seem . . . different. Is it their clothes?'

'It is everything, Simon. It's the clothes, the language, the countryside. Do you not feel that it is special? I think it feels cleaner, more wholesome somehow, than England.'

'What, you mean Devon?'

'No – I was thinking of England near here. London and Kent. They are curious places compared with this lovely landscape.'

Simon looked about him. 'What is so lovely about this?'

Baldwin snuffed the air. 'The scent of garlic, of grilled fish, of lavender, of wine . . . all these things and more.'

'You can get all those things in England.'

'True enough, but in this country they seem more natural, in some way. Look about you!'

Simon did. He huddled his chin down against his gorget and shook his head to resettle his hood over his ears. 'Yes. It's very pleasant. Except just now I would prefer to be at home in Lydford with a great fire roaring on the hearth and the smell of woodsmoke and spiced wine to warm my heart.'

Baldwin said nothing, but smiled to himself for a few moments. Then a picture came to his mind of Jeanne sitting at his own fireside, with Richalda and little Baldwin nearby, and suddenly the vision brought a lump to his throat.

Pontoise

Le Vieux was feeling sick again. He had to stop at the side of the road and throw up. That was all his lunch wasted, then.

'Come, Vieux! We have to—'

'Shit! You go on, Arnaud. I am too old for this.'

'You? I never thought I'd see the day you said that!'

Arnaud was staring down at him with a mirthless grin on his face. He wasn't bothered by the sight of the dead men. No reason why he should be – as executioner as well as torturer, it would have been a surprise if he had been. Yes, Arnaud was a hard man, certainly, but so was le Vieux. He would not submit to this sudden weakness. He'd seen dead men often enough before. 'Very well, but I'm exhausted and hungry. You go on. I'll follow and get myself some plain bread. I'll see you at the baker's outside his house. You know it?'

'Of course I know it. I will be there as quickly as I may.'

Le Vieux nodded and slowly made his way to the bakery. It was some little way from the town's gate, and there was a bench not far away where the older men of the place were wont to sit in the sun during the warmer months. At this time of year it was mostly deserted, but that was all to the good, so far as le Vieux was concerned. A man had a brazier nearby on which he was roasting small pastries, and le Vieux bought one, breaking it open to let the steam burst out and cool it, eating it quickly, mouth open, to save his lips and tongue from scalding. It was delicious. He sat back contentedly, his mouth full of the flavour of nuts and spices, his belly comfortable, for a while.

His head was still hurting appallingly, but there was nothing to be done. He would have to wait until it was cured. Perhaps it would help to have his blood let out a little. Maybe he ought to seek a physician or barber in the town.

There was a thump at his shoulder, and he was startled awake again, finding himself looking up into the eyes of Arnaud.

'Well enough rested, eh? We have much to do.'

'What? Why?'

'To catch that bastard Jean, naturally. If he escapes, there will be trouble for us. We have to catch him, silence him.'

'What do you mean?'

Arnaud sighed. 'Look, do you remember anything?'

'Of course I do! Just because I was knocked on the head doesn't mean I've forgotten what happened! I remember *everything*! We were guarding the King's bitch, but when she'd gone, we were all sitting about, and then . . .'

'Yes. And Jean escaped, and he knew all that happened in the castle. So we have to catch him or kill him as soon as we can before he can tell anyone else about us.'

Le Vieux nodded with a grimace. Jean knew too much about their actions.

Arnaud looked up at the sky, then to the north. 'This weather is going to break soon. It'll be snow in a couple of days, you mark my words. We have to move fast to tell him.'

'Who?'

'The Comte de Foix. Our master has ordered us, Vieux.'

Boulogne

Fortunately there was much to distract them as they began to make their way on horseback down through the steep old streets, and out into the open countryside.

'Christ's bones!' Simon gasped as they passed under the city gateway, and Baldwin could see that he was not alone in shock. Among the English party many were just as surprised to see that there was a large gathering of people here to see the Queen off. Many were knights and squires, all mounted and caparisoned, with gaily coloured flags fluttering in the cold breeze. It appeared that many wished to honour the sister of their king, and the knights and other nobles were to join Queen Isabella's party.

Their leader was a tall, powerful knight with the bearing of a man born to command: Pierre d'Artois, a senior member of the French nobility, to whom the other knights and counts submitted. Greying, he was plainly not a young man, but the blue eyes in his brown face were shrewd and confident.

For the English, to see so many war-like Frenchmen was somewhat alarming. True, they had papers promising safe conduct, but all too often such papers could be ignored. Although there was some pride in the Queen's face at the sight of such an honour guard, Baldwin was less happy. Poor Queen Isabella had suffered the indignity of having all that made her life pleasant removed from her in recent months, and one thing she had sorely missed was the respect that she had been used to since birth. Under Despenser's rule, even her children had been taken from her. Now, here in her homeland, she was being treated as a queen once more.

However, where there were many warriors there were equally many threats. In theory the first was the threat to the Queen herself, but looking about him Baldwin judged that she was safe enough. With the small force of Englishmen surrounding her, any enemy would have to cut through a ring of steel comprising not only Lord John Cromwell and his knights, but also the men-at-arms. Richard Blaket in particular was glowering about him ferociously at all the French as though longing to wield his bill. Except the French were all behaving with impeccable courtly manners. There was no possible danger to the Queen from these people.

No, it was not she who was in the most danger. It was he himself, Sir Baldwin de Furnshill, the renegade Templar. He must look to his own defence before almost anything else. Thus, while quickly glancing about him for any possible danger to Queen Isabella, he was also careful to study all the faces for any which might seem familiar. He had no wish to be arrested by the Church for supposed past offences.

There were none. Some fellows looked a little suspicious of these English knights, as though considering them little better than supplicants come to beg alms from their king. One in particular was especially haughty in his manner. He looked over the Queen's entourage with simple disdain, and Baldwin was sure he made a comment – something about it being no surprise that his king had taken back his Gascon lands if this little band was the best the English could produce to serve his own wife.

The man's arrogance irked not only Baldwin. He could see that others, even Sir Charles, were eyeing the fellow closely. Baldwin jerked his head to Simon, and spurred his mount to close the distance between them and Lord John Cromwell. If that man was a threat, he was already nullified if all had spotted him. The menace Baldwin feared was the one that had not been seen.

Lord John was riding with his own squire and a groom, and as Baldwin drew nearer he saw that Sir John de Sapy and Sir Peter de Lymesey were also already close to hand. It was in the way of things that men of war would automatically look to the security of their charge.

For Simon, seeing such a gathering was petrifying, and he knew only gratitude for the presence of Baldwin and the other knights and Lord John. If there was a threat to the Queen, these men would soon quell it. They certainly looked the part, with their armour shining, and the rattling and clanging of their weapons a constant accompaniment.

All had brought their own horses, of course. Each knight had brought a destrier with him, and for the beginning of this journey to Paris all were mounted upon their mightiest beasts. Now Simon could see why. The Queen's company might number only some thirty-one people, but with four knights and one lord sitting high over all others on their great horses, haughtily looking about them grim-faced, few would have been bold enough to attempt any sort of action against the Queen.

However, even as he considered that, Simon realised that

one face was missing. Although Sir John and Sir Peter were already with Lord John immediately behind the Queen, Sir Charles now was not. When Simon looked for him, he saw the knight over at the flank, as though riding along in parallel with the Queen's party, but not a part of it. It made Simon wonder again about the man.

Simon and Baldwin had first met this handsome, tall, elegant knight while the battle at Boroughbridge was still a painful memory. Earl Thomas of Lancaster had been accused of treachery by the King, his armies chased about the country until he was forced to surrender. And after that came the appalling retribution.

In the past, men who committed the disgraceful crime of raising arms against their king tended to be punished with a degree of tolerance. They might be imprisoned in the Tower, then forgiven, so long as a fair ransom was paid and a fine against their lands imposed. This was not so in the case of the King's cousin, Thomas of Lancaster. He had not merely raised an army with the intention of subduing his lawful king, he had deliberately insulted the King's best friend and adviser, Sir Hugh le Despenser. The two men, Lancaster and Despenser, were determined to snatch whatever power and money they could. And Thomas lost.

Earl Thomas had been the richest and most powerful man in the country save only the King himself, and the King was determined to make an example of him. The Earl was executed shamefully, without consideration of his position, and before his body had cooled the reign of terror began.

Any men-at-arms, knights or even barons who were thought to have been allied to Earl Thomas were hanged, drawn and quartered, bloody sections of their bodies boiled and tarred before being despatched to all parts of the kingdom to be put on display at the gates to the King's cities as a permanent reminder of the punishment that would be meted out to any who dared challenge his authority. The country was filled with the stench of rotting corpses.

And one of the good earl's senior knights was a certain Sir Charles of Lancaster.

Sir Charles had been a most devoted knight of Earl Thomas's household, so he clearly had no place in the England that was ruled by the men who had executed his master. He had fled to France, and eventually come to rest in Galicia. When Simon and Baldwin returned homewards, he had joined them, hoping to find some new lord to serve. He declared himself heartily bored with foreign lands. There were not enough tournaments and wars to pay his expenses. Better to give up the mercenary life.

It was that aspect of his career which had given Baldwin the most concern, Simon remembered. Baldwin had always had a powerful dislike of men who served for cash. He had been brought up to believe in a life of service and duty. Mercenaries who would go wherever the money took them were the enemies of all that was good and honourable.

Now, Sir Charles looked like a man who was at the edge of the company so that he would be able to ride off at a moment's notice if danger presented itself. But then, when Simon cast a suspicious look over the crowds again, he noticed that Paul, Sir Charles's man-at-arms, was not near his master but instead towards the rear of their column, and on the other side of it. So one was at each flank, ready to warn the lord of any threat to them all, and probably in a better position to protect the Queen than many of the others who huddled nearer her.

After all, Simon told himself, Sir Charles was one of the King's household knights now. His days of mercenary warfare were over.

Or so Simon hoped.

Chapter Twelve

Feast Day of St Edward the Martyr[1]

Pois, France

Ricard was no nearer even *liking* the man as he sat frowning in the pre-dawn greyness. All about them there was the noise of men striking camp, knocking down the great beams that supported the tents, pulling up the pegs, some shouting for more trunks to store the blankets and drapery, others bellowing for help to fold the heavy canvas, while grooms saw to the horses. Donkeys brayed their protests, dogs barked, and only the Queen's tent was an island of calm as she ate a sedate breakfast and prepared herself for the continuing journey.

'He can bloody sing, though,' Janin said placatingly.

'I don't think that's all there is to it,' Ricard countered. 'Look at the way he behaves! Disappearing like that just when we were supposed to be entertaining the Queen.'

'Look, truth is, I never really liked him much,' Adam said. 'I think we ought to try to get on with him now, though.'

'You never . . .'

Ricard was too shocked by the blatant dishonesty of the comment to do much more than gape, and it was left to Philip to snort: 'You are a prick, Adam. You know that?'

---

[1] Monday 18 March 1325

'Sod you, Philip!'

'Shut up, both of you. The fact is, we were all asked to go and play yesterday, just for the Queen and Lord John, and he wasn't here.'

He kept himself very much to himself, this Jack of Ireland, and wandered off at the worst possible times. Ricard would have dearly loved to know where he came from, and why it was that William de Bouden had wanted him to join their little group. There must be some reason for it.

Last night was the worst, though. They'd all been summoned to entertain the Queen because there was some local dignitary visiting whom she had wanted to impress, and Jack had just – *gone*! He could have melted into the surrounding countryside, except there was bugger all for a man to melt into. Hardly even any trees just here, where they were camped. That was why they'd picked the site, of course, but it still made things that much more confusing.

Not only confusing. Bloody irritating! Ricard and the lads had played their fingers raw, so it felt, with a good few tunes which the Queen declared she had never heard before, and there were some knights there who'd been tapping their feet rather than chatting as they usually did, the heathens, and smothering the sound of any music with their laughter. No, last night they'd *listened*, as though they couldn't help it. In some way, Ricard wondered whether it was partly the first tune he'd struck up – the one they'd called 'The Waferer' in honour of Peter. It seemed suitable, some-how, as if they were bringing a bit of Peter with them on this great journey of theirs. Not that it was the happiest of occasions for them. They were hemmed in by dangers, so he felt.

So he'd gone to see William de Bouden as soon as he'd had a chance, and what had he said? Only 'The man is a member of your troupe. Nothing to do with me. You brought him, so you deal with him. If you're unhappy with his performance, you should discuss it with *him*. I have enough on my plate.'

But there had been no sign of the man.

It was full dawn when Adam looked up and pointed. 'There he is.'

'Where the hell have you been?' Ricard demanded as Jack strolled casually towards them.

'I found a lovely, lively little French whore. Why?'

'We were supposed to be singing to the Queen last night, and you weren't here.'

'I am sure you will have done well without me.'

'Perhaps we'd have done better with a drum-player,' Janin said irritably.

'You had Philip there.'

Ricard saw that this was not productive. The man was not exactly laughing at him and the others, but neither was he giving way or apologising. Instead he appeared to be preparing himself for a fight. Yes, he was! He was happy to fight them all, from the look of him, rather than submit to responding to their questions. The fellow must be demented!

'Where were you?'

'I have told you.'

'No, you just said you were with a French wench. Who? Where did you find her? Where did you go to lie with her?'

'These are all interesting questions, but I'm afraid I have much to do. I haven't packed my things yet.'

'It's all right. I packed your stuff,' Adam said, and had the decency to look ashamed as all the other men of the group turned to stare at him. They'd agreed Jack would have to do it himself. It wasn't as though he'd tried to endear himself to them even remotely since their first meeting with him.

'Why, thank you, Adam. That's good to hear. You are a real friend.' Jack smiled at Adam, and when the smile was not reciprocated, it broadened until Jack looked close to outright laughter. 'Well, lordings, I'd best be preparing myself, eh? I'll see you on the road.'

'That bastard,' Philip snarled. 'Why don't we just push him under a cart's wheels?'

'Because if we tried to, we'd have to explain his death to William de Bouden. You want to do that, when we've enough problems already, what with those two dead in London?' Ricard returned. 'No? Then get your gear together. I don't like it any more than you, but we're stuck with the shit.'

They stopped late in the morning to rest their beasts and take a brief meal, and Baldwin and Simon found themselves near to the Queen's favourite guard, Richard Blaket.

'How is the Queen?' Simon asked. All knew that Blaket was wooing one of the Queen's maids, the blonde called Alicia.

'She grows ever more keen to see her brother, I think. Nothing will give her greater satisfaction than meeting him and feeling that for once she's truly secure,' Blaket said, his dark eyes moving over the men around them. His air of lowering truculence had not diminished.

The other two nodded. There was no need for any of them to suggest that she was safe enough with the knights provided for her escort. Only Baldwin was sufficiently independent to be determined to protect her no matter what. The others were all creatures of Sir Hugh le Despenser.

Simon nodded towards a man walking to the woods at the side of the clearing. 'He one of her musicians?'

'Yes.'

'Friend, you sound less trusting of them than you do of the French,' Baldwin chuckled.

'One of them once molested my Alicia.'

'He would be a brave man, who tried that against her will,' Simon said lightly.

Baldwin was about to laugh, but something in Blaket's expression made him hesitate. 'She was all right, though? There was no rape?'

'No. She assures me that she was perfectly all right. It doesn't make me look on them with a joyful spirit, though.'

'Naturally.'

'The one who did it is dead now, anyway.'

'Really?' Baldwin asked sharply.

'Yes. He was drowned in the ditch outside the city. In London, I mean.'

Baldwin winced. 'A nasty way to die.'

'Ach, a man like that, he probably deserved it. Climbed into some girl's bedchamber, I expect. Her father found him there and did it to him.'

'When was this?'

'Day or two before we set off. Why?'

'Just curiosity.' Baldwin smiled.

It was that same afternoon that Baldwin had his argument.

At first it was little enough. He had been riding along gently, his mind wandering slightly, as any rider's will after several days in the saddle, his hips automatically swaying with the horse's gait, his body fully accustomed to the dip and roll, when there was a sudden explosion of noise behind and to his left.

His rounsey, a dependable, stolid creature generally, was as startled as himself. The large bay jerked to the right, almost unseating Baldwin, and was about to plunge when Baldwin jerked his head back into line. If a horse the size of this one decided to charge off through all the people in the column, his steel-shod hooves could kill someone.

Hearing a laugh, he turned to see a knight grinning amidst a small cloud of evil-smelling smoke. Even from here Baldwin caught the whiff of brimstone. About the man were his men-at-arms, a couple of ostlers, a short, smiling priest and some others. All appeared hugely amused by his reaction and near-fall from his horse.

It was that same Frenchman whom Baldwin had noticed at Boulogne. He was strong and well muscled, with a neck that was almost an extension of his head, it was so thick. Like Baldwin, he too was bearded, and he had a scar that reached down from his ear to his jawline. When he laughed, Baldwin could see that his front teeth were little more than stumps. The man had been a fighter, and had taken powerful buffets, from the look of him.

'*Mon sieur*, you have me at a disadvantage.' In the past Baldwin had always felt that the French language lent a certain air of gaiety and elegance to what might otherwise have been tedious discussions. Just at this moment he was less convinced. It felt a barbarous language if this fellow was born to it.

'That is true, Sieur Baldwin,' the man said, and made a mocking bow, one hand at his breast. 'I am Enguerrand, the Comte de Foix. Pardon me if I respond slowly, but it is a little difficult to comprehend the words as spoken by you English. Your dialect and the pronunciation, they make it very hard, you understand?'

Baldwin felt his face blanch. He was too angry to be cautious. At his age, insults were seldom received, and even more rarely noted, but this man had deliberately snubbed him, and now he chuckled again with his friends. More, Baldwin had lived in Paris for long enough to recognise a provincial accent. He affected his best Parisian tones.

'Perhaps so, *mon sieur*. I understand your difficulty perfectly. I also find your dialect hard. Perhaps that is because I am unused to rural language? Or possibly it is your teeth,' he added more quietly. He did not wish to provoke the man too harshly.

'*Nom d'un chien!*' The Comte de Foix flushed a deep mauve colour, and spurred his horse to join Baldwin, but even as he did so, Sir Charles of Lancaster suddenly appeared between them.

'Sir Baldwin, I do believe you are taking over my responsibilities here. Isn't it my duty to be the cantankerous, disputative fellow, and yours to be the rational, sensible justice from the country?'

'*Mon sieur!*' de Foix cried with genuine anger. 'I must insist you apologise for that ill-thought comment!'

'*Mon sieur*, what ever can you mean?' Baldwin said with icy calm. 'I thought especially carefully before speaking. I would not wish to think that I could upset you unintentionally.'

'Caution, Sir Baldwin,' Sir Charles muttered. He looked over at Lord John Cromwell, who was watching with keen interest. Cromwell nodded and motioned to Sir John de Sapy.

De Sapy was an arrogant fellow at the best of times, but he was undoubtedly a good fighter. Still, Baldwin had no need or desire for others to join in a battle on his behalf. 'I can manage this man,' he hissed at Sir Charles.

'I am sure you can. However, I am less certain that the Queen's party can cope with the whole of France, old fellow. You can scrap as much as you like, and as far as I am concerned you can wipe out the whole of France. Yes. But beforehand, please wait until I've reached a safe location, eh?'

De Foix was still riding alongside, but, prevented from reaching Baldwin by de Sapy and Sir Charles, he gave a sneering gesture, and trotted back to his companions, as though to say that Baldwin was not worth fighting.

'Ignore him, Sir Baldwin,' Sir Charles said. He spat over his left thigh, from where he could keep an eye on the French knights.

Baldwin had fought often enough, but he did not like to be forced to retreat from an insult. He held de Foix's eye for a while, keeping his face expressionless. Looking away at last, he caught sight of Pierre d'Artois, who was watching them closely. Baldwin inclined his head stiffly, and Artois did not acknowledge him, but pulled his horse's head about and trotted away

'Yes. That is fine, Sir Charles,' Baldwin said quietly. 'I can do my best to avoid him, but he may be able to do even better at seeking me out. And I shall not surrender to a man such as he.'

Sir John de Sapy trotted alongside Sir Charles of Lancaster. 'What was all that about?'

'I think the fellow over there enjoys unsettling Englishmen. He had a hand *gonne* of some sort, I think, and set it off as Baldwin rode past. Nearly had Sir Baldwin on the ground.'

'A *gonne*, eh? I've seen them a few times. Interesting toys.'

'Aye. Damned noisy, though. It was foolish to set it off as a man was riding past.'

'Unless he wanted to provoke.'

'Why should he?' Sir Charles frowned.

'I don't know. But he seemed to know Sir Baldwin's name, didn't he?'

Simon was blissfully unaware of the altercation. He too had heard the noise, but had no idea what could have caused it. It sounded like a hammer striking an anvil very hard. No: worse than that. He had once been in a smithy when the old devil had wanted to shock him. The man spat on to his anvil when Simon wasn't looking, then held a red-hot bar over the spittle, and hit it with a six pound hammer.

The resulting explosion had been much like that noise: an enormous crack which had almost made Simon leap from his own skin. But there was no anvil here on the march, and

Simon was wondering what could have made such a loud noise when he saw Paul, Sir Charles's man-at-arms. Paul had been with Sir Charles from very early on, when the knight was still with Earl Thomas of Lancaster.

'Paul – how goes it?'

'Well enough.'

Paul was an unlikely-looking warrior. He was shortish, and plump, and had almost black hair with white feathers at either temple. From the Scottish March, he spoke with a soft Scots accent, a lilting, pleasant sound, which did not match the quizzical expression he commonly wore.

'So, tell me, what are you and Sir Charles doing in the King's service again?' Simon said. It was the question he had been burning to ask. The last he had seen of Sir Charles, the knight was returning to England with a view to trying to beg pardon for his crimes as a loyal supporter of Earl Thomas of Lancaster.

'We never raised pennon or steel against the King,' Paul said. He kept his eyes fixed ahead as though musing to himself, rather than speaking to a companion.

'But you were thought of as an enemy. We all saw the devastation of the country after the death of Earl Thomas. Knights from every county were hanged or beheaded . . . I heard there were more than two hundred, all told. And the killing carried on for months. Yet you are back in the King's service?'

Paul tilted his head and shot a look around him. 'Look, you see that knight with my master and Sir Baldwin? Sir John de Sapy? He was a household knight along with us in Earl Thomas's castle at Pontefract. Listed as a rebel in '22, he was. Now look at him. You know what got him his position here? He's a friend of Despenser. That's got him back in the King's favour. And Peter de Lymesey? He was one of Earl Thomas's men too. Now, though, he's a respected man in the King's household.'

'But how?'

'You think the King has so many loyal knights, he can afford to lose men like these? They may not be the most reliable compared with some others, but while the King dispenses *largesse*, they'll be there with him.'

'And you?'

'I'm easily pleased. All I crave is a bed at night and enough money to fill my belly.' Paul grinned and patted his belt. 'It takes some filling now.'

Simon laughed aloud. 'So does mine. At least during this journey we appear to have access to the best victuals in the land.'

'Aye, that's true enough.'

Paul was a good companion. For some while he and Simon spoke of matters that concerned them, from the sudden chill that both felt, perhaps a precursor to snow, to the best means of protecting leather from the ravages of a journey like this. If a scabbard was to protect the sword within, its leather needed good and careful treatment. It was as easy to be silent in his company, though, and soon the two men rode along without speaking, content to let the countryside pass by them.

Not until much later did Simon see the man who strode onwards so forcefully, and wonder about him. He had not noticed the musicians specifically since his talk with Richard Blaket – they were merely a band of men who happened to travel in the same part of the column as the servants, and were not particularly relevant to him – but now he watched Jack of Ireland with some puzzlement. The man moved like a man-at-arms, not a musician, for all that he carried a drum wrapped in leather and waxed linen on his back. There was no sword at his belt, only a long knife like the ones the Welsh men carried, but he looked the sort of fellow who would be adept with either sword or axe. 'Paul – do you know who that man is?'

Paul followed his pointing finger, and gave a dry smile. 'You miss little, Bailiff. I have seen him, yes.' He stopped and studied Simon speculatively for a moment. 'There are men you get to recognise after a while. Some, the more honourable ones, are the men you see in the King's service and in his hall. Others, though, you see on the outskirts of things always.'

'I don't understand you.'

'Oh, I think you do, Bailiff. The King has one household. There are others near him who have their own. And if a man didn't trust the Queen, he'd want a spy in her camp, wouldn't he?'

'I see,' Simon said coldly. Clearly the man was one of Despenser's.

Chapter Thirteen

Arnaud was in little doubt when he saw the van of the column that this must be the party in which his master was travelling. 'Look!'

Le Vieux lifted his eyes to the horizon, squinting into the bright sunshine. 'Yes, I see them.'

There was no need to hurry. The Comte would soon be with them. Men on horseback were trotting along easily, their ladies rocking along in a group together behind them on their specially trained *amblères*, while the provisions and essentials were brought along behind them in the great wagons and carts. It was a magnificent sight. To see the richest people from the two kingdoms, all displaying their wealth in their bright clothing and the quality of their wonderful dresses and tunics, was something that not even le Vieux had experienced before, and the two men stood quietly, a little overwhelmed, as the great party drew nearer.

It was when the first third of the column had already passed them that Arnaud saw their master and darted in amongst the people and horses to reach him. He pushed a donkey from his path, making the fellow leading it snarl at him, but Arnaud was used to the attitude of others towards him. No one ever showed him any sympathy, which was part of the reason why he never gave it to anyone else. He was content with his own company, and had no need of companions. He could sit back with pleasure with a knife and some wood, and whittle. His delight was to invent, especially tools that would aid him in his chosen profession – torturer and executioner.

'My lord? Comte de Foix. I have news from the château for you.'

His lordship was not happy, from the look of him. His dark eyes were flashing with rage, and he was pale, which was never a good sign. Arnaud looked up at him with interest. The Comte was usually so cool and collected – this temper might mean that Arnaud would have a job to do for him soon, with any luck.

'Follow on with the baggage. See me in my tent this evening. I won't talk now.'

Woods south-east of Pois

Jean shivered in the cold night air. This was the worst night of his life, he was convinced.

At first, he had been content to spread his blanket under the stars, well wrapped in a thick cloak with a heavy second blanket over the top, but then the dampness had started to fall. At first it was only the light drizzle that would irritate but not kill a man. Now, though, light, soft flakes of snow were slipping through the air, their very touch a stinging threat.

He had lived through worse. When a lad, he'd been a shepherd in the mountains back in his homeland of Languedoc, and there, in the winter, he had been accustomed to the dangers of the snow. On occasion he had seen the after-effects. It was not unusual to find a man huddled into a foetal shape in the morning, all warmth gone from him, all life fled. Sad, but it happened every year, especially among the youngest and the oldest.

Jean had been lucky. His father had been a sensible man who had taught him how to make himself safe in the worst of weathers. There was no point in having a son and then leaving him to endure a Spartan existence on the mountainside without allowing him the most rudimentary protection. A little knowledge went a long way to secure a man's life, after all. That was his father's opinion. Later, when they went to war together, when there was nothing left for them in their home town, that education was very useful. Now it was still more so.

He rose and looked about him. He was on a hillside. A short way up the hill was the roadway which led from Beauvais to Pontoise and on to Paris, but he had chosen this hillside because it was well covered with small trees. Ideal for a man who needed fire and shelter.

Grunting reluctantly, he rose, folded his blankets, and began to hunt around. Soon he had selected two little saplings which were standing close together. If he'd been less lazy earlier he could have saved himself this grief now, but there was little point in reminding himself that he had grown lax. Better to simply get on with things.

He gathered up a long pole and set it to rest on corresponding branches to form a lintel. Then he started collecting more branches. These he set aslant on his lintel to form a lean-to roof, the open doorway facing away from the wind and safe from the snow. More boughs leaned against this roof to form walls, and finally he could gather some leaves and throw them over the top. He didn't need too many – there was no need for the roof or walls to be waterproof or insulated. The snow itself would soon achieve that. However, he was not going to suffer frostbite unnecessarily. Looking about, he persuaded himself that no one else would be foolish enough, or desperate enough, to be out in this weather, and began to gather up twigs and dead branches. It took him a little while to gather enough, and then he had a stroke of luck when he stumbled over a length of wood. It was a sapling which had fallen, dead, and was well dried. Pulling it back to his shelter, he began to break it up into sticks and constructed a small fire. He took out flint and tinder, and soon had a tiny flame, which he tended assiduously. It took an age, or so it seemed, but at least the act of fetching and carrying the wood had kept him warm, and now he could sit back a little and enjoy the flames that licked up from his improvised hearth.

Yes. His father had taught him well. But then, all those who were condemned heretics had to learn to survive. This was just one of the sets of skills he had been forced to learn as a follower of Waldes.

Peter from Oxford, the chaplain, had finished his last service of the day, and was cleaning his portable altar when he saw the cloaked and hooded figure wandering about the place.

'You are the chaplain?' the man asked.

'To the Queen, yes,' Peter said warily. He didn't know this man. His face was unfamiliar, and any sensible man of God was also cautious. There were enough footpads who were prepared to break into a church to steal what they might. A bold one could easily knock a man on the head and take his plate and silver.

Not that this little fellow looked too dangerous to him. He had the appearance of a mild monk. Small in stature and amiable in appearance, the chubby fellow was all smiles. 'I wonder, would you welcome the companionship of another priest on your way?' Opening his cloak and bringing out a large skin, he added, 'I have a warming drink of burned wine, if that will aid your decision, Father.'

Peter smiled and set aside his little altar. 'Father, it'd be a pleasure to have you with me. What may I call you?'

'Pierre. Pierre Clergue.'

'That little arse wants his backside leathered,' Baldwin grumbled as he rolled himself in his blanket in their tent.

'I think you have made your feelings perfectly clear,' Simon said with a low snigger.

'You didn't see his face, Simon.'

'I don't need to. I saw yours,' Simon said. 'Talking of faces, did you see William de Bouden's today?'

'What of it?'

'He was like a man who'd eaten a bowl of sloes.'

Baldwin winced at that thought. 'Why should that be?'

'I think he's chewing through the money faster than he had hoped.'

'The Queen was given a large sum, I think. The King finally gave in and allowed her a decent sum for this embassy.'

'Well, you wouldn't think so to look at her comptroller.'

'Maybe so. At least he's a decent fellow, not like this Comte de Foix.'

'Him again?' Simon grunted despairingly.

'He was thoroughly dishonourable,' Baldwin muttered. 'I should have allowed him to challenge me. It would have saved much time.'

'Baldwin, from what you've told me, the fellow was twenty years younger than you – possibly more. I don't think that it would save much time to seek out a suitable site for your burial, and it most assuredly wouldn't have made my journey any faster to have to go to your home to explain to Jeanne how it was that you died.'

'Oh, so now you don't think I can protect myself against a young brute like him?'

'What was it made that noise, anyway?'

'The noise? I don't know. I have never heard an explosion like that before. It was a curious thing – like a small cannon.'

'I did see some smoke,' Simon said thoughtfully. 'But that was all. It reeked.'

'Yes. I smelled brimstone,' Baldwin said. 'Ach, there's a root under me.'

'Move, then,' said Simon, content in the knowledge that his own bedspace was comfortable. At least they had the benefit of good tent canvas overhead. It was considerably better than being stuck out in the open. He could hear the tiny pattering of snow hitting the material. It was like the sound of individual grains of sand . . . no, it was quieter, softer, more soothing.

'I do not expect much in the way of sympathy, luckily,' Baldwin grumbled.

'That may be as well.'

'However, you are fortunate to be younger. A man of my decrepitude also has to contend with the tribulations of old age. Such as a weak bladder!' Baldwin said, rising. He eyed his sword, but it seemed foolish to strap on his war belt. Still, he did not like to wander about a camp without any means of defence. After pausing, he took his dagger and held it in his hand as he ducked beneath the awning, then stuck it, sheathed, into his belt.

It was darker than he had expected. This late in the evening, only a couple of fires were lighted still. The others had been put out for safety. Some years ago, when the Queen was here with her husband on another diplomatic visit, her tent had caught fire, and she had been badly burned about the arms as she tried to rescue some trinkets – jewellery and other valuables. The injuries had affected her for years afterwards, and she had been most insistent on camp safety during this journey. Which was why Baldwin kept stumbling into discarded items of camp trash or almost tripping over guy ropes in the dark.

The area he was heading towards was a ditch between two fields. There were bushes and trees on the farther side of the ditch, which gave a useful marker to him now as he made his way somewhat unsteadily over the rough ground, icy and snowy as it was. Then he found himself at the lip, and lifted his tunic to make his own mark in the snow before sighing, hitching up his hosen again, pulling down his tunic, and setting off to return.

A small cry made him pause. There was a short gurgling sound, rather like a mill's leat chuckling over stones, except there was none here. The river was at the other side of the camp. Baldwin looked about him sharply, wondering if it was another man writing in the snow, but he saw no one.

That noise was all too much like another he knew well: a man trying to shout when his throat was filling with blood from severed arteries. Baldwin had heard it too often ever to be able to forget it. He felt his scalp move with the atavistic fear that affected any man, no matter how old, when hearing another slain in the darkness. But Baldwin had been well trained. Although he wanted to return to the tent, to Simon's companionship and safety, he was a knight, and, more than that, he was here to protect his queen. He would prefer to be damned for eternity than submit to night terrors.

He gripped the hilt of his dagger and pulled it free of the sheath, then started to make his way towards the place from which he thought the sounds had come, although the going was tough, and reaching the place quietly would be extremely difficult. Rather than fall over guy ropes again, he took a wide berth around the tents and made for the source more cautiously.

The noise had seemed to come from the small stand of trees that marked the edge of a little stream. Baldwin had noted this, as he had noted the lie of all the land as they arrived. One aspect of his military training while in the Knights Templar was always to make careful observations of the ground near a camp, and never had it proved so useful.

Beaten into the soil here, was a pathway, and he followed along the track until he came closer to the trees. Once there he slowed, listening intently.

There was little to hear. From all about there came the muffled snores and grumbles of a camp at night. In the short pauses between, when the wind blew from the north and took all such sounds away, there was nothing at all, only the soft, insistent sussuration of snowflakes settling on the ground, like a gentle hissing. A horse whinnied, a dog barked, and a man muttered, cursed and rolled over, trying to get warm, but there was nothing else.

Baldwin closed his eyes to hear the better. The clouds were so thick and low, there was no light from the moon whatever. Not a stray gleam shone in the midst of the clouds. His eyes were all but useless. Slowly he crouched down, frowning, wondering whether he could have been mistaken when he had thought he had heard something. He took a step, his foot crunching on a patch of ice, slipping into the puddle beneath, the mud squelching, and stood utterly still.

There was a sound there . . . *there*! He set off more quickly. The man was moving quietly, but his passage would conceal Baldwin's approach. And then he saw something ahead. It was a man, bent down, so he thought, and there was a little spark of light in his hands. He called out, and ran on, but the man was up and away in the darkness, and Baldwin saw a short flash, a sizzling burning, and then there was an appalling explosion, a vile gout of fire, like raw energy. Flames gushed towards him from the ground, searing his eyes and leaving him blinded, and he screamed as he turned away, falling to the ground, his hands over his eyes, trying to squeeze out the vision of hell leaping towards him.

The screams woke Charlie first, and he shot upright, staring about him wildly, adding to the noise with his own shrill cries of terror.

'*Jesus and all the saints!*' Janin burst out, springing from his bed. 'Ricard? Are you all right?'

All the musicians were together in the one tent, and as Ricard held little Charlie close to him Philip stared about him blearily, gathering tinder and striking a spark. As it glowed, he was able to light a taper, and then looked round at the other faces.

Looking at Jack's bedding, Ricard summed it up for them all. 'So where has the little shite got to now?'

In his tent, Peter of Oxford woke gradually. The screaming and shouting on all sides was enough to startle him, but he had been so deeply asleep, ready to wake before dawn to celebrate Prime, that it was hard to gather his senses.

'Do not panic,' came a voice, and he was about to bellow for help when he realised it was his guest, Pierre Clergue.

'Father! Do you know what has happened?'

'No idea, my friend,' Clergue said. He was at the tent's flap, and now he turned to peer out. 'An alarm of some sort, but probably just a squabble over a game of merrills.'

Simon heard the detonation and the scream from his friend, and threw off his blankets. He tugged on his boots, pulled a cloak over his shoulders, and grabbed his sword before hurtling from the tent.

There were some men already standing in a group, talking loudly, and Simon made his way to them quickly. 'Let me through! Baldwin? *Baldwin!*'

'Simon, my Christ, but that flame seared my eyes!'

'What flame?' Simon asked. Peering closely, he saw that Baldwin was sitting hunched, his face frowning, eyes squeezed tightly shut. Simon took his hand, and helped him up. Peering closely, Simon could see that there were black powder marks on his friend's face, and his beard looked as though it had been singed. 'You reek of the devil, Baldwin! Can you see me?'

'I don't . . . yes. Yes, I can. Thanks be to God! I saw flames coming towards me, Simon. Huge yellow flames which scorched my face. I was blinded for a moment . . .'

'You are sure you are all right?'

Baldwin put out his hand shakily and took hold of Simon's arm. 'Help me walk, Simon. My legs feel as though they're made of aspic! I do not think they will support me. In Christ's name, I never thought I should be so . . .'

There was a muttering behind Baldwin, and Simon saw torches approaching. Men were gathered together in a group, and Simon was alarmed to see that the men were bending down over something. 'Christ's ballocks, Baldwin! What have you done?'

'Me? What do you mean?' Baldwin demanded, blinking wildly, but he could hear the footsteps approaching solemnly.

'Sieur Baldwin, what explanation do you have for this?'

'Sieur Pierre?' Baldwin asked. 'Is that you?'

Sieur Pierre d'Artois peered at him. A servant with him was gripping a large flaming torch, and he held it up as the ageing French knight stooped slightly. 'What has happened to you?'

It was left to Simon to try to explain. 'He was attacked by a flame. . . they burned his face, look.'

'He has been attacked by something,' d'Artois agreed. He looked up as a heavy tread announced the arrival of Lord John Cromwell with Sir Charles and Sir John de Sapy. 'My lord, *mes sieurs*. We have an embarrassment.'

Lord John bent to peer into Baldwin's face. Baldwin was still blinking furiously to try to clear his eyes of the stinging grittiness. It felt as though someone had thrown a handful of hot sand in them. He had been fortunate, he knew, but he wasn't prepared to let anyone else know that.

'I agree. This is an outrageous state of affairs. When an English knight, here to guard the Queen, with plenteous letters of safe conduct, is assaulted within the camp, it makes for a grave situation indeed.'

'It must have been the Comte de Foix,' Baldwin grated. 'The flames; I am sure that they were his black powder. He set it off as I drew nearer him. He wanted to embarrass me!'

'You see?' Lord John said. 'Where is this comte?'

Sieur Pierre looked at him. 'You are right. It is very grave. Especially since the Comte is dead.'

Chapter Fourteen

Robert de Chatillon stared down at the body with mixed feelings. This had been his master, his mentor and the source of his livelihood, and although he was never a greatly affectionate lord, yet he was the man who had taken on Robert and maintained him. Without Sieur Enguerrand, Robert was unsure what might happen to *him*.

However, it went further than a lack of affection. The Comte de Foix was a powerful magnate, a man fully aware of his importance and his place in the world. He had provided food and clothing for Robert, and in return Robert had given him his service, but there was no love in the relationship. Theirs was the companionship of a feudal lord and his servant, nothing more.

Still, it was hard to lose a master, even when he had not been kind or particularly generous. There was a void in his place, a void in which all was uncertain. Robert had no family to which to turn, and he was not convinced that the Comte's wife would want any reminders of her husband. He had been cruel to her, too. Thus it was that even as he bent a leg at the side of the corpse, he was not certain what his feelings were for this man, who had provided for him during his life, but without grace or gratitude. His tongue had been harsh, and, when he found a fault or a weakness, he took pleasure in exposing it to all.

'Stand aside!'

Pierre d'Artois was behind him, and Robert scrambled to

his feet as the great lord peered down, motioning to men to bring their torches lower that he might study the body more closely. 'Did any man here see what happened?'

Beside him was the Englishman, the Lord John Cromwell, and he gazed suspiciously at all the men present, rather than staring down at the body, his cold, grey eyes as keen as a hawk's as he studied the expressions of those nearby.

No one answered, and soon Pierre's attention left the body and rested on Robert. 'You were his *escuier* What was he doing out here in the middle of the night? Did he have to rise from his bed each night?'

'No, my lord. He was never wont to get up. He would sleep through the night without difficulty.'

'Then what was he doing here?'

'I don't know. I was asleep. But I am not aware of any reason for him to come here.'

'Very well,' Artois said, and turned his attention back to the body, shaking his head and grunting. 'So perhaps someone bethought himself that this was a stranger, possibly a danger to the Queen, and killed him.'

He would have continued, but now there was a soft voice from behind Robert, and he bowed low even as he turned to face her: Isabella, queen of England.

'My Lord Cromwell? There has been a disturbance?'

'This man has died.'

'And it would seem,' Pierre d'Artois added silkily, 'that one of your knights may have had a part in his death. I noticed earlier today that Sir Baldwin and he had been arguing, and now, within a few hours of their cross words, one is dead.'

The Queen gazed over to where Simon and Baldwin stood. 'I know this knight personally. He would not be guilty of an underhand or dishonourable action, of that I am sure.'

'My Lord Cromwell, would you have him come here, please?' d'Artois asked.

Lord Cromwell nodded and beckoned to Simon, who brought his friend with him.

Baldwin was still shaky. His legs were unreliable, and he felt as though he had been riding in a tournament, his heart had been pounding so hard. Now it was calming a little, and he could look down at the body dispassionately, noting the position of the arms and legs, the relaxed expression on the dead man's face. Nothing odd there. Most corpses had the appearance of calmness. He thought it was the way that the muscles loosened and settled once the energy of the soul had left the body. His eyes passed over the face to the throat. In the flickering torchlight, the pool about his neck looked black on the snow. He had been right: de Foix had drowned in his own blood as his throat was cut. Then, from the look of it, he'd been stabbed as well. A dagger protruded from his breast. And then his eyes locked on the hilt of the knife, and his hand shot to his belt. With some disbelief, he looked down at the empty sheath.

The dagger planted in the man's breast was Baldwin's.

Morrow of the Feast of St Edward the Martyr [1]

Pois, France

It was a cold, cold morning. The sky was leaden with the heavy clouds covering it, and all looked up, fearing more snow.

Robert had not slept well. Since the discovery of the body, his mind had been unable to disengage from the overriding consideration that his own future was in the balance. Ideally he should ride back to Foix with the body, but in the absence of a murderer, he thought that he should ride with the Queen's

---

[1] Tuesday 19 March 1325

party to the King with the body. If nothing else, the matter could be discussed before the King.

No one had confessed to the murder, but Robert was sure that there was something shifty in the English knight's eyes when he was questioned by Artois. Artois was considered one of the King's most intelligent knights, a man with courage, but also a shrewd mind. Often he could read a man's heart and see what lay within. And today Robert wanted him to study Sir Baldwin and see what he uncovered. There had to have been something. Robert had not been with his master all that day, but he had witnessed the anger and heard the brief but sharp exchange between the two on the road. He'd asked Baldwin about that the night before, in front of Artois.

'The argument? Yes, we had some words, but it was nothing that could justify my slaying him. He did something that made a noise and scared my horse. That was all.'

'What did he do?' Artois had asked.

It was Robert who had been best placed to respond. 'My lord, the Comte had been demonstrating his new hand-cannon. He fired it and the sound disturbed this noble knight's horse. But I believe this knight was significantly discommoded by the sound. Perhaps he sought to take revenge on the man who had so scared his mount?'

Artois had nodded, his eyes on Baldwin. 'Do you know whose dagger that is in his breast?'

'It is my own. Someone must have stolen it earlier.'

'You expect us to believe that?'

'Yes.' Now it was the other man, Lord John. 'You do not forget that we travel under the protection of your king? This man is as safe and as free as he ever has been. He knows that, and there is no need for him to dissemble. If he says it was taken from him, you have to believe him.'

Artois had ignored the lord. He had gazed fixedly at

Baldwin. 'I saw you with this man earlier. I ask you: did you have any part in his death?'

'I did not. He disturbed my horse, and we spoke briefly, but there was no threat in me.'

'He did not fire his cannon at you?'

'My lord, I do not know what this hand-cannon is. We do not have them in England, so far as I know.'

'Really?'

The disbelief in his tone had been plain to all about them. Robert, though, was intrigued by the detail which no others appeared to have noticed. 'Was there not a loud report here tonight?'

'I was scorched by the flames he threw at me,' Baldwin had admitted.

'You certainly have the appearance of a man who has been burned by a cannon's flames,' Artois had agreed.

'You say his cannon was here?' Robert had asked. 'But where is it now?'

That was a question which no one had answered last night. It was not lying near Enguerrand's body, that was all anyone would say. Now Robert looked over at the racks of weapons at the rear of the tent. The *gonne* was there, on its long pole.

There was a scratching at the tent's opening, and he turned to see a pair of scruffy churls waiting. He was ready to shout, but the bellow died as he recognised them. 'What do you two want?'

Arnaud smiled. 'Is that any way to welcome us back?'

Neither Simon nor Baldwin had slept since returning to their own tent late in the middle watches.

'Simon, I swear I do not know how my dagger came to be in his breast,' Baldwin said again as the sun rose and the walls of their tent lightened. He was lying back on his rugs, a cloak over him as he worried at the problem.

'You are safe, anyway. Even Artois accepted that while you are a member of the Queen's retinue, you are safe from prosecution.'

'Yes. Even if all consider me guilty of murder in the middle of the night.'

'I am sure the Queen doesn't.'

'No. She did graciously confirm her trust in me.' Baldwin nodded. 'But how did my dagger come to be used to kill him?'

Simon grunted. 'I suppose you are sure that it was yours? Not merely a similar one?'

'I took my dagger before leaving the tent, and the sheath was empty when you found me. No, there is no doubt.' Baldwin scowled again with the effort of memory. 'I remember that I had it with me – I took it out when I first heard the noise. And then there was the flash . . . the cannon . . . and I was blinded. I covered my eyes . . . I believe I must have dropped it then, but I cannot remember.'

'So the man took your dagger and stabbed the count as he came closer.'

Baldwin could hear the doubt in his voice. 'Either Foix was dead already and my knife thrust into him to throw suspicion on me, or he was not there, and hurried up after hearing the cannon go off, only to be stabbed.'

'It seems unlikely. You always say that you dislike coincidence – here you propose that you and he, the only two men who have argued on this journey, should have met by chance in the middle watches, and a murderer happened by and fired a hand-cannon at you, then took your dagger and killed de Foix. He took your dagger only because you happened to drop yours after his *gonne* was fired. And he missed you, although he was close enough to singe your beard.'

'Worse than that – the killer had no reason to guess that I

would be up from my tent in the night. I do not believe it myself. If I was sitting in judgement over my own case, Simon, I would not consider my evidence credible either.'

'No. It means someone knew you had a problem with de Foix, that he saw you get up from your tent, and already had the *gonne* prepared. He discharged it, scorching you, grabbed your dagger when you dropped it, and could then go and stab de Foix.'

'Put like that, it hardly makes more sense,' Baldwin said heavily. 'It's light, Simon. Let us go and see whether there is anything else we can learn.'

Simon nodded, and followed his friend outside. In the chilly light, he sucked in his breath at the sight of his friend's face. 'In Christ's name, Baldwin! You have been speckled with flame.'

'It feels as though someone has flung a panful of cinders at me,' Baldwin said ruefully, gingerly touching his cheek, his brow and his nose. 'The effect was most disconcerting.'

'Yes. That I can easily believe,' Simon said. His friend's face was raw in some places. 'It's a miracle your eyes are all right.'

'There is a little residual pain, but not much,' Baldwin said. He squared his shoulders and set off towards the place where de Foix's body had been the night before.

Under the orders of Artois, the body had been gathered up last night to protect it from marauding animals. Baldwin had been too tired and fractious to argue, although he did bitterly point out that any evidence in the area was likely to be lost in the dark. Artois had given him a not friendly stare for that comment, and Simon had hurriedly led him away.

Now it was plain that his words had been all too accurate. The whole area about the body was trampled into a mess of mud and broken stems of grass. Baldwin looked at it all in silence, before grunting in disgust. Still, he crouched down and peered at it closely for some little while.

'Nobody found the *gonne* last night, did they?'

'I don't think so. I didn't see it myself, but I'm not certain what it would look like.'

'It was a cylinder of metal set atop a length of wood. Probably ash or beech, I would think. The pole was thrust into the rear of the cylinder, so it looked like one long staff, thicker at one end than the other.'

'How long was the length of wood?'

'About two and a half feet. And the cylinder itself was another foot or so long, I think. I saw it only the once, when he was discussing the explosion with me. Then I had no idea what it was, but a hand-cannon makes sense. It was like that.'

'And it went off, burning you like that?' Simon asked dubiously. 'Surely, even if it was only a tiny cannon, there would have been a small stone or something in it. Shouldn't it have hit you when it went off? Did it just miss you?'

'I don't know,' Baldwin said. He could remember the scene again. 'I saw the man as though crouched on the ground, and then there was a flash and flames were rushing towards me.'

'That is all you recall?'

'I seem to . . .' He closed his eyes to aid his memory. 'Perhaps there was a small glowing ember of some sort.'

Now he thought about it, he was almost sure he had seen a little red glow before that enormous burst of flame. And a sizzling line, like an incandescent, spitting snake. 'Come with me!'

'This is where you found me last night?'

They had stopped at a slight hollow in the ground. Nothing much, and in the snow it would have been hard to see, but there was a muddy puddle at the bottom which showed its curvature, and Baldwin could see where he had stood, then fallen, his hand prints showing distinctly in the mushy snow at the upper lip. And then he saw the blackened mess.

'There was no *gonne*, Simon. The fellow simply set fire to a pile of black powder on the ground,' he said. 'That was why I was uninjured.'

'But why would someone have done that?' Simon said, hunkering down and prodding at the black residue.

It had lain on a flat board, a half-inch-thick plank of some light wood about three feet long. Simon ran his finger over it. There appeared to be a groove cut into it from one end to the other, and where the black residue was thickest there was a distinct hollowing, like a shallow dish.

'This board would keep the powder away from the damp,' Baldwin said musingly. 'And the depressions would hold the powder in one place to be fired.'

That would make sense, so far as Simon was concerned. He had heard of black powder, the strange, explosive material that was used to fill the lethal cannons that hurled rocks at walls. Siege trains in the hosts of any king must always have their cannons now, no matter the fact that the damned things seemed to be the invention of the devil. From all he had heard, they were more dangerous to the labourers who loaded and fired the hellish things than to the enemy. But the powder was as temperamental as a girl on the cusp of puberty. Like his own daughter – although now she was a little older, thanks to God, she seemed to have calmed a little . . .

No. He must concentrate on the matter at hand.

Baldwin was frowning with perplexity, he saw. 'Baldwin? What is the matter?'

'Look at this, Simon. Whoever put this here was intending some mischief. What was it, though? Did he intend to disturb the camp, and perhaps put the Queen in fear of her life, or did he intend to waylay someone?'

'And when you stumbled into him, he saw an opportunity,

took your knife, and when someone else came to see him, stabbed him to death?' Simon guessed.

'It is more likely than someone trying to harm me personally,' Baldwin admitted. Then he straightened and gazed about him. 'Although I think the Comte was already dead. I guess he was met here, killed, and then set down. When I turned up, I made the killer panic. He set off the powder, and then saw me lurch away and drop my knife. He took it and thrust it into the Comte's chest.'

'Why the powder, though? What was it doing here?'

'Let us go and talk to de Foix's servants. Perhaps a little of his spare powder had been mislaid? If not, who else might have some of it here?'

Chapter Fifteen

Janin was pouring some water into a dish preparatory to washing his face, which still felt sticky and rough from the previous day's journey, when he heard the soft footsteps behind him. Turning, he saw the Irishman. He gave a short, piercing whistle, and Ricard and Philip both stirred and grunted themselves awake.

'So you decided to come back, then,' Ricard said grimly. 'Where were you last night? Another French bint?'

'I am lucky to be popular,' Jack said easily.

'There was a murder last night. You hear about that? Strange how things happen when you aren't around,' Philip said.

'Coincidences. I find them refreshing. Your boy. He is not here – you haven't lost him, have you?'

'Never mind him. He's safe enough,' Ricard spat. 'What do you mean, refreshing? You realise . . .'

'You realise that the man responsible is an English knight called Furnshill? He was there, his dagger was found in the man's breast, and it was only his position as a guardian to Queen Isabella that saved him from arrest.'

Ricard glanced at his companions. 'That true?'

Janin shrugged. 'How would I know?'

'Well, just stay back with us, so we don't have to be suspicious about you at least,' Ricard said flatly. 'We don't need all this shite. It's bad enough we were forced into coming away.'

'Forced into coming here? You were persuaded to bring me, but someone made you come as well? Who did that, then?' Jack asked. There was a smile on his face, but no reflection of it in his voice. That was as cold as the ground all about.

Janin shivered. 'It was before we met you.'

'And it's none of your business,' Philip added.

'No problem. I was only interested. After all, we musicians need to keep together, don't we?'

As he smiled and moved away, his feet as quiet as a cat's, Ricard exchanged a look with Janin. 'I really, really don't like him.'

Robert de Chatillon knew he had to prepare the tent to be taken down. His eyes were drawn all too often to the shrouded body on the table, considering all the messages which must be composed and sent hither and thither. He managed to persuade the two churls to leave the place at last, and could begin to start work.

No sooner were Arnaud and the old man gone than he heard someone else scratching at the canvas.

'This is the tent of Enguerrand de Foix?'

'What do you want, Sir Baldwin?'

'You know my name?'

Robert gave a dry smile. 'I think that there will be few people in the camp who don't recall your name by now, sir knight. Now, if you don't mind, I have to strike camp and prepare my dead master's body for the journey. There is much work for a man whose master has been murdered.'

His shot hit the mark, he saw. The bearded knight coloured slightly. Not with anger, but a kind of shame.

'When your master died last night, I had been fired on by a charge of that powder you use for *gonnes* and cannons.'

'You have my sympathy. Was that an excuse to kill him?'

'I killed no one. I was attacked. Someone tried to kill me, then took my dagger and stabbed your master while I was blinded.'

'So you say someone was out there to kill him and waited until you happened by? I don't think—'

'Or, more likely, they set the charge and only fired at me because I came by at an inopportune moment.'

Robert stopped at that. 'Why would they do that?'

'Tell me about this charge, and maybe I can find out why – and *who*!'

'They aren't the same, you know.'

'What do you mean?'

'The powders. You couldn't use cannon powder in a device made for your hand. It would burst out of the barrel without exploding. I have seen it. For a smaller *gonne*, you need smaller grains of powder.'

Baldwin was holding the board on which the charge had been laid. 'Which was this?'

Robert decided there could be no harm in telling him. 'It was the finer type.'

'You can tell that without even looking at the board?' Simon snapped.

Robert had kept his eyes on Baldwin. Now he looked at Simon without emotion. 'Master, it is easy to see. I can see each flake marked on this knight's face.' Still, he took the board and studied that too for a short while.

'Can you see anything on the board that could help find the man responsible?' Baldwin asked.

'Well, it's possible, I suppose. Certainly the grain was fine, just like our own stores. When the charge went off, did you see it go up, or just out in one large puff of smoke and flame?'

Baldwin gave a half-grin. 'All I remember was the flash. It was like a gush of hellfire rushing towards me.'

'I think you are lucky, then. The man who set this did not

know what he was doing, if he intended to kill. He should have set the charge in a pot, or a small barrel. Then the explosion would have been constricted, and that would have given it more force.'

'Why?' Simon asked.

'It makes the *gonne* work better if the charge is held back.' Richard went to the rear of his tent and returned with a barrel. 'Watch.'

Simon had heard of this powder, but never seen it. As a fine trickle poured from the small wooden barrel, he eyed it without enthusiasm. It was just a dirty, black, uninteresting powder. 'It looks like fine, dry soil.'

Robert glanced at him as he set the barrel aside and tapped a bung into it. 'You think so?' He took a spoon and carefully scooped a small amount onto Baldwin's board. Then he walked to the rack in the corner of the tent, at which were set some polearms and de Foix's swords. From here he took up the long stick Simon had seen before. This he brought to the table, and scooped another spoonful of powder into it, using a funnel of leather.

The *gonne* was about eighteen inches in length. At the back it must have had a socket, because the long hazel stock protruded from the rear end. The *gonne* itself had been made like a barrel, Simon saw, with strips of steel staves gripped tightly by some heavy steel bound about them. He presumed the whole had been fired in a smith's forge, because he could see that the metal appeared to have welded together. Underneath the barrel itself a forged hook protruded.

'What's that for?'

'If you're firing near a tree or a wall, you can hook that over so that the gun doesn't knock you down. Now, see this?' He had a shred of linen. He wrapped this around a little pebble he had in a leather purse, and pushed it into the barrel on top of the powder. Taking a pinch of powder, he wandered outside, strolling to the limit of the camp. There was a fire, with two guards warming their hands by it. Robert stood at the side of it, then set the stock under his right arm and sprinkled a little powder into a dimple on top of the barrel near the stock itself. Then he asked Simon to pick up a glowing stick from the fire.

Simon took up a long branch with a well glowing tip, and stood in front of Robert.

'It might be better if you stood behind me,' Robert said, gently pushing Simon aside with the barrel. He took the branch, blew on it to make the coals glow, cast a look around at the others, and set the tip of the branch to the dimple.

Intrigued, Simon was peering at the *gonne*. There was a sudden flash, a *whoomph* as a cloud of smoke burst upward, and then a loud boom that made Simon step back hurriedly. Clearly in the dim light he saw a tongue of yellow flame lick out, at least six feet, and a thick blanket of fog sprang out, hiding everything from view.

'Mother of Christ!' he heard one of the guards shriek as he sprang back. For his own part, Simon was reaching for stronger words.

'That, you see, is how it reacts when you put a flame to the powder when it is confined. It explodes and the bullet shoots off into the distance,' Robert said.

'Where will the bullet have gone?' Baldwin wondered.

'Over there,' Robert said tersely, and set off back to his tent.

Inside, he took the pile of powder and swept some into a line. He thinned it, tapping it with his fingers until it formed a narrow length less than a quarter inch thick. 'Watch.'

He took a flint and his dagger and struck some sparks. On the fifth blow, a spark caught the line, and it spluttered and fizzed, sparks flying off in every direction, while Simon yelped and jumped back, trying to evade the thick roiling smoke. 'It smells like the devil himself!'

'Yes, it stinks,' Baldwin said, but thoughtfully. 'I see what you mean. It is clearly safer when it is not enclosed. May I?' He motioned towards the remaining powder.

Robert nodded. 'Of course. Yes, I think it is less lethal when it is free. There is some force of nature – it is like a beast. If you have caged a bear or a lion, and it escapes, it will be a great deal more dangerous to men than if you had not. Even wild animals in the open will tend to avoid a man, knowing their place in God's plan. As their wild nature is concentrated when confined, so is the powder's vital essence.'

Baldwin had made another straight line of powder. He took Robert's flint and struck a spark. At the first attempt, flame rushed along it quickly. 'This is a marvel!'

'Just be careful you do not leave an actual pile of it,' Robert warned.

'When you said I was fortunate, I can understand your meaning now,' Baldwin said, forming another line, this time a series of curves one way and another. He struck a spark, and watched eagerly, smiling, as the flame coursed from side to side like a snake. 'This is a wonderful thing! I have never been able to toy with it before, but it gives an extraordinary sense of pleasure to be able to guide it along the route you wish.'

'Yes. Well, so long as you are careful,' Robert said. 'If you will excuse me, I have work to do.'

'Of course,' Baldwin said, forming a fresh pattern, a broad coil of powder. 'Look at this, Simon.'

He struck a spark. There was a fizz as the first length of powder caught, and then a loud report as the entire coil detonated, a thick fume rising and making Baldwin cough and stand back, waving his hands to clear the air.

Robert gave a great sigh without turning to look at him.

'Yes. If you don't leave a decent gap between the threads, sparks fly from one to another. It is not a toy for fools!'

The Queen's tent

Rousing herself, for Queen Isabella, was never a great problem. Not for her the slow, languorous climb from sleep to a gentle wakening; she had always been aware of all that must be done in the day. The march to chapel for her Mass, the riding for her exercise, the listening to petitions and business about her varied interests must necessarily take up many hours each day, and as soon as she became aware of the sun cresting the horizon and heard her servants begin to stir, she would be wide awake herself.

All through her married life she had been the centre of a large establishment. In the very earliest days, of course, her husband had refused her the private household she had craved. That she had insisted upon her own servants, her own knights and cooks, grooms and burners, was no more than natural for her, a princess of France. During her childhood those small symbols of wealth and importance had been granted to her as a matter of course, and when she was old enough to marry she had expected similar proofs of respect, just as she had provided for each of her children.

The eldest, naturally, had been receiving such marks of esteem all his life. Dear Edward, the Prince of Wales, the heir to his father's throne, had never been left in any doubt as to his own position in the scheme of things. He would become the next king on the death of his father, and the lavish lifestyle which he would come to enjoy was already being emulated in his household. He might be only some thirteen years old, but her son was fully aware of his rank.

Even in the recent hard times she had found herself waking early. Despite the loss of so much, with her household disbanded, her servants all arrested or exiled, she had naturally woken swiftly, though less because of the amount of work that was necessary to manage her interests than from the urgent need to plot her revenge on the evil, avaricious and dishonourable son of a peasant, Sir Hugh le Despenser, her husband's *oh, so close* friend.

She could mimic that hideous, sly tone in her own mind. There was so much which she had grown to detest in that *cretin*. Not only the way in which he had wheedled his way into the King's affections, leaving no space for Isabella herself, but also how he had gradually excluded her from all which lent her life lustre. He had taken her lands, her mining interests, and after he had managed to insinuate to the King that she might one day become a threat to him, with war looming against France, he had even managed to see to it that her own little darlings, her three youngest children, had been removed from her protection. That was so cruel, so unthinkably vicious, that her hatred for him had threatened to burn so harshly that any could see it, but she had taken as her model that creature of guile and intelligence, the fox, and concealed her rage.

In all the last hard weeks and months, she had tried her utmost to remain collected. At all times, even when she had been convinced that the murderous churl was planning to have her removed – murdered – she had remained cordial towards him, until at last she had succeeded in persuading him that she held no grudge. Oh, he was not totally convinced, naturally. The monster that he was could never conceive of any person being motivated by anything other than greed or personal interest. To behave otherwise, he thought, was entirely contrary. But he did have one blindness: he thought that women were constant and loving as a matter of course; it was in their natures. He found it impossible to believe that a mere woman could fool him.

That was the root of his foolishness. For, believing that the weak and silly queen had almost forgiven him, since she had paid him some flattering attention in recent weeks, Despenser was prepared to allow her to go to France to negotiate. He was as certain as any arrogant man that she would never dare to connive on her own part. She would not scheme to bring down Despenser's deplorable rule of the country her husband was supposed to reign over. She was a mere woman, who wanted to run home to see her lands one last time, Despenser thought.

It had been hard, but even on that last day, she had dissembled as professionally as any whore. She had spoken with Despenser, displayed her sadness on leaving her children behind, begging 'good Sir Hugh' to look after them for her so she could see them as soon as she returned, and even sealing her farewells with a kiss, while her husband looked on approvingly. He only ever looked on *approvingly* when the horse's arse was in the room – or on the hillside, as he was then. In God's name, that kiss had been the hardest thing she had ever had to do.

But all simulation was now over, so far as she was concerned. She had a diplomatic mission to Paris, to see her brother, and to discuss with him the return to England of the lands and provinces which he had confiscated last year. That task was given to her by her husband, and she would faithfully honour the trust put in her.

Until she had achieved her ends, at any rate.

'My lady? Wine?'

Yes. She arose swiftly. There was so much to do. Especially when plotting the death and utter destruction of the man who had stolen her husband from her.

Chapter Sixteen

Janin sat back on his haunches and eyed Ricard with his lip curled doubtfully. 'You sure about this?'

'What else can we do?'

'Tell the Queen's comptroller.' Adam was grumpy. 'I'm sorry, but I never liked the man.'

'What good would that do?' Ricard protested. He spread his hands emphatically. 'De Bouden told us to bring this bastard when he was the last man we wanted along with us.'

'I still don't like that,' Philip said.

'What?' Ricard snapped. He was watching Charlie throwing stones at a temporary target made of a pile of sticks. The lad was hopelessly inaccurate. Well, he was only three or so.

'The way that he appeared just after poor Peter died. It was odd. Such a coincidence.'

'My arse!' Ricard spat, turning to look at him. 'Look, Peter just happened to get himself killed. It happens every night in a city like London. Nothing new in it. So he was unlucky. Yes, I can live with that. I can miss him, too – I do! – but it's still only a coincidence that Jack was there to replace him.'

'And was wanted by de Bouden,' Janin observed.

'Yes, yes, and was wanted by him. I dare say he has good reasons.'

'Like what?' Philip wondered. He was gazing into the middle distance and tapping a rhythm on his thighs. Then he stopped and stared into the fire. 'I fear the long arm of the Despenser.'

'Oh, for the love of Christ and all his saints!' Ricard threw his hand up in disgust. 'Look, do you honestly think that the Despenser would send one of his henchmen along with us? What would he want a man with us for? We're a bunch of bleeding musicians, not fighters. You think he wants to spy on us? Win over all our secrets, like Adam's ambition to play a bloody tune without screwing up? Learn how it is Philip can't tighten the skin on his nakers? Or maybe he wants to learn how to get the hurdy-gurdy to play without sounding like two cats strangling each other?'

'Or what the Queen is doing,' Philip said quietly. His fingers played a simple ripple of sound and stopped. 'Perhaps that's what he wants? De Bouden must be Despenser's man now, after all. He's not the Queen's, is he?'

'De Bouden? He's the Queen's own comptroller, for Christ's pains!'

'The Queen hasn't had her own household in a while, has she?' Janin noted. 'If de Bouden was put in charge of things for her here, surely that's more to do with Despenser than her own choice.'

'Oh, in God's name, if you're so damned scared, then we won't. I just thought it would be safer for all of us if we knew what the hell the bastard was after.'

'And that we ought to jump him to find out,' Philip said. 'But how can we do that when we don't even know where he is at night?'

'He walks with us during the day,' Janin pointed out.

'Yes,' Ricard said, 'and when we halt he helps us get the tent up, doesn't he? So that's what we'll do. We'll jump him tonight before he runs off and disappears for the evening.'

* * *

Jean awoke with the chill settled deep in his bones. The cold was clean and dry, but none the less freezing for all that, and he had to blow on his hands to warm them before he could even think about leaving his little shelter and beginning to prepare a fire.

At least he had been safe enough here. His thick leather jerkin and the old frayed cloak had been enough, with the protection from the wind that the walls afforded. Now, with a small fire lighted, he could take the worst of the chill from his hands and arms.

It was curious, the way that a man would seek a fire before any other comfort. He had learned when a lad that a shepherd who kept moving needed fewer clothes, felt the chill less, than an idle, indolent one. And later, when he was a grown man, and fought, he never felt the cold. When marching across the mountains to pass into other villages, or travelling down into the snowy valleys, he still survived with a good leather jerkin and cloak, while others, merchants and men of their kind, rich, pampered, *Catholic* men, would shiver and complain from within their furs and expensive velvet clothes. They were the swiftest to call for a halt, a fire, and a heated drink. Well, for Jean, the most delicious drink in the world at this time of year, for a man living in the wilds, was a pot of warmed water made from ice melted over a fire. Fresh, clean, and invigorating.

Only when he was sure that the fire was lit and he could start to feel the warmth did he rest on his haunches and begin to take stock again.

Yes. He was safe enough. The last days had been a panic, what with the discovery of Arnaud's insane murders, and then bolting as he had had to. But surely now he was secure, because if everyone thought he was dead anyway, they wouldn't bother trying to find him.

It had been many years since he was last safe from instant

arrest. Once it had been the murderous devils under that cool, calm, outwardly kind Bishop Jacques Fournier. At least the man gave the impression that he was actually interested in his victims. He didn't merely arrest them, torture them quickly and pass them on to the waiting executioners. There were plenty who would do exactly that, after all.

Fournier was a man who saw it as his duty to destroy every aspect of their heretical faith. He arrived without the apparent desire to execute many people. That was itself refreshing for the Waldensians of the area. Why should they be burned at the stake, anyway? What was their crime? Their faith was no less Christian than any other. They believed in preaching, they believed in the same seven principles of the Catholic faith and the sacraments, but they did not believe in Purgatory. That was a mad invention of a venal pope, so Jean's father had told him. And it was matters like that, matters of deep philosophical significance, that had made the whole Church turn against them.

But what was Purgatory? It was a Catholic invention that allowed corruption and greed to rule. If there was Purgatory, there was an opportunity for the living to pray for the dead, and if they could pray, they could pay the Church to help them do so. Masses for the dead could have little impact – a man was judged by his life, not by the number of Masses that were paid for by his last will. And Indulgences were nothing more than an appalling proof of cynical avarice on the part of the Pope and his bishops. Who could think that paying money into a religious body like the papacy could influence God? No, that was a purely human matter, not something for God.

God would not be impressed by His people today. That was why the Holy Land had been lost to Christendom thirty-odd years ago. When Acre fell in 1291, it was proof, if any were needed, that God had lost all love for Christians. How could He have allowed the land of His son to be taken over by the heathens who now inhabited it? If the Christians had been more honourable, less sinful, more obedient to His will, they would still own the kingdom of Jerusalem and all the other Crusader lands. But no, the Christian faith had fallen into shame and ignominy. Priests would take money and concubines, and with felons and sinners holding Masses supposedly in honour of God, was it any surprise that the faithful should start to emulate them?

For Jean's family and the other 'Poor of Lyons', it was crucial that the Mass should be held by those who were without sin. Those who were pure, who were uncorrupted by the world, should officiate at the religious services. What benefit was there for a man or woman who received the sacrament from a corrupt priest? None. Only a virtuous man could intercede for their souls. Even a woman who knew the correct words was better than a priest who was sunk in dishonour.

His breakfast completed with a handful or two of flour mixed with water and roasted on sticks, he rose. If there was no need to worry about where he went, he would have to make a choice. In the past he would have bolted southwards, back towards the warmer lands and the mountains, those places where a man might live free and safe, away from anyone. No need to wear the yellow cross on his back to mark him out as a heretic, so long as he avoided towns. He should be safe enough.

Except, if he were seen, it could be still more dangerous for him. Fournier had tried to avoid killings, but he might have gone. The man in charge now could be more dangerous. The idea of being captured by someone more fervent than Fournier didn't bear thinking about. Men like that would break limbs and kill peasant folk without a qualm, and order wine to celebrate the destruction of a soul afterwards.

South was his own homeland. He missed the high

mountains, the bright sunshine, the deep blue skies, the freshness of the pastures in springtime, the flowers, the cold, clean streams . . . his wife and family.

If all he had there was his memories, there was little point in worrying about it. Better to go somewhere else.

Sir John de Sapy was delighted to learn that at last they were going to be riding on. He had little interest in the route they were taking; all he wanted was to reach Paris, complete his mission, and rest with some of the whores in the wine shops that abounded in the city.

'You don't seem keen to get there?' he enquired of Sir Charles of Lancaster.

'Hmm? Have you been to Paris?'

'No. It is a place I have heard much about, though. The French sluts are supposed to be more inventive than the wantons from Aragon.'

Sir Charles glanced at him. His eye was amused. 'You have not been there either, then?'

Sir John was defensive. 'I have travelled widely in our kingdom. I've not had the opportunity or inclination to wander farther.'

'Then you will see and learn much.'

Sir John frowned quickly. He was of an age with Sir Charles, so he was unsure how to take the man's insouciance. There was an arrogance in his manner that implied a degree of experience which Sir John could only guess at. 'You have been there before – what were your impressions?'

Sir Charles smiled openly at that. 'How to explain?'

How indeed. The last time he visited Paris, he had been a renegade, a fugitive from the wrath of King Edward II. He was only one of hundreds who fled the kingdom in order to save their lives, terrified of the King's retribution. They had supported the man he loathed more than any other,

Lancaster, and once he had executed him, the King set upon any who had served him. Hundreds were captured and executed as traitors, their limbs and heads decorating spikes all over the realm, and the few who escaped, like Sir Charles, were glad to find a country where they could live awhile in safety.

Never one to seek peace for long, Sir Charles heard of some who were planning to return to England by rescuing Roger Mortimer from the Tower of London. They thought that this mighty general could perhaps save both England and them. Mortimer was known for his courage, his intelligence, and his integrity. It was his relentless campaigning in Ireland which had protected that part of the kingdom from Edward the Bruce's invasion, thrown the Bruce back, and finally led to his death.

But when Sir Charles got to Paris, those who declared themselves co-conspirators were so inept and foolish that he had soon realised that there was no possibility of saving Mortimer. Better by far to save himself, because it was plain even to Sir Charles that such a group must have been deeply infected with the King's spies. And a man who was known to the King as a member of the conspiracy was likely to have a very short life expectancy on returning to England.

He was in Paris for long enough to lose all his money and his plate to the pawnbrokers. Everything was so expensive, and no matter how much he or Paul, his man, tried to haggle, the prices appeared to remain high for a foreign gentleman in that city. In the end they were forced to leave. And then they had got into a little trouble at an inn, when a fight started. It was long ago, now, but the memory still rankled. A swarthy little toad-like shite had spat at him, and he and Paul had killed him and his friends.

After that, there had been a certain urgency about leaving the area before anyone could catch up with them, and they had made their way to Galicia, to Santiago de Compostela, which was where he had met Simon and Sir Baldwin.

'All I would say is, dicker like hell for anything you want to buy. Last time I was here they tried to fleece anyone with an English accent in Paris,' he said after a moment's consideration.

'What about the women, though?' Sir John demanded.

'I was talking about the women,' said Sir Charles.

Jack was aware of their looks long before they sprang their attack. If only all enemies were so transparent.

They had reached a town called Pois, and here they were allocated rooms in a tavern, while most of the other members of the honour guard, and the Queen herself, were given rooms in the better inns.

It was a nuisance that the entourage was always so spread about. Jack had been hoping that all their halts would be in larger inns so that he and the others would always be billeted near the Queen and the maids. It was next to impossible for him to keep an eye on her while he and the others were housed over a half-mile away. The distance was no trouble, naturally, but it was difficult to cover it without being observed by the watch. Every time he walked about in daylight, he was aware that he was different from the locals. His dress, his looks – even his ruddy manner of walking – set him apart. The folks here dressed more flamboyantly, they were darker of hair and skin, and Christ's teeth, they all swaggered as though they were God's own gift to the land. In contrast, his gait was as sober as his clothing. Dull, dull, dull. And it added insult to injury that that should mark him out as different. Usually, it would make him stand out not at all. He would fade into the background, unnoticed. Not so here.

Ah, he caught a glimpse of Philip circling round behind him. Meanwhile Ricard was right in front and trying to hold him in conversation – that was a first. Did they really think that they could jump him?

Philip began his move in a lumbering manner, just as Jack would have expected. Probably the most dangerous of them, and clearly the most ruthless, Philip was still built more like an ox than a greyhound. He was not built for speed. Where was the boy? He must have been left with someone else.

Jack turned, almost audibly sighing when he saw that Philip was still a couple of yards away. 'Did you mean to surprise me?' he asked.

His contempt turned to indignation when his legs were suddenly yanked from under him, and he was thrown to the ground. Only his elbows stopped him from bashing his face on the rough timbers of the floor, and that did not improve his temper. 'What do you think you're doing?'

'It's what you're doing that we mean to learn,' Philip snarled.

His anger was plain enough, but Jack was not about to surrender without a battle. He was on the ground, his face pressed to the boards, and Janin and Ricard had his arms. Adam or someone was on his ankles, holding them together. All in all, it was a remarkably successful assault for a bunch of pathetic, incompetent musicians. Which made it doubly humiliating for a man like him.

'So? What now?'

Ricard was at that moment staring at a rope which lay on the table some feet away, and mouthing to Janin that he should try to reach it. He looked down at his captive. 'What?'

'What do you intend to do with me? Torture me? Pull out my nails? Or just break my legs? Sirs, this is uncomfortable.'

'We want to know what you're doing here,' Philip said. 'And yes, if you don't answer, I'll be happy to tap splinters under your finger- and toenails. It's up to you.'

'I am travelling with you and playing music, of course. What else have you seen me do?'

'Nothing – because every time we stop for a night, you disappear.'

'What of it?'

'Nothing. Perhaps. But the fact that you were so enthusiastically pressed upon us makes us all a little nervous,' Ricard said. The rope was still on the table, and Janin was paying him no attention. 'Why was de Bouden so keen for you to be a part of our band?'

'You'd have to ask him that. All I know is that you were coming over here, and I was asked to travel with you to aid in the defence of the Queen.'

'Who by?' Philip demanded, simultaneously with Janin's: 'By whom?'

Janin peered round at Philip, who studiously ignored him. 'Eh?'

'That is for you to guess.'

'No. It's for *you* to tell us,' Ricard said, and looked at Janin for approval. He felt quite proud of the way that had come out. He sounded quite firm, he thought. Firm and definite. Then Jack's next words burned any pride away like acid.

'Since if I tell you, it's likely you could be killed, I think it's for you to guess, don't you? I wouldn't want Charlie boy to be orphaned again.'

Chapter Seventeen

Beauvais

Baldwin and Simon were glad to be installed in a large, comfortable bed. The previous night had been uncomfortable before the adventure of the explosion and Enguerrand de Foix's death, and sleepless thereafter, so a bed with a real rope base and a soft mattress over it was an almost undreamed-of luxury. It was worth the risk of lice and fleas to sleep in comfort again.

'How's your face?' Simon asked.

'Not too bad. The Queen's salve helped.'

'It was good of her to bring that stuff to you.'

'Yes.'

It had been late in the morning when Alicia appeared before them on a little mare.

Baldwin had bent his head to her courteously. He had liked the Queen's lady-in-waiting when he first met her in London. 'My lady.'

'My queen saw how dreadfully scalded you were after last night. She thought a little of this salve might help you,' Alicia said, holding out a small pottle of some thick juice.

'The Queen?' Simon repeated, awed.

'She was once burned badly,' Alicia said by way of explanation. 'She found this mixture always soothed her and took away the pain.'

'I see. That is most kind of her. Would you give your lady my deepest thanks.' Baldwin bowed. He could remember hearing that ten or eleven years ago Queen Isabella had been caught in a fire in a tent, and her arms had been dreadfully scarred. She still suffered from burns, it was said.

'I will.'

'Do you find the journey pleasing?'

Alicia gave a small smile. 'How could I fail to? We are out of London and away from all the trials and sorrows that place has brought us.'

'I only pray that our queen may find more ease when we are returned,' Baldwin said with feeling.

'That is not likely,' Alicia said with a regretful shake of her head. She graced them with a smile each before riding away to rejoin the Queen.

'She meant Despenser?' Simon said.

'Of course. He poisons all whom he meets,' Baldwin said.

'But if the Queen succeeds in her mission, that will surely put her back in the King's favour?'

'Does he have favour for her any more?' Baldwin had responded.

Now, though, as he sat on the edge of the bed and contemplated the candle burning on its spike set into the wall, he wondered whether he was being unreasonable. Maybe he was doing his king a disservice by assuming the worst of the man. After all, King Edward had fathered four children on this woman. If she could return to England in honour, with a treaty that did not shame him, would that not make him respect her again? And when a man respected a woman, love was surely never far behind. Possibly this would be the making of them both.

There were only the two options: if the Queen failed to win back the Gascon territories her standing would be destroyed, for if she could not even benefit the King in his dealings with France she was of little value; but if she managed to win back Guyenne and agree a peace, then the whole reason for her marriage to King Edward would be confirmed, and she could go home to England with her head held as high as the skies.

And yet . . .

The few times Baldwin had seen her during this ride, her excitement, her apparent repressed glee, had been a little out of place. It must be that she was glad to be free again, he thought.

He would have mentioned it to Simon, but when he turned to look at his old friend, he saw that Simon was already asleep.

Baldwin blew out the candle and lay staring up at the ceiling. All he could see was the body of Enguerrand, Comte de Foix, the blood forming a cushion for his head on the snow. Two dead men already, he told himself. The musician in London, as Blaket had said, and now the Comte.

There was nothing for him to trouble himself about, though. No. He rolled over on the bed, and was soon asleep.

They had let Jack go. There was little point in trying to maintain the charade that he was in danger, not when he lay on his belly and smiled at them, as though knowing that they would like to harm him but in truth did not dare. Disgruntled, Ricard had jerked his head, and all had released him.

Philip was the last to speak. He held his fist under Jack's nose. 'See this? See this, little mystery man? When I have the chance, one day I'll use this on you, and you'll not know what day of the week it is, I swear!'

'Fearful,' Jack said, eyeing the clenched fist closely. 'Wash it first, would you?'

'You . . .' Philip swung twice, hard, the fist striking on the cheek, the nose. Jack was just able to roll his head enough to absorb the blows, but the blood began to trickle from his nostrils.

Ricard grabbed the fist before it could swing again. 'Philip, get out of here.'

'Just leave me with him for a little. I'll find out what he's about.'

'Leave him! You want the Queen to hear you've been brawling? She'll abandon you here without a penny. You want that?'

'He's a spy. He killed Peter, and now he's here to spy on us all.'

'Who'd want to spy on us?' Janin asked reasonably.

'I'll bet he killed the Frenchie too,' Philip spat, pointing at Jack. 'And because he says he'll see us dead, you let him get away with it all!'

Jack watched him throw his hands in the air, then stride angrily from the room. The others were eyeing him cautiously, as though he might at any moment turn and kill them all.

'Is there any truth in what he says?'

'What, that I may have killed this man Peter? I never even met the man. And as for the Frenchman – why would I do that? No, I'm innocent, just an ordinary drummer. That's me.'

Alicia was content enough with the large room she shared with the Queen and the other ladies.

It was hard to find a moment to speak to the Queen without being overheard, but as she washed the dust from her mistress and brushed it from her hair, she could whisper a little.

'Have you seen him again?' Isabella asked. Her lips scarcely moved.

'Yes. There was a shadow down in the doorway when I fetched the water, and Lady Joan was there.'

'Joan of Bar. My husband's niece. He does me the honour of a noble spy, at least.'

Alicia smiled at that. Of all the ladies-in-waiting, she was the least by birth, and if it were not for the fact that the Queen had insisted on her presence, she would never have been brought along. The Queen already had Lady Joan of Bar and Alice de Toeni, the Dowager Countess of Warwick. King Edward had pointedly asked why she should need any more people, and Alicia had smiled to herself at the Queen's indignant response.

'Why, would you have the King's ambassador arrive at my brother's door like a beggar? If you seek a peace with my brother and would have me treat with him as an equal, you will need to allow me to appear as though I have some status in your eyes, my lord. You would grudge me my own maid?'

It was a telling comment. The Archbishop Reynolds supported her, as did Henry Eastry, prior of Christ Church. There were enough men who would be unwilling to see her humiliated before her own brother for the King to acquiesce, finally, albeit with a bad grace.

But there were spies about her at all times.

'Is she back yet?'

'No, my lady.'

There was another pause while the Queen considered. 'She is the King's lady. She could be sending information to him, but if so, she is also telling Despenser. We must remain careful.'

'Yes.'

'Did you see him?'

'Thickset, broad-shouldered, with a slow sort of mien. I would not think him a nobleman. He didn't have that kind of breeding.'

'His face.'

'Didn't see it. He was in shadows. Lady Joan was between him and the torches.'

Queen Isabella nodded faintly. 'Watch her, then, and let me know if you see him again.'

'I will, my—'

'You are taking your time, child. Is our queen's toilet complete?'

'Lady Alice, I think I can decide for myself when my toilet is complete. Where is Lady Joan?'

'I do not know. She went out a little while ago.'

'Perhaps you should send someone to ensure that she is quite safe? And while you are out there, you could send for my musicians. I think I need a little music to lighten my mood. I find myself a little *distraite*.'

'Very well. Alicia, you go and—'

'Countess Alice, I think I asked *you* to go,' the Queen said. In her voice was a hint of steel. Although she did not turn her head to look at the Dowager Countess directly, there was enough menace in her tone to make Alice de Toeni colour.

'I should insist, my lady. I am of noble blood, and it would be better if I did not leave you alone. We are in a foreign country, and—'

'Lady Alice, this is the land of my birth. You suggest that my own countrymen would harm me? For *sooth*! Now, begone. If there is any trouble, you may point out that it was the absence of Lady Joan that forced you to leave me alone. Now, *go*!'

As soon as the door had slammed, she gave herself over to giggling. 'Did you see her face? She was like a stuffed frog!'

Alicia was more concerned. 'But what if she causes you trouble? She could tell the King that you sent her away like a serf.'

'She will. With fortune, it will be too late,' Queen Isabella said with a cold certainty, and Alicia wondered at that. It was not the first time she had heard that hard, ruthless edge to her mistress's voice, but it was the first time that she had seen the glitter of certainty in her eyes.

While the Queen waited for her musicians, Alicia noticed that she appeared unsettled. Usually Alicia would leave to go about other duties while the musicians played, but tonight she was unusually tired. The effect of the journey and the feeling that she must spend her time in cautious observation of all those about her, she supposed.

The men trooped in, a very motley band. Still, as the first struck a tune on his gittern, and another started to saw on his rebec, she warmed to them. They might be the tattiest churls ever to have been scraped from the kennel, but they could certainly play their instruments. Even when they had been in a fight. The man with the bodhran was looking quite battered, although he stood there with his head turned away from the drum, his ear near the skin as he beat out the rhythms, like a man with nothing on his mind whatever, other than the urgent need for the music he had to play. Then the rebec player glanced over at the others in turn, each nodding to him, and he ducked his upper body and sawed faster on his fiddle, and as though by magic all the others joined in at the same time, this time playing a furious, quick dance tune. Alicia's foot could not keep still – it began to tap in time.

But all the while her mind was not on the music. It was on the Queen, sitting here so close to her, her head moving, smiling all the while.

There was a fresh change of tempo, and now it was the gittern player who initiated it. He looked at the rebecman, then to the drummer and the recorder. All nodded.

And then she saw something else. It was so swift, so fleeting, that at first she thought she had been wrong. The bodhran man looked up quickly. Just for a moment, but Alicia saw it, and she also saw his slight nod. It was a momentary thing, but enough, she thought, to be over-familiar. Except Isabella did not seem to mind. Instead, she too nodded. A spasm of the neck that made her head move a fraction, only for an instant.

Alicia felt the breath in her lungs turn to ice. Isabella had a plan to which even Alicia was not privy. It was the first time Alicia had realised that there could be secrets which the Queen would keep even from her.

In the street outside the Queen's apartments, Adam and the other musicians stood and counted their coins again. Ricard knew he ought to go back to their room and make sure that little Charlie was safe, but somehow it seemed hard to move his legs just now.

'My God,' Adam breathed. He stared at the coins glittering and shining in Ricard's hands.

'I know,' Janin said. He could not believe what he held. He stared at the coins with a kind of longing. They were so beautiful, he hardly dared to put his rosin-stained hands near them. Large, solid coins. Fifty of them.

For his part, Ricard was all but speechless. It was only after he had stood there with the pile of coins in his hands for a while that he shook his head and muttered, 'Keep this up, we'll be able to retire in comfort.'

'She must have been in a good mood tonight,' Jack said.

'She's a queen. What's there for her to be anxious about?' Adam said, his eyes still fixed upon the mound in Ricard's hand. 'Can I feel one, Ric?'

'She usually gives us a few coins, doesn't she? One or two shillings for an evening's banging and scraping. And tonight she gives us ten apiece, and you're not interested in why?'

'Just leave her alone, is what I say. She's a lady, and she doesn't deserve some arse like you sniffing around her,' Philip said.

'Me? Ho hum. So you still think I'm a spy now, do you?'

'I don't know what you are, but I know damn sure I don't trust you,' Philip snarled.

'Ah, now, there's a pity. When I could be such charming company, too,' Jack said lightly.

'Just leave the woman alone. She has enough to cope with.'

Adam gave a small sniff of contempt. 'Like what? She's a queen, Philip. She's never been left out in the open with her instruments getting warped in the rain, has she? Never had to worry about where her next meal's coming from, neither. Don't see what you reckon—'

'Have you wool in your head? You heard what Peter used to say. She's been suffering a lot recently, what with her children taken away and her friends all gone. Despenser hates her, that's what they say. So yes, she has plenty to worry about, I'd reckon.'

'Let her worry. What do we care, as long as she keeps paying us?' Jack said.

'You shouldn't keep talking about her as if she was just some slattern from the stews!'

'Was I disrespectful, old man? Ah, now there. I hadn't realised that talking amongst friends could be so dangerous. If I've upset you, that's a shame.'

All was delivered in a calm, disinterested tone, as though Jack was absolutely unconcerned what Philip might think, and it was enough to make Philip forget where they were. Here, in the street, in the dark, it was hazardous to brawl where the Watch could catch a man, but he was past caring.

He growled low in his throat, and launched himself forward, his hands reaching out like a campball player's[1] to grab Jack. But as he sprang at him, Jack slipped aside and punched once, sharply. His fist connected with a solid-sounding thud just under Philip's ear, and he fell to the ground like a pole-axed ox.

---

[1] Campball was an ancient form of football which was more like modern rugby.

'I think you'd best take care of him now, fellows. Don't think he'd like me to be around when he wakens, eh?'

The last they saw of Jack that night, he was strolling away as though he had not a care in the world. It was only Adam who saw the figure slip from the shadow of a doorway further up the street and join Jack, walking in step with him as far as a bend in the road. They both stopped there and turned back to look at the musicians before walking on.

'Who's that?' he asked.

'What?' Ricard had been carefully replacing the coins one by one in the neat purse, and looked up now as Janin tried to lift Philip to a sitting position.

'Up there. I could have sworn it was William de Bouden, but . . . they've gone now.'

'What of it?' Janin demanded, puffing a little as he rolled Philip on to his back. 'Give me a hand, Ricard.'

'De Bouden was watching us, as if he knew Jack was going to be here,' Adam said. 'When he wandered up, Bouden stepped out, all friendly, and joined him. Why?'

'Because the bastard's in league with Despenser, that's why!' Ricard snapped. 'So what's new? He's probably spilling all he's seen in the Queen's chamber tonight. Then Bouden can relay it all back to London.'

'You really think that he's dishonourable enough to do that?'

Ricard stopped, turned, and stared at him.

Adam coloured. He felt foolish enough. But if he'd seen round the bend in the street, to where de Bouden and Jack had halted as they met the third man, he would have felt still more confused.

As would Ricard.

Chapter Eighteen

Wednesday after the Feast of St Edward the Martyr[1]

Jean had tried to find a small room, but the sudden influx of people in the town had soon put paid to that. All the sleeping chambers were taken, and even the haylofts and stables were occupied by grooms and servants, because every knight travelling with the Queen – those in her entourage and those French men who had met her on her way to celebrate her journey – had a squire, two horses for riding, and a sumpter horse or two; and then there were the assorted hangers-on: musicians, cooks, procurers, carters. There was not a foot of floor available anywhere, he was told at one point.

In the end, he had been forced to accept an offer of some boards up in the eaves of a peasant's hovel. The peasant was content to sleep on the ground on his palliasse, and Jean was forced to make the best of it on the man's bed without a mattress. It was only a little harder than the ground outside, and reeked of the man and his wife, smoke, and urine from some creature which lived in the thatching, but at least it was consistently warm – until the middle of the night, long before dawn, when a combination of the cold, the man's wife's snoring, and a wooden dowel sticking in his kidneys, all conspired to wake him.

---

[1] Wednesday 20 March 1325

He glanced about him quickly, alert as always to the risk of a sudden attack from a stranger, but when he looked down, the peasant and his wife were both still asleep. Others he had known had been stabbed at night and robbed by poor folk such as these, but he felt safe enough. He did not look to them like someone worth robbing; he had little enough to steal. Rolling over, he slept until dawn.

The Queen's company might have made his search for a bed problematic, but at least he had the pleasure of witnessing the cavalcade depart the following morning. He was sitting outside the peasant's hovel on a rock when the men began to gather, and he left it to trail after them and watch what was happening. It was many years since he had seen a grand party like this lot.

That was down in Pamiers. When the bishop arrived. He had not realised then how the man would destroy his life. How could he? It was difficult to conceive of a single person's bringing so much ruin on so small a community of believers.

He couldn't think of that again. There was too much sadness in the memory. He was a man who had been trained in fighting, who had witnessed the deaths of all his family in the wars, and yet he was still persecuted by that vicious, cruel, and above all *honourable and pious* damned bishop! All he had ever done was try to live a decent life, and the bishop had destroyed it for him.

Ach! No. There was no point raking over those coals again.

When he reached the town's marketplace, he had recovered his equanimity. There was a shop with some pastries for sale, and he could see that it had been all but cleaned out already. The *patissier* was running about seeking fresh supplies to bake more for his regular customers, and Jean thought he might wait awhile to buy something himself. Leaning against the doorway, he watched the people gathering.

The richness of the clothing and uniforms was quite shocking here in this little town. There were some merchants who might own some moderate garments, he thought, but nothing in comparison to all this magnificence. Velvets, scarlets, silks, fine woollens, the softest pigskin gloves – these people had everything a man could hope to acquire. And they wore it with such *élan*, too. As the men sprang on to their great horses, they looked as elegant as kings in their own right. And then he saw the Queen.

Such beauty was blinding, he thought. A woman of some thirty years, with fine, fair hair gleaming under her headdress, seated on a horse rather than in a wagon, wearing a long cloak trimmed with ermine, she looked almost heavenly. Jean had to pull his eyes away with an effort. She was so magnificent, it almost seemed a crime to watch her, him clad in filthy leather and linen, as though he could pollute her with his glance.

'Christ's pains!'

He carefully sidled back into the shop's doorway, wary and anxious at the sight of the two men standing at the opposite side of the square: le Vieux and Arnaud! They must have followed him somehow, and now they were here with this party. He must escape them again!

Thursday before the Feast of the Annunciation of Our Lady[1]

Pontoise

To Simon's eye, the buildings were growing wealthier and more splendid with every day. The last night they had spent in a little town called Beauvais, and he had been struck by the

---

[1] Thursday 21 March 1325

richness of all the people living there. Admittedly, everyone would have been made aware that the English queen was on her way by the arrival of the heralds sent ahead to book rooms and food, and they would have decked themselves out in their best clothing in honour of the sister of their king, but even so, looking about him now in this little town, he was almost shocked by the displays of wealth on every side. It was so blatant and unashamed. Much, he had to remind himself, like London. Except cleaner.

This place was only a few miles from Paris, he had learned. Baldwin had described the journey which they were to take before they left England, but he had hardly listened to much of it. At the time he had been concentrating on the appalling thought of climbing on to a ship again. He had seen enough of ships for his life, so far as he was concerned.

The town was pretty, though, built on the banks of the River Oise, with the steeple of the cathedral towering high overhead. There were plenty of trees and orchards, he saw, as they approached the great bridge over the river.

'We should go to the cathedral and give thanks for arriving here in one piece,' he muttered.

'An excellent idea,' Baldwin said, 'except I rather think we'll be expected to carry on to the castle.'

'Why?'

'I thought you knew already – the Queen is to be introduced to her latest sister-in-law.'

That explained all the flowers and decorations, then. Simon frowned a little. 'She had several brothers, didn't she?'

'Yes, but her siblings appear to be short-lived. Her father died eleven years ago, cursed to death by the honourable Grand Master of my Order.'

Simon had heard of the Grand Master de Molay's curse. As he burned, in agony, he called on the King to join him before the throne of God to answer for his crimes in destroying the

Order of the Temple, and the King had died within the year, as had the Pope. 'What of the others?'

'Her oldest two brothers both died soon after taking the throne. The first, Louis X, survived only two years. Then there was poor John, his son, who lived five days after becoming king, and the throne passed to Philip V, but he died three years ago, so he was only on the throne for six years. Now we have Charles IV.'

'And this is not his first wife.'

It was not a question. Simon remembered that he had been married already.

'That is so. The first wife was caught in adultery, and he had the marriage annulled two or three years ago. I think he was married after that, but the lady died, and so now he is searching for a new bride.'

Simon set his head upon one side. 'With all these deaths, could the throne come to our queen? If this king dies without children, presumably the crown must pass to one of the women in the family?'

'I fear not. The idea that the two crowns could be joined like that has intrigued many for several years, I think, but I doubt that the French peers would allow it. They are jealous of their authority, Simon. The idea that the English queen, as they see her now, could come here and take power would make them . . . well, they would be happier to drink poison together than allow that to pass.'

Simon pondered this awhile as they entered the cobbled streets of the old town. It had been here for centuries, he was told, guarding the bridge over the river, and the King himself liked the town so much that there was a royal castle here. It was here where they were to meet Jeanne d'Evreux.

It was a gay occasion. Flags flew from every staff, and the number of knights about the Lady Jeanne was proof of the value the French king placed upon her. The two women walked to each other and greeted each other with gracious delight, as was obvious to all about.

'They are first cousins,' Baldwin answered when Simon asked. 'Although I do not know whether they have met in the last ten years or more.'

Musicians played, and there were magicians and tumblers demonstrating their skills in one corner of the square, which gave the whole affair something of a feastday atmosphere. Certainly today at least there was nobody who appeared to have any animosity for others. French and English knights mingled and joked with each other, and even de Bouden appeared less anxious than Simon had seen him for some days. Money was always tight for the Queen, ever since her monies had been confiscated by the King, but it seemed that de Bouden had been given some form of assurance that the French king would not see his sister embarrassed by lack of funds. That would be a relief to many.

Glancing about him now, he wondered where de Bouden had gone. The comptroller was not with Baldwin or the other knights. He could see Lord Cromwell a short distance off, and he, like everyone else, had his attention fixed firmly on the Queen and her cousin. And then Simon caught sight of de Bouden's face a little farther on, at the front of the crowds, but his eyes were not on the Queen – not all the time. No, he was watching someone at the other side of the crowd, a man who was in among the friends and guards of Lady Jeanne. A tall man with dark hair trimmed in a military cut, with broad shoulders, a powerful neck from wearing a steel helmet, and the arrogant swagger of a knight. Or perhaps more than a knight.

'Recognise him?' he asked, pointing.

'Who?'

It was plain enough from the blank look on his face that Baldwin had no idea who the man was. He glanced up at

Cromwell, but could tell he was too engrossed to be interested.

'Ach. It's nothing,' Simon said. 'I just wondered. De Bouden seems to be staring at him – or at least in his direction.'

'Really? Why should that be so?' Baldwin said. He glanced at de Bouden, and for a moment their eyes met. De Bouden appeared to colour, blushing slightly as he looked back towards the Queen, and his demeanour was enough to make Baldwin wonder who the man could be. Whoever it was, de Bouden seemed to know him.

'He's gone,' Simon said.

'*Don't* point, Simon,' Baldwin muttered sharply, and he put his own hand out as though to bring Simon's arm down.

'Why? What on earth is the matter?'

'That man . . . I don't know. But if de Bouden is ashamed of knowing him, I think perhaps we should be cautious.'

Jean had arrived in the town a few hours after the Queen herself. Not because her wagons and trains moved any faster than a man on foot but because he took care to remain some distance behind them. He had no desire to allow le Vieux and Arnaud to catch a glimpse of him.

The more he thought about it, the more he was convinced that they were planning to kill him. All he had seen when he looked down was Arnaud chasing after his last victim. The others had been dead just outside the guards' room. He'd assumed that Arnaud had gone berserk and killed all the others in a fit of madness; he'd assumed that le Vieux had died from his injuries. It hadn't occurred to him that le Vieux had lived. How had he escaped, in God's name? The way that Arnaud had slaughtered all the other men, it seemed incredible that even the most proficient of them all had survived.

But if Arnaud had beaten le Vieux over the head with a jug or a cudgel, the old man would have fallen quickly enough, and that would have given Arnaud time to despatch all the others. Perhaps le Vieux had no memory of the attack. Perhaps he woke later with a dreadful headache, and had no idea who had killed all the men there. But he would surely have thought it must be Arnaud. Arnaud was the only survivor apart from him. Whom else could le Vieux suspect?

It was then that the cold truth hit him, and hit him hard. He had to lean against a wall, breathing slowly and deeply with the shock.

'You all right, master?' a young urchin called to him.

'Yes, blessings on you. I am quite well,' he lied.

How could he be well, when Arnaud must have told le Vieux that he, Jean, had been the murderer who set upon all the guards and killed them?

So now they were after him. Not because he hadn't reported the murders, but because le Vieux thought he was responsible. They were going to kill him, as they might slay a rabid dog. A man who could kill with such ferocity was plainly insane, but that was no reason to spare him. He was a danger to everyone.

He wouldn't let them. There were two choices, either to flee again, and keep on running, or to get to le Vieux and hope to persuade him that he, Jean, was innocent. It wasn't he who was responsible, it was the foul-minded Arnaud, the executioner and torturer. Jean must get to speak to le Vieux and explain. The old man would understand.

Poissy

The day was busy. Soon after their rapturous reception in Pontoise, they were all back in the saddle again to make the short journey to Poissy and the King's palace.

'At least here we won't have to hunt about for rooms,'

Simon grumbled. The last few towns had been too small to accommodate such a grand party, and what with the Lenten fasts and so much effort being devoted to ensuring that the Queen herself was comfortable, their own journeying had been harder. Even Sir Charles had been heard complaining about the quality of the rooms in which he was expected to rest. As a seasoned campaigner, he usually thought such 'whining' to be beneath his dignity.

Baldwin was less sanguine as he looked up at the magnificent palace. 'I hope so. Often you find that a great palace like this has two qualities of chamber – the very best for the king and queen, and stables for all others.'

Fortunately the rooms were significantly better than his worst fears. They were billeted with the other English knights, Sir John de Sapy and Sir Peter de Lymesey as well as Sir Charles. Lord John Cromwell had his own room close by.

Just the sight of the bed had Simon closing his eyes and dreaming of the comfort which he would find lying in the cool sheets with a heavy riding cloak set over the top, but as usual there were more celebrations to be endured first.

Although it was the middle of Lent still, many fish dishes were permitted. Simon was gladdened by the sight of a white porray, a thickened soup of leeks and onions with milk of almonds to give it some flavour, as well as several pottages. Especially good to Simon's taste was the one made from old peas; he also enjoyed dishes made from fresh sprouts, spinach, and *craspois* – strips of heavily salted whale flesh that had been boiled and added to a dish of sweetened peas with some sprouting leaves at the side. All in all, very tasty.

It was late by the time the Queen left the table and all the men rose to their feet. Simon was pleased. After all the noise and excitement of the day, he was keen to make his way to his bed. The memory of the clean white linen made his muscles ache afresh. 'I'm for my bench,' he said to Baldwin when they stood alone together. 'I'm too tired to carry on.'

'You go. I doubt not that I shall be going to my own bed before long,' Baldwin said with a grin, and he watched for a moment as his friend left, hoping that Simon would not become lost in the labyrinthine corridors of the palace.

He filled his cup with some water, and drank deeply. The salted whale was a little too strong for him, and had left a thirst which he found it hard to assuage. He had taken some rissoles to try to ease the effect, but they were too salty for his palate as well, and only served to exacerbate the problem.

Walking outside, he unsuccessfully sought the privies. There was a wall near the great hall which would serve, though, and from the scent others had been forced to the same expediency.

Finished, he was walking back inside when he glanced to his left. Beyond a lean-to building that had been added to the hall, he saw a couple of men – de Bouden and the man Simon had seen de Bouden staring at earlier. There was something about their manner which struck him as odd – furtive, like conspirators – and it put him on alert.

Carefully he eased himself backwards into the shadow by a buttress, peering round the stonework. The man with de Bouden clearly made the comptroller anxious, and he was gesticulating as they conversed, while the other was cool and collected, listening a little, and then making a brief comment. He concluded with a few words, leaning down towards de Bouden as though to whisper, but Baldwin was convinced that the movement had little to do with keeping his words secret, and more with the fact that his leaning down made him seem more intimidating to the shorter man.

Whoever he was, he stepped back, holding de Bouden's eyes all the while, before stopping and glancing about them quickly. He turned on his heel and strode away but, Baldwin noted with a spark of concern, not away from the palace complex. Whoever the man was, he was here inside the palace and staying put.

De Bouden was walking back towards the entrance now. He was pensive, Baldwin could see. The light from a torch flared at the lines on his face, and he shook his head as he walked, as though carrying on an internal debate.

'Comptroller, you look disturbed.'

'Christ on a cross!' de Bouden blurted, startled, and shot backwards. His heel snagged a cobble, and he all but fell, but righted himself at the last moment. 'Dear heaven, Sir Baldwin, what do you mean by leaping out at me like that? You could have stopped my heart, I swear!'

'Perhaps I could. My apologies if I shocked you. It was not entirely my desire to do that.'

'Entirely? You did mean to a little, you mean?'

'Oh yes. I wanted to see whether you looked guilty, you see. And you do.'

'What nonsense is this? You think you can upset me like this? Excuse me, Sir Baldwin, but I have work to be getting on with.'

'Wait a moment, Comptroller,' Baldwin said, moving to stand between him and the entrance. 'Who was that man with whom you were conversing?'

'I don't know what you mean.'

'I was watching you, de Bouden. I saw you talking to a man over there. Who was he? I did not recognise him.'

'No one. There was no one you need worry about. It is my business – only mine.'

'Then you will not mind my mentioning it to Lord Cromwell?'

'You'd tell him?'

'I am here with other knights charged with the protection of the Queen. You appear to be holding clandestine meetings with a stranger, and refuse to tell me who it is. That is surely enough to warrant my informing the leader of our party.'

'He wants to meet the Queen.'

'Who does? Come along, man! Speak out!'

'Lord Mortimer of Wigmore. The rebel.'

Chapter Nineteen

'And what did he say to that?' Simon asked.

Baldwin had gone to Simon in their room, and since, fortunately, none of the other knights had retired yet, he could tell Simon all about the conversation.

'He begged me to keep his association secret. Secret, in God's name! The Queen's Comptroller meeting with the King's most detested traitor!'

'What will you do? You should tell the Queen herself, or at least tell Lord Cromwell. He's charged with her safety. The traitor Mortimer tried to have the King assassinated, after all. It would be perfect for him to embarrass the King by harming the Queen here. He might have her killed, or capture her and take her away. What could a man like that do to her?'

Baldwin said nothing for a moment, and Simon shot him a look. 'Baldwin? Did you hear any of that?'

'Well yes. Yes. I suppose you are right,' Baldwin said.

'There was a "but" at the end of that sentence, wasn't there?'

Baldwin rose and walked to the window. Staring out, he spoke as though musing to himself. 'I know that the King would expect me to tell Cromwell about Mortimer's being here. But in truth, all know this is where he has been hiding. He sought sanctuary with the French king as soon as he escaped from the Tower of London. There is no surprise to anyone in the fact that he is here. This is a royal palace. So his presence is not news.'

'Even if that were true, Baldwin, the simple fact that he appears to be on friendly terms with de Bouden, the Queen's own clerk, is surely enough to raise warnings in the minds of any who have her interests to heart.'

'Simon, I know you are probably right, but let me just ask you to consider this more deeply. This man Mortimer, whom all eagerly declare to be a traitor, was a close friend of the King's for twenty years or so. He has backed the King in everything, even supporting his friendship with Gaveston, when all the other lords and barons had the man exiled. He served the King with his body and arms in all the King's wars.'

'I know that, Baldwin. But if you have a good, loyal dog, you still kill it if it develops the rabies. You can't trust it after that. Mortimer has lost any rights because he raised a host against the King.'

'He never raised his standard against the King, only against the rapacity of the Despenser – and we both have had experience of that devil!'

'I don't say I don't agree with the aim of removing Despenser. But we're here to protect the Queen, and if Mortimer's here, he is a threat to her. He is the King's own stated enemy, he was held under sentence of death, for Christ's sake! Now he's escaped from the Tower, he's more dangerous than ever. We have to tell Lord Cromwell.'

Baldwin said nothing for a few moments, but then he turned away from the window. 'And what will that achieve? John Cromwell will be determined to find the man and execute him, which will lead to more bad feeling between the French and the Queen's party. I have already experienced the trouble that a killing can bring, Simon. People still look at me askance, thinking I killed Sir Enguerrand. The men who killed the Comte de Foix endangered my reputation. If another man is slain here, we shall be put in a dreadful position. It may well ruin the talks about Guyenne, and then we would be guilty of harming English interests and the King's.'

'So you would keep this secret?' Simon demanded. 'I tell you now, Baldwin, I cannot agree to that. I believe that the danger must be pointed out.'

'I agree. However, I think that we should put the news in the hands of the one person here who knew Mortimer and can form a judgement on the degree of the threat he presents to the Queen – and that is the Queen herself.'

'You seriously believe it's better to tell her than Lord John?'

'John Cromwell is a good man, but he takes his orders from the King – and in his case, I think that many instructions actually come from Despenser. Despenser hates Mortimer. The conclusion is clear – Despenser would command John Cromwell to have Mortimer murdered. The Queen knows Mortimer, though. She would surely understand him better.'

Saturday before the Annunciation of Our Lady[1]

Poissy

The King had arrived in his royal palace a little earlier, but it was important for a king to ensure that all was prepared before he made his entrance. Jeanne, his bride-to-be, had already welcomed his sister to France, so King Charles IV could give himself up to making the preparations for the welcome feast.

And at last all was ready on the Saturday.

To Baldwin's embittered eye, it was as unprompted and natural as any play-actor's performance.

---

[1] Saturday 23 March 1325

The King was a tall, handsome man. He had the natural grace of a man of authority, and the lightness on his feet of a trained man-at-arms. This was a noble who was experienced in the lists, he thought. And he was genuinely interested in people.

'You are?'

Lord John Cromwell gave his name easily enough. He was used to speaking with kings, and he bowed low and respectfully, gruffly introducing the other men from his party. De Sapy was careful to bow low, as was Peter de Lymesey, but Sir Charles, Baldwin saw, was less reverential in his approach. He bowed, but in an almost perfunctory manner, which made some in the chamber eye him suspiciously. For his part, Baldwin bowed as low as he would to any king. There was no point in making a show of rudeness. It could all too easily make an enemy of a ruthless man in the lands where his power was absolute.

'Sir Baldwin de Furnshill,' Lord John intoned.

'I am delighted to meet you,' the King said in that soft voice of his. His tone was light, but Baldwin had the impression that it would carry clearly a great distance.

'I believe you have all looked after your queen, my sister, well. I am most grateful to you all for that. If there is anything you require while you stay here in Poissy or in Paris, let my servants know and I will ensure that they will provide it for you. You are all my honoured guests.'

He had turned to return to his throne when the doors opened at the far end of the hall, and the Queen stepped in.

She was clad in black, a dress rather like a widow's, Baldwin thought, and then his mouth twitched cynically. No fool, she would have carefully considered what to wear before entering. This was designed to make men question her state of mind. Everyone knew of Despenser's relationship with her husband, and wearing widow's weeds would allow them to appreciate the depth of her own disgust and shame.

The King stepped forward as she entered, and taking her hand asked how she fared, how her journeys had been. 'Welcome, my fair sister!' She attempted to kneel before him, not once, but three times, at each occasion held up by him. 'You are my sister, my equal. You shall not kneel for me.'

Baldwin saw the tears running down her face as the King led her to a seat and installed her, commanding wine and sweetmeats for her, and for all his loyalty and devotion to her, he could not help but reflect that she was a more consummate actor than any he had seen displaying his craft on a wagon at the miracle plays each year.

'Well?' Simon demanded as Baldwin walked out into the yard later. As a mere yeoman, Simon had not been invited to the audience. Not that he cared a whit. As far as he was concerned, kings were above his usual rank of companion, and he was content to leave such people to Baldwin's acquaintance.

'It was tedious. The Queen met her brother. That is about it.'

'What did she say? Was he excited? What is he like?'

'She said hello. He was happy as any monarch who now holds the secret to upsetting a rival; and he is tall, handsome, and as ruthless and avaricious as any king,' Baldwin said.

'Ruthless and what?'

'Simon, he has one interest and one interest only. He is a devoted Christian, and he is determined that he shall become the Holy Roman Emperor. His only rival for the position has already been excommunicated, I hear, so he is likely to win that race. And then no doubt he will launch a new crusade. I think that is what he desires above all else.'

'And meantime, if they get on so well, then with fortune we can leave here and get back home before too long?' Simon said optimistically.

'Perhaps so,' Sir Charles said. He had followed Baldwin from the room, and now stood at the bottom of the steps to the hall. 'I should not hold out for that to be very soon, though, old friend.'

'Surely, if he still loves his sister, he will not refuse anything she asks for?'

'Simon, dear fellow, that is what we must hope will happen if he wants peace with the English. It has little to do with his sister's wishes, though. If she were to win what *she* desired, we'd be in great trouble, and would be forced to remain here a damned sight longer.'

Simon frowned. 'I don't . . .'

'What the king of England wants is his territories returned, at no cost, and without having to pay homage to King Charles. What King Charles wants is any pretext to keep the lands *and* force the English king to pay allegiance to him. What the Queen wants is somebody to remove and preferably execute Sir Hugh Despenser so that she can return to her husband again.'

'But the French have no power over whether our king turfs Despenser out.'

'Quite so. Which means that the Queen must be disappointed. Will that make her keen to assist her husband? I somehow doubt it. No. You have to pray that the self-interest of the French will make them try to force our king to agree to accept back his lands, while still coming here to pay allegiance for them.'

'But he won't,' Baldwin said. 'The last man he would ever trust is his brother-in-law.'

'Why?' Simon asked, baffled.

Sir Charles sighed slightly, glancing at Baldwin as though unbelieving that any man could be so far behind the realities of the nation's politics. 'Simon, the two of them are neighbouring kings. Both wish to lead Christendom. That means that they hate each other. It's not helped by the fact that the English still rage about the French stealing Normandy from us; now they want to steal Guyenne. They are dishonest and unreliable.'

'You do not like the French, do you?' Baldwin asked mildly.

'When dead, they make tolerable companions,' Sir Charles said with chilling amiability.

'Baldwin, you don't believe all that, do you? I mean, we'll be home again early in the summer, won't we? It shouldn't take long for the Queen to knock together some sort of deal with her own brother, will it? They love each other, after all.'

'Simon, I don't know what he feels towards her. You have heard of the matter of the silken purses?'

'I think so, but I don't know . . .'

'There was a meeting in France some ten or eleven years ago. The Queen, our Queen Isabella, was there, and she met her father. Now she had given some purses to her sisters-in-law a while before. They were all embroidered in silk, so easily recognisable to her. Imagine her feelings when she saw them, not in her sisters-in-law's hands, but bound to the belts of some knights with whom they were dancing.

'She worried about the matter for some little while, I expect, but her conscience wouldn't let her be. She decided she must tell her father, for if these women were committing adultery it was not only a matter of cuckolding their husbands, it meant that they could be compromising the succession of the royal line of Capet. They could be raising bastards to take the crown. That was enough to make her, a daughter of that royal house, bridle. She told her father, he arrested the men concerned, and they died as any man would, guilty of such an appalling crime.'

His tone was reflective, precise, unemotional. Simon knew

that although Baldwin was a firm believer in justice, he also detested unnecessary cruelty, to man or beast. He knew the necessity of eating, but he preferred his venison to be killed swiftly and cleanly. That was why he maintained a good pack of hounds and raches, to bring down game quickly and kill it cleanly.

'The women, though, were made to suffer still more, perhaps. The two women who were found guilty of adultery were imprisoned in the Château Gaillard. One was her brother Charles's wife. He has been unfortunate. Some little while ago he managed to have his marriage to her annulled, and I think he rejected any children she'd borne in case they were sired by another. The second wife died in childbirth last year, I believe, and now he hopes to marry again. Given those circumstances, Simon, how glad would you be to meet your sister again? How keen would you be to grant her any favours?'

'But the fact that the favours she craves are to please her king? Surely the king who is Charles's closest neighbour must have some impact?'

'I think I need not reiterate the words of Sir Charles,' Baldwin said lightly. 'Consider this, Simon: the man is already insulting King Charles. He has accepted as his own closest adviser and friend a man whom King Charles has declared outlaw. Sir Hugh le Despenser robbed French shipping for a while when he was exiled from England. Taking him as a close confidant is a gross insult. Just as is King Charles's response in taking in and protecting our king's worst enemy, Roger Mortimer. The two have no desire to help each other. No, I think that King Charles will have all the English territories, and our mission here is a farce. I do not know why I agreed to come!'

Jean gave up for the day. He had been inside the town,

watching the gates carefully to see if there was any sign of Arnaud or le Vieux, but as he wandered the streets it became clear that, if the two were here, they must be staying in the palace itself.

Well, no matter. He could be patient. There was plenty of time. He found lodgings in a mean little chamber not far from one of the town's gates, and settled down to sleep. But his dreams were not good. He woke, stifling a scream, as once more he saw Arnaud and Berengar running from the castle, and walked down to find the bodies outside the guard rooms again. And he wept for the men who had been slain by that madman, Arnaud.

He must kill Arnaud.

Saturday before Palm Sunday[1]

Poissy

To Baldwin's relief Simon's worst fears were not realised.

From the day that Baldwin had spoken to de Bouden, Simon had maintained a cold silence. To him, it was clear enough that they should make Lord John aware of de Bouden's meeting, but when Baldwin had spoken to the Queen it was clear that no useful purpose could be served by doing so.

'You say that my clerk spoke to Roger Mortimer?' she had asked.

Baldwin had nodded. 'He would not say what they discussed.'

'I am distressed to hear this,' she said.

'Would you like me to tell Lord Cromwell?'

'No!' she snapped, eyes blazing. 'I would ask that you obey me, sir knight.'

---

[1] Saturday 30 March 1325

'My queen, I always try to do all to serve your interests,' he protested.

She gave a short smile. 'Rather than my husband's, eh?'

'I hope I can serve both equally.'

'That I doubt. However, my annoyance is not with you, Sir Baldwin. It lies with de Bouden himself. He should have told me that you saw him.'

'I . . .' Baldwin had closed his mouth. She had not said that de Bouden should have told her that he had met Mortimer, but that he had told Baldwin about meeting Mortimer.

'Yes. You comprehend, I think?'

'When did you first begin to negotiate with Mortimer, your highness?'

'That is none of your concern . . . and yet, why not? Roger Mortimer has been known to me for many years, Sir Baldwin. And when I was last staying in the Tower, I visited him there. The poor man has seen all he has built up over the last years removed from him. Believe me, I know how loss of privilege and lands and *respect* can hurt a man or a woman.'

'I am sorry.'

'You are not the man who took away my possessions and gave me a pittance to live on. Yet I thank you for your words. You are a kind man, Sir Baldwin. Yes, but worse than what was happening to Mortimer, I also knew of his poor wife, Joan. My husband had her arrested too, and imprisoned. She is allowed only one mark a day for food and expenses. One mark a day! Their children have been taken from her and imprisoned, all but Geoffrey who is here in France.'

'I understand.'

'No. You cannot, Sir Baldwin. You cannot know what it is like to be taken from your home, to have all your pretty little possessions stolen away, to be forced to become a beggar, and you cannot understand – no man can comprehend – the horror of having your children taken from you. All else is bearable, my sir, but to have your children stolen from you, to be refused permission to see them, to hold them ... that is cruelty beyond torture.'

He could recall so clearly the brightness in her eyes as she spoke. She knew about the pain of loss. Baldwin was tongue-tied standing before her as the tears formed and trickled down her cheeks. In his heart he wondered how his own wife Jeanne would cope with the destruction of their family, with seeing their little manor broken up, their belongings taken away to be sold or destroyed, and her children torn from her embrace, to be carted away, perhaps never to be seen again. All because of offences caused by their father – offences of which they were entirely innocent.

'I shall not tell Lord John, my lady,' he had said stiffly.

'Lord Mortimer is a good man, Sir Baldwin. He has a loving wife who misses him dreadfully, and he her. You know that in all their married life, he never left her? When he was sent by my husband the King to fight in wars all over the King's lands, he always took Joan with him. She and he are devoted.'

Her eyes were distant, a woman considering the fortune of another. A cause for jealousy, perhaps, but all Baldwin could see was a whimsical respect. Or a sadness for the love she had not felt for so many years.

'Sir Baldwin, I know what it is to have a lover taken from me. I know how Joan must feel to know that her marriage has been ravaged. Her husband was stolen from her by the fiend Despenser, may he rot in hell! Despenser has done the same to me. He is the third person in my marriage. I *know* how poor Joan feels because I have suffered the same fate.'

'I think I now understand you better, my lady,' he said. And for the first time, in his heart, Sir Baldwin de Furnshill cursed the king who could have ordered such injustices.

Chapter Twenty

Jean had seen nothing of them. The little store of coin which he had in his purse was all but used up, and now he was husbanding the remainder by working in a little cookshop not far from the palace gate. The money was poor, but he could eat as many pies as he wanted while the cook was in the front of the shop, and there was enough to pay for his room and buy a cup or two of wine each day.

He couldn't stay here for ever, though. The whole town was full of talk of the protracted negotiations which were continuing here between the King and the English queen, she who was his sister. Not that it meant there was too much love between them. She had new loyalties now, to her husband, her son, and her adopted country. So the haggling went on, and meanwhile the men who had travelled here with her were all closeted up in that palace. And all he wanted to do was get to see le Vieux and explain what had happened so that they could both overwhelm and kill that madman, Arnaud.

It was ironic that he should have come to this conclusion now. In the past, all the while they had been guards at the Château Gaillard, he had loathed Arnaud for what he had done to Agnes and Raymond.

Jean had known many men who had killed. He had done so himself. When a man joined his lord's host, he must expect to be sent to fight; unless he went with the intention of dying, he must expect to kill. But that was in hot blood, when the energy fizzed in a lad's arms and legs, when he shouted, his heart warmed by the thought of standing with friends and comrades in defiance of another's will. It was easy to kill when a man ran at you trying to cut your throat.

Others were put in the hideous position of having to kill in cold blood. He was fortunate, he'd never been forced to that, but he knew other men who had. Men who'd been told to execute prisoners, thrusting a sword down into their bodies while they knelt with hands and feet bound, like cattle waiting to be slaughtered. Yet that was removing dangerous enemies. Even that was more acceptable than the actions of a man like Arnaud.

An executioner could show pity, sympathy, compassion or even regret. Any display of that nature was good for the heart of the victim. And no one would wish to be killed by a man who had no feeling at all. That would serve only to denigrate the entire life of the condemned. Yet there was one worse possibility – a man like Arnaud.

Jean had seen him. Yes. He'd seen him when Agnes screamed and wailed in the flames. It was inhuman to kill a woman in that way. Worse than bestial. The law must be upheld, of course it must, but to kill like that, in a way specifically designed to terrify, was no form of justice.

Some executioners went out of their way to prevent too much suffering. Jean had seen them: men who cast a rope about the throat of the victim, so that as the flames crept higher they could strangle the man or woman before the pain became unbearable. Others came to their duties with fear; weakly souls, these, who would cause the prisoners untold anguish because they detested what they must do. Often they would be drunk, intentionally overindulging in wine or ale so as to be incapable of feeling when they set the pyre alight.

Arnaud was that worse type, though. He gloried in killing. He enjoyed it. He would go to the executions with a smile on his lips. He would listen with delight to the pleading of the condemned; he would laugh and caper in appalling mimicry of their death throes; he would revel in their horror.

Jean had been arrested within hours of Raymond's death. It was one of the few things in his life he had done for which he could be proud, standing up in the tavern and declaring Raymond and Agnes innocent. But it had cost him dear. Christ! *So* dear.

Sir Charles was in the main court before the castle's hall when he saw the man.

Many men would have bellowed for guards, demanded that the fellow be arrested immediately, or, more shrewdly, slowly sidled away to seek for more English knights to help capture the man. After all, Roger Mortimer was no felon by French law.

But Sir Charles of Lancaster was an astute, thoughtful man. Years of wandering after the destruction of his earl's host at Boroughbridge had made him cautious about over-hasty action. Especially when it came to French sensibilities. He had been overwhelmed in a tavern because of some French peasants who were insulting him. He'd killed them all, with Paul, his man-at-arms, and a Portuguese man they had met. Since then he had been a little wary of bringing attention to himself.

He saw Mortimer leave the court and walk out through the main gate. Strolling as though idly, he followed the man out into the town itself, and was doing well enough, until his careful passage was obstructed by a cart that happened to shed its load in a narrow part of the street. Immediately people blocked the way, and he could only stand and curse quietly. Coming to a quick decision, he turned round and made his way back to the castle.

He took a little passage near the main hall, and walked down the corridor to the chamber where the servants tended to meet. It was a large room like a calefactory, in which there were several barrels of cheaper wine and ales. After peering about him, he caught sight of Paul negotiating with a friendly woman in a corner.

Seeing his master, Paul hastily concluded the haggling, and marched to see his knight. 'Sir Charles?'

'When you've finished here, I'd like to walk about the town a little,' Sir Charles said.

'I am ready, sir.'

'Good.'

He led the way through the gates, under the strong portcullis, and out into the town's streets.

The weather had improved steadily in the last few days, and now all around there was the proof of springtime. Flowers were bursting open everywhere. Lent was still in force – Easter was to be late this year, and was still over a week away – but the scents and colours of the renewed year were enough to lift everybody's spirits.

'Do you know why I asked you to join me?' Sir Charles asked.

'No.'

'An elegantly simple response. Very well, then. I am alarmed to have noticed a man in the town who appears to be all too familiar. Roger Mortimer. I've seen him.'

'What's he going to be doing around this place?'

'That is a good question – but I have a much better one: how much would the King, or my dear friend Sir Hugh le Despenser, pay for his head on a plate?'

'A large amount, I'd think. They'd pay well to see Mortimer destroyed. He must be the King's most feared enemy.'

'I should think so.'

'You sure you've seen him?'

They were entering a little alleyway. Sir Charles looked at

him, and did not answer. Paul pulled a face. It had been a foolish question. They both knew Mortimer. Any man who had fought with, for, or against the King in the last twenty years would know the King's general. Shrewd, quick-thinking, an excellent strategist, Roger Mortimer had cowed the Irish and the Welsh, and had probably been the best warrior to begin planning an invasion of Scotland. All in all, if there was a fight anywhere within the King's lands, it was likely that Mortimer had been there, and had succeeded in winning victory for the King.

'What do you want to do?'

'Find him, kill him, conceal the body, and send you with the head back to London. Or Beaulieu in Hampshire – I believe the King is there presently. That way you and I can reap the reward without anybody else's being aware. I shall remain here, naturally, so you'll have to hurry back with the money. Clear?'

Paul nodded. 'He'll be in a not-too-lowly place, I assume.'

'He may well be inside the castle – but I doubt it. I think if he's here, he isn't here with the King's approval. No, I tend to the view that he's here because he wants something. Perhaps to attack the Queen? Whatever the reason, we must catch him when there's no one else about to share the winnings. Is that clear? Good. You know what he looks like as well as I do. I think we need to wander about the town and see if we can spot him.'

They had reached the cart. The crowds had thinned, and they could pass by it without trouble.

'This is where I lost him, Paul. He was going down this street somewhere. All we have to do now is find him.'

Abbey de Maubisson

Blanche de Burgundy was delighted to have arrived, but the experience was still overwhelming.

The smell of fresh flowers greeted her every morning from the other side of the wall. She could hear birds singing in the trees, the gentle sussuration of the wind in the corridors, the occasional bark of a dog – and voices. Voices raised in song, the words irrelevant to her in God's own language, but the sounds of the tunes uplifting and wonderful to ears which had only heard the rasping voices of gaolers for a decade.

There had been times in that cell when she had seriously considered the final, irredeemable sin. She was guilty of so much already – adultery, fornication, pride, envy, gluttony . . . there was little she had not done, and for which there could be no forgiveness in a cell beneath Château Gaillard. At the last, she had thought of taking her own life. She could throw herself before God, if He allowed her, to beg forgiveness. The priests said that suicides would all be damned, but she already suffered so much that the thought of eternal damnation was not so terrifying. At least it would be a release from the misery she had been forced to endure every day already.

She wasn't sure what it was that stopped her. Perhaps a mortal fear of so irrevocable an act, or maybe it was the thought that by dying she would indeed make her husband's life – her ex-husband's life – a little easier.

If he had wanted, he could have pardoned her. He didn't need to keep her down there in the dungeon. It was three years ago that the marriage was annulled, they told her. So he could have removed her at any time, and stopped the appalling degradation she was forced to endure.

But that was a part of her punishment, surely. The rapes and indignities. And then the birth of her child.

Lord Roger Mortimer heard the two men approaching long before they actually appeared along his alleyway, and he had plenty of time to turn back and march up the alley.

There was a distinctive sound to men-at-arms. It was the

clattering of their metalwork, the rattle of spurs, or simply the ribald laughter and foul language. They were like troopers in any host from that point of view. Usually he was more than happy in the company of men from any lord's retinue, but not here and now. The King had clearly ordered him to leave the environs of Paris while the English queen was here, and he had deliberately ignored King Charles's command.

It was stupid, perhaps, but he had responsibilities. At least Queen Isabella had shown him pity before. When he had been stuck in the Tower of London two years ago, without any hope of regaining his freedom, she had visited him, and generously offered to try to help him.

Ach, she was a lady, and a kindly gentlewoman at that. It shouldn't have surprised him, but it did none the less. Poor Queen Isabella had enough problems of her own. Everyone in the blasted country knew that. The King had turned from her to lie with a man, from all accounts, and there she was, her authority eroded, without the company of her own husband.

Still, even with her own tribulations, she had made the effort to help him. She'd heard of poor Joan's predicament: all her clothes and possessions confiscated, and a meagre pittance given for food and drink. The Queen had written to the treasurer to persuade him to be generous; and knowing her own position in the hierarchy of the palace was already diminished, she also enlisted the aid of Eleanor de Clare, Despenser's wife. Roger only hoped and prayed that his darling Joan would have been accorded slightly better treatment as a result.

Perhaps it was a forlorn hope. When the King's father, Edward I, had captured the sister and mistress of one of his bitterest enemies, Robert Bruce, Edward in his wisdom had seen fit to have them both caged and put on show. Mary Bruce, the sister, was held in her cage at Roxburgh Castle, while Isabel, Countess of Buchan, was held in a similar cage at Berwick. The sole token of privacy these poor women were accorded was the use of a hidden privy. Apart from that, both must suffer the indignity of constant display for more than three years.

He had mentioned that to the Queen, and she had confessed to being appalled by her father-in-law's treatment of the two. It was one thing to take vengeance on a knight or some other man who had been disloyal, but this extension of revenge on to the womenfolk and children, both of whom were clearly innocent, was distasteful in the extreme. Still worse was to come, though.

After Boroughbridge and the King's successful quashing of the attempted insurrection of Lancaster, he had launched an attack on Scotland again to quell the rebels there. But the Scots soon outflanked him, and the King and Despenser were forced to beat a very hasty retreat – leaving in their wake Isabella, trapped at Tynemouth. In her speedy escape by boat, two of her ladies-in-waiting were killed.

That, Roger reckoned, was the turning point for Isabella. Up until then she had tolerated Despenser's ruthless tyranny. She despised his tactics, his terrorisation of any noblewoman who stood in the path of his single-minded avarice, but she was prepared to be coolly polite for the sake of her marriage. But not after Tynemouth. That her husband could desert her to the mercies of the Scots after the treatment his own father had meted out to the Bruce women showed he no longer had any feelings for her.

It was after that, really, that she had begun to work for Roger Mortimer's release from prison. After all, as she said to him, once Mortimer was in the ascendant Despenser must be deposed and destroyed, and that could only be good for her marriage, for the kingdom, and for all who lived in it.

He only hoped that Joan was all right. Apparently she had been transferred to a fresh prison, but he had heard that her treatment had improved. Perhaps Despenser was a little troubled by the thought that Mortimer could return to take his revenge for the treatment of his family.

One son at least was free. Thanks to God, when Roger had escaped from the Tower Geoffrey, his third son, had been in France to take over the lands he had inherited from Joan's mother and swear his allegiance to the French king. Both Geoffrey and his money would be needed if Roger's plans were to come to fruition.

But he would have to be cautious. He had no wish to suffer the fate of men like Robert le Ewer. When it was learned that Ewer had helped plot to assassinate Despenser, he was taken and condemned to die in the slowest, most horrible manner. He was chained to the ground and iron weights were set upon his breast, slowly crushing him until he died several days later.

Roger Mortimer would not see his family suffer any more. He had already paid his debt of honour; he would see his family released.

The sound of the men's footsteps was quite loud, but Roger was confident he could escape them. He increased his pace, took a quick right turn into a short passageway, bore right again into a wider thoroughfare, and then went left and down towards the town's gate. He would double back in a short while.

He didn't want to be caught by the French *or* the English.

Chapter Twenty-One

Arnaud had an annoying habit of humming when he was thinking. It wasn't something le Vieux had noticed overmuch when they had been together in the Château Gaillard, but now that the others were gone, perhaps it was natural that Arnaud himself should be more irritating. The more time a man spent with a single companion, the more likely it was he'd become intolerant.

The best way to escape was to leave him behind. Le Vieux went through to see Robert de Chatillon.

Since the burial of Enguerrand de Foix at the church on the day they arrived here, a service that was honoured by the presence of Jeanne d'Evreux, Robert had been busy with the many little affairs that must be tied up. Two clerks had travelled with the Comte, and they had been going through all his papers in detail. It was slow, frustrating work for a man like Robert, but he must only endure it a little longer, and then he would be able to return to Foix. The Comte's heart was in a sealed box, and this he would take back with him so that the Comte's widow would have something to bury. A woman needed something like that. This way, she'd have a small spot near home at her own church where she could go and pray for him.

Le Vieux entered the room just as Robert was finishing another box of papers. He was peering down at the scroll in his hand, a frown of incomprehension on his face. Looking up and seeing le Vieux in the doorway, he raised his eyebrows. 'Yes?'

'Do you have any instructions for us?'

Robert shrugged. 'I have passed on your report. All the men there at the château are dead and the woman has been taken to the abbey of Maubisson as arranged. I think that all is completed satisfactorily.'

Dismissed, le Vieux wandered from the room. He stood outside, wondering what he should do. The castle held little attraction for him. It was a place of rest, but he was bored with rest. Give him a decent march, some wine and women at the end of it, or a fight, and he'd be happy, but this lazing about for day after day was driving him up to the moon. He needed some action.

He couldn't face returning to Arnaud and that appalling humming. Instead he walked under the gate and out into the street, and went to a cookshop for a pie before aimlessly passing down the lane, glancing at the food displayed on the shutters as he went.

An urchin slipped past him, a hand whipped out, and the lad ran off with a small loaf of bread, haring along the lane like a small greyhound. It made the shopkeeper roar, and he bolted into the lane, shaking his fist over his head, but others, le Vieux included, laughed. The boy was quick and clever. So long as he wasn't caught, he would have a great future ahead of him. A lad like that could get far.

That was when he heard the 'Psst' and urgent whisper of his name.

He turned, and, to his horror, there was Jean.

'You didn't expect to see me again, did you?'

'You! What are you doing here?'

'I followed you. I had to. The men at the château – I had to make sure you knew what had happened.'

'Eh?'

'I saw them. I was up on the wall, and I saw them.

Berengar and Arnaud. Arnaud was after him like a demon, waving a knife, and murdered him just outside the castle. And then I went back to our room, and the others were all dead.'

'Wait, wait!' le Vieux said, his hands up. He was not panicked yet. There was space between him and Jean, and he had his sword on his hip, but Jean was dangerous. He knew that full well. 'I don't know what you're talking about.'

'I had to run. I – er – I thought you were dead like all the others, and I fled to get help. But I couldn't. I was going to come here, to tell the King what had happened, but then I thought I'd be suspected myself, so I just ran. But then I saw you in the Queen of England's party with Arnaud, and I knew I had to do something to warn you, so you knew it was Arnaud who'd committed the murders. What did he say? Did he say it was me?'

'Well, that was what I thought.'

'What happened to you?'

'I was knocked out early on. I didn't see what happened,' le Vieux admitted.

'That was why. He knocked you down, then started to kill the others. It must have been easy enough if they weren't expecting him. He's a lunatic – he must be. You've seen how he was with the prisoners. Torture and murder is his delight. You have to help me – together we can stop him.'

'Stop him?'

'Kill him. He's mad! I know him. I saw him years ago, back in my home town, down in Pamiers. He burned some folks there, and he *enjoyed* it. He was dancing about them, taunting them as they died. He has to be stopped before he can kill any more. You are still with him, and you can't tell when he's likely to push a knife into your heart! You aren't safe until he's dead, and neither am I, because while we're alive, the truth about what he did in Château Gaillard may come out. He can't take that risk.'

Le Vieux nodded slowly. There was a slowly dawning horror on his face. 'I thought you had done them in. It never occurred to me . . . The idea that Arnaud could have knocked me down and killed all the others . . . I hadn't even considered it.'

'I didn't think you could have,' Jean said. 'What was worse was that when I got to the town to get help, they already knew the garrison was dead.'

'Come with me. I think I know what to do,' Le Vieux said, and set off at a trot towards the palace.

Baldwin had been for a long ride that day, and when he returned he dropped from the saddle with the bounce of a man who had enjoyed a day's exercise after too many days of lassitude. He cast the reins at a waiting groom, and only when he'd seen the man start to rub down the beast did Baldwin leave and go to find himself something to drink. It was deeply ingrained in him that he should always see to his mount before attending to his own pleasures. A horse was more than an animal – to a knight it was his principal weapon as well.

The French did not believe in weak wines. Those served here in the King's palace were magnificent, and it was good for Baldwin, so he felt, to be reacquainted with them. It was many years since he had last lived in Paris, and the opportunity of drinking the wide variety available was proving to be immensely pleasurable.

He watched as a man-at-arms crossed the court with a younger fellow behind him. They went quickly, men in a hurry, as so many did in this great royal palace. Everybody appeared to be in a hurry here.

Lord Cromwell was standing in the doorway, and he walked over to Baldwin. 'This is a peculiar place, eh, Sir Baldwin? Everyone is so busy – except for me. I feel useless here.'

'I had to go for a ride to remind myself what a horse feels like.' Baldwin smiled.

'The Queen is here to negotiate with the French, hoping to rescue some fragments of our once great Angevin empire from her blasted brother, the French king, but you and I, we kick our heels, while the French run around as though there're not enough hours in the day. There's nothing for us to do, not until we get the signal. Either we send messengers back with new proposals for the King, or we gradually slide into irrelevance. If there's no movement, nothing's going to win back Guyenne for us,' Cromwell said sadly. 'I always loved that territory. I have been there several times. Have you?'

'Yes.' Baldwin could remember a green landscape, hilly like Devon, but with long, tree-lined valleys, and hillsides covered in vines. He remembered warm sun and cool evenings. A blessed land. 'It would be a great loss to the kingdom.'

'Amen to that. Dear God, how much longer must we wait here? I have lands to manage, business to see to for myself.'

'I have a son just born,' Baldwin agreed sadly. 'I wanted to spend the springtime with him and my wife – instead I am out here.'

The lord nodded glumly. Then he looked at Baldwin with a slight frown. 'Did you ever make sense of the death of that count on the journey here?'

Baldwin bridled, and Cromwell noticed.

'I am not blaming you, Sir Baldwin. But you are more experienced than any others here in investigating murders.'

'I am sorry, my lord. It's just that every so often I catch a sidelong look from someone I've never met which seems to suggest they think I did it. In truth, I know nothing about him. All I know is, he and I had words on the way here. That is all.'

'No one has given us any trouble over his death, anyway, which is a relief,' Lord John said. 'It could have become embarrassing were someone to have taken it into his head to accuse you of murder.'

'There are many who consider I did it.'

'Damn their souls! It doesn't matter, in any case. It was an odd event, though. I've never heard of a similar one. Firing a charge of powder, then stealing your knife – that is strange.'

'There is nothing new under the sun,' Baldwin said with a grin. 'When there has been a murder, I always tend to find that it was because of some obvious reason. Usually it's money, or a desire for power, and sometimes a lover removes a competitor for some woman's affections. Only rarely is it a chance encounter.'

'This wasn't chance, then.'

'No. Clearly somebody had planned something. They had the powder there before they took my dagger to thrust into the Count's chest.'

'Was it your knife that killed him?'

'No. His throat was cut, and I believe that was done some while before the murderer realised I was there. I think I heard the man die. By the time I reached the scene he was already dead; my dagger was only a distraction.'

'I wonder what he was doing there, then.'

'So do I. I was called out there by a weak bladder, but he was a much younger man. And there is that one thing that concerns me.'

'What is that?'

'My lord, the assassin had an elaborate explosive set up. Surely if someone desired to kill a man like the Comte de Foix, they would have to ensure that he came along at the right time.'

'The assassin knew he would be there that night?'

'Not just that night. He must have known that the Comte would be there at that time. Which implies an arranged meeting.'

The lord was silent for a few moments as he absorbed this. 'I understand you have had much experience of inquiring after murders?'

'I have had some success.'

Lord John nodded. 'Do you have any suspicions as to who might have wanted to do this?'

'I hardly knew the man, and don't know his enemies. However, I think I know how the assassin planned to kill him: he intended to cut his throat, and then make it look like an accident with a hand-cannon. He had the powder and the board. He cut the Comte's throat, and was going to position him over the board to make it appear that the powder had been fired up into his throat. How would anyone have shown otherwise?'

'There was no *gonne*.'

'Taken away when the plan went wrong. When I turned up, the killer had to distract me, so he fired his board in a hurry, and that gave him a swift idea: to take my dagger and make it seem as if I had stabbed the Comte. He had no way of telling it was me, but my dagger was a useful device. Then he snatched up his *gonne*, but forgot to collect the board, and was off.'

'I see. An interesting theory. Be careful, Sir Baldwin.'

'I shall,' Baldwin said. He watched the lord walking away, and in his mind there was a feeling that Cromwell had been trying to put him on his guard all through that conversation. Perhaps he was warning him that the matter of the Count's murder was not yet over. Someone wanted to punish him for it still.

Jean had to hurry to keep up with le Vieux. There was something in his movements that spoke of anger. It was just a relief to Jean that his story was believed. He'd expected to have to argue for much longer, but, thanks to Christ, le Vieux had realised he was not lying almost immediately.

Then they were inside. Le Vieux took him up a tiny staircase that wound round and round inside a tower, the stone flags crisp and perfectly cut, unworn. They came out through a narrow doorway, and then they were out on a brief walkway at the top of the main walls, before diving into another, larger tower. Here they descended one flight, and passed along a short corridor to a door. Le Vieux knocked, then walked inside, beckoning Jean to follow.

It was a good-sized room. A wealthy-looking man stood inside reading a scroll behind a table, a large window behind him. Jean didn't know who he was, and looked over his shoulder enquiringly to see why le Vieux had brought him here. As he turned, something made him move.

The heavy cudgel missed his head by a scant inch. 'Le Vieux! What are you doing?'

'What in the name of heaven is going on!' the man at the table shouted.

'This is the man we told you of. The last guard to survive,' le Vieux snarled.

To Jean's horror, the man looked at him with empty eyes and began to draw his own sword.

He was almost a third of the way into the room. Le Vieux was between him and the door. If he tried to leap for it, he would never make it. Le Vieux would knock him down, and if he failed, there was that sword at his back.

But Jean had been a fighter for many years. He sprang into the room even as the stranger swept his sword from the scabbard. Jean lifted the front of the table high, thrusting forwards, and slammed it against the man. He was crushed against a mullion, and the air left his lungs even as a crunching sound told Jean that at least one rib was broken. The sword fell from his hands.

Jean moved quickly away, to his left, further away from le

Vieux, even as the cudgel came down again. It splintered fragments from the table as it hit the old beech, and then Jean was against the wall. There was a fireplace here, and his questing fingers found a steel poker. He kept it behind him.

Le Vieux had recovered already – he had great powers in a fight. Now he was approaching a little crabwise, left flank and arm forward, cudgel high in his right.

Jean could think of nothing else. He switched his hands on the poker, and leaped forward, aiming a fist at le Vieux's face. Le Vieux caught hold of the fist with a fierce smile, the teeth shining in his brown face. Then he brought down the cudgel.

Too late he saw the poker. It crashed into the side of his head, and as it thudded dully, Jean saw an explosion of blood spray outwards. Le Vieux's eyes rolled up instantly, and he fell to his knees, the cudgel falling to crack on Jean's shoulder with little force behind it. Jean tried to move away, but he seemed fixed there. His hand was on the poker, and he remained staring down at le Vieux, the older man apparently peering back at him, but with eyes fogged and dull.

Le Vieux was dead. Attempting to retrieve the poker, Jean found that it was stuck in his head somehow. When he tried to wrest it loose, le Vieux's head moved with it. It would have been comical if it weren't hideous. He was forced to push le Vieux to the ground, set a boot on his cheek, and tug hard.

At last the poker was free, and Jean went to the other man. He was breathing harshly, trapped by the weight of the table over his legs. One was twisted at an impossible angle, and he looked at Jean with an expression of horror and the terror of a trapped animal.

It was sickening. 'Why?' Jean demanded. 'Why did you want to kill me?'

There was no answer. The man stared back at him but said nothing, and Jean could already hear steps approaching. Someone must have heard the sharp encounter. He swore to himself, then clenched the poker in his hand and went to the door. Opening it, he could see no one about, and he darted out, bolting back the way he thought they had come, but he had only gone a short distance when he realised he had missed the stairs to the top of the wall. He ran on, blindly, praying that he would find an alternative, but there was nowhere obvious.

And then, behind him, he heard the shrieks from the man trapped under the table.

Chapter Twenty-Two

Baldwin heard the screams from the court where he was still standing, contemplating Lord John's words. As soon as he heard the noise, his first thought was to run to the source, but a moment's reflection told him that would be pointless. Others would be running there. Instead he turned left to head for the Queen's chambers to make sure that she was safe.

He found her in the main hall, pale and anxious.

'What is that, Sir Baldwin?'

'I do not know, your highness. I heard the first cry and came here to assure myself of your safety.'

'I am most grateful, Sir Baldwin. It sounds like an animal in pain.'

'It is a man,' Baldwin said coldly. He had heard similar cries of agony often enough in battles.

There was a heavy knocking at the door, and Baldwin went to it, calling, 'Who is it?'

'Me.'

Baldwin unbolted and opened the door to Lord Cromwell, who stared at Baldwin fixedly as he came in. Baldwin lowered the point of his sword and closed the door as the noble spoke quickly to the Queen.

'Sir Baldwin. Would you go, please, and see what is happening out there?' Queen Isabella said.

Baldwin nodded. He listened a moment, then opened the door. 'Lord John, bolt this after me.'

Cromwell agreed, and Baldwin was away.

The noise came from the tower over the main entrance, so far as he could tell. He hurried along the path, entered the tower, and climbed the stairs. It did not take long to reach the chamber. Robert de Chatillon was slumped on the floor, his breath rasping in his lungs, and the body of an aged warrior lay over by the fireplace, close to a heavy-looking cudgel. Blood was splattered over his shoulder, and there was a foul, matted mess at his skull just above his ear.

'What has happened here?' Baldwin asked wonderingly. He recognised the man-at-arms he had seen crossing the yard earlier.

'Someone came here and attacked me and this man,' Robert said haltingly. He was very pale.

'Did you see who it was?' Baldwin asked. Perhaps it was the same man he had seen following after this fellow. There had been two.

'A guard from the Château Gaillard. This man was another of the guards from there,' Robert said, motioning feebly towards le Vieux. 'He broke in here and attacked us both.'

'Why would he do that?'

'All I know is there was a small garrison there to protect the castle, and some weeks ago that man went insane. He took a knife and slew all the other guards in the château. We don't know why. Le Vieux was the only survivor at the time. Clearly the fellow learned where le Vieux was, and came here to finish his task.'

'But why would he do so?'

'Who can explain madness?' Robert demanded with a ferocious anger. There was a fevered gleam in his eyes now, and if it were not for the twisted and broken leg, Baldwin could have feared that he might leap up and set upon him for asking ridiculous questions. 'Just find him, Sir Baldwin. Find him and kill him, in God's name, before he murders anyone else.'

Baldwin nodded. 'What does he look like?'

Yes. It was the same man.

As he left the chamber, his brow was furrowed. The killer and the dead man had walked happily together across the courtyard, and then come to blows in the chamber with Robert. Robert had lied for some reason, Baldwin felt, but he was unsure why.

Jean had found his way to an undercroft, a crowded storeroom filled with barrels of food and drink, with bales of other goods set over the top to keep them dry. He bolted along it, hoping to find an escape, but the only way in was the one by which he had entered. He ran at the farther wall, and crashed into it, his arms up, still gripping the poker, his eyes firmly closed. The crash forced him, sobbing, to his knees, and he crouched there a while, gasping with shock and terror, before reaching out with his hands and touching the stone-work before him, fingers rippling over the plaster, seeking crevices as though he could have insinuated himself into the rock and passed through it. But he was human. Such feats were for God, not for him.

He relaxed, easing himself down again, and as his eyes grew acclimatised to the darkness in the chamber, he stared at the poker. It was a long log-poker, with a one-inch spike protruding to one side. That was what had hit le Vieux. It had punctured his head as easily as a pin bursting an inflated pig's bladder.

Jean was not upset at the thought of killing a man. Once he would have been, but he had fought in enough battles since then to know that sometimes a man must kill. Le Vieux had wanted to murder him . . . and he had no idea *why*! That was what had so shocked him: not the attack, but the man who had launched it. He had thought le Vieux was a friend, a comrade and an ally. All he'd tried to do was warn him about Arnaud.

The only thing that made any sense was that Arnaud had convinced him that Jean had killed all the other men at the château. Le Vieux must have believed him implicitly.

Jean groaned to himself. The thought that Arnaud could be so persuasive hadn't occurred to him before. And it wasn't only le Vieux who was convinced, either. That other man had obviously been persuaded as well. Jean was marked out for death. If he was seen or captured, he would be sure to be killed. There was no escape for him.

'Who was he?'

The man behind the table. He had drawn his sword when le Vieux had said that he was the last of the men from the château, hadn't he?

Suddenly Jean started to wonder if his initial impression of that last day at the château was as clear as he had thought. Le Vieux had been hit, surely, for there was no faking that bloody seeping wound, but that didn't necessarily mean he had been hit by Arnaud. Now it seemed to make more sense for him to have been hit by one of the other men as he and Arnaud *together* tried to kill the guards. But why would they do that?

The only person whom he could ask was probably the one whom he was most keen to kill. He would have to catch Arnaud to question him. But just now the likelihood was that he wouldn't even be able to escape the castle, let alone run off and later find Arnaud to learn what had actually happened.

Then again, he considered, there was less need to run away to hide when you were already in a large undercroft filled with barrels of food and drink. This was probably as good a place to hide as any other, and it had the added attraction of being cheap.

He would stay and formulate a plan to gain his revenge.

Louvre, Paris

King Charles IV was not known for his patience, but the reputation was unfair. There were times when he was capable of explosions of rage, just like any other monarch, and others when he was content to be still and watch other men's actions. This was particularly true when he felt sure that someone had failed in their duties to him.

'Alive?'

The cardinal smiled, but warily. Thomas of Anjou knew when the King was displeased, and today the man could have frozen a sea with his stare. 'I am afraid, so it would seem.'

'I seem to remember you telling me that the entire matter of the château was over,' King Charles said, his attention moving to the face of his adviser.

François de Tours nodded, his eyes fixed on the floor. 'I relayed the news to you as soon as I was told. The men of the town went up there and found all the guards dead, or so I thought. Now it would seem that one of them has miraculously returned to life. He found Robert de Chatillon and killed one of his men in front of him, as well as hurting Robert.'

'He killed my executioner?'

'No. The other one. An old soldier of Enguerrand's.'

'Oh, I recall. Well, he was to die as well soon enough, wasn't he? But my man is not hurt?'

'Not yet. However, if we do not act to remove any other witnesses, matters could become more difficult.'

'See to it. And François? No more slip-ups, my friend. All witnesses, all of them, must be removed. I want no surprises in the future.'

Poissy

'D'you hear that?' Adam asked.

'What?' Ricard demanded, staring into his cup. On his lap Charlie was resting, snoring softly with his mouth open. He had started snuffling today, and Ricard hoped it was only a cold. He had grown rather fond of the little boy.

'He's right,' Philip said. 'There's some sort of disturbance up there.'

'So what?' Ricard belched. 'There's always something going on. It's a bloody castle, isn't it? Some fight between men-at-arms, I dare say. I'm not getting up to go and look.'

Philip scowled. 'And where's our friend? Eh?'

Ricard looked up at him. His eyes were bloodshot and he was finding it hard to concentrate. 'If you mean our illustrious companion, Philip, I don't know, and I don't care. The arsehole has left us alone. Far as I'm concerned, that's good news. You won't find me complaining. In fact, I think that rather than complain we ought to celebrate. Yes. Let's have another drink!'

'Before you do that, let's make sure he hasn't gone and killed someone else,' Adam said nervously.

Janin leaned back on his seat. 'What makes you say that? Adam, what is it with you? You always have to bring out something unpleasant, don't you? There's nothing to say that anyone's died, is there? And nothing to say Jack's involved anyway.'

'I told you all when he arrived,' Adam said. 'I'm sorry, but that's how it is. He's a bad one.'

Ricard frowned and shook his head without looking at Adam. '*No*, actually you didn't, Adam. You never said he was bad. In fact, I seem to remember you were the only one of us who wanted this fellow to join us, because with your usual grasp of the unimportant, you thought it was essential that we had another drummer to replace Peter.'

'I didn't!' Adam declared, and shot a look at the others. They studiously avoided his gaze. 'Oh, if you're going to be idiots, then blame me. You always do anyway.'

'No one's blaming you for anything,' Janin said soothingly.

Philip pulled the corners of his mouth downwards in a gesture of denial, shaking his head slowly. 'No. We aren't blaming you, Adam. But we all wish you'd stop blaming *us* for everything.'

Adam sank back, his face bleak. 'It's not my fault.'

'So where is he this time?' Philip asked. He drained his cup.

'God only knows,' Ricard said. 'All I know is, he's bloody dangerous. If there has been some crime up there, I pray someone will catch him and slay him quickly so that we're all a little safer.'

Janin was thoughtful. 'He was strange about that, wasn't he? I would've thought . . .'

'What?' Philip demanded.

'I was just thinking: all the men I've met who've been allied with Despenser have been proud about it. They've boasted.'

'I suppose you've met a lot of them, eh?' Philip scoffed.

'Quite a few,' Janin said. 'You remember the man in the glovemaker's house? He was not too secretive, was he? He was determined to have us spy on the Queen, and he told us how.'

'Although he told us to tell everything we learned to some man with a peacock picture,' Philip said, scowling.

'Who never appeared,' Janin agreed. 'Perhaps that was only while she was in England still, and he couldn't get his comrade to join us out here?'

'For my part, I reckon that fellow Jack is a friend of his, and he had Jack placed with us so that Jack could keep an eye on her all on his own. There was no need for us then.'

'Except,' Janin said, 'he had a man who was a competent musician, so he had to find a means of installing the fellow into a troupe of Queen's musicians.'

The others said nothing. There was nothing much they

could say. All knew what he meant: Jack or an accomplice had murdered their friend Peter in order to ease his route into the Queen's party. Kill Peter, then Jack could join the musicians.

'We aren't fighters,' Philip said, with blatant dishonesty.

'If Jack is one of Despenser's men, why did his mate have the glover and his wife killed? That man told us the glover was a loyal servant to Despenser,' Adam said.

'Who else told us that?' Janin demanded harshly.

'Hmm?'

'Did anyone else corroborate what he said about the glover? The man might well have been uninterested in politics for all we know. The mention of Despenser's name was handy to scare us into being obedient, but that doesn't mean he told us the truth, does it? I'd guess he was a Despenser man himself, and Jack is too.'

'Which means de Bouden is. He forced us to bring Jack,' Ricard said, and belched.

'So he was telling the truth when he told us to leave him alone,' Janin said. 'He could have had us caught and executed, if he's one of Despenser's men.'

'In England he could,' Ricard said. 'Maybe we ought to just stay here in France.'

'What?' Janin shot out. He looked up. 'Stay here?'

'Become wandering troubadours. With the number of castles in the country, we'd make a good living, I'll bet. As much wine as you can drink.'

'They're a bit odd over here, though,' was Philip's considered opinion.

'The weather's warmer,' Janin mused.

Adam stared. 'You reckon this is warmer than London?'

'The summers are longer and warmer,' Janin amended.

'At least here in France we're out of the reach even of Despenser's arm,' Ricard pointed out. 'The only person who hates him more than the Queen is the French king.'

'What of Jack?'

'Swyve him with a blunt stick. As soon as we can lose him, I vote we do,' Ricard said. 'At best he's a spy against our queen. I don't want to aid him in any way.'

For some minutes the group was silent, drinking slowly, each immersed in his own thoughts. But then Ricard's fingers began to tap out a beat. Janin watched intently, frowning as he strove to recognise the tune, then nodded, and took up his hurdy-gurdy. Adam pulled out a small whistle and set it to his lips, while Philip began to beat on the tabletop.

'Space for another in your session?' Jack asked as he entered the room.

'Where have you been?' Janin asked as they all stopped playing.

'I wanted to learn what all that noise was about. Did you hear it? Apparently some guard has been murdered.'

Ricard sprang to his feet, and was about to jump on Jack when Jack held up his hand and laughed outright. 'Not again! No, there was a witness to the attack, a squire. He's described a Frenchman from the south, wearing a worn leather jack and red hosen. Do I fit that description? No? Then calm yourselves.'

'Why should we?' Ricard said. 'We don't trust you. You suddenly appear, just after our mate's been murdered . . . did you have him killed?'

'Me? Christ in a bucket, no! That was our enemy did that. No, I'm your comrade.'

'You?'

Jack shrugged, but then he stepped nearer their table. In his hand he held his bodhran, wrapped in its leather case. He took it out and showed it to them, then reversed it. At the back of the skin, near the rim where his forearm lay while gripping it, was a picture. 'Look at that. I'm told it's a very good picture, although I'm no judge. Ach, I can't understand pictures and what people see in them. What do you think?'

Ricard could not speak. The little picture of the peacock was perfect, he thought dully. So this was the spy to whom they were supposed to report. All along, he'd been the spy for the man who'd killed the glover and his wife after Ricard's drunken fondling in the London tavern.

'Who do you work for?' he asked.

'Ah, now. That you have to work out. Let's just keep things all good and professional.'

It was Janin who asked the one question they all wanted answered. 'Why show us that now? You could have told us at any time, but you kept it hidden until now. Why?'

Jack looked from one to the other of them measuringly, finishing with Janin himself. 'I didn't need to before. I thought to keep quiet and just stay with you. That way I could keep a close eye on the Queen. But now odd things are happening. The man who died today was one of a small garrison in a castle downriver. As far as I can tell, all his companions have died except one.'

'What of it?' Janin asked.

'This castle was a prison. It held an important lady, and the men there, so it is rumoured, raped her. It is a foul story. To think that a high-born noblewoman could be thrown into a gaol is bad enough, and the more so when it's a place like that, but to have the guards rape her too, that is particularly repugnant.' He held up his hand. 'I know. I'm getting to the point.

'The thing is, gentles, that the woman who was thrown into gaol went there because of our queen. And that's a little worrying, because it could mean that the dear lady we serve could herself be in danger. Someone has killed those who harmed this prisoner. So she has some fellows who want to serve *her*, perhaps. They are punishing those who hurt her.'

Adam made an impatient noise. 'What of it?'

'Ah, perhaps I'm making a little heavy weather of my

story. They do say it's a curse of the Irish, after all, never to tell a story quickly when it can be spun out. Well, I'll try to be brutally swift, then. Just for you. You see, young Adam, if someone is out to punish all those who hurt their lady, and if our queen was the very person who had her imprisoned, it's not too much of a leap of intellect, lad, is it, to think that our queen could very well herself be next on this fellow's list. Eh?'

Chapter Twenty-Three

Back at the Queen's chamber, Baldwin took little time to explain what had happened. 'So if you see a tatty little churl from the far south, carrying a poker and clad in worn red hosen and old leather jack, stab first and question him later,' he said lightly.

The Queen nodded and showed relief. 'For a moment I wondered whether there was something a lot worse.'

She was sitting in a high-backed chair. There were no other chairs or stools in the room, so Cromwell and Baldwin were standing before her.

Lord John glanced at her. 'You thought the peasants had risen?'

'It is not unheard of, but no – my fear was another fire. Sir Baldwin, that reminds me. How are your burns?'

'Much better since I've been using the salve you kindly sent me,' he said with a bow.

'A curious thing, that,' Lord John said. 'I have found no one who can tell why someone should have wished to have de Foix killed. He was pretty universally liked.'

'Except by me, I fear,' Baldwin said. He caught Cromwell's eye, and shook his head very slightly. 'But it is probable that this was just a chance encounter. Someone intended to set off the charge there to tempt men from their tents so that he could enter to rob them, and the Comte happened to catch him in the act. I dare say it was nothing more than that. The main thing is, there was no threat to the Queen, and that is all that matters.'

'It was,' Cromwell said. 'But now we've had two murders in the space of as many weeks. Surely that is too many for coincidence.'

'I do not see how the Comte de Foix and an ageing prison guard could be related,' Baldwin said. 'They must have been unconnected.'

'The Comte de Foix, you say?' the Queen mused. 'His territories are in the far south of France, are they not?'

'Yes, I believe so,' Cromwell said.

'Which is where this little tatty guard came from, I think you said, Sir Baldwin?'

Baldwin nodded.

'So perhaps the same man was responsible for both deaths? What of the dead guard – did you learn anything about him?'

'Only that he was a guard in a prison-castle in Normandy, near the borders. The Château Gaillard. The man who killed him was from the same garrison.'

'*That* place!' the Queen hissed, and looked into the fire's flames. 'I would have you leave me, my lord, Sir Baldwin. I am tired.'

'What do you think she meant by that?' Simon asked a little later.

He had risen on hearing the noise, but he didn't know the palace well enough to go haring about the place. Confident that he'd get lost if he tried to find the Queen's quarters, he took the sensible option of remaining in his room with his sword unsheathed. After all, guards would be pelting up and down passages seeking the source of those screams, and a foreigner with an odd accent would be an easy target. Better by far to remain safely out of the way. It was a relief to hear Baldwin return.

'There was something about the castle which upset her, I think. I do not know why,' Baldwin admitted.

'And meanwhile there is this strange, scruffy churl wandering the place. Do you think he was there on the night the Comte died?'

'It is possible. There were a lot of strange men and women on the journey here, weren't there? The hangers-on formed a large train at the rear of the column, and there were all the knights and nobles. He could have been attached to any of their parties.'

'And this other man, the one he killed. He was in the room with Robert de Chatillon? Curious that people near that Robert seem to keep dying. First his Comte, now this guard.'

'I want to learn more about the Château Gaillard. There must be some reason for the two guards to have had a dispute.'

'We could always try to speak to Robert again, I suppose,' Simon said. He was doubtful. 'He was not overly keen to discuss affairs with us last time we spoke, though. Do you think he has given up any thoughts that you could have been responsible for the murder of his master?'

'Oh, I think so. I think my inane playing with the black powder was enough to convince him of that.'

'Maybe he thought you were so incompetent that you'd be likely to burn yourself out in the wild at night?' Simon guessed with a mischievous smile. 'Just as you did!'

Paul had passed up the road twice before he decided to give up on the search for now and find a small wine shop.

The nearest was a scruffy little building that suited his mood nicely. He entered and ordered a jug of the local wine. It was the peasant drink, rough and potent, but that was how he liked his wine. The smooth, sweeter wines on offer in the palace were no doubt more expensive, but he preferred a harsher variety.

He'd always liked France, since the first time he'd come here with Sir Charles three years ago. That journey was curtailed after they had got into a fight with some locals and killed them all, but it hadn't affected his feeling for the country. Only for some of the peasants. They were as rude as any others.

That attack and the consequent flight from France had been exciting, but much of his life had been like that. At first, with Sir Charles in Lancaster, he had only ever been on the right side of the law, but as soon as they found themselves declared outlaw everything changed. They were forced to run from the country and seek refuge in France, where for a while they had survived on the proceeds of Sir Charles's store of silver and pewter, but all too soon that was expended, and they had decided to try their luck with the Germans. It was said that the colonies in Lithuania were lucrative. Teutonic knights were overrunning the heathen eastern lands and turning them into productive Christian territories, apparently. Except they'd never made it there.

Instead they had travelled back to England with Simon and Baldwin. They had endured enough wandering by then, and it was to be hoped that the King's rage against all those who had been loyal to Lancaster would have burned itself out.

Returning had been a strange experience. At first Paul had reckoned that they would suffer the fate of so many others, and be hanged for their treachery, but they had been fortunate. Apparently only a short while before their return the reign of terror had come to an end. Many said it was the Queen who intervened. She was certainly a kind, gracious lady, so it would be no surprise, Paul thought. Sir Charles reckoned that the King had sated his desire for blood, and one morning awoke to realise what horror he had inflicted on the kingdom. For his part, Paul doubted it. He had enough experience of warriors and rulers to know that those who wielded immense power tended to believe in their right to use it to the exclusion of all other considerations.

Anyway, they had managed to find themselves billeted in the King's household at last. Along with many others who had dubious pasts, they had been accepted, and their crimes forgiven. Not that they'd been guilty of many crimes in England. Most of them had been committed in France.

Which was why he was still a little nervous as he walked the lanes about here. It was near enough to Paris for him to feel that sense of wild danger, as though someone was watching them constantly, ready to call the hue and cry to arrest them both, or kill them. Even though he knew that they should be perfectly safe here, his eyes kept flitting over the crowds walking past.

No sign of Sir Charles. He would be farther up, nearer the river, if he had kept on walking. Paul hoped he was all right.

It was a strange thought, but one which had returned to him more regularly recently: if it was bad enough to lose Earl Lancaster, what would he do if Sir Charles were to die? Without his master, he would be as lost as a cork bobbing about on the sea. Sir Charles gave him purpose, his life meaning. Without Sir Charles, he didn't know what he could do. He was no farmer, and he had no trade. Perhaps, he considered, glancing about him idly, he could start up a wine shop, or take on a tavern in England? There were always people who wanted a drink, and provided he didn't fall foul of the ale-measurers, it was safe business, too.

A flash, nothing more, just a brief glimpse of a cloak, and his attention was focused again. He stood slowly, drinking from his cup, eyeing the figure. It was a tall man, with the build of a rich one. Not someone who looked as though he'd ever been forced to go hungry.

Paul drained the cup, regretfully left the remains of the wine in the jug, and hurried off after his quarry.

* * *

Robert de Chatillon groaned as he levered himself up from his seat. Painfully, grimacing, he hobbled over to the sideboard.

If anything, the pain was worse now. It felt as though his back was turned against his body slightly, like a bar of steel that was bent out of true. Standing and walking were difficult, and even when he lay in his bed of an evening, matters were not improved. The dull pain would always be there, and no matter how he turned or rolled, he would be aware of it. Somehow the fact that it was unchanging seemed to make it more unendurable.

He poured more wine, hoping it might make a little difference. The knock, when it came, was welcome as a distraction. 'Yes?'

'Do you remember me, my son?' Père Pierre Clergue asked as he stepped quietly into the room. 'Our friends are anxious that our plans appear to have gone astray.'

Roger Mortimer kept a smile on his face as he walked quickly along the cobbles. He had to be cautious, aware always that any eyes with black suspicion in them might belong to his enemy's men. There were so many who'd be prepared to slay him and carry his body back to Despenser for a reward – and he had no doubt that the reward would be large. Despenser hated him enough to share his wealth with any man who destroyed him.

The King, too, was keen to see him dead. It was terrible, that. The man whom he had served devotedly all his life was now seeking to have him killed. All because of the poison that evil whelp Despenser was pissing in his ear the whole time. Mortimer had made it very clear that he wanted to remove Despenser, but that was no more than common necessity. The thieving bastard was ruining the country with his avarice and

ruthlessness. Trouble was, just as before with Piers damned
Gaveston, the King was blind. He was in love, and nothing his
lover did could be wrong in his eyes.

And therein lay the problem. If only the King would pick
suitable advisers. He always selected the pretty men, the ones
with the ready charm – for him – and the same love of high
fashion and clothing. A man who was merely obedient and
honourable didn't rank nearly so highly in the King's esteem.

What was truly insulting was the King's love of play-acting
and peasants. He would much prefer to join a group of churls
laying a hedge than get involved in a good boar hunt. He had
been known to go swimming, in God's name, when his
knights were off after venison. What sort of example was
that?

There was a figure in a doorway, and Mortimer turned his
head just a little, so that as he passed he could still see it from
the corner of his eye, but there was no movement to show that
the man left his shelter to follow him. No, he was still secure.

His conversation with de Bouden had been fruitful. It was
good to know that the Queen herself was as keen to see him
as he was to meet her. How they might manage it was a
different matter, of course. It was hard to see what they could
do, with so many about the palace. Perhaps they could simply
stick to using de Bouden as a go-between? Mortimer was not
very keen to do so, since de Bouden had been put in his place
by the King. In the past he had been in the Queen's household,
but now he had been reinstated by others, and that made his
motives suspect in Mortimer's eye. You didn't stay alive in
this environment without being very cautious indeed.

There was a step behind him that appeared to be hurrying.
Mortimer slowed his own pace, and the pattering of boots
also slowed. He stopped to tie a lace, and the steps stopped
too.

'Shite,' he muttered. Very well. He must remove another

obstacle. Without glancing round, he set off again, back towards the palace grounds. He knew where he could go safely.

With Paul's footsteps echoing behind him, he marched quickly to the palace gate, then inside. There were extensive stables and guard quarters over to the left, and he made for them, opening a door and peering inside. A ladder was leaning up against the hayloft in there, and he shinned up it quickly. There was a window for ventilation at the farther end. He went to it and peered down. It was a long way to fall. Instead he darted back to the ladder inside, pulled it up, carried it through to the window and waited.

As he had hoped, soon he heard steps in the chamber below. Smiling, he thrust the ladder through the window, careless of the noise. The man below began to run about the place, as Mortimer let the ladder out, and carefully clambered onto the upper rungs.

At the bottom, he looked at the thick wall that encircled this little orchard and smiled to himself before sauntering away towards the rooms he was renting.

After all, even a man hunting him for a bounty would find it hard to persuade the hard-faced guards installed here by his son Geoffrey to let them past. There were advantages to having money.

Chapter Twenty-Four

Palm Sunday[1]

Next morning, Jean woke with a sore back and a stinging hand. The fight had used muscles which were not accustomed to hard effort, and they were all complaining in unison.

It took him some moments to remember where he was when he opened his eyes. The curving ceiling of the undercroft spread overhead, while the barrels on his right were entirely out of place in any bedchamber he had ever used. The wall on his left was strange, too. He was more used to the sight of lathes and plaster in recent weeks. Even at the Château Gaillard, the guard rooms were all thin-walled. The castle itself might be built of strong rock, but not the outlying servants' quarters.

Then he remembered the previous night, the assault by le Vieux, the mad, panicked flight along the corridors and passages until he reached this undercroft, miraculously avoiding all the people on the way. He looked about him again now as he clambered to his feet. It was cool down here, but not so cold as the nights on the mountainsides all those years ago when he had been a peasant and met his first traveller.

Oh, to be in the mountains again. It had seemed such a hard life in those days, but at least then he had been able to

---

[1] Sunday 31 March 1325

rely on himself, without having to worry about politics or the lies of anyone else threatening his life. He should have stayed there, but the lure of money tempted him away into the service of the Comte. His father had heard about the possibilities of *largesse*, and he'd persuaded his sons to join him, all making the long, arduous journey with the Comte's men up to the far north, where the weather was cooler, and the land terribly flat. And there they had fought alongside the Comte to defend French lands against the rebels.

The bastards were infernally lucky. No one looking at them would have thought that they could have survived. After all, they faced the might of Christendom's most powerful king, with the massed arms of the best equipped cavalry in the world. And what were they? Merely peasants. Fullers, weavers, butchers, all men with filth under their fingernails. Untrained rabble. That's what the men in the French host were told. Robert Comte d'Artois himself came along to tell everyone that the battle was already won, before a French horse had so much as trotted in the general direction of Courtrai.

Even now Jean wasn't entirely sure what the fight was all about. He'd heard that those Flemings were rebelling, but he didn't know what they were rebelling about. Still, they'd bottled up the French garrison in the town, and now the men of Ypres, of Bruges and God alone knew where else were all lined up in front of the walls.

His father had been to other battles, and he laughed when he saw their position. 'Look at them! The fools have the town's walls behind them to their right and rear, and the river blocks their escape to the north! They couldn't have picked a worse position if they'd tried!'

It was true. Jean and Bernard had looked at the enemy and could see, even they, untrained and unblooded, that the land gave all the advantage to the French cavalry. Oh, there were a couple of obstacles, two small streams, and some other minor distractions – rocks and such – but for all that, the knights should be able to form up in no time, and once they did they'd be able to thunder at the gallop towards the Flemings, and no man, none, could face that. Jean's father told them, and he'd been in plenty of battles: 'When you have a mounted man-at-arms riding at you, you can't defeat him. You can dodge and try to run away, but if he wants you, he'll prick you with his lance. You can't save yourself on the flat. On this sort of field they'll have no chance at all.'

At first it seemed he was going to be right, too. It all started a little before noon. Jean and his brother and father were with the crossbowmen, and moved forward with the *bidauts* and shield-bearers to a position just short of the streams, where they settled down to exchange bolts with the enemy. Initially it looked as though many on either side would be slain, but then the Flemings began to give way. It seemed they didn't like the look of the horsemen forming up behind the French crossbows, and chose to retreat before they could be cut off.

It had seemed an auspicious moment. With a shout, the French crossbowmen began to hurry forward, firing as they went. Bernard was unused to the bow, but he managed to loose all his bolts early on, and he was one of the first to reach the streams and yell his defiance. It was as he turned to grin at Jean that Jean heard the loud, wet sound of a cloth hurled against a rock, and knew in his heart that it was Bernard. A long bolt had been fired at him from a great artillery crossbow, and had penetrated his leather jerkin with ease, the heavy wood slamming through bones and muscle of chest and arm until only the last few inches remained. Bernard fell, a thick bloody mess erupting from his mouth as he tried to call to Jean. He was already dead, Jean knew. He couldn't breathe, because of the blood in his lungs, and the quarrel that had destroyed his whole upper body. Instead he fell back, thrashing about on the ground.

But the first of the men were wading through the water now, yelling and screaming their defiance, calling the Flemish peasants to come on, if they dared, cursing them, insulting their mothers and sisters, shouting that they would steal all their belongings by nightfall. However, the Comte d'Artois bethought himself that this was a good time to launch the main assault. If all the crossbowmen made it over the water, they would be easy prey for the Flemings. That was what Jean heard later, anyway. As it was, all he knew was that the standards suddenly appeared before the Comte's *bataelge*. Almost immediately there was the bellowed command for the foot soldiers to retreat, and they needed no second warning. The terrible sight of those men and horses approaching was enough to send all who could rushing to escape. A few were trampled by the knights – as was poor Bernard's body.

The Flemings saw the horses, too. They retreated into close-packed lines, each bristling with the sharp tips of lances, all butted carefully into the ground.

Jean could see that some of the horses were refusing to jump the streams. It was almost comical to see the knights spurring their mounts, trying to scold them into obedience, but the simple fact was that although the stream was only some four yards wide it was broad enough to deter a heavy war horse hampered by all its armour and a massy knight. Still, in short order the knights were over, and they began their charge.

Any remaining Flemish crossbowmen in front of the lines took out their knives and cut through the strings of their bows, rendering them useless, before hurling them down and scurrying for safety.

'Poor fools!' Jean heard a grizzled old warrior declare. 'They'll be cut to pieces.'

By now the horses were kicking up so much rubbish that to keep an eye on them was like watching a salmon in a vigorous river. All Jean could see was the line of horses making for the rebels like a living wave, ready to wash all from its path. As he knew, all the men on those horses had been trained from the age of five or six in the use of weapons to kill. And the Flemings? They'd picked up the nearest tool, probably, and like as not didn't even possess a helmet. It would be all over in a short space of time.

He waited to see the line of bristling steel points waver, but couldn't see over the top of the knights. Still, no man could stand before an irresistible foe like that. No one could. It was a rule of war.

The horses were rearing now, and he could hear the sounds of war; the neighing and shrieking, of thundering *goedendags*, the fearsome Flemish war-hammers with their long handles, the clatter and crash of swords, pikes and lances, the rattling of mail, the screams of terror and agony. And then he saw some of the horses pushing forward in the centre. The breach in the Flemish line had been effected at last.

'The beginning of the end,' his father muttered, pulling a grass stem from the ground and chewing the sweet, blanched part. 'Soon over now. Best get moving.'

The other crossbowmen slung their weapons and made their way over the water, ready to carry out the foot soldier's duty, using their long knives to put the wounded enemy out of their misery. It was the part which Jean had most dreaded beforehand. He had killed enough sheep to be able to do so without letting the poor creatures suffer, but that was different from killing a man. A man could look up and plead. He didn't want to have to slay a man begging for his life. Now, though, since seeing his own brother's horrified agony, all sympathy was flown. He *wanted* to kill Flemings. He hoped to be able to, to see a man pleading with him for his life, because Jean would pay no attention. He would kill and keep on killing until they were all dead. No mercy, no compassion, no sympathy for the rebels who had killed his brother.

There had been a fresh charge. They saw it over on their right, a pounding wave that broke farther through the line of pikemen. It gave them all a burst of enthusiasm. It was bound to crush the Flemings. Nothing could withstand that sort of onslaught. They said that one knight in his armour was worth at least a hundred ordinary warriors, and this was why.

And then he saw something that made his entire body shiver. He saw a French knight wheel round, dart back towards him, and then turn to gallop at the line once more.

'What's he doing?'

'Just giving himself some space,' the grizzled warrior said, and spat. 'Give 'em that. These Flemings know how to fight.'

Jean nodded, but even as he turned to watch, he saw a small group of Flemings rush forwards. Three had the dreadful *goedendags*, hideous sledgehammer-like weapons set on seven-foot poles – some even longer – and he saw one swing, then the others, all at the horse's head. There was a little puff of red smoke from beneath the horse's armour, and although the knight swung a long sword, he couldn't reach them. The horse collapsed to kneel, and the hammers again slammed into its head, but already one of them was turning to the knight himself. Then pikes were stabbing up under his helmet. Even as the horse began to fall to one side, Jean saw a jet of blood squirt from between the breast plate and the helmet. The knight dropped his sword, and scrabbled with his gauneleted hands at the blade in his throat, but it was too late. He could expect no quarter, and even as he tried to prise himself free the hammers rose and fell, and he disappeared from view.

There was the sound of horns, a blaring, raucous noise,

and he turned to see the last *bataelge* trotting down towards the streams. There they stopped and waited, their flags and pennons flying merrily in the breeze.

The Flemings nearest saw them, and Jean saw them challenging the knights, daring them to come on. 'Father, are you sure we should . . .'

'What?'

The foot soldiers with them were aware now that not all was going as they had anticipated. Their forward trot had slowed, and some of the men were watching the little scene on their right.

When the taunts and challenges failed, some Flemings started to cross the river to attack the French, and as they reached the other bank Jean felt a hideous heaviness form in his belly.

The main body of French knights wheeled, and rode away, their shields still on their backs. A few apparently felt so revolted by the idea of leaving their comrades on the field that they charged forward, only to fall to the hammers and pikes.

And then they were all racing away before the Flemings could reach them. They ran as though the hordes of the devil himself were behind them; they ran as though hell would take any who dithered. And then some knights came through the foot soldiers, fleeing the slaughter among the Flemish lines. Jean saw the knight who, enraged, terrified, and desperate, hacked at the men of his own side who stood in his path as he tried to escape. Jean saw his sword whirling, saw it slice down, and watched with a kind of disinterested fascination as the tip appeared at the other side of his father's body, sweeping around and out. He continued to watch, all feelings dulled, as his father's body toppled, his head rolling away, the lips bared, the teeth clicking together pointlessly.

Ah God, yes, Jean had endured enough of war. The terror, the running away, the appalling realisation that the men who had been a part of your life since birth were gone for ever, and there had not even been time to say 'Farewell' or 'Godspeed'. All were terrifying in their own way. And then the relentless hunting down, the horror of being prey to a pack of marauding humans. It was hideous.

And it was all happening to him again; all over again. If he allowed it.

Well, he wouldn't. He was going to stop this. Someone had lied about him. Someone had deliberately set him up. He would find out who, and why. And if possible avenge himself.

Wednesday before Good Friday[1]

Paris

There was a lull in the negotiations during the new month, and Baldwin found himself growing more and more irritable as the days passed, eager to be home. He wanted to see his wife and children again. Already it felt as though he had been idle for too long, when he could have been in their company. This enforced indolence was grating at his patience.

He had thought he must be back at Furnshill by the middle of the summer. It was not that he had promised it to Jeanne; more that he had promised it to himself. The King, when asking him to come here with the Queen, had intimated that he had made it clear to her and to Lord Cromwell that he expected their business to be completed by then, and wanted the Queen to hurry home. It was never explicitly stated, but the clear implication was that he did not trust her while she was away from his side. And of course the mission to France was growing ever more expensive.

The cost would not have been diminished by the state

---

[1] Wednesday 3 April 1325

entrance into Paris two days ago. Baldwin and Simon had been there to witness the Queen's arrival, as befitted members of her guard, but although Baldwin had glanced at her he had spent more time watching others in the roads, ensuring that there was no enemy of the King or herself in the throng. Simon had not been so conscientious. As she rode in towards them, Simon had simply stared. He was not alone. Her appearance induced awe.

Flanked by the Comte de Dammartin and the Lords de Coucy and Montmorency among others, she cut a dashing figure astride her horse, clad as she was all in black velvet. Simon could only guess at the price of such a wonderful garment. It was layered, and so long that only the tips of her riding boots were visible. Her headdress was so modern that Simon did not even know what it was termed, and he had to ask Alicia. She was happy to inform him that Isabella was wearing crespinettes made of gold fretwork dangling from a narrow fillet. Simon nodded knowingly, not knowing what such items were. All he knew was, the Queen looked glorious and utterly beautiful.

But now they had been in Paris for two days, and still there was no possibility of returning home. Negotiations had continued, and even as the King prepared the Easter feasts, letters had been sent back to England with the main proposals. The Queen had carefully prepared each, and Baldwin had no doubt that they would show how hard she had been working on Edward's behalf. Meanwhile she danced, feasted, and generally enjoyed herself. If she had a care in the world, it was carefully hidden.

Simon, for his part, was enthralled by the city. 'It is not so great as London, of course, but you cannot deny that there is a certain . . . liveliness to the place.'

Baldwin cast a dull eye over him. 'You think so? A dunghill is also full of life.'

Simon glanced at him. 'Come, friend. What is the matter?'

'I used to *live* here. I will never be able to forget the horror. It was here in Paris that I witnessed the execution of my Grand Master,' Baldwin said quietly. There was a rasping quality to his voice that spoke of his emotion, and Simon grunted and looked away.

He ought to have remembered. There should have been no need for Baldwin to explain his mood, for Simon knew his history. A Knight Templar until the dissolving of the Order, he had witnessed his Grand Master being burned to death on a pyre for so many alleged crimes, the world had been appalled to hear of them. And yet, even as he died, he asserted his innocence and the innocence of the Order. Ever since they had arrived in the capital, Baldwin had grown increasingly grim, and Simon should have realised it was this that was on his mind, rather than some mere petty annoyance at being apart from Jeanne.

'Where did it happen, Baldwin? I have heard that the execution grounds are at a field outside the walls.'

'You mean Montfaucon. That is where most died, I suppose. It's up there. North-east, roughly.'

The two were walking about the Châtelet, near the river, and Simon could see his friend's eyes turning every so often back towards the Louvre where they had left Queen Isabella.

'That is fine!' exclaimed a voice behind them, and both cast glances over their shoulders to where Sir Charles was standing with a new sword in his hand, sweeping it through the air with satisfaction. Paul was perched on a trestle nearby, eyeing his knight's antics with a sour expression.

'At last!' Baldwin muttered, and Simon grinned.

They had come here with Sir Charles and his man Paul as soon as the Queen had told them that she had no further use for them that day. Usually Baldwin would have remained nearby, but by now his temper was all too plain, and the

Queen had instructed Lord Cromwell that she would be happier were the 'grim and despondent' knight given some little time to wander the city and soothe his bitter spirit. Sir Charles had suggested that they might come here, to the area of the city where the armourers plied their trade, for, he explained, he had a need of a new riding sword. His old one had been dropped during their journey here, and a cart had rolled over it, bending the blade severely.

'Yes. Try the balance on this, Sir Baldwin.'

'I am sure that you are more than capable of assessing the quality yourself, Sir Charles,' Baldwin said evasively.

'Hah! If you are sure. Then I shall take it myself.' So saying, he began to dispute the price with the armourer, and once they were both content, Sir Charles pulled the coins from his purse and handed them over.

The armourer pulled a face and shook his head. '*Livres parisis, mon sieur. Celui-ci sont livres tournois.*'

Sir Charles smiled gently. 'Sir Baldwin, you're so much more competent at this, would you mind assisting me?'

'He is telling you that those coins are *livres* from Tours. He wants coins of Paris. There are about four Paris pounds to five Tours, and he is telling you that the price was fixed in Paris, so he wants Paris *livres*. You owe him another quarter.'

Sir Charles's smile spread and he took a small step forward, the sword now pointing at the armourer's throat. 'I see. And could you explain to this gentle that I did not fall from a boat on the Seine this morning? I know a fair price, and I know when I am being shorn for my fleece. Kindly explain that to him.'

Baldwin looked away, then shook his head. He spoke rapidly, in a manner which Simon could not follow. The bailiff was used to many of the dialects of France now, having dealt with many Frenchmen during his time at the Port of Dartmouth, and could even understand the strongly accented language of the butchers of St Jacques, but Baldwin's speech was incomprehensible to him.

The armourer scowled, but finally nodded. 'Oui.'

'Pay him one eighth more,' Baldwin said. 'He'll accept that.'

'Another eighth?' Sir Charles asked as though deliberating.

'It is up to you. It is a very good price for a sword of that quality. He has been reasonable, and he is still trying to be so. However, if you wish, you can instead test your steel.'

Sir Charles allowed a passing confusion to mar his elegant features. 'Test it? You mean stab him?'

'No. I mean, if you are wearing your cuirass, you will have a chance to test its strength against this man's friends, who are preparing their crossbows to fire at you, should you try to harm him.'

'Are they within reach?'

'Sir Charles, I am no knave. This man has asked a reasonable price. I would not attack him or those who seek to protect him, just because you want a bargain. If you want cheap goods, seek them elsewhere. If you want this blade, pay the price and be thankful you have acquired so splendid an example of Parisian craftsmanship.'

'I think you have a point,' Sir Charles said after a moment's thought. He nodded to himself, and then relaxed, allowing the sword to fall to point to the ground. 'I should be most glad if you could tell this gentle that I shall be glad to pay the full price in *livres Parisis*. As you say, craftsmanship is worth its price.'

Chapter Twenty-Five

Paul watched his master pay and followed him as Sir Charles set off after Sir Baldwin and Simon.

Sir Charles had not spoken to him much in the last few days. The ridiculous way in which he'd managed to lose Mortimer had unsettled them both. It wasn't something Paul had ever done before. Stupid, stupid bloody thing to do – let him climb up into a hayloft and thence into the grounds of a private house. Soon as he'd seen where the man had gone, Paul had gone to the door to demand to be allowed inside, but there were plenty of guards there to prevent him. He'd even considered calling Sir Charles, but it was plain enough that even with Sir Baldwin, Sir John and Sir Peter, and even Lord John Cromwell too, they'd not be able to get in and capture the bastard without people hearing and stopping them. So he'd been forced to give up, and Sir Charles had been distant. Disappointment was not an emotion Sir Charles enjoyed.

There had been no sign of the traitor since that evening. Probably keeping his head down, in Paul's view. Still, he'd be looking out for him now. There was a possibility that a man like him would be so arrogant, he'd think himself safe from attack in the French king's capital. Well, let him show his face, and Paul would introduce him to a whole new experience – a sharp knife, and a swim for the headless corpse in the Seine.

* * *

'What was the point of that?' Baldwin grumbled a little later as they walked away from the Châtelet, up the road known as the 'Grande Rue'.

'He would not wish to be seen to succumb to any form of trickery,' Simon reckoned. 'He is an enormously vain man, Baldwin.'

'True enough – but to try to gull an armourer in a place where armourers congregate is foolish in the extreme. All could see him dickering like a wife buying fish, and all could see he desired the sword, so what was the point of calling attention to himself like that?'

'I do not pretend to understand the behaviour of knights,' Simon said with a grin. Then, 'So where does this road go? I do not think I have been along it as far as the walls.'

'It takes you up as far as the Porte Saint-Denis. From there you can look north towards the plain of Saint-Denis.'

'What is up there?' Sir Charles had paid, and now he walked at their side, a happy smile on his face, his left hand resting on the new sword. Paul wandered at his left flank, a man-at-arms to the last, his eyes wary as he kept an eye on the people thronging the streets.

'Simon was asking earlier about the place of execution, the hill called Montfaucon. It is up there.'

'I have heard of this place,' Sir Charles said. 'The people of the city often go there, I understand. A curious place to sit and chew on a leg of chicken.'

'It is good that people should remind themselves of their own mortality,' Paul muttered.

Simon controlled a grin. Plainly the man had similar feelings to Baldwin about his master's negotiating stance.

Baldwin was walking a little faster now, and Simon cast a look at him now and again as they marched up the Grande Rue. Baldwin had lived here, as Simon knew, in the great fortress of the Temple. That lay to the north of the city walls, so he had heard, and it was there the Knights Templar had been held and tortured, and many had been killed, before the Pope took pity on the survivors and suppressed the Order.

This city held many sad memories for Baldwin. It seemed peculiar to Simon that the man would want to head up this way, towards the focus of all the misery and horror of those days, but then he understood. This was not only the place where his Order had been destroyed, it was also where they had lived for hundreds of years in glorious isolation from Paris itself.

Passing beneath the Porte Saint-Denis, a fortification that shocked Simon when he saw the outer face: set into the wall at ground level was a large, glazed window! He stopped and gaped at it, before pointing and calling the attention of the others to that incongruous feature.

'This city is too great to be attacked,' Sir Charles explained. 'Have you ever seen so magnificent, so ostentatious a place? It would be worth sacking, but what host would dare to attempt to march on such a town?'

'When was it last assaulted?' Simon asked.

'More than a hundred years ago,' Baldwin said shortly. 'In their arrogance the Parisians believe themselves impregnable. No city is so safe that it may give up all its defences without tempting an enemy.'

Simon nodded, but the others were already walking onwards.

Here, the road was still lined with small houses. When Simon asked Baldwin, he was told that the city limit was in practice farther to the north, where the *rue* met the foul stream called La Pissotte, into which all the refuse and sewage was thrown.

Baldwin took them eastwards, pointing to some towers looming over the houses, and Simon realised that this was the

Temple – the most important building for Baldwin's Order outside the Kingdom of Jerusalem itself.

It was a vast fortress. Standing slightly isolated in marshy ground, it reared up a little like the Tower of London, but apparently taller. There were round turrets at each corner, thinner, smaller ones in the middle of the wall facing Simon too, and each was roofed with a conical cap, flags fluttering from every one. It was a strange-looking place, which gave Simon an impression of elegance and beauty, with its stark, spare lines. This was a building constructed for function, and that function was defence and intimidation.

Not that it had achieved its aim. Simon was glad when Sir Charles gave it a cursory glance, and remarked, 'I should not like to stay there. It looks like a gaol. Let's walk on and see this place of execution. I assume that's it there?'

Simon followed his pointing finger and frowned. There was, only a matter of a few hundred yards away, a flat, almost uninhabited area through which their road passed, which held a low rise in the ground to the north and east. At the top of the hillock was a curious construction. 'Are they building a house up there?'

Baldwin's voice was cold. 'No. Not a house.'

They carried on, and in a few minutes they were standing at the base of a series of some sixteen large rock pillars. Some were already in position, but others lay on the ground, and there were cranes and windlasses all about, and scaffolding set up to assist in the erection of the massive structure. Part of it had been completed, and now Simon realised what its purpose was, for across the top of the four upright blocks lay a thick beam of wood. Dangling from it were fifteen men.

'The idea was that this hill should be visible from most of the city,' Baldwin said. He was peering up at the men. None had a broken neck; all had been gradually throttled as they hanged. Now their features were unrecognisable. They had been so badly attacked by the crows and other carrion birds that all were pecked to uniformity. The ropes suspending them creaked and groaned as the bodies swayed.

'How long do they stay there?' Sir Charles asked.

'Until another batch arrives to be hanged,' Baldwin said. 'Then they're brought down and cast into a grave over there.'

'No women,' Paul commented.

'It would be indecent to hang women,' Baldwin said cynically. 'So they are buried alive instead.'

It is a sad place, Simon said to himself. He had never been good in the presence of death, and he averted his eyes from the noisome group, forcing himself to look at the scaffolding which supported those pillars which had not yet been set in place. A man was walking about with the labourers, instructing them, casting words about him like darts, expecting each to hit its mark. From the look on the faces of the men with him, Simon seriously doubted that more than a few would succeed.

'Good day to you, master,' Baldwin said slowly.

The man seemed to notice them for the first time, and he scowled. He was a good-looking fellow, with shrewd, intelligent dark eyes. Although he had a narrow face, there was nothing of the ferret about him – he was more of a greyhound, Simon thought. A low, but strong, narrow head and slender shoulders, but a powerful torso and well-muscled arms. Now he had his head set low as he eyed these strangers.

'And to you,' he said at last, his attention on Paul, who was returning his stare with fixed intensity.

'You are rebuilding this gallows?' Sir Charles enquired.

'I am Pierre Rémy. I have been set the task of constructing a new gallows with stone.'

Simon nodded towards the site. 'How many pillars are there?'

'You are not Parisian? Ah, English?' He appeared

reassured by their agreement, as though a Parisian who was unaware of the law was suspicious. Ignorant foreigners were a different matter. 'Ah, you look at this, and you realise that you are in the presence of the gallows of a great leader of men. It is all a matter of rank. A lord is permitted a gallows with only two uprights. A baron may have four, but the King can have sixteen. These will be set in four rows of four, so the King can hang sixty-four men at a time. And with the whole built in stone, it will last for a hundred years. Much less maintenance than a normal gallows.'

Sir Charles was nodding, and Simon could understand the logic. He had seen that the Tavistock gallows which executed the felons of the abbey's ecclesiastical court had recently had to be replaced. The damn thing was growing dangerous, and could have collapsed in a bad gust of wind with a body on it.

Baldwin alone appeared unimpressed. He stood staring at the gallows with a sardonic expression. When Simon gazed at him, he saw that there were tears in his friend's eyes.

'Are you all right, Baldwin?'

The knight waved away Simon's enquiry. 'You should be cautious, friend. All too often a man can be executed while declaring his innocence.'

'No one would willingly go confessing his sins, would he?' Rémy laughed.

'The most innocent might,' Baldwin said.

'I am sure I am safe enough. I haven't committed a crime.'

Simon was watching the men who were supposed to be building the gallows. One in particular caught his attention. He was an ill-favoured fellow with a thick leather jerkin, and he was laughing to himself as he carried a ladder towards the line of corpses. 'Who is he?'

'Arnaud? A King's Executioner,' Rémy said dismissively. He appeared to have little time for the man. 'He's got some more prepared for their last dance. Has to make space for them.'

As he spoke, Arnaud reached the gallows. He set the ladder against the beam and climbed until he was at the same height as the dangling bodies. Seeing the men on the ground watching him, he stared back for a moment before shrugging to himself and starting to cut through the rope holding the most decomposed figure.

Baldwin glanced up, his eyes narrowing slightly. 'He looks familiar, Simon. Where have I seen him before?'

'Him?' Simon stared at the man on the ladder. 'I don't know . . . are you sure?'

'His is not the sort of face a man could easily forget – and nor is his style of dress all that common. No matter. It can hardly be important,' Baldwin said.

Simon could not pull his eyes from the sight of the man's knife sawing through the old hemp until the rope began to fray, the body jolting and spinning faster. He shut his eyes and looked away, only to see that there was a party of crossbowmen at the nearer pillar, watching the body. There was a crack like the hand-cannon of the Comte de Foix, and the rope parted. The body fell like a sack of coal to thud into the ground, and to his horror Simon saw that the bone of one thigh was thrust through the softened meat of the leg, protruding vertically while the soggy sack of bones and flesh lay back untidily. It was a revolting sight, but the archers apparently thought it a source of immense humour.

'Why are they here?' he found himself asking.

'The archers? To stop witches coming here and stealing the felons' hearts to make their philtres and potions. The bitches would steal the skin from your back if you were swinging up there, my friend,' Rémy said. He noticed a man hauling on a rope at the far side of the site and swore to himself, running at the man and bellowing.

'Well, lordings, I think we may return to the city, eh?' Sir Charles said with a disdainful look about him. 'Until they bring the next wagonload of men ready for their execution, there's little enough to see here.'

'Yes. Quite right,' Baldwin said. Simon was reluctant to speak. He was still averting his eyes from the fleshy mess lying on the ground as Arnaud went to it, eyed it contemplatively, and then grabbed a bare foot and started to haul the body away to where the mass grave was. It was the leg with the bone sticking up, and as Simon watched he saw the dark, rotting skin at the groin begin to tear as Arnaud pulled. He turned away quickly, hearing the man swear a short while later. From the corner of his eye he saw Arnaud walk to the pit and toss in the leg, before returning to collect the remainder of the dead man.

When they had left, Arnaud leaned against a pillar and watched them as they wandered back to the city. He wiped the blood and muck from his hands on to his leather jerkin, and sat back to wait for the man he had been told to kill. No one he knew, just someone who'd irritated the King or someone.

He often held the power of bringing death, but Arnaud had only once had the power of bringing life. He missed the feel of the child in his arms. Killing was easy, but *creation,* that was different. There were times when he wished he didn't have to concentrate on only the one.

Shame le Vieux was gone. The old twit was a good companion. They understood each other, and it was always hard to lose a friend. Arnaud hadn't had too many of them in his life. He'd thought that Jean was going to be a mate when they'd met. They came from the same part of the country, down in the Comte de Foix's lands. Of course, some people disliked Arnaud just because of his job. That was stupid. Everyone appreciated the order that the law brought, and if there were laws, someone had to carry out the punishments. And Arnaud was good at his job. He knew he was. Anything that was well done was good for all. It must give God delight to see a man excel at his duties, so why should Arnaud not take pleasure in his skill?

There was little more satisfying than achieving a good death, one that made all the crowds howl. Some men took pride in their carpentry, others in the quality of their clothes-making, or their ability with a horse. Well, Arnaud was no different. He enjoyed just the same pride and satisfaction as they.

Sometimes he thought he was like a player with the mummers. They would don odd clothes, disguises to hide their real personalities, and in the same way he would often sport a hood to conceal his features. After all, the people weren't there to see him, but to watch the spectacle of an execution.

Some of his victims were bold, and stood resolutely, as though daring any in the audience to laugh or make sport with him; others whimpered, wet themselves, soiled themselves, fell and rolled on the ground. They were the more rewarding ones, Arnaud felt. They showed people the true result of their misdeeds. If they broke the King's laws, they would suffer the torments of Arnaud's punishments. Terror was important. Without fear of the consequences, any man would dare to act the felon.

Back up the ladder, this time to throw a fresh rope over the beam. As he did so, the nearest body was caught and turned slowly in a gust of wind. The face, leering and bloated, skin blackened, came to peer at him as though it was studying him from its empty eye sockets.

Arnaud grinned. He patted the face's cheek and giggled. 'Don't worry. Soon have another companion for you up here!'

* * *

Roger Mortimer was not at the Louvre, but at a small inn nearby. It had been made abundantly clear to him that the King preferred him to keep well out of the way and avoid any diplomatic incidents. The last thing he wanted was to endanger the discussions directly. That would mean two kings wanting his head, and that was not a good idea. No, far better that he should keep to the shadows and away from the negotiations.

Not that it was easy. He had always enjoyed cordial relations with the Queen. Isabella was a kind woman, understanding ... sympathetic. She understood what it was to lose a love. Of course, in Roger and Joan's case it was an enforced separation by that madman the King. More or less the same for her, actually. The King had separated himself from her.

It was hard to conceive of a man who could have started out in life with so many advantages and squandered them so swiftly, he thought. The King had enjoyed the love and devotion of a loyal wife; he had the benefit of a country which had endured too many wars and wanted only peace, a strong barony which would support its king no matter what, and in the space of only a few years he had lost it all. He had destroyed the faith his barons had held in him and in the office of the crown, he had lost the trust of the people by passing too much money and treasure to his lovers, and he had even managed to alienate his wife, the mother of his four legitimate children.

Mortimer should know. He had been one of King Edward's most devoted servants. Christ's bones, he'd been to Ireland to fight the King's wars, he'd supported Edward against all his foes, and yet he still got kicked in the teeth when the King decided to give all his trust to Despenser instead. What was the point of a man's risking his life and livelihood for a king, if that same king showed no loyalty to him? A man had a right to expect his king's *largesse*, but in Roger Mortimer's case the

King had worked to deprive him. Gradually, all authority was passing to Despenser and Walter Stapledon, and in the end Mortimer would be killed. There could be no other outcome.

The evening was drawing in. Soon it would be time for his meeting. He rose from the fireside, glancing about him. There were four men with him tonight, and as he passed out from the room to the roadway they followed him. Then, with one before him, one behind and one either side, he set off towards the Louvre.

It was a marvellous castle, this. The powerful Philip-Augustus had constructed it in the days when his great enemy, Richard Coeur de Lion, had threatened. This was the point where Richard was most likely to attack. Later, when the city walls were built, the castle was left outside them, so that Philip-Augustus should always retain the capacity for defence without concern for the people of the city. But Roger was not going straight to the King's great castle. In preference, he was walking to the secondary seat, the Château du Bois, which lay within a short walk to the west. Here, in the gardens which surrounded the castle, the King was wont to wander. It had been a place of especial pleasure for all the kings since Philip-Augustus, a place of rest and relaxation, where the hunting was second to none.

He reached the city walls and passed out with his men. Now they bunched together about him a little more closely. Any man walking out in the wilds at this time of night was at threat of attack, and the fact that Roger Mortimer had more enemies than most was a cause for extreme caution. He kept his own hand near his sword hilt.

The houses had come to fill the gaps between the walls of the city and the Louvre, and now they had rippled out beyond, so that the Château du Bois was an island of calm in a sea of small houses. True, to the south was the great castle of the dukes of Brittany, but the houses lapped even about that.

There were so many who were keen to live in this greatest city in Christendom, that any space must inevitably be filled.

'I am here,' he muttered at the gate to the Château du Bois. The gatekeeper at the postern gate nodded, eyed the four guards, then opened the gate. Mortimer hesitated, then slipped through, almost expecting to receive a blade between the ribs as he did so.

'Your royal highness,' he breathed, bowing low.

'My lord,' Queen Isabella responded.

Chapter Twenty-Six

Jean picked up the bowl of pottage and supped from it. God, that was good! A pleasing, thin soup of spring leaves with some lentils, and a sausage with bread alongside, and a man could sit back in comfort.

He had made his way here slowly, wary at every stage in case he was being hunted for le Vieux's murder, but there was no sign that anyone was seeking him. Nobody appeared to have the faintest idea that he could still be in the area, and he had found it remarkably easy to make his way down to this part of town.

The undercroft had saved his life. Surely everyone who had sought him would think that he must have escaped from the city after le Vieux's death. It was like the last time, when he had been marked as a heretic.

He ought to have learned to keep his mouth shut. Anyone who was prepared to stand up for the truth was automatically a suspect in the eyes of the Church. Not that it was entirely due to evil men – he had no doubt that the bishop believed in his little crusade. He thought he was saving people. Jean didn't doubt that. But when a man saw people being executed, he had a duty to think about their reactions. And if their behaviour didn't seem suitable, bearing in mind their crime, he should consider that.

That was why he had reflected long and hard after witnessing the death of Raymond de la Côte and Agnes Franco five years ago.

What was their crime? Only that they had sought to honour and worship Christ in a way that was in keeping with their beliefs. The people of the mountains had followed the way of the Poor of Lyons for hundreds of years, but now they were to be persecuted for the way they worshipped God because the Church disliked the fact that they preached against corruption among priests and the sale of indulgences. But Jean knew that the 'friends' were right. No man should presume to sell remission of sins here on earth. Only God could decide to do that, and He was all-powerful. He would scarcely consider Himself bound by some contract made here in this imperfect world.

But Agnes and Raymond had been deemed guilty. They had been questioned, tortured, and had their crimes recorded by the zealous Bishop Fournier. And finally, they were passed over to the secular arm for their destruction.

It wasn't only Jean who spat on the idea that they had died sinful. Others were of a like mind. When he stood and drank his wine at the inn in Pamiers, it was not merely the bitterness in his soul which made him denounce the bishop. He wasn't foolish or brave enough to try that. No, it was the general feeling in the room.

'Who thinks them evil now?' asked the innkeeper.

'Who could?' one customer asked, and belched.

That was the strange thing, Jean thought. He'd felt it even under the elm tree at Ornolac earlier, when the village worthies gathered to discuss the executions. The man Raymond had sobbed, but never begged forgiveness for his crimes. Instead, when the ropes were burned away, he held his hands aloft, clenched together in prayer, and entrusted his soul to God.

It was that which made Jean bear witness. 'Any man who could do that, who could suffer the flames and still call on God to take his soul, that man was no heretic. He must be a

Christian. Any man dying in such pain and calling on God must surely have had his soul accepted. God would *treasure* a soul freed in such suffering in His service.'

It was the other customer there who'd shaken his head at Jean then. 'Jacques Fournier is a good man, though. He's a good bishop. Do you know, he wept when he heard that Raymond wouldn't recant? It was Raymond's fault – all he had to do was apologise, beg forgiveness, and return to the Holy Mother Church's arms. There he would have been welcomed. He had fallen prey to heretical beliefs – perhaps from his own stupidity; maybe he was just gullible, and others took advantage of him with their lies – and he should have seen that he should give them up. It was ridiculous of him to hold fast to that which could not be true!'

'A good man? A *good* bishop? He is a murderer! I would wager that Fournier would be less keen to hold to his faith than Raymond, were he to be put to the flames! Ha, there were two good Christians there, but he had them both burned.' In his heart, he had added that it would have been better for all had Fournier been burned, and Raymond and Agnes saved, but saying something of that sort would only have served to ensure his own arrest.

Not that he need have worried. Within the hour, he was held by the bishop's men. He was accused, denounced, and gaoled, and there he would yet be, were it not for the good offices of my Lord Enguerrand de Foix.

The Comte's men had negotiated his release in little time, and provided that Jean left the gaol with a yellow cross stitched to the breast of his tunic to show that he was a reformed heretic of whom others should be wary, he was permitted to go with the Comte's men. One was le Vieux, although the old man-at-arms would not talk to him for many a long month.

He had been taken up to Château Gaillard, and there he

learned that he was himself to turn gaoler rather than prisoner. Others would suffer, but he was assured by le Vieux that the people in those cells deserved their punishment. Especially the poor woman who would have been queen. And even when he realised Arnaud was to remain there too, he swallowed the revulsion he felt. The alternative was to return to the bishop's gaols himself. He couldn't do that.

In the bishop's cells, and then guarding those at the château, he had come to appreciate the fact that often the gaolers were little happier than those in the cells. All those in the guard rooms were rather like him. All had spent time in suffering. Some, like him, had been in trouble with the Church, others, like Berengar, had been guilty of some other crime. Berengar had married a maid in the Comte de Foix's household without permission, and the Comte had sought to punish him by separating him from his wife. But all debts would be discharged as soon as the last prisoner had been taken away.

The good thing about his time in gaol, and then spent guarding Lady Blanche, was that when he was forced to hide in the undercroft there was little that could alarm him. Not rats nor dark could concern him after the dank misery of Bishop Fournier's cells at Pamiers. Apart from anything else, the room was very well stocked with food and drink, and no one need ever realise he had stolen from it.

It was two days before he dared leave the castle, and by then the Queen was long gone, but at least her movements were not kept secret. Jean was able to hear that she had travelled with her entourage to Paris itself. Surely, he reasoned, Arnaud must have also gone there. It seemed that Arnaud and le Vieux had been with the Queen's party thus far, so it was unlikely he would have left now.

But all the way as he walked from the castle through the town and out on to the road, his pack over his shoulder, he saw in his mind's eye how le Vieux had glared at him as he tried to brain him. It was almost as if le Vieux hated him – had always hated him. That wasn't how it had been, though. Le Vieux had been friendly towards him – towards all of them – from the moment he'd first rescued Jean from his prison cell. There was only kindness in him, or so Jean had thought. Of all the guards, le Vieux was the only one he would have trusted. The others had all spent time in gaols, for one thing. They were hardly responsible, respectable fellows. Le Vieux had always been different. And he'd seemed to have more respect for Jean, because he'd heard that Jean had been in the battle at Courtrai. A fellow man-at-arms was someone to honour.

The more he thought about it, the more he tended to the view that someone must have poisoned le Vieux's mind against him. And the only man who could have done so, surely, was Arnaud. Arnaud must have told le Vieux that he had gone mad, killed the men in the guard rooms, and then run away. He had no idea what Arnaud could have wanted to achieve by such lies, but there was no other explanation of le Vieux's behaviour. There had been such loathing and disgust on his face as he tried to brain him with that cudgel. It wasn't like the old man he'd come to know over the months at Château Gaillard.

But Arnaud was capable of anything. He enjoyed seeing people suffer. He had set the rope about Agnes's neck, but when she started to scream in anguish and he could have strangled her to save her further torment, he hadn't done so. He had allowed the rope to dangle in the flames so that it burned away before he could use it. And left her to shriek in the intolerable horror of death by fire.

Yes. Apart from the murder of the guards at the château; apart from the lies told about him to le Vieux; apart from all these and the rape inflicted on Lady Blanche, Jean wanted to meet Arnaud again, and make him feel the anguish of a slow death for what he had done to poor Agnes.

He finished his pottage, wiped his bowl with a little of the remaining bread, and left the inn.

Arnaud was dead. No matter what, Jean would hunt him down and kill him.

When the others were all back in their rooms, Paul went out once more.

At times like this, a man must be cautious and look to his safety. In truth, there was no city in Christendom which was fully safe. The curfews protected many, but when a man walked abroad after nightfall, his life was in his hands. Anyone might defend himself against a dark shape in the shadows, and with good reason. It was better to attack first than wait until someone drew blade against him. Each morning there was a fresh crop of bodies waiting to be found and collected – and here many were lost for ever, simply dropped quietly into the Seine. Like London's Thames, the river could clean up a multitude of untidy murders.

But Paul was sure that his master was correct when he said that there would be a good price for the head of Roger Mortimer. Sir Charles could take it to the King, and they would share the proceeds; Sir Charles would take the larger share, of course, but that mattered little. Since both lived on the profits of his ventures, any money in Sir Charles's purse tended to benefit Paul as well.

Paul had no idea where the man could be, but he had spoken carefully with all the grooms and other servants, and was, after all, seeking a stranger who should stand out a little. It was a man, he said, who had been a warrior, who had a certain carriage about him, like a knight, and did not appear to arrive and depart, so was probably staying nearby.

One man seemed to have an idea. He had been asked by William de Bouden, the Queen's comptroller, to deliver a note to a servant staying at an inn. At the time the fellow delivering the message had been surprised, for it seemed peculiar that the Queen's comptroller should want to speak to such a man, but when he arrived at the inn, he had caught a glimpse of a tall, warrior-like man in the background.

It was enough to interest Paul, and that was why he was making his way to the place now. The man had not taken only the one message. In the last evenings, there had been three all told. Likelihood was, so Paul reasoned, that there'd be another tonight. So he was going to the inn to watch.

The inn was set in the maze of small alleys and lanes behind the butcheries of St Jacques north of the river, and he walked cautiously in case he met the watchmen. Anyone found this late in the evening could be arrested with impunity, and Paul had no false hope that an Englishman from the Queen's guard would be safe if found out here. More likely, he'd be stabbed and killed the more swiftly and his body thrown over a bridge. Better to dispose of him than have the King's men come and seek retribution for scaring one of his sister's men-at-arms. No, if he saw the Watch, he would either bolt or fight. He reckoned he should be safe against most watchmen.

Narrow-fronted, the building was placed in the midst of a series of ancient little houses. It had only recently been converted into a tavern, from the look of it. Waxed parchment covered the windows to keep out the worst of the cold night air, but while it no doubt gave a warm glow to the dim lighting within, it served only to make Paul feel colder. He settled into the shadow of a doorway opposite and gazed at the place, waiting. That was one thing about being a fighter for so many years: waiting patiently came as second nature to him now.

Steps came down the cobbles, and he stirred himself silently. He had been dozing with his eyes open, but at the first sound he was wide awake. Soon he could make out the shape of his informer.

The man scurried along the alley like a rat walking down

a corridor of cats. His eyes were all over the place, as though he expected to be jumped on at any moment. Quite right, too. The bloody fool should have had a couple of men with him. But then, as Paul knew, he would have been a still more attractive mark. A man who walked abroad at night was a possible target to a cut-purse. A man who walked at night with two henchmen was clearly guarding something of value, and so was still more attractive.

He pulled the door open and slid inside around it. The hinges were rotten, and the door scraped badly on the ground, opening only about halfway. Orange candlelight flooded out into the lane, to slip to a knife-blade as he tugged the door closed after him.

It was only a matter of a few minutes before the door was opened again, and then the man hurried out and set off up the road to escape back to the Queen's household. Paul watched him with a slight frown on his face, wondering what could have made him hurry so urgently. Then he pressed himself back into the darkness as the door opened again. Three men came out and stood in the lane looking up and down for a few moments, before two more figures emerged. One was a tall, well-favoured man, a cap on his head, pulling gloves on as he came. He stopped in the doorway, looked about him, nodded, and then marched off after the messenger, his guards fanning out behind him.

Paul pursed his lips. This would clearly not be so easy as he had hoped. He would have to have some help. He nodded to himself, and as the men disappeared round a curve in the lane, he left the shadows, peering up after the group.

As soon as he began to trail quietly after them, the door of the inn scraped again. Too late, he saw his peril, thinking to leap back to the shadows.

'So, master. You were wanting to see our lord?'

Two men, both with swords drawn, blocking his path that

way. He turned to flee up the lane, but even as he turned he saw the men back at the corner. Roger Mortimer made a gesture with his hand, and the four men with him began to walk slowly towards Paul. He put his hand to his sword, but before he could grasp it he felt the two behind him jump forward. One took his sword arm; the other beat him about the head, three, four times, with the hilt of his own. Paul stumbled, but could jerk his elbow upwards, and he felt it crunch against a nose. That caused a short curse, but then there was a hideous crashing thud against the back of his neck, and sparks were thrown up in front of his eyes, sparks that pinwheeled about before his gaze as he toppled forward to rest his face on the cobbles.

'Who do you work for?' The voice was calm, but determined.

'I work for no one.'

'You were seeking me. The messenger told us. He at least was loyal. Who do you work for, the King? Are you with him?'

'I was just looking for a pot of wine! You lot attacked me,' Paul protested.

'You have two choices. A fast death or a slow one. Slow will be painful. Tell me who you work for, and you will not suffer. Refuse, and I will see to it that you have a bad death.'

Paul tried to clear the fog in his head. The back of his neck was on fire, with flames of pain searing the rear of his skull. It was hard to think straight, and he certainly couldn't think fast enough to save himself. 'I don't . . .'

'Take him back. Question him. Find out all he knows, then kill him,' Mortimer said. 'Sorry, friend. I don't have time for this.'

Chapter Twenty-Seven

Thursday before Good Friday[1]

Château du Bois

The next morning William de Bouden was early at his sheets of parchment, yawning regularly. There had been a storm in the night which had left the whole area damp. As far as he could tell, he was sleeping in a room which faced the wind. The shutters had rattled and banged all night, the rain sluicing in through the slats, the wind was blowing so hard, and the water had pooled on the floor inside. It left him unable to sleep, with the result that he was crotchety and petulant this morning. Still, he was nothing if not assiduous in his duties, so while he grumbled to himself, he continued counting the money.

Some people thought that so long as the Queen was in France there would be no need of a formal accounting, but they were dolts. The simple fact was, the King had allowed her a budget to come here as ambassador, and he, William de Bouden, the Queen's Comptroller, had a duty to ensure that the money spent was all accounted for. Before he had left England, he had been given a thousand pounds by the King, but Edward had known that more might be needed, so William had a letter allowing him to draw on the house of the

---

[1] Thursday 4 April 1325

Bardi in Paris. Not that he wanted to pull out too much from there.

Still, the Bardi were competent – very competent – bankers. And the first rule of banking was, as William knew only too well, to keep a careful eye on those who borrowed. To do that, they maintained some of the most efficient spies in the world. That was how they kept themselves briefed on whether a man had enough money to justify a loan, or whether someone had become a bad credit risk.

They scared him.

William had been given the post here by the King because he knew the Queen. Until the King had dissolved her household, William had been her treasurer, but now that he had this new post Edward appeared to believe that he would be automatically loyal to him. Yet no, he was not. He had been the Queen's man for years, and just because the King ordered him away and then gave him his job back changed nothing. He was still the Queen's man. There was such a thing as loyalty, in God's name.

But in royal politics there was little in the way of trust. That was why William was convinced that the Bardi had been paid to keep an eye on him *and* the Queen. There was a man who appeared to be watching him wherever he went. It had scared him half to death when he had been accosted by that knight in Poissy, and it was even worse when Queen Isabella confronted him with his confession to Sir Baldwin that he had been talking to Roger Mortimer. That had gone down like a bucket of cold sick. Still, as she agreed a little while later, at least it demonstrated that they had one ally among the knights who made up her guard. Or if not an ally, at least someone who was prepared to remain loyal to her interests over here.

It was ridiculous, frankly, that anyone could look on Roger as any sort of threat. The man was an old friend of the Queen's. William had been in her service long enough to know perfectly well that she and Roger had met plenty of times when she was still happily married to her husband. Roger had visited her often. Nothing suspicious; it was always with his lady, Joan. Joan and Queen Isabella had got on well, and Mortimer was utterly devoted to his wife. She went with him on all his travels, even when he was marching with his warriors in England, Wales or Ireland. They were one of those terribly rare things, a man and wife who were genuinely in love.

Made it all the worse to see him like this. Now he was a pale reflection of his earlier self. William had seen him in those days when he was the King's most trusted general, but now he was a renegade, a traitor. Untrusted and despised by the king he had served for so many years, he was eking out a living, kept in the background by the French king in case he might become useful at some point in the future, but really a prisoner. He could not leave the French king's protection. To do so would make him nothing more than the target of every cut-purse, draw-latch and robbersman who was bright enough to see how much bounty his head could bring.

It was enough to make a man sigh in sad reflection, of course. He did so now. The mere thought of all that cash, just waiting for any fortunate fool to claim, was enough to make any man of moderate ambition sit back and think of all the fine clothing, the wine, the food, that such treasure could bring. It would be as much as, maybe, a hundred pounds. Good God, a hundred pounds . . .

With cash like that a man would be free indeed. But William did not have a hundred pounds. He didn't have two pounds of his own. Only a matter of a few hundreds of the Queen's money which was all that remained of her thousand. When that was exhausted, William would have to go to the Bardi. Not until then, though. Best to keep away, especially while the Queen was set on meeting Mortimer every so often.

He opened the great steel-barred chest with the huge key he held about his neck, and began checking the money. Satisfied that it all still tallied with his calculations, he closed the lid and relocked it, listening to the great bolts sliding into place.

It was his morning's duty, and now, duty done, he could consider his other tasks. But even as he was seating himself once more at his table, there was a knocking at his door.

'Yes?'

'Master. There's been a murder! An Englishman is dead!'

Sir Charles had been in the hall when the men began to scurry about.

'Something happen?' he murmured to Baldwin at his side.

'It rather looks like it,' Baldwin responded, looking up. 'They are all quite busy. Anyone might think that they were fearful of an assault on the city.'

Simon sipped his weak wine and beckoned a servant. The man was one of the French servants set to watch over the English guests and ensure that they were comfortable, and the fellow came to Simon with a wary expression in his eyes, as though expecting to be assaulted. Simon smiled at him. 'What is the alarm?'

'There is a man dead.'

'What, here in the castle?' Simon asked. There were too many deaths, he thought to himself. This whole embassy could end in disaster.

Sir Charles shrugged. 'What of it? Many die each day. In castles as often as in a city or the countryside. What did he die of? Fall in a well? Fall from a wall? I suppose he was drunk?'

'*Non, mon sieur.*' The servant explained that the poor fellow had been stabbed.

Baldwin cast an eye about the room. There was a

suppressed excitement about the men present. It was not like the anxiety which was the normal companion of a corpse, in his experience. No, it was more like the thrill of watching someone else who would shortly be distraught as the news of a loved one's demise was delivered. 'Who is it?'

There was no answer to that question. The servant gave them to understand that someone would be there to tell them more as soon as he had learned all he might.

Sir Charles was smiling as the man left them, but Baldwin rose. 'I wish to see the Queen and assure myself that she is safe. God forbid that this dead man might be one of her entourage, or even one of the knights with us here.'

'You think it might be Sir John or Sir Peter?' Sir Charles asked. He felt that Baldwin's concern was a little overdone. 'Sir Baldwin, there is nothing to fear. It's probably one of the grooms. Nothing more than that. We can soon hire a fresh one, if need be. Please, sit, and do not trouble the Queen with a matter which may well be completely unimportant.'

He watched as Baldwin stood, undecided. Then Baldwin saw Sir John de Sapy walk into the room with Sir Peter de Lymesey and Lord Cromwell. The sight of the three of them made up his mind. 'Is there no one with the Queen?' he demanded rhetorically, and was gone. Simon rose and hurried after him.

'Where are they going?' Cromwell asked.

'Sir Baldwin has very chivalrously gone to the aid of the Queen in case she is downhearted to hear that someone has died,' Sir Charles said with some amusement. 'Do you know who it is who has been killed?'

'Has no one told you?' Sir John said, his face registering his surprise.

Lord Cromwell was the man who stepped forward and rested a hand on Sir Charles's forearm. 'I am sorry, Sir Charles. It was your man-at-arms – it was Paul.'

* * *

The Queen left them both in no uncertainty about her feelings. She was perfectly well, and if they had not run to her chambers and woken her with their infernal knocking, she would still be blissfully unaware that anyone had been harmed, let alone someone from her delegation.

'So who was it?' Simon wondered.

Baldwin was unable to answer, but as they left the Queen's chamber and could look across the yard towards the entranceway they saw a throng of people. 'Perhaps the answer is out there.'

'You think so? It looks a little dangerous.'

'It is just the street people of Paris looking at a corpse, I think,' Baldwin said, but he joined Simon in splashing through the muddy puddles towards the gate.

Simon gasped when he caught sight of the dead man's face. 'Christ's ballocks, Baldwin, that's Paul!'

'Dear Christ! If you see Sir Charles, keep him away, Simon.'

In the roadway near the castle's gate the throng of people stood watching while a man in *sergent's* uniform studied Paul's corpse. He was asking questions that seemed to go unanswered. 'I said, did anyone see him dumped here?'

There was no response from the people gathered there. Simon could understand enough of the local accent to follow the questioning and the lack of answers from the folk watching, and could sympathise with the poor official trying his best to find the killer.

When he had clearly given up hope of getting any information from the people standing about, and returned to his study of the body, Baldwin stepped forward. 'I do not know if I can help, but I have had some experience of murder and seeking felons in my own lands.'

'I would be very grateful for any aid,' the *sergent* said. 'But

I fear that this is one of those killings which will go down unsolved.'

'Do you know anything at all?'

'As you can see for yourself, he was beaten, and then stabbed. The wound was a cruel one, up from his belly, and straight into his heart and lungs, I imagine. A quick enough death for the poor devil. Not that he would have looked on it as that, I suppose. Nobody saw him die, nobody heard him die, nobody saw a killer – in short, nobody knows anything at all. Hardly surprising, since anyone who saw the man who did this could expect something similar to happen to him.'

'Why do you say that?'

'This was a professional killing.'

'There is no possibility that it could have been a common cut-purse?' Simon asked.

'I shouldn't think so,' Baldwin answered. 'He's been too badly beaten up. And since when did a cut-purse kill a man like this?'

'Oh, God,' Simon said, and turned away from the corpse. He had taken a glimpse, and that was enough.

Paul lay on his back, arms outspread, legs sprawling. The whole of his stomach area was a reddened mess, with blue-grey coils of intestine pulled out and smeared with blood. A thin, oil-like slick of blood pooled over all the puddles in the roadway. Some had coagulated, but much was so diluted with the rainwater that it could not, and merely gave its own pink coloration to the water.

'Yes,' Baldwin said as Simon retched. 'The poor fellow suffered first.' He was about to bend to study the body more closely when the cry made him stop.

'*Paul!*' Sir Charles shouted, and would have run to his servant had Simon not grasped him first and pulled him back. It was a relief to be able to move away from

Paul's body and have something – someone – else to think of.

'Wait, Sir Charles. Let Baldwin see if he can learn anything from him first.'

Sir Charles was incapable of coherent thought, let alone speech, and he struggled at first to free himself.

In the fog of his horror, he did not appreciate that it was Simon and one of the guards from the gates to the château who were holding him back. He roared with anguish, and at one point even tried to reach for his long dagger to cut the pair of them off him, sensing them as enemies trying to stand between him and his man, but Sir John de Sapy was already there, and pulled his hand away. 'Wake up, Sir Charles. Wake up!' he bellowed, and slapped at Sir Charles's face, once, twice. 'Sir Charles! You are being stared at. You have made yourself an object of scorn. Control yourself!'

Sir Charles came to himself. He stared, appalled, at Sir John, but then his eyes slid back towards the body. Sir Baldwin was at Paul's side, respectfully kneeling, and he glanced back at Sir Charles with an expression of such infinite understanding and sadness that Sir Charles knew at once there was no hope. He sagged in the arms of his restrainers, head hanging, feeling as though his own life was ending. A dreadful lassitude came over him, and he felt an urge to spew over the pavement.

How could he waken from this nightmare? Paul – Paul his loyal servant from the days when they were both living in the service of Earl Thomas of Lancaster; Paul who had gone with him into exile rather than be captured and slain by the King's men; Paul who had been with him when he was forced to leave Paris and take pilgrimage to Santiago de Compostela; Paul who had with him been forced to the island of Ennor – in all the long months of wandering, the only man who had remained his devoted servant and friend was Paul.

He had learned to cope with the loss of so much. All his wealth and lands had gone when Earl Thomas had been taken and executed, and gradually during his exile he had grown accustomed to the steady, slow diminishment of his pride as time and again his attempts to find a new lord had failed. Eventually he had sunk so low as to demean himself by offering himself as a mercenary – the lowest form of life. Yet all through those dreadful days, at least he had enjoyed the company of his servant, guard, cook, procurer – Paul. And now he was gone, it felt as though there was a terrible hole in his breast. The man whom he had valued above all others was dead, and now Sir Charles was entirely alone. There was nothing and no one to fill that gap.

'I swear that I shall find the man responsible and cut his heart out,' he said thickly. The words gave a little consolation – just a little – and he was able to stand upright again, pulling his arms from the two at his sides, and forcing his chin up. He remained standing in the same place, unsure whether to trust his legs to take him the short distance to his man's body, but unable to draw his eyes away as Baldwin shook his head, stood, and made his way back to join them.

'Sir Charles, I am truly sorry.'

'He is dead?'

'Yes.'

'Did they make him suffer?'

'I am afraid so. He was beaten before being killed.'

'Thank you for your candour, Sir Baldwin. I appreciate that. Excuse me, I must go and arrange for my man's burial.'

'Of course.'

Baldwin and Simon watched as Sir Charles walked stiffly towards the body.

'He is devastated,' Simon said, his voice hushed.

'He will manage,' Baldwin said harshly. 'We do.'

Simon shot him a look. His companion was gazing after

Sir Charles, but his eyes scarcely appeared to see him. There was an inward-looking emptiness in his face, as if he was thinking of that time, less than ten years before, when he too had been forced to witness the death of men who had been very dear to him.

Lord John Cromwell swore as he stumbled over a loose cobble. 'In Christ's name!'

This was the last thing the mission needed. The embassy was doomed, damn it, and he was the man who was going to be called to account by the King and Sir Hugh le Despenser when they returned. No one else. It could hardly be laid at the Queen's door this time. No matter how much the King hated his wife, the idea that she was responsible for such a breach of security as allowing one of the embassy's men-at-arms to wander the streets and be captured by someone was absurd. That was all Lord John's area of interest. His *fault*.

Diplomacy was fraught with dangers, naturally. When two great kings negotiated matters of such vast importance, there were always factions who sought to assist or thwart. In this case, there was such a preponderance of vested interests on the French side, with barons determined to get their hands on the English king's lands, properties and wine production down in the province of Guyenne, that it was hardly surprising that someone sought to destroy the English mission.

And how better to destroy it than by embarrassing the English? Kill off an Englishman, and you instantly create tensions between the two negotiating teams.

He reached the oaken door to the Queen's hall, and stopped a moment to draw breath. There were two guards here, both from his own entourage, and he nodded at them before reaching forward and opening the door.

'Your royal highness.'

A sword swung in front of him, and he would have

grabbed for his own were it not for the surprise of Blaket's blade-point at his chin. 'Get that away,' he snarled.

'Where have you been?' the Queen demanded as Blaket withdrew his sword without apology.

She was standing close to her fireplace, a book in her hands. A short distance from her was the blonde, Alicia, while Alice de Toeni and Joan of Bar were a little further away, close, as though they had been discussing matters themselves.

'Your highness, I've been talking to the men at the gate, making sure of the facts.'

'What are they?'

'The dead man was one of ours. He was a man-at-arms who rode with Sir Charles of Lancaster. The knight doesn't know when he might have died, but apparently this man Paul was out last night. Probably out seeking the . . .' He quickly decided not to speculate on what kind of woman the fellow was hunting for. 'Anyway, he was captured, I suppose, and robbed and killed.'

'How?'

'How killed? Someone put a knife to his belly and paunched him like a rabbit.'

'I see. And you have examined the body?'

'No. I left Sir Baldwin de Furnshill to do that. He is experienced in such matters. But I suspect that there is little likelihood of finding the man responsible. There are so many alleys and lanes between here and Paris. The body was placed outside the gates at some time during the night, so it could have been anyone. Not necessarily someone from within the castle.'

'A killer from the city?'

'It is said that the city is less vigilant about the walls and gates than it might be. It has not been attacked in the last hundred years.'

'But you are sure that here in the castle we are secure?'

'It is my own men who guard this place, my lady,' he said with a trace of coolness. 'I trust them.'

'So you are sure it was someone from without the castle. Who would want to attack a man like him? Was he rich?'

'No, not at all. I think it was an opportunistic assault. The fellows saw him, bethought themselves that this was a stranger to the town, a foreigner, and therefore an easy mark. Perhaps he had a few pennies on him, but nothing more than that, I should think.'

'Then it was not possible that this could have been a deliberate attempt to damage the talks between the king of France and me?' she asked sweetly.

'I am sure it could not have been, your highness.'

'You are? I am glad. I should hate it to be only me who has considered such eventualities,' she snapped. 'And pray, what is your conviction based upon?'

'Why would a man from the French delegation wish to kill a person of no consequence? Surely, were they to try to damage our embassy, they would have killed a knight, or myself. Not some unknown man-at-arms.'

'Tell me, my lord: we are here because my brother invaded Guyenne, are we not?'

'Yes. Because of the affair over Saint-Sardos.'

'Quite. And when that little war over Saint-Sardos began, was that not over the death of a French official?'

'Yes. The French marched into Guyenne and began to build a *bastide*, and when the locals stopped them, it grew ugly, and a Frenchman was hanged.'

'What was his name?'

Cromwell looked at her blankly. 'Eh?'

'What was this man's name? After all, we are here to negotiate a peace as a result of that war, but you say that a man of no consequence has died. That is a relief.' Her tone rose and her eyes flashed with anger as she finished, 'And yet, my Lord Cromwell, *this whole war began because a man of no consequence – a nonentity – was slain*! And you tell me not to worry, that this man is unimportant? Do you think that solitary dead Frenchman was unimportant too?'

Chapter Twenty-Eight

The Queen's Men were all still abed when the summons came. A man banged on the door, and Charlie squeaked with fear at the sound, hurling himself at Ricard and burying his head in Ricard's breast. 'Hey, little man, little man, calm down!' he said, stroking the boy's head and back. Charlie clung to Ricard like a small limpet, though, hiding his face.

It was a man like this, then, someone who knocked loudly, who had scared this little fellow more than any other. If he had to guess, Ricard would reckon that the boy had not seen his parents die, but he couldn't ask. It would have been too shocking if the boy had admitted seeing his mother raped and murdered. No, Ricard couldn't put that question. So far as he knew, Thomassia, her husband, and the Queen's Men had arrived at her house some time about dusk or later, and the musicians had repaired to the garden almost immediately. So perhaps a little while later Charlie had heard a knocking at the door, and went down to see his parents arguing, or being threatened, and went to hide in the hutch. That would make sense.

Only, didn't boys who saw their parents being threatened usually go to them for protection? If a man was upsetting them, surely the lad would go to his father?

Who could tell how a little boy like this would react?

The messenger was summoning them to the Queen. Her demands must have speedy responses. He took up his gittern as the others quickly gathered up their own instruments, and hurried with them to the Queen's chamber.

Panting as he ran with them, Adam scowled to himself. He'd told them all. It was clear as the nose on his face that this 'Jack' was a dangerous fellow. Plainly not a real musician, no matter what he damned well said. No, he was a danger to them all, he was. A *murderer*. And probably not just some killer-for-money, either, but a much more dangerous type, one of those who killed for Despenser.

There were few men in the kingdom whom Adam feared as he feared Despenser. Who wouldn't? Despenser was the most powerful, the richest, the nastiest, the greediest bastard in a country where instant gratification was the norm for knights and their kind. Didn't matter that some poor devil stood in their path. Any obstruction was there to be removed. A husband of the wench they fancied? Kill him. A widow who owned good property? Kill her. A musician who stood in the way of a man being sent to spy on the Queen? Kill him. And that was why Peter was lying in a grave now, just so that bloody Jack could make the journey with them.

That sign of the peacock was all very well. What did it mean, though? Just that the man had access to a decent artist who could colour a picture on a skin. There were plenty of men who could do that kind of work. Didn't need to be an honest man. And the fellow who'd suggested that they should look out for a man who'd have that sign wasn't necessarily a friend to them. He'd just killed a glover and his wife, after all. Life was cheap, but there was no need to execute someone for no reason like that. Sweet Mother of God, no!

'Hurry up, Adam!' Ricard snapped.

They were trotting over the courtyard now, but when they reached the middle they were halted by French guards with their polearms levelled to hold them back.

'Christ! Are we arrested?' Adam squeaked.

'God's ballocks, just shut up, you fool!' Philip grated. 'Anyone would think you'd been off and killed Paul yourself. What's the matter with you?'

Adam glowered at him. They were all on edge, obviously. It had been bad enough when they had to leave England after Peter's murder, but to have first that Frenchman killed on the way here, and now their own countryman slaughtered outside the castle, well, it seemed to show that things were getting worse. Made a man wonder if he'd be next. In God's name, he didn't want to see any more blood. It had been bad enough in the house in London. That poor woman's body lying there like a discarded bloody rag. It was enough to make a man throw up. Certainly made him spew.

Oh, shit. That's why they were being held up.

Adam stared, lip curled in disgust, as the bloody body was carried past on a bier. Four men carried Paul's remains, all in French uniform, and Adam wondered why, until he realised what a diplomatic disaster this could be. Sir Charles of Lancaster walked along behind the body, eyes fixed on the corpse like a man staring into hell.

As soon as the cortège had gone by, the nearer guard lifted his bill, and the musicians darted past. Ricard was in front, and Jack almost at his side on his long, loping legs. It made Adam feel a flash of anger that the man should be up there in front. Should be him, or maybe Philip or Janin, at Ricard's side, not this interloper.

He glanced back at the bier, and for an instant he could have sworn it was Peter there. The boots were the same, the clothing was much like an old tunic Peter used to wear for different musical events, and there was a tatty old green cloak covering much of him that was so like Peter's it was uncanny. And then he nearly fell over. The bier was being manhandled at the door to the chapel, and had to be tilted slightly to make it through the doorway. As the men eased it inside, one of the corpse's hands fell away, as though to point. And when Adam looked ahead, he knew perfectly well what was being pointed at.

It was the murderer – Jack. The man who had appeared after Peter's death, and who was here to spy on the Queen. The bastard! How could they all play music with the man who'd killed their mate?

After passing by the guards, they reached the Queen's chamber at last. And as Ricard installed the boy at the rear of the room with a wooden ball he had fashioned himself, Adam eyed him with contempt.

Ricard was weak. Since Peter's death, he'd been confused and undecided about everything except taking this little brat everywhere with them. He was useless; couldn't even see how dangerous Jack was.

He'd speak to Philip about Jack. Philip was still a man. He'd help kill the bastard.

Baldwin joined Simon at the bar in the buttery of the castle's main hall, and both drank deeply as soon as their beer arrived.

'Baldwin, are you all right?' Simon asked.

'I am perfectly well,' Baldwin said.

Simon studied him briefly. He didn't want to thrust his nose where it could be bitten off, but he was worried about his friend. 'It was a dreadful murder.'

'Paul's? Oh, I don't know. The man was a known killer, who has murdered plenty in his time, I dare say. Do not forget, Simon, that he was a mercenary when we first met him. A man like that is not going to change his habits. Who can tell, perhaps he was trying to rob someone himself?'

'Baldwin, that is hardly likely.'

'He was never the most communicative of companions. He was a close confidant of Sir Charles, but I would put him no higher than that in my own esteem. For me he was only an acquaintance, and not a welcome one.'

Simon was nonplussed by this cold analysis. 'But surely his death should be investigated?'

'Yes. Without a doubt, but that is what concerns me. It is a question of what may be learned.'

'What do you mean?'

Baldwin looked at him very directly. 'I am an ageing cynic, I think, but I find it hard to understand why a member of this embassy should be set upon late at night. He was not wealthy, and his clothing spoke of poverty. A poor man might attack someone like him for his boots or cloak, especially in this weather, but nothing of the sort was taken. And there are reasons to suspect that it was no poverty-struck man who killed him.'

'You are meandering, Baldwin,' Simon said with a slight chuckle. 'What are you on about? Why not a poor man? His purse was taken.'

'All I mean is, no one who wanted a good purse would bother with his. A successful cut-purse would take his victim's money without the victim's knowing, so it was no professional thief. A poor man wanting better clothes would steal boots or cloak, shirt or hat – but none were taken. Only the purse. A felon might kill if he saw a well-filled purse, but Paul never had one. So who did attack him?'

'A chance encounter, and someone was fearful of being assaulted, so struck first?'

'Paul was many things I disliked, but I respected him for one thing: he was a highly competent man-at-arms. A man would be justified in being nervous of him, but if he sought to draw a weapon at speed Paul would have had his own out first. He was a thoroughly competent fighter. We have both seen that. In any case, this was surely the action of more than one man. Someone must have held him while the second opened him up. Unless, of course, he was already dead when the belly was slit?' He mused a moment, eyes narrowed.

'Then who could have done it?' Simon asked.

Baldwin drained his drink. 'That is what concerns me.'

Lady Joan of Bar winced as the nondescript group of musicians appeared and took up their places. The Queen, damn her, was taking up all the warmth of the fire, with that young hussy Alicia attending to her, and the rest of the room was chilly. But no matter. So long as those two were comfortable, all the other women could go and hang. The Queen wouldn't give them a thought.

The men looked at each other and then struck up a melody. One of those infernal dance tunes they played so often. It grated on her nerves, for she had heard it many times already on this embassy. Gracious Mother, if only the fools could learn something a little more interesting, or at least something that had a little more sobriety. This constant tinkle, tinkle, tinkle, plink, plink was beginning to make her feel like screaming 'Enough!'

She had been brought up to a more genteel lifestyle. The granddaughter of King Edward I, she felt all of her thirty years today. True, since divorcing her foul, cruel, capricious and sly husband, John de Warenne, a man for whom the term 'brute' might well have been invented, she had found her life growing easier, but then she had been thrown back into the politics of the realm by her uncle, the King, and told to keep a close eye on the Queen during this embassy.

It was not a duty she relished. Her cousin Eleanor had monitored the Queen in England, which had not been onerous but was very time-consuming. It was that, Eleanor had said, which made the journey to France so undesirable to her, much though she loved France.

Joan was unconvinced. In her opinion Eleanor had other

reasons for wishing to avoid this duty: first and foremost was the fact that she had been acting as unofficial gaoler to the Queen for the past four or five months. She had taken custody of the royal children – all except the heir, Edward – and was in charge of Isabella's seal, so that all letters must be passed to her to be sealed. The Queen was allowed no secrets. And here they were in the French capital, where the Queen's brother was king. He would be able to make Eleanor's life uncomfortable.

There was another thing, of course. While Eleanor protested that she adored France, and would dearly like to visit it again, she knew that her husband, Sir Hugh le Despenser, would be unable to accompany her there. His actions some years before, when he had been exiled from England and turned pirate, had caused some friction between the French and him. There was the matter of the shipping he had captured, the men he had killed. He dared not visit France, and without him Eleanor would be reluctant to do so.

Which had all conspired to see to it that Joan was forced to come. Well, at least Isabella was congenial company generally, and more so since arriving here in France. She could converse with all about her with a gay easiness that was entirely out of keeping with what the lady Joan had known in England.

Yes. It was strange to see someone who had been so downtrodden only a short while ago flower into this vibrant, beautiful woman again. She was more or less of an age with Joan, but when Joan had seen her in London before departing for the coast, she had been unrecognisable. She looked like Joan herself before that blessed year of 1315, when she had at last managed to dispose of the Earl of Warenne and regain her freedom. Seeing the back of John had been marvellous. Joan could imagine no better moment in her life. And it was sad to think that this queen, this wonderful, attractive woman, should be similarly afflicted while in the presence of her own husband.

At least that was one thing about these accursed music-killers. Queen Isabella appeared to relish their playing. God alone knew how she could tolerate it, but she seemed to like it. Well, the poor woman was here to work her will on the embassy. As soon as that was over, she would be taken straight back to England by Lord John Cromwell, and her peace would be shattered. She would be held once more in the miserable Tower in London, or at the palace on Thorney Island. There she would have her seal taken away once more, and she would be held under the guard of Eleanor.

Joan set her jaw. Since her suffering at the hands of her own husband, she was less inclined to see another woman put to the same slow, intolerable torture of a loveless marriage. Isabella had lost her husband to another lover – all knew of it, there was no point denying the fact – and could never find peace in her own country. She deserved the little relaxation she had discovered here.

The brat who scampered about in the wake of the musicians sent his ball rolling along the chamber, and Joan almost shouted at the miserable churl, but then the ball hit the delicately booted foot of the Queen. She glanced down, startled, and stared at the ball, then over her shoulder at the boy.

For a moment all was breathless and expectant. The lead musician's mouth opened in horror, the fiddler made a squawk by accident, and Joan herself allowed a smile to touch her mouth. But then the Queen beckoned the lad over and held out his ball to him.

You could not ever tell how Queen Isabella would respond, Joan of Bar told herself. She decided that she would have a strategic headache and retire to her rooms the next time these musicians came to play.

* * *

Baldwin and Simon were hailed as soon as they left the buttery, and Simon heard his companion groan to himself as they recognised the tones of Lord John Cromwell.

'Can we escape?' Baldwin whispered.

'I think not,' Simon said with a chuckle. 'Why else were we brought here if not to answer the call of Lord Cromwell?'

Baldwin grunted and turned, fitting a smile to his face. 'My Lord Cromwell. How may I serve you?'

'That man who was killed. I don't want some sort of diplomatic incident. You are used to investigating murders, Sir Baldwin. I want you to show that it was nothing political.'

Baldwin blinked. 'Pray, Lord Cromwell, since you have decided the conclusion, how precisely would you like me to begin my study?'

'Don't be clever, Sir Baldwin,' Cromwell snarled. 'This isn't some easy-going footpad knocking a man on the pate. This is murder, very clearly. We appear to have suffered from rather too many of them of late, don't we? First the poor devil Enguerrand de Foix, then the guard from the Château Gaillard, and now our own man-at-arms. Sir Charles is devastated, and quite capable of causing mayhem in the attempt to kill the man responsible. But having the brain and reasoning capacity of a bloody Lancastrian, he'll be likely to find that the man responsible was the personal steward to King Charles. That cannot be permitted. I will not have our entire purpose ruined because of one man's desire to avenge a blasted servant. Is that clear?'

'Perfectly. However, if you want me to research this latest death, it may be a problem, bearing in mind that the land is strange to me, the people more so, and I have no knowledge of French law. Really, Lord Cromwell, I believe—'

'You will have to do your best.'

'One thing: if you wish me to do this, you must be aware

that I will be truthful. If you expect me to investigate, I will investigate to the very best of my ability. You understand? And if I am questioned, I shall tell the truth.'

'You will remember that you are here on a diplomatic mission, Sir Baldwin. If someone asks you about this crime, you will remember your status, and you will advise your questioner to come to *me*. You will answer nothing, except to *me*.'

The lord scowled ferociously at him, then barely glanced at Simon as he wished them both God speed, and strode away, his boots splashing in the little puddles left by the previous night's rains.

'And that, I think, told me, eh?' Baldwin said with a dry chuckle. 'Come, let us see what it is that the good lord wishes us to see, and try to blinker ourselves to all other possibilities.'

Chapter Twenty-Nine

Jean sat and counted his coins. One *livre* and a few *sous*. Hardly enough to keep him going for long in a city so ruinously expensive as this. It was tempting to try to gamble his way to some money – there were bear pits and cockfighting pits here – but he knew only too well how easy it was for a man to lose his all in such ventures. There was no straightforward way to keep a man's soul together other than slow, steady employment.

There had been many times since leaving the south when he had wished that he had not gone away to war with his father and brother. It would have been so much better to have stayed at home with his wife and lived the contented life of a shepherd. He would never have made himself rich, it was true, but that was by the by. If he had stuck to it, he would have a small family now, his wife would have given him boys to keep the sheep, and he would have been able to build a smallholding. Left something for the children when he died. As it was, what did he have to leave? A few *sous*. Nothing more.

His wife had been raped before she died. Oh, at the time the folks had said it was someone who'd sought her out. The local priest, they reckoned. He made advances to so many, that one. He was safe, a Catholic in an area where so many followed Waldes. If he picked on a Waldensian, she might not defend herself, because he could declare her heretic and perhaps see her burned. And if she was not one of the Poor of

Lyons, that would hardly help her if he denounced her. She would still be interrogated by the bishop.

When he returned, still ravaged by his memories of that dreadful campaign, the only thing he sought was the solace of his wife. It was the one thought that kept him together during the long march from the far north of the kingdom to his own southern home. One battle had shown him his father's destruction, his brother's too. It was plenty enough for a young man. He had had his fill of war and death. Never again. All he craved was the springtime in the mountains, with the little flowers bursting forth in the meadows. He could recall the scent now, if he closed his eyes. It was always so wondrous.

His Huguette had been a beautiful woman. Sixteen when they married, seventeen when she was killed, she had long, lustrous black hair, eyes of an unusual grey hue, and a slim build that was voluptuous when naked, and he had worshipped her.

When he returned, they told him all about it. Strangers with carts who had passed through, all wearing the insignia of the bishop's men. They'd stopped the night and departed early the following morning, and later that day one of the men of the village had discovered Huguette's body. The villagers told him all. No one held back. Why should they? He was the injured party. He deserved to hear the facts.

But as he sat in his empty house, staring at the bed on which she had died, feeling the cold of the night sinking into his bones, thinking about her, about their happiness, he knew that the one thing his Huguette would have wished was that he should not launch himself into some vain attempt at revenge. There was no point. She was a devoted Waldensian, and the idea of seeking a man in order to kill him was alien to her. If a man were to insult her, she would not defend herself; if he struck her cheek, she would turn and offer him the other. It was her faith, and it would be a heretical act for him to assume the responsibility of avenging her injuries. He couldn't.

Perhaps it was not only the desire to comply with her own wishes, though. He had just seen his father and brother die, and had been forced to flee the butchery of the battlefield. The simple fact was, he had seen enough horror. He wanted to have some peace, and the thought that he might himself draw steel to harm a man, even in justifiable revenge, was too appalling to consider.

So in the morning, he had packed all his belongings and gone to the door. He had found one little reminder of the mountains – a small pale yellow flower which had always been one of Huguette's favourites was blooming in their little garden. He picked it, and carefully pressed it between two pieces of horn which he liberated from a lantern. Over time, the flower dried, but it still looked lovely to him. Years old, it was now, yet it still held a little freshness for him. Of course, when he bore witness to the death of Agnes and saw the dreadful result of the bishop's execution, he lost it together with all his other belongings. A convicted felon has few rights to anything – ownership of trinkets was not possible.

He wished he still had that little flower. No matter. There were more immediate matters to concern him. Such as, how to earn a few *sous* and keep his body and soul together?

When Simon and Baldwin entered the chapel, the corpse was already lying cleaned and tidied before the altar, and both bent the knee and crossed themselves with a little holy water from the font before marching along the pretty tiled floor to the bier.

'Sir Charles, do you object to our looking at Paul's body?' Baldwin asked.

'Why? He's dead, man!'

It was so unlike the usually urbane Sir Charles that Baldwin gave a fleeting frown of surprise, but then he nodded to himself. 'Yes, I understand, Sir Charles. However, it is possible that I may be able to learn something about his death which could help me to discover his killer. You want to find whoever was responsible?'

Sir Charles moved away from Paul's body. 'Very well. But when you learn who did this, I want to know *first*. You understand me? I want to know who it was.'

'Sir Charles,' Baldwin sighed. 'If I could, I would be delighted. But there are some here who would be happy to see you seek out the killer and disrupt the talks here. Do you really want to see the negotiations fail?'

'The talks? Pah! You think I care about all this horse shit, when my man has been murdered?'

'And what if someone killed Paul deliberately to provoke you? What if this entire affair is nothing to do with you or Paul, but was intended to upset the truce between the two countries?'

'Why would someone want that? If a Frenchman wished to damage the peace, he would advise Charles to demand that our king come over to pay homage. He would not do it, so the matter would be resolved. No need to kill my man.'

'No need, perhaps. But if the same goal could be achieved without embarrassment to the Queen, a Frenchman would prefer it. Killing an English servant would be one effective method of provoking an English knight if that knight was known to have a temper. Do you want to achieve their aims for them?'

'Sir Baldwin, you misunderstand me. I care nothing for them or their plans. All I want is the chance to avenge my man. I will do that. You find out who was responsible, if you wish, but when you do, I want to be told who it was. I will not want to learn that someone else has been given the name so that another can take the fellow. It is for me.'

'You think it was one man, then?' Baldwin asked, moving about the body. It was obvious that he would get no joy from Sir Charles. The man would have his revenge, no matter what.

'I had thought it was a cut-purse whose attack went wrong.'

'How could one man do this? Knock Paul down, then kill him in this manner? There were surely at least two. And in any case, if he was murdered at the gate there, wouldn't the guards have heard it happen?'

'Over the noise of the storm last night?' Simon pointed out.

Baldwin considered. 'Perhaps. But is it likely someone would want to commit a crime like this just outside the walls of a castle? More probable by far that he'd do it elsewhere, and then dump the body. I could imagine killing a man in a house, in a street, in the open countryside – but right outside the King's own palace? That stretches my credibility too far.'

'So? What of it?' Sir Charles snapped.

'Just this: if it was not an attack outside the castle, then it becomes a premeditated murder. Someone had planned it – possibly to avenge some form of insult real or imagined which Paul was supposed to have delivered, or to get to you, Sir Charles, or to damage the negotiations. Discover the motivation and we will be close to learning who was responsible.'

'Find him, then. Find him for me.'

'Him. Him, or them?' Baldwin mused. He shook his head. 'It is thoroughly unlikely that this was the crime of an individual. I cannot believe it.'

He pulled the sheet aside and peered at the wound while Simon averted his gaze. Sir Charles gazed on, unbothered by the sight. It was the fact of his friend's death that concerned him, not the actual manner of it. He had seen death in too many forms, and inflicted too much of it himself, to be overly bothered by the sight of another corpse.

'Here is the wound,' Baldwin said. He enlisted Sir Charles's aid to roll the body over. 'Nothing on the back. No mark at all.' Gently he allowed Paul to return to his recumbent position. 'Only this great slash in his belly.'

'What of his neck?' Sir Charles asked.

'Nothing there. No cut in his throat, no stab down from his collar. I've seen that often enough. No indication of throttling, either. No, just this one slash at his gut.' He eyed the massive wound again, and then he frowned. 'The *sergent* was right – this wound is aimed upwards. I suppose the killer could have thrust to the heart, and made the slash opening his belly once he was already dead.'

'What would that tell us?' Sir Charles demanded.

'Perhaps nothing. Perhaps a lot. Until we have more, we cannot tell,' Baldwin said thoughtfully. Then he beckoned Simon. 'Come. Let us go and view the place where he was found.'

The place had been washed clean of most of the blood by some thoughtful person who had hurled some water over the spot. Baldwin stood and eyed it, but he could discern nothing from the general mess.

'If there was anything to see, I rather think it would have been washed clean by now,' he said as the two of them walked away.

They asked an old peasant woman, who directed them to a small house along an alley nearby. There, she said, they would find the *sergent* who had been at the scene that morning. It took little time to find the house, and the man was eating a late breakfast of peasant bread and some soft cheese. He eyed them as Baldwin spoke, and then shrugged.

'There is nothing for me to do. The man was found, but no

one saw nor heard anyone. I have reported already.'

He could, or would, say no more. Baldwin and Simon soon found themselves outside his little cottage. 'What now?' Simon asked.

'I would think that we have more or less exhausted our enquiry already,' Baldwin admitted. 'If we were in England, I could round up all the neighbours in the hundred and interrogate them until someone broke. I would have the King's authority to question whomsoever I wished. Here, though, I am powerless. Our king has no power here to compel people to respond. What should I try?'

'Well, there was no evidence on the body,' Simon mused. 'In the absence of that, and with no witnesses, perhaps we should simply return and apologise to Lord John. He won't like it, but at least there's no evidence of a deliberate attempt to ruin the negotiations.'

Baldwin pulled a grimace. 'That is what is niggling at me,' he admitted. 'There was the explosion in the night when Enguerrand de Foix died, which annoys me since it implicated me in the murder; then the death of that guard, too, in the castle on the way here. It makes me suspect more, perhaps, than I should.'

'What possible connection could there be between Paul and the other two?'

'In God's name, I wish I knew. Perhaps they are all unconnected? Three random murders that just happen to have taken place when the Queen came here to see her brother. But that would militate against the careful planning of the murder of the Comte de Foix. That man was dead before I arrived at the site of the killing and frustrated the attempt to make it look like an accident. When the charge blew up in my face, the killer took the opportunity to seize my knife and stab the Comte with it to divert suspicion from himself. That was the impulse of the moment – I think his plan had been carefully thought out, but he had no time to put it into execution.'

'Then there was the murder of the guard from the château.'

'Yes. We have no idea why that should have happened.'

'What about the man who was injured during the attack – the fellow who told us about the powder,' Simon wondered. 'Perhaps he could help us?'

'What would he know?'

'Baldwin, I have no idea. But the fact is, the man was connected to both of those incidents. Perhaps he knows something that could help us.'

'He's not involved in this, though, is he?'

'It was you who postulated a connection between all three, Baldwin, not me.'

'True enough. All these sudden deaths. And might there not be more?'

'What do you mean?'

'Blaket told us, didn't he, about a man who was killed in England – a waferer to the King? Why not include his murder as well? It is as explicable as all these other deaths,' Baldwin said with exasperation.

Robert de Chatillon winced as he leaned back in the chair, his hand at his side again. Dear Christ, the pain was unbelievable! He would never have thought that so much could have been caused by a wound that did not even bleed.

The physician had looked at him carefully, and then declared that from the colour of his urine he was severely choleric, a diagnosis which Robert was keen to reinforce by kicking the fool downstairs. If only he'd been able to. Choleric, indeed. Who wouldn't be bloody angry after a sudden attack like that? If anything could have made it worse, it was the fact that the killer of the old guard had escaped as well. Nothing could have been more surely guaranteed to make his ire increase. The damned fool of a physician had hurried out of the door almost immediately afterwards, prescribing a course of blood-letting and a poultice for the rib, and Robert had been content to ignore him.

Maybe he ought to get a second man in, though. This pain was so sharp, it was impossible to think of leaving the city for some while. He ought to go with Enguerrand's heart back to the *comté*, but he could not face the idea of getting on his horse again. No, it was plainly mad to think of such a thing. He would have to stay here for a while longer.

The knock at his door came as a surprise, although not an unwelcome one. He knew few enough people here in Paris, and any company was preferable to sitting here alone. Calling to them to enter, he pulled himself upright again, wincing at the stabbing sensation in his flank.

'Robert, I am glad to see you looking a little better,' Baldwin said.

'And I am glad for a guest. Bailiff, I am pleased to see you too. Could I offer you both some wine?'

The innkeeper was a surly soul, but at the thought of selling some wine at inflated prices he almost smiled. Soon he had returned with a tousle-haired lad and two jugs of wine.

Robert waved him out as soon as all had a cup in their hands. 'This is little better than vinegar with water added, but it is better than nothing. I shall have to ask that the city sends someone here to investigate the quality of his stocks. There are laws against poisoning clients even in Paris.'

'You do not like it here?' Simon asked, surprised.

'How can I tell? I am nearly bedridden just now. Every time I move, I feel a pain here,' he said, gingerly holding a hand above the area. 'I cannot ride, cannot walk . . . in short, I may as well be a prisoner.'

'It is about that attack that we wished to ask you,' Baldwin said. 'Would you object to speaking to us about it?'

'No. What do you want to know? It was a shock when it happened.'

'I can imagine that. The man who died, he was a guard from a prison, you said?'

'I did?'

'I heard he was from the Château Gaillard, a castle in Normandy. Is that right?'

'Yes, but he was just an old man-at-arms my baron had known for many years, really.'

'So he worked for Enguerrand de Foix?'

'Of course.'

'And the other man?'

'The other . . . ?'

'The man who killed him? What actually happened?'

'Well, I was in the room with the old man, and then the other fellow jumped in and set to. He shoved the table into me, and broke my rib here, and then broke the old man's head with a war-hammer or something.'

'That was what made the wound?' Baldwin nodded. He had seen le Vieux's head after the attack, and remembered the puncture in the skull. A war-hammer would make exactly that kind of injury. But then he frowned as he recalled seeing the two men in the yard that day.

'Something wrong, Baldwin?' Simon asked.

'No, no,' Baldwin said. He decided to hold that information back, wondering whether it was a failure of Robert's memory, or a deliberate attempt to deceive. 'Tell me, Robert. The Château Gaillard. Did your baron visit the place?'

'Occasionally. We had been there a few times.'

'But it is a royal castle? I seem to recall hearing of it. Did not the French king capture it shortly after Richard Coeur de Lion died?'

'You have a good understanding of history, Sir Baldwin.'

'Yes.'

Robert was nonplussed. The flat response was not what he had expected. 'Well, I believe the castle was one of the last of the Norman castles held by the English before King Philip-Augustus invaded the territory and took them all back. Château Gaillard was the key to Normandy, though. Once that fell, Normandy became French.'

'So it is a royal castle?'

'Oh, yes.'

'So what was your baron doing up there?'

'Ah, I couldn't say.'

'And the old guard who died, he was there too?'

'Well, I couldn't . . .'

'At the time you were hurt, that is what you were saying.'

'Was I?'

'And more than that, you also said that the man who killed him came from there, too. Do you not remember?'

'I could have been raving, Sir Baldwin. I was in a great deal of pain.'

His evasiveness was apparent. Baldwin nodded again. 'Is there anything else you would like to tell me about the castle, or about the two men?'

'No, I know nothing, I fear.'

'Oh. That is a shame. Never mind, though. Tell me, do you have any more of that powder, by any chance?'

'Some, yes. Why?'

'I would be glad of a small barrel,' Baldwin said. 'Where could I acquire some?'

'You can take one of mine, and welcome,' Robert said, trying to conceal his reluctance. In truth, he did not like the idea of sharing such a dangerous substance. He pointed to a chest. 'There are three barrels in there.'

'I am grateful,' Baldwin said. He stood, the barrel in his hands, frowning slightly, staring down at the container.

'There is something else, Sir Baldwin?'

'I am sorry to test your patience, my friend,' Baldwin said slowly. 'But I was just thinking. You may not know, but another man has just died. Perhaps he has nothing to do with the Château Gaillard. I do not think he does. However, it could well be that there is someone who seeks to harm all those who had any dealings with the place. Somebody did tell me that it was a place of imprisonment, and that the King's enemies were sometimes incarcerated there. It seems to have been viewed with some horror by people. Do you know aught of this?'

'There were some prisoners there,' Robert admitted. 'But that can have little to do with this affair.'

'Which affair is that?' Baldwin said.

'Why, the old guard being killed in my chamber, of course. What else did you think I might mean?'

'I wondered. It could have been the man killed this morning – or your master on the way here. There seem to have been so many deaths, do there not?'

Chapter Thirty

Adam was reluctant even to walk at the side of Jack as they returned to the chamber where they were staying. Instead, he fell back until he was in step with Philip.

'What's up?' Philip asked. 'You never usually seek my company.'

'Well, what's usual is variable. I don't like that man. Don't like him at all.'

'Jack? Nah. Neither do I. There's something bad about him.'

'He was out again last night, wasn't he?'

'Was he?'

'While you were still at the bar, yes. He was out for some while. It must have been gone the middle of the night when he came back, because I was already asleep. Did you see him?'

Philip shook his head slowly, considering, his eyes firmly glued to Jack's back up in front of them. 'No, I didn't notice him,' he said. The suspicion tarred his voice. 'Where was he, then? Do you think he killed the knight's man too?'

'Who else?' Adam hissed.

'You liked him at first,' Philip taunted him. 'Now, all of a sudden you reckon he's a murderer.'

'That's not true! I'm sorry, I never liked the man. He always struck me as odd.'

'You can't make up your mind who's a friend and who isn't, that's your trouble,' Philip said disdainfully.

'I've made up my mind about him now,' Adam said with conviction.

'Then we have to decide what to do with him,' Philip said. 'None of this half-arsed ballocks about catching him and holding him to get some answers. We need to just kill him and throw him over the bloody walls.'

'What about the peacock?'

'That? It only proves the bastard was with the man who killed the woman and her man at the house in London, doesn't it? Maybe even had something to do with killing Peter. Sod the peacock. He's dangerous to us. Let's get rid of him.'

Baldwin and Simon were discussing the matter as they left Robert's inn, the little barrel of precious powder in Baldwin's arms. Over the way was a man in a pale orange jerkin leaning against a post, and Simon nodded at him. It was a matter of courtesy, nothing more.

'He was keeping back a lot of things,' Baldwin said as they marched along the street.

'I didn't feel he was a dishonest man,' Simon said.

'That doesn't mean he'll tell us the truth about everything, though. It depends upon who he thinks is his real master,' Baldwin considered.

'True enough. So who do you think he serves?'

Baldwin grinned. 'Ah, now that would be nice to know!'

'I . . . Baldwin, are we being followed?'

Baldwin glanced at Simon, but his friend was staring back the way they had come. Behind them was the man at whom Simon had nodded. 'No, I doubt it.'

They slowly ambled along the streets until they reached the castle again, paying no attention to the people about them. There Baldwin carried the barrel to their chamber, while Simon sat out in the yard. After the rains of the previous night, the weather seemed to have made up its mind to be more congenial, and now there was a hot springtime sun blazing in a clear blue sky. Simon leaned back, letting the sun strike his face and warm him. This weather was a great deal better than the chill rain of the moors back at home, he told himself as he closed his eyes.

There was a step close behind him, and he grinned. 'Stored it safely, Baldwin? We don't want you to wake in the middle of the night to hear a loud explosion. Next time you may lose more than your eyebrows!' And then he felt the sharp prick of a blade at the top of his neck, where his skull met his spine. Instantly he stilled.

'Shut up and stand. Move too quickly or too obviously, you bastard, and you'll never move again.'

Robert sat back as the two left, and felt his heart pounding. This was growing dangerous now. It was bad enough before the death of his master, but the risks were growing greater and he was beginning to feel seriously threatened. Damn Jean for escaping. If only Arnaud and le Vieux had managed to silence him at the same time as all the others. There would be no problem now if they'd done their God-cursed job properly. But no one could expect cretins like them to do things without screwing up.

One had paid for his incompetence. Now Robert had to rectify matters. And quickly. How?

He bellowed for the innkeeper. 'Get my man. Bring him here.'

The innkeeper, surly as ever, nodded and left. He didn't like Robert. Well, that feeling at least was mutual. And Robert did not care much what the man thought about him. Or anything else. He was merely handy because he had a room, and that was all. If he wanted a hard life, all he needed to do was make Robert's difficult.

* * *

Baldwin was in the yard again after only a few minutes, and he looked about him in some surprise, expecting Simon to be resting on the benches where he thought he had said he would wait. There being no sign of him, Baldwin crossed to the hall, and made his way to the great buttery, but although he peered about in the busy chamber there was no sign of Simon either, and suddenly Baldwin felt the first stirrings of alarm.

Turning, he went back outside and looked all around. With no sign of his friend anywhere, he trotted over to the gate. Simon was not to be seen up and down the street, so he went to a guard who stood leaning on a polearm near the entrance and asked whether he had seen him.

'Yes, he walked out a little while ago,' the man said, when Baldwin had described Simon. 'He was with a fellow in an orange jerkin. Strange-looking fellow. He was holding your friend's arm.'

The prickling of alarm became a steady thrill. Baldwin demanded where the pair had gone, and when the guard pointed he started running off to the north, in the direction the man had indicated.

He had gone only a matter of a few yards when he saw a flash of colour between folk up ahead. It was pale orange, and he saw it for only an instant. He hurried his pace until he was running. There were lots of people here, and the way was all but blocked where they stopped to view the wares on the shutters outside the shops. At one point he heard a sudden alarm, and saw a man pelting away, a cook giving chase, hurling imprecations at the motherless son of a cripple who'd filched his cakes. All the people in the way moved to gain a better view, effectively cutting off his path. It was only with the use of curses and his clenched fist that he was able to force a way through. Then he saw the orange again, and now that the street was a little more clear he could dart after his quarry, slipping between men and women, biting at his lip, hoping against hope that he would not be too late.

The orange jerkin disappeared. Baldwin slowed, peering about him carefully and cautiously. There was an alley on the right, and as he drew level with it he edged towards the wall. With a wary glance to make sure that there was no one behind him, he cast a look along the alley.

There, in a doorway, he could see the orange. Taking a deep breath, he thrust himself after the man, and pelted down the cobbles. The man was alone. He was the one whom Simon had pointed out, but there was no sign of Simon. He would tell Baldwin, though. Baldwin drew his sword as he ran, and when he reached the fellow the blade rose until it lay across the man's throat. 'Where is he?'

'In here, Sir Baldwin.'

Baldwin narrowed his eyes. This was not a Frenchman. The accent was clearest London, and the man was unafraid. His eyes were steady as he met Baldwin's stare.

'You know my name?'

'Oh, yes. We know all about you and Bailiff Puttock. Follow me.'

Baldwin did so, the sword's point at the man's kidneys. The house they entered was a dark place, with no natural light in this front chamber, but the man led the way through a short passage to a rear room, which was lighted by a large window facing south over a small court, to which the door lay open.

'Simon!'

His friend was sitting on a stool in the yard, a man at either side of him, both holding long knives in their hands. Baldwin reached out and grabbed the man in the orange jerkin, and snarled, 'If anyone hurts him, you will die – you understand?'

There was a low chuckle from behind him, and Baldwin whirled about, still gripping the orange jerkin. Behind him, sitting on a bench beside the doorway through which he had just passed, sat another man. A most familiar man. Tall, strong, with the sunburned face of a man who had spent many years out on campaign in all weather. A man who was used to command and respect.

'Sir Baldwin, your friend is perfectly safe. He was merely a lure to attract you. Now, please, set your sword aside and sit here with me. I only wish to talk to you.'

'Really? My Lord Mortimer, I do not know whether I can speak to you.'

'I know. The greatest traitor of the realm, eh? Never mind all that nonsense. I swear to you on my honour as a knight, you will come to no harm, and neither will the good bailiff. I have news for you – news of a highly important nature. It concerns the safety of the Queen. And you.'

Arnaud left the chamber fuming with rage. How could the fool have put them all into so much danger? They'd been so close to safety, and now he'd ruined everything.

It was all because the Comte de Foix had died. If only he hadn't. He was clever, the Comte. He understood things, told them what was needed, and gave them the tools to make sure that it could be accomplished.

The whole scheme had been so carefully worked out, and now there was the distinct possibility that everything could go horribly wrong. *Merde!* Robert had known all along that there was an especial mission for le Vieux and Arnaud, but no one had thought it necessary to tell him any details. Well, for why would they tell him? He was a lazy churl with the brain of a peasant, when all was said and done. Never wanted to exert himself in his lord's service. Not like Arnaud and le Vieux. They would do their lord's bidding and be glad. Not that they were in any great danger. Their master could protect them against all accusations. Any at all. There was no need for them to fear the law.

And now the Comte was dead, le Vieux was dead, and there was only Arnaud left to carry out the plan.

Well, he would do it all on his own, then. He had before, and he could do so again. There was a gap in the legal calendar just now. No more hangings for a while. So Arnaud had all the time in the world.

Chapter Thirty-One

'Release my companion,' Baldwin said, his teeth gritted.

His rage was fanned by his own sense of stupidity and culpability. If only he had listened to his own heart, he would not be here in France at all. Surely he could have declined the King's demand that he should come . . . no. No, he couldn't. Not unless he had wanted his family to become the focus of the King's interest, and that of the Despenser. No man wanted that sort of attention.

But he could have been more sensible. If he had thought even a moment, he would have accosted their pursuer on the way back from Robert's inn. Stopped and caught him. There had been ample time to do just that. It was ridiculous that he should have put himself into this position. A demonstration of utter stupidity.

Roger Mortimer nodded towards the window. 'Sir Baldwin, your friend is already released. This is nothing to do with him. It is more to do with you, I believe. Please, won't you sheathe your sword and sit?'

'What is more to do with me than him?' Baldwin demanded. He ignored the suggestion that he might sit or cover his blade.

Mortimer was a man of about Simon's age, Baldwin knew – a couple of years short of forty years old – and yet his face showed none of the ease of Simon's. A man of forty should know what it's like to have loved, to have fought, to have lost. In Simon's eyes there was all of that maturity, as well as a calmness that came from acceptance of life – good and bad.

In Mortimer's eyes there was no ease, because all the good fortune he had enjoyed had been swept away by the change in the King's attitude towards him. Despenser had poisoned the King's mind against him, and now Mortimer lived under the sentence of death. The King had signed it. All Mortimer had grown to know and accept had been taken from him. His wife, children, homes, wealth – all were gone, and that loss was there in his eyes. They were wary, yes, but they held an unfathomable sadness too.

'The man who was found outside the castle this morning. There will be allegations that it was my doing that left him dead. I have heard already that you are to mount an enquiry into his death. You will find much evidence pointing to me, I am sure.'

'Why should you be so certain?'

'Because I am evil. I am the man who has betrayed the King, according to Despenser, that devil's whelp! Look at me, Sir Baldwin. Do you have children?'

'I miss them.'

'Mine have been arrested. I know my wife is being held in a castle, while my daughters have been thrown into convents. My boys are imprisoned too. How would you feel to know your family was being so cruelly treated?'

'Guilty, perhaps. All is your own responsibility.'

'I sought to protect the realm and my friend the King. But no matter what I did, his mind was poisoned against me by Despenser.'

Baldwin stared for a long moment, but then he nodded. 'I have a boy too. He is my pride, his sister my joy.'

Mortimer looked away, and Baldwin was sure that there was a slight moisture at his eyelids. 'I remember my boys being born. I taught them how to wield sword and lance, how to ride a horse – everything! In all my life, the only things I am truly proud of are my sons.'

'You imply evidence against you will be fabricated?'

'I am the King's traitor. What else will happen? I tell you this, though: last night I captured the man, and would have killed him, were it clearly not in my interests to do so. I had meant to, I assure you, but then I saw that his life would be of more use to me. So I allowed him to live. There is no point ending a life unless there is an advantage in doing it. You may imagine my disgust this morning when I learned that someone else had destroyed him. It was irritating.'

'Why did you want to kill him?' Baldwin said without thinking. He was grinning at Simon, who had joined the two in the chamber. Simon was rubbing his wrists ruefully, and he shrugged shamefacedly at Baldwin without speaking.

'My dear sir knight, if a man wished to murder you, throw your body in the Seine, and ride post-haste for London with your head bouncing at his saddle-bow, wouldn't you feel justified in being keen to return the favour? The fellow was searching for me in order to cash in on the King's reward. The King is less concerned with appearances than most, and I believe has not bothered to mention the "alive" part of the "dead or alive" offer for me.'

Baldwin understood. He had always disliked Sir Charles's mercenary tendencies. 'He was seeking to claim the reward, then?' It made sense. No man interested in money could turn his nose up at the thought of the reward for the King's most implacable enemy. He had thought the two of them had been quiet in recent days – this explained why.

'He saw me the day that the King met the Queen Isabella. I was in the crowd.'

'You wanted to see her. I spoke to de Bouden.'

Mortimer waved a hand as though dismissing de Bouden. 'She has been very kind – both to me and to my wife.'

'I do not need to know this.'

'Very well, but please hear me out. I cannot talk to others in the Queen's guard.'

Baldwin frowned. 'Why should you wish to?'

'There is danger here for her. She is not held in universal regard, you know. To some she is a symbol of the English power. It is clear enough that she is the one with the independent spirit and the intelligence in that family. No one who knows them can doubt it.'

Baldwin was about to demur, but Mortimer shook his head.

'Sir Baldwin, you know how the King has failed in every military expedition bar one. He is not competent to lead. Men distrust him, especially his choice of adviser. Many over here think that Isabella is the key to the crown of England. They think little of her husband, but believe that they can influence him through his wife.'

'Hardly likely.'

'Quite right, Sir Baldwin. I agree. But that is the thinking here. They wish to bring the King of England to his senses and force him to capitulate, probably demand the whole of his French assets and his homage to the French king, and expect that they can do so by keeping the Queen here. At least she is the bright one, they think.'

'Where is the danger in that for her?'

'The danger lies in England. There is another who seeks to destroy her. You know that as well as I.'

'Who?'

Mortimer sighed. 'Why, your friend and mine, Sir Hugh le Despenser.'

'Why should he want to harm her?'

'You know that, I think.'

He was right. It was easy to see why Despenser would desire to destroy Isabella. She was his most dangerous enemy, the one person who could potentially win back the affections of King Edward and leave Despenser in the cold again. All Despenser need do was see to it that the mission here in France was ruined, and her credibility would be destroyed. Her whole reputation just now was built on a precarious foundation; the success of this negotiation. Failure would justify the King in treating her still worse: there would be enough men who would suggest that her failure was caused by a lack of commitment to the Crown. She was French born, they would say; it was hardly surprising that she sought to support her brother and France against her adopted country.

'What exactly are you saying, Lord Roger?'

'Thank you for that courtesy, Sir Baldwin. It's the first time I have heard an English voice call me that in many months. What I am telling you is this: Despenser has decided already that this mission must fail, and fail catastrophically. To bring that about, he is very happy to incite trouble.'

'Why would he do that?' Simon asked. 'He is English, for Christ's sake. Why try to harm the King's interests?'

'Because by doing so, he will ensure that the King never comes here and leaves Despenser all alone; because by doing so, he concentrates the King's mind on England, which is where Despenser's money and personal interest lie. Because he cares nothing for anyone else, so long as he protects his own lands and treasure,' Mortimer said coldly.

'What of the Queen?'

'You are a singular man, if you hold the Queen's interests in your mind. Lord John Cromwell is a loyal servant of the King. The knights with you? They were put in place by Despenser and the King. They are here to protect the King, not Isabella. And even her own ladies-in-waiting are related to the King. They will see to his interests. Isabella is all alone, with only you to turn to. All I ask is that you help her. She needs all the help she can win, Sir Baldwin. And only you can be trusted.'

'What makes you so sure that I can be trusted, though?' Baldwin frowned.

Mortimer gave a guffaw. 'If nothing else, that answer alone! Nay, Sir Baldwin,' he added, his tone suddenly sombre. 'I cannot joke on such a matter. You are known to be a devoted servant. You have sworn to support the Queen, so it is known that you will die in her defence, if necessary. The others with you? De Sapy and de Lymesey have both served Lancaster as well as the King. They move from one allegiance to another. Charles of Lancaster? He's only recently become a household knight, and he won't upset his master. But you? You are devoted to the Queen.'

'So I am at risk?'

'Despenser has decided to destroy you utterly. Your life, your reputation, your existence will be erased. The reason is this: the Despenser has decided that the Queen threatens his ambitions. If her mission here is embarrassed, it will fail, and possibly she will return to England in disgrace. Of all the men guarding her, they sent you, Sir Baldwin. You, who are no ally to him, from what I have heard. He perhaps thinks you are a danger to his ambitions.'

'And how can he embarrass the Queen through Baldwin,' Simon scoffed. 'Sir Baldwin is a noble man. There's nothing the Despenser could do or say that would hurt him.'

Mortimer did not look at Simon, but kept his eyes firmly on Baldwin. 'It has been suggested that you are a renegade Templar, that you are a heretic, and that you should be hunted down and captured, and executed. I am sorry.'

At last, Jean saw him again!

He had been all over the city, searching high and low, and it was only when he had a sudden flash of inspiration and learned that the public executions were all conducted on the King's massive new gibbet at Montfaucon that he had seen a way to learn where Arnaud was.

A guard there had eyed him suspiciously when he arrived, staring with disgust at the sixteen-odd dangling men. Some were close to falling from their ropes, they were so putrefied and decomposed.

'What are you after?'

'I was looking for the executioner. He's called Arnaud of Pamiers, I think. Is he here today?'

'There's no one to be killed today. I heard that someone was going to be branded in the main square outside Notre Dame, but not until tomorrow or the day after. Hold on.'

Bellowing up to another guard, the helpful fellow soon learned what Arnaud's itinerary for the coming week was likely to be. In the end, he and his companion suggested that Jean may find him near an inn not far from Saint-Jacques. He gave Jean directions, and Jean was soon on his way. At least the city was still a small, compact area. And laid out on flat land, fortunately. When he had been a lad, any walk would take him right up the hills into the mountains. A short journey as the crow flew could take a day or more, scaling the peaks – or, more likely, walking down to the end of one valley, around the spur of the mountain, and up the next. This, in comparison, was easy.

The inn was a nondescript place that catered for butchers. It opened before dawn for the tradesmen who worked in the butchery. They needed their breakfast before light, when they had been hacking and cutting the carcasses for some while already. Even now, although it was still early, several in the inn were drunk. Two stumbled and almost fell against Jean as he entered, but it was natural enough. It was almost time for them to go home, their day's work done.

Jean bought ale and took it to a dark corner from where he

could keep an eye on the men all around, and then he *saw* him!

Arnaud had been in a second chamber at the rear of the inn, and now he was walking out. He crossed the room with scarcely a glance to right or left, viewing all the butchers there with contempt, as though their work was but a pale reflection of his own, but Jean also saw that one or two of the men, perhaps those less drunk than the others, crossed themselves and withdrew from him as he passed them.

No one liked the executioner.

Baldwin felt as though the earth had trembled and fallen from its mount. His legs were suddenly weak, his heart pounding as though he had run a great race, and he felt physically sick. It was one thing to be an escaped Templar at home, back in England, where no one truly cared about such matters any more, but something quite different to be accused of such an offence here, in France – in *Paris* – where the foul lies had first been invented and bruited abroad, used to destroy that holy, honourable and godly Order of men. It was obscene that the Order had been condemned on the basis of malicious lies. And now suddenly he felt his vulnerability. Because they had been invented here, by the French king. This was the heartland of his enemies.

'I am sorry, Sir Baldwin. It will be no consolation, I know, but the man responsible was, I am sure, Despenser. It shows you whom you can and cannot trust, I fear. He sees you as a useful means of ruining the Queen. Whether he knows or thinks you may once have been a Templar doesn't matter to him so much as the benefit that can accrue to him by damaging you.'

'I see,' Baldwin said. He was almost lightheaded in the face of this shock, although it should not have been a surprise. The Despenser was an especially ruthless and cruel foe, and he viewed all as his enemies unless he had a specific use for them. 'I am grateful to you for your warning. I cannot imagine why he should think to accuse me, but I can understand that it could benefit him to harm the Queen. Do you know who has been told of this allegation about me? Is it held within the English court?'

'No, I don't think so. So far as I am aware, no one in England has been told. No, the rumour has been spread over here. King Charles knows it, my friend.'

Baldwin shoved his sword into its sheath and wiped a hand over his brow. This was worse than he could have imagined. He could be arrested for this, no matter that he had a safe conduct. Even with a letter giving him diplomatic status, the Church could arrest him. There was no safety from an inquisition based upon the concept of heresy. A Templar who had not submitted to the Church's authority was to be arrested no matter where he was found.

If the French king was aware of Baldwin's past, he was doomed.

Janin was in their room and practising a new tune when the two men found him, and he looked up with a faintly suspicious lifting of his eyebrows.

Philip said nothing, but went to stand leaning against the wall by the door. It was left to Adam to speak, and he looked at Philip as though searching for some support before beginning.

'Janin, it's that man Jack. I think we have to be rid of him. If he's the man with the peacock, we know he's been involved with the man who killed the glover and his wife in London, and he probably had poor Peter killed too, just so he could join us. And why? So he can spy on the Queen, is what we have heard, but what if he's here for something else? Eh? He might be looking to do something much worse. Perhaps hurt her? Kill her, even? What could we do if he was to hurt her, and we got the blame?'

'It'd save us having to keep looking for new rooms to play in,' Janin said lightly.

'Be serious, Janin! How can we keep on with him here? At the least we ought to tell someone, so that if he is a bad 'un, at least we're covered.'

Janin laughed at that. 'How long ago did he join us, Adam? Back in England, wasn't it? And we've been quiet all this time, just waiting to see whether he's going to do something to hurt her, is that what you want us to say? That we've been hanging around all this time, but now we can see he's done nothing so far we want him taken away. Why, because we're *disappointed* to see he's done nothing? Or should we say that it's because we didn't think he was so much of a risk before, but now we've learned he is the man we are supposed to report to while spying on the Queen we aren't so happy about him? How well do you think it'd go down, the Queen hearing that we were intending to spy on her?'

'We don't have to tell anybody anything,' Philip said.

Janin glanced over at him. 'Philip, what are you on about?'

'We could just slide a knife into him and drop his body into the Seine. It's been done before.'

'Well not bloody by me, it hasn't!' Janin spat with a wince. 'Christ's nuts, do you think it's that easy to kill a man? And we're in France. You know the different ways they have of executing people for murder over here? You can be broken on a wheel, burned alive, hanged on the King's gibbet . . . you want me to carry on?'

'Are you with us or not?' Adam demanded. 'We can't carry on like this, Janin. He's a dangerous man, and he's threatening all of us. We have to get rid of him.'

'You do it if you want to, but I'll have no part in it,' Janin said coldly. 'You put your own heads into a noose by all means, but don't expect me to as well. You do it on your own. And I am not sure I won't warn Jack that you'll try it. Murder! Since when did murder solve anything?'

He picked up his instrument and strode to the door, but as he reached it, Philip put a hand out and held it closed.

'Don't go talking to anyone else about this, Janin.'

'What, are you threatening me now, Philip? After all we've done as a team, now you threaten me in case I do something to help another man? Is that it?'

'If we do decide to kill him, I don't want to have to kill you as well. That's all. If you go talking about this to anyone, we'll have to see to you as well, won't we? Neither of us wants that. So just keep quiet.'

'Leave the door alone, Philip. Let me out. You, friend, can go mad in your own way, but don't presume to take me with you,' Janin said quickly, opening the door.

Philip smiled, but as Janin stepped forward to leave the room he felt the prick of a knife's point at his groin. 'What are you doing?'

'I'm serious, Janin. Keep it quiet – all right?'

Janin met his gaze resolutely, and then stepped around Philip's hand and left.

Chapter Thirty-Two

Baldwin was walking like a man who had been struck about the head, and Simon kept an anxious eye on him as they made their way back towards the castle.

'Are you sure you're all right, Baldwin? You don't look it.'

'I am fine.' Baldwin sighed. 'Dear God, how could I have been so foolish as to think that the Despenser wouldn't take advantage of my position here? I must have been lunatic.'

'How could you tell he would spread word of this sort?'

'Because I should have realised what sort of man he is! He saw my sword when we were in London. Remember?'

Simon did. Earlier in the year, when they had been to London with Bishop Stapledon of Exeter, they had been invited to a meal with the Despenser, and he had seen Baldwin's sword. On one side, Baldwin had caused a Templar cross to be cut into the blade. It proved nothing, of course. A cross was a cross, and there were only a few tiny indications that showed a cross was Templar and not any other, but that little symbol was enough to damn Baldwin. If his sword was seen by the French king, Baldwin was lost.

'Perhaps Mortimer overplayed the story? It's possible that Despenser doesn't intend to blacken your name.'

Baldwin merely looked at him for a minute.

'Very well. But you are still here under diplomatic protection. No one can arrest you here.'

'Even if that were true, it would still damage the whole embassy were the negotiators on the other side to hear that I

had the reputation of being a renegade Templar.' Baldwin
spat. 'No. I must leave, I think. And immediately. There is
nothing I can do here.'

'But how can you do that?'

'Well, I shall have to see Lord Cromwell and tell him . . .'

'Yes. Tell him what? You cannot tell him the truth, can you,
Baldwin? If he were to hear that you were once a Templar, he
would be duty bound to see you arrested too.'

Baldwin swore under his breath. There was nothing he
could do that was safe.

'Even if you make it back to England, what then?' Simon
said. 'Won't you still be in the same danger there?'

'It is possible,' Baldwin allowed. 'But what else can I do?'

'Stay here, remain with the Queen, and perhaps she can
protect you.'

'I don't think she can . . .'

And that was the rub. If the King of France decided that
there was money or some other advantage to be gained by
destroying Baldwin, he would do so instantly. He was
ruthless, the last of the Capetian line. It was his father who
had utterly broken the Templars, and Charles would be
content to see another Templar burned at the stake. No matter
how much Isabella tried to protect Baldwin, in the end, even
if she desired to, she must succumb to her brother's authority.
Not least because her embassy about Guyenne was so
important.

'I am sure Queen Isabella would protect you,' Simon was
saying earnestly.

It made Baldwin smile to himself. The idea that anyone
could protect a Templar against King Charles IV was so
innocent, so entirely *wrong*, that it was enough to make a man
laugh aloud.

Still, even laughter was a form of defence. If he showed no
fear or concern, it would make any such allegations less

believable. Were he to ride suddenly for the coast, it would surely make him an easy target. A fleeing man in a strange country must be suspicious, and the suspicious would all too often be arrested. Better perhaps to brazen it out, if there were any accusations. So long as he was not forced to lie. To deny his Order would be hard, but to agree that the Templars were evil, that they committed terrible crimes, would be all but impossible.

'What is it?'

'Very well,' Baldwin said. 'I shall remain. We shall do all we can to seek the killer of Paul. Not that there is much we can hope to achieve. We know no one here.'

And it was that thought which occupied his mind as they meandered about the streets of Paris. There was little point in stopping men to question them. There was nobody who had a motive, so far as Baldwin knew, other than the man he had already spoken to. And Mortimer had been convincing. Much though he disliked admitting it even to himself, he found himself instinctively trusting Mortimer. He had seemed rather too much like Baldwin himself a few years ago. Baldwin knew what it was to lose everything; to have position, wealth, even friends and comrades, ripped from him. Mortimer had suffered the same. He even had a death sentence hanging over him, just as Baldwin did.

Yes. Wandering aimlessly around the greatest city in Christendom, Baldwin came to be convinced that Mortimer was more likely than not to be speaking the truth.

It was as he decided to trust the man that Baldwin caught sight of a familiar figure.

Simon saw his eyes narrow. 'What is it?'

Baldwin was frowning ahead. 'That man, there. See him?'

'The executioner from the King's gibbet, isn't he?'

'Not him, no. The slender fellow in the tatty clothes behind him. I think he's the man I saw on the day that the old man was killed and Robert de Chatillon injured. It looks like him.'

'Are you sure?'

'I saw him momentarily – I can't be certain, no, but it definitely looks like him.'

'Then let us catch him, Baldwin,' Simon said.

They moved off after the fellow. Observing him with great care, Baldwin felt convinced that the man was moving with a set purpose, and it was no time before he came to the conclusion that the fellow was himself trailing the executioner.

At this time of the morning, the streets were filled with the noise of the population. It was not a market day, but the shops were doing a brisk trade in bread, cakes, pies and other foodstuffs, and the raucous shouting of wares was deafening.

It was not only their ears which were assaulted, though. The people of Paris enjoyed wearing bright colours, and in the sunlight after the last few days of rain Simon felt as though his eyes were being burned out by the garish clothing worn all about him. And the odours! Poorly tanned leather, sweat-soaked wool, old, slightly rancid linen that had been bleached in fermented urine once too often without being washed properly, and over all the smell of excrement, that pervasive tang that spoke of any city anywhere.

A sumpter horse clopped past, and Simon lost sight of their man for a moment, but then he caught sight of the executioner, and a matter of only two or three paces behind was the man Baldwin had last seen at Poissy. 'Come on, Baldwin!' Simon exclaimed, and darted off again.

The executioner turned left now, and the two saw the stalker's elbow rise beneath his cloak, and then seem to move as though concealing something.

'He's drawn a dagger, Simon,' Baldwin breathed, and then he bellowed: 'EXECUTIONER, 'WARE THAT MAN! SHEATHE YOUR KNIFE, CHURL!'

The executioner turned in surprise, and saw Baldwin, but then he noticed the man who was just a little too close behind him, and saw the blade. He threw himself sideways as the knife slipped by where his belly would have been, and bounced off the wall. In a moment, he had his own knife out, but already the attacker had retreated into the Paris mob. Amidst the screams of women who thought they had witnessed a murder, he bolted up the street.

Simon and Baldwin took off after him, pelting up the cobbles, but in a short time it was obvious that they would not catch him. The throng was too tightly packed in the narrow thoroughfare, and whereas one man could slip from one side to the other, and gradually make headway, two men together could not. Baldwin and Simon tried their hardest, but in a short time had to accept defeat.

'Master, I am indebted to you,' Arnaud said, bending low and introducing himself. 'You saved my life.'

'And you can return the favour by telling me about that man there. Why did he want to kill you?'

Arnaud looked at them over the rim of his cup, sipping slowly.

To Simon's mind, he had the look of a cunning toad. His wide-set eyes were quick and shrewd, and the bailiff instinctively disliked his appearance. A lot of the brutality of his way of life had been scored into his flesh, from the look of his cold, unfeeling expression. There was little enough there to commend him, certainly. And the thought of the number of men he had killed or maimed in his life made him repellent. Simon had the feeling that were he to touch the man, a little of the misery and anguish he had caused over the years would pass on to him.

Baldwin was clearly much less bothered by him. 'So you are called Arnaud? And you are a public executioner?'

'Yes. I punish those the King tells me to. I've been working for the King for many years.'

'But that man? Who was he?'

The executioner snorted and sat back in his seat, shaking his head slowly. 'He is a devil. *The* devil, perhaps. He was a guard at a royal castle with me—'

'Château Gaillard,' Simon said flatly.

'Yes,' Arnaud agreed, his cold eyes going to the bailiff with a measuring assessment. He appeared not to like what he saw, and transferred his gaze to Baldwin. 'I was there too. His name is Jean. Often called Jean de Pamiers. He was a guard at the castle while I was there as the King's gaoler.'

'So you were in charge of the prisoners there?'

'Sort of.'

Simon snapped, 'What does that mean? You were or you weren't.'

'I was mostly responsible for one prisoner.'

'Ah,' said Baldwin. 'And here, I think, we come to the point, don't we?'

'He was intensely jealous of me. I think that's what started to send him mad,' Arnaud said reflectively. 'But it wasn't his fault. You can't imagine what it was like there in that castle over the cliffs, stuck there for month after month, and never a chance of being freed. For me, it wasn't so bad. I am used to such jobs in the King's service, but for men like Jean it was much more difficult.'

'Why?'

'I was allowed to wander, but the other guards were there for a set time, and weren't supposed to consort with the townspeople or anything. But they were men, just like you or me, and they had the need of companionship. Women.'

'You didn't?'

Arnaud looked away. Then he suddenly closed his eyes and

his shoulders began to shake a little. 'I didn't feel the need to leave the castle.'

'What do you mean?' Baldwin asked.

'I fell in love,' Arnaud said simply. 'She was so beautiful, so brave and soft-mannered, it was hardly surprising. She always spoke to me kindly. You know? No one has ever spoken to me like that before,' he added quietly, staring into his cup. After a moment's reflection, he up-ended it and drained it defiantly. 'Yes. I fell in love with the King's wife.'

'Christ's ballocks,' Simon breathed. 'You mean to say you . . .'

'She loved me too. Ach, I couldn't do much for her. When all's said and done, she was used to living with silks and decent beds. What could I do to provide that sort of thing? No, but at least I could make her life a little more comfortable. I found her some sheepskins, some warmer slippers, and an undershift to ease the pain of her rough sackcloth. Oh, and a warm woollen cap to cover her poor head. They'd shorn her of all her hair before she was brought to the prison.'

Simon shook his head. The idea of this fellow pawing at the poor woman was revolting. Simon remembered Montfaucon, with all the corpses lined up on that hideous gibbet, and this man up there among the rotting faces, cutting one down to make room for a fresh hanging. It made him feel sick.

'And she was grateful to you,' Baldwin said.

'I suppose so. Although, maybe it was something else. She was always very polite, very respectful, but all the other men just took the rise out of her. They joked about her, you know, offensively.'

'All of them? You were the only man there who was kind to her, then?' Simon asked sarcastically.

'Simon!' Baldwin hissed. Then, 'What of Jean?'

'He wasn't like the rest. I think he said once he'd lost a

wife. Maybe that made it easier for him to be nice to her. What would she see in him, though, any more'n she'd see something in me? That was why he got jealous.'

'Why?'

'Because her and me, we got close. Used to go there to the cell door and talk to her. She told me all about her life in castles and palaces and that, and I told her a bit about me.'

'Like, "men I have killed"? "Women I have tortured"? "Children I've slaughtered"?' Simon demanded sharply.

Arnaud looked over at him. 'You want to know about the people I've killed? I've killed many. Very many. But where would the law be without the punishments? If you don't have men like me, you don't have the law, and without the law the world is mad. You need me and my kind, master. You think you're so much better than me? You're happy enough to see people sent to the gallows, aren't you? But you just don't want to do that last little job, do you? Actually kill them. You want to know someone's done it for you. I suppose it's like meat. You're happy for a butcher to kill a steer, but you don't want to do it yourself, nor skin it and gut it. You're happy to know that a murderer has been captured, glad to see he's been punished. I dare say you like going to watch him dance his last on the King's evergreen tree, eh? But you hate me because I do it and save you and others the effort. I wouldn't like to think you'd be upset by having to put the rope round the man's neck. That would be *nasty*, wouldn't it?'

'You kill for a living. I am happy to know that the law is upheld and punishments are carried out, but there's a difference between that and enjoying the job.'

'You think I like what I do?' Arnaud stared at him, long and hard. 'Yes. You think I'm a monster because I end lives. But at least I do what I may to ease their ends. I don't leave men to suffer without need.'

'Enough! We are talking about the Château Gaillard,'

Baldwin said. 'This man Jean – what more can you tell us about him? What happened between you and him? Why did he try to attack you?'

'Jealousy. He saw how well I was getting on with my Lady Blanche, and he wanted to have time with her too. But then the orders came.'

'What orders?' Baldwin asked, eyes narrowed.

Arnaud shook his head, staring down at the table. Baldwin beckoned the innkeeper, and soon a fresh pot of ale was placed on their table. 'The King wanted a divorce. At any cost. So he asked that she be proved to have been an adulterer.'

Simon shrugged. 'Why ask you? There must have been others he could turn to who were used to spying, surely.'

Baldwin glanced at him with a face blanched in horror. 'Don't you understand, Simon? The King ordered his wife to be raped so that they could show her adultery in gaol. Whether she had been forced or not, the fact that she had had intercourse would demonstrate that she was no longer chaste and perfect. She could not be queen. Her marriage to the King would have to be annulled.'

'I couldn't let it happen to her, sir. I *couldn't*. I love her. So . . . I told her what had been suggested, and she was glad to . . . to let me. And some months later, there was proof.'

'She was delivered of a child?'

'Our little boy. Yes. He was a lovely little thing, sir. Beautiful, and sweet.'

'Where is he now?'

'He died. Youngsters often do.'

Simon looked away. He had lost his own son to a fever. It still hurt to think of it.

'I had heard that Lady Blanche had taken the veil,' Baldwin agreed. 'But what of that man Jean?'

'He wanted her. He was mad with jealousy, sir. When he

heard that Blanche was with child, he went berserk. And then, later, Blanche was taken away from us all. Ah, God, that was a terrible day. I was driven mad myself. I *love* her, sir. The idea that she was going was bad, but to know that I'd never be able to see her again, that she'd take up the veil at a nunnery, that was just . . . I could hardly bear it. And Jean was worse. He wanted her. So did some of the others. Berengar worse than most.'

'Berengar?'

'One of the other guards. He'd been there since the Queen first arrived. A week or two after she'd gone, he suddenly went insane. He started shouting that there were evil ones all about him, and drew a knife. Well, we were all handy with our weapons, like any man, but when you see a fellow start dribbling and foaming, and then he begins to lay about him with a long blade, well, it's enough to make you stand back and be cautious, you know? So we all stood back, like I say, and our oldest, le Vieux, went to try to calm him down.'

'Le Vieux? The Old Man?'

'Never knew his real name. He was always called that. Anyway, he went in, and was struck down by a knock on his head. Fell like a poleaxed bull. Thump, straight down. And Berengar got the rest of us in a corner and started to stab at us all. He killed three, I think, before running off. I went after him to try to get him – he only scratched my arm here and here.' He pulled up his right sleeve to show two long scars, each four or five inches long, both of them badly healed with thick, ugly stitch marks where the flesh had been pulled together. 'But he got nearly as far as the town. Luckily, he saw some men in a field, and tried to kill them too, and I caught up with him and put him on the ground and cut his throat. Had to do it. At least I was trained in how to do it and end his misery before anyone else was harmed,' he said, staring hard at Simon.

'And Jean?'

'He wasn't in the guard room at that time. When I got back, he'd gone. I think he saw the bodies and just bolted in terror. There's not every man who can cope with a slaughterhouse like that. Luckily I found le Vieux and pulled him out. He was all right after a while, and I was able to get him to a physician and have him seen to. And my own wounds, too. The man I saw was more used to healing calves, though, I reckon,' he said with a rueful grimace before pulling his sleeve back down over the wounds.

'Why would Jean hunt you down here?'

'He had attacked and murdered le Vieux at Poissy already.'

'I thought so. I saw him there with le Vieux.'

Arnaud shrugged. 'I think he is still jealous of me with Blanche. Don't know why he did that to le Vieux.'

'And the other man, Robert de Chatillon. Why would he attack him?'

'Well, Robert de Chatillon was the Comte de Foix's man, and he hired us all to go to the château. Perhaps he blamed him for setting us all there? Or blamed him for allowing the lady to be molested.'

'But you stopped her from being attacked,' Simon said. 'Or so you say.'

Arnaud looked a little shifty. 'I stopped the others from raping her.'

'It was only you did that, then?' Simon noted. He curled his lip. Now he was sure of the facts: the woman had been forced to lie with this man. He raped her alone. Better that, perhaps, than a gang-rape by some number of guards, but for a woman born noble it would be an indignity close to horror. It would be a wonder if her mind hadn't been broken. And her heart.

'You can think what you like. I love her, and I petitioned the Comte to allow me to sleep with her and save her from the others. He agreed. Robert de Chatillon came to tell us all, and perhaps that made Jean even more bloody pissed at me. So he tried to kill me.'

'But why follow you all the way here and try to kill you here?' Baldwin wondered.

'He is a southerner. You can't tell what goes on in their minds half the time.'

'Well, he is free now, and wandering the streets. You must be careful.'

'Baldwin, I do not trust this man at all. Why should that guard come seeking him? Why should he begin a blood feud after this man raped the King's wife? If he did, surely it's because he wanted to stop an executioner raping a noblewoman.'

'You don't trust me? All I've done is walk down the street today, and you had to save me from an assassin. Now I've told you my story, and in return you call me a liar?' Arnaud spat. His face had grown black with anger, and now he set his hand to his dagger's hilt.

'Leave your knife sheathed, Arnaud,' Baldwin said sharply. 'What you say is fair – but so is what my companion said. How can we confirm your words, bearing in mind we shall need to decide how to respond?'

'Ask Robert de Chatillon. He can confirm it all. He was the man who relayed our orders to us and paid us. Or don't you trust the knight who gave us our instructions either?' he finished snidely, looking at Simon with contempt. 'Look at me! I have only ever obeyed my betters when they commanded me to do their work. Yet you look down on me because I was obedient. Well, in this case, I followed my heart. I love that lady and would do nothing to harm her. That is why I did what I did. You think I polluted her? Blame those who are in power, who commanded all the guards to rape her. It wasn't my doing. I saved her from that.'

Chapter Thirty-Three

Baldwin was feeling distinctly waspish. It was partly Simon's distant rudeness that had made him throw a whole *livre tournois* at the man as he stood and stalked from the room, ashamed of his friend, himself and his all too ready dislike for the man. After all, as Arnaud had pointed out so cogently, if he did not perform his function, some other man must do it. There was no point in dislike of the functionary. It was the reality, whether he liked it or not, of the way of all societies.

To an extent, he recognised that his anger with Simon in that little alehouse had been a reflection of his anger at his own feelings. In his case, he knew that it had come from the knowledge that the man sitting there in front of him, drinking his ale, had been exactly the sort of man who would have tortured his comrades and hanged a number, or burned them at the stake. The thought was repellent. To be seated at the same table was worse: the idea that he could consort with one of the men who had helped to destroy his friends and comrades was enough to bring a tear to his eye.

He waited outside for Simon, and couldn't help but snap grumpily, 'What makes you think that you have some right to question him? He gave us a lot of information that he need not. In some ways he condemned himself.'

'Baldwin, look at the man. I wouldn't trust a word he said.'

'His comments about looking down on a man who takes life legally were close to the truth, weren't they?' Baldwin said. 'I cannot think how many men I have ordered to be executed over the years, and yet I feel justified in despising him for carrying out the orders of men like *me*! How can I be so hypocritical?'

'It is easy. You and I can command a man's life to be ended, and we can send men to the gallows, but the man who turns them off the ladders to die does not need to enjoy the task. Did you see his face up at Montfaucon? He liked those corpses. He is a sick man, Baldwin. His mind is warped and twisted. I trust him not at all.'

'Before you make judgements about him, bear in mind that those who do such jobs will often be hardened. They have to be to continue causing such suffering. They drink themselves to oblivion before each execution, and then, afterwards, hope to forget. What you see as pleasure may be no more than a front to protect himself. A carapace that he uses to conceal his own horror.'

Simon looked at his friend. 'You think so? I do not, and I have a good record of seeing into men's hearts.'

'Well, while we are here still, let us return to Robert de Chatillon to ask him, as Arnaud suggested. If he verifies Arnaud's story, perhaps that would also explain a little about Enguerrand's death. If this guard felt that the orders coming from Enguerrand were detrimental to the lady in the prison, and he did adore her, as Arnaud hinted, perhaps this fellow was following Enguerrand and killed him too?'

Robert de Chatillon was not gracious when he saw who it was who had returned. 'Am I to have no peace today?'

'Perhaps you will shortly,' Baldwin said. He perched on the edge of a small table. 'We have been talking to one of your men.'

'My men? Who, one of the servants?'

'No,' Simon said. 'The executioner. Arnaud.'

Robert twisted his face into a grimace. 'What on earth did you want to talk to him for? I find the stench of noisome body fluids tends to follow him around a little too closely for my liking.'

That was a sentiment with which Simon concurred only too heartily, Baldwin knew, so he broke in quickly. 'Arnaud made several allegations: that Enguerrand de Foix was responsible for all the guards at the Château Gaillard, that there was a specific order relating to the woman held there, that Arnaud himself persuaded de Foix to allow him to be responsible for carrying out this, um, order, and that there was a kind of mutiny there. Is it all true?'

'You have hardly been specific enough for me to say whether it's accurate or not. I can tell you this, though. The man Arnaud was there. My comte did hire the guards for the castle, most of them from the south or somewhere. As to the orders about the – ah – lady . . . I do not know that you need to worry yourself about them.'

'Is it true, then, that it was ordered that she should be raped?'

'It is true,' Robert said, fiddling with a pot of sand on his desk, 'that proof was required that she had been guilty of adultery. Obviously it would be unthinkable that a queen could reign with our king if her honour was questionable.'

'So it is true, then,' Baldwin said coldly.

'If you wish to think it so,' Robert said. He would not meet Baldwin's eye, and instead seemed to find the sand pot astonishingly fascinating.

'Is it also true that all the men were chosen by the Comte?' Baldwin asked. There was something about this that made little sense to him.

'I believe he may have had a part in selecting them. I couldn't say how far he was involved in the choice of the men.'

'Who was, then? You?'

'Me? Do I look the kind of man who would sink to choosing the guards for a castle dungeon? I may not be so senior a nobleman as you, *sieur*, but I have not sunk so low as to hand select staff for that sort of position.'

'Then who did?'

'I do not know. I have heard that it was Arnaud himself. Well, a man used to living amongst the dregs of society, it's not surprising.'

'You are saying that your master, Comte Enguerrand de Foix, asked Arnaud to seek out the guards for the château, and then used these miserable creatures to staff the place and guard the Queen? And then he ordered them to rape her so that her infidelity could be in no doubt?'

'I think that sums it up well enough.'

'And the man who was killed when you were injured. Who was he?'

'I only ever knew him as "le Vieux". He was an old warrior who'd served in the King's host a few times. It is said that it was he who, with Arnaud, picked the men individually.'

'But why should he be willing to do so?' Simon asked. 'What would it benefit the Comte to get together a band of men, and then have them rape the Queen?'

'Politics is a dangerous game,' Baldwin said, watching Robert closely. 'If the King asked him as a favour, you can all too easily imagine the eagerness with which the Comte would have set about his task. And Arnaud was surely a most enthusiastic ally. If the Comte had been asked to assist the King, he would have agreed in a hurry, just as any number of friends of King Edward and the Despenser will rush to their aid, in the hope of great rewards to come. There is nothing surprising in that, surely. And yet the act itself was so shocking that . . .'

'That the idea that it should ever come to light is deeply concerning,' Robert said, still avoiding their gaze.

'So the King would prefer never to hear that news of this has been spread about.' Simon gave a twisted grin. 'I can understand that. It would be a little embarrassing for any man to have it known that he would willingly subject his own wife to multiple rapes, just to help him end the marriage.'

'You think that the King entered on this scheme easily? My master was as reluctant as any noble knight would be to put this plan into effect, but when a king is as desperate as Charles must be to produce an heir, what will he not do? What must he not do to be married and raising sons?'

'Did your Comte meet the King himself?'

Baldwin's question seemed to calm Robert a little. He shrugged and slumped back in his seat, wincing as his rib shifted. 'No. It was his trusted adviser who suggested it. It was a good plot, after all. She was already guilty. We know that from the confessions.'

'This was the confessions of those who were accused of adultery with the two princesses?' Baldwin said. 'The D'Alnay brothers? They were tortured, I recall.'

'Perhaps so. But the princesses both confessed too, and they were not tortured. No, the men were guilty, as were the women. There is no doubt about that. So Lady Blanche was already shown to have committed the offence. All the King wanted was to have proof – after all, if the Pope was granted incontrovertible evidence that she was guilty of adultery, he could have no objection to annulling the marriage. As did happen. The King and Blanche were divorced three years ago, and now she has been sent to Maubisson. She's taken the veil.'

'And the child?' Simon asked with deceptive gentleness.

'What of it?'

Baldwin thrust out an arm and gripped Simon's forearm

even as Simon began to move forward. He adored his children, and the thought that any man could consider the life of a child so unimportant as to merit little if any consideration was enough to drive him into an almost blind rage.

'Robert,' Baldwin said, 'do you mean to tell me that all the guards were killed apart from these three – Arnaud, the old man who is now dead, and the other fellow, the one who killed him?'

'Yes. So I understand.'

'That is intriguing,' Baldwin said, 'and a little alarming for you, of course.'

'Why me?'

'Well, this man called Jean, who killed your old guard at Poissy, is here today. He tried to kill Arnaud. It was our intervention which saved Arnaud's life. But I do not understand all this. Arnaud told us that the guards were all killed by some fellow called Berengar. Yet now this other guard has turned up and is trying to kill the other men involved.'

'What of it?'

'Perhaps nothing, but I should be worried, if I were you. After all, the guards are all dead bar two, who seem keen to end the lives of each other; the man who commanded this plot was Enguerrand, and he is dead. Perhaps all those who have had any involvement in the plan are to be removed.'

'Oh, that would only be—'

Robert was suddenly silent.

'Only be whom? Perhaps only the guards, eh?' Baldwin smiled wolfishly. 'Aha! Yes! Arnaud picked the guards himself, didn't he? An executioner and a gaoler sent to select gaolers for a disgraced princess. Who better than the dregs of society? After all, it would be likely that one of them would try to rape her anyway, without any intervention. So much less embarrassing. And then, because they are all criminals from the gaols of France, they can be dispersed, returned to

their gaols ... oh, but that is not what you meant, is it?'
Baldwin's tone hardened as he took in the full meaning of
Robert's words. 'You meant that they could be removed
permanently, didn't you? They were never going to be
released, were they, these poor devils who aided you so much.
They were to be gaolers for a little while, until they con-
veniently raped Blanche for you, and then they could be
removed and killed and forgotten. The King would not like it
to become known that he had conspired to have his wife
treated in such a manner, after all. So he arranged it in a way
that ensured that all evidence could later be destroyed. Isn't
that it?'

'I believe so.'

'Be very afraid, then. Because if Jean has learned or
guessed this, your life will become worthless. He will seek
you out and kill you too.'

Simon had been silent, but now he smiled kindly, and
Robert thought for a moment that he was going to offer some
comfort. But no.

'It is worse than that, Robert. If Jean could guess that you
would seek to kill all those in the castle, do you not think
Arnaud would also guess?'

'He was to do it,' Robert said scathingly. 'You think he'd
be worried? He is an executioner.'

'Yes. And yet I wonder how long it would have been before
he realised that of all those who were actively involved, one
man would still remain. Himself. And there is only one man
alive who knows the full chain of command. You. For his own
defence, if he is sensible, he must kill you. And I did think
him very sensible.'

Jean had no idea who the two men had been, but he had
cursed them roundly, their parents, their children to the third
generation, and still his anger knew no bounds. Whatever

may have happened, if only he had been able to kill Arnaud, he would have felt fulfilled.

He damned the day he was selected by the bastard. Down in Bishop Fournier's gaol, where he had been installed after his spirited – overspirited – defence of the poor devils burned on their pyres, declaring them to have stronger religious faith than Jacques Fournier himself. His words had been overheard by a zealous servant of Fournier, of course. There were spies everywhere in those days. So Jean had been hauled off to gaol, and there he would have remained for months, if not years, had not Arnaud made his surprising offer.

'My master remembers you. Weren't you with the host that travelled to the field of the Golden Spurs? To Courtrai?'

He agreed, nodding. 'My father and brother died there in the service of the King and Comte Robert de Foix.'

'That same comte's son remembers you. He wishes to reward you. Be ready, and when I return, you will fly this coop.'

Jean had nodded, but did not believe him. He had seen the woman being left to die hideously on the pyre instead of being granted the kindness of a rope about her neck first. He did not trust Arnaud.

But the executioner had been as good as his word. When he came back, he carried a tunic and a new cloak, hood and cowl, together with a good leather belt and a dagger. 'Best I can do,' he had explained apologetically, pointing to the roughly sewn star at the breast. The yellow star of a heretic.

Jean cared nothing. He grabbed the clothes and pulled them on, overjoyed to feel the weight of a dagger at his hip once more. Then, quietly, the two men walked out of the gaol, up the stairs, along a passageway, and finally out into the sunshine.

Arnaud walked like a man with the power to have a man

sent to the gaol, and none of the guards troubled him. In the courtyard there were two horses waiting, and Arnaud went to the first, a gentle-faced mare. He set his foot in the stirrup, and then hoisted himself upwards.

It had been the most embarrassing moment of Jean's life, having to confess that he had never sat upon a horse.

Arnaud had soon introduced him to le Vieux, and Jean had thought the old man the perfect example of a lower-ranking man-at-arms in the King's host. He even went so far as to run through his memories of men in the host he had accompanied to Courtrai, thinking that le Vieux must be a comrade-in-arms from that earlier war, but without success. No, le Vieux was just one of those men who was so archetypical of the kind of warrior the King sought to keep that he appeared familiar.

'Another one, eh?' he'd said as he caught sight of Jean and Arnaud. 'What were you in gaol for?'

'I said that two folks the bishop burned were better Christians than him.'

'Do you still think that?'

Jean cast a sidelong glance at Arnaud. *Merde!* It was possible that the wrong thing said now could have him returned straight to gaol. But Arnaud must know what he had been thrown in gaol for. There was little point trying to hide it. 'Have you seen Bishop Fournier?'

Le Vieux stared at him for at least five beats of his heart, and then, to Jean's relief, he began to chuckle, loud and long. 'You'll do for me, boy.'

It had been the beginning of a companionable friendship, so Jean had thought. Le Vieux seemed to look on him as a slightly wayward apprentice. It didn't matter that Jean was already almost thirty years old; in the opinion of the ancient warrior, he was a mere stripling. When there was any duty to be performed, le Vieux would help him with advice or would actually knuckle down and assist him. More than he would with any of the others, anyway. Men like Berengar he ignored. They didn't deserve more than occasional comments or harsh bellows. And sometimes the threat of the lash.

He hadn't been like that with Jean. Le Vieux seemed to think, after that first encounter, that there was more to Jean than he would have guessed. It must have been his defiant first comment. That and the fact that Jean had stood up to the bishop. There were not too many people who would repeat derogatory comments about a man like Jacques Fournier in front of him, and fewer still who would then challenge a man to deny them even after spending time in his gaol. That was what made le Vieux and him get on: the way that Jean was prepared to stick to what he believed.

Le Vieux admired that. Possibly because he believed in nothing himself. Except the Comte de Foix, of course.

Chapter Thirty-Four

Philip and Adam had tried to find Ricard, but the man was nowhere to be seen. It was Adam's belief that Janin had already found him somewhere, and the pair of them had decided to have no part in any attack on the blasted bodhran player.

'Doesn't matter,' Philip said. 'We can do it ourselves. Why do we need any help? There's two of us.'

'Yes,' Adam agreed, unconvinced.

'Wait until he turns up in our room, and we can jump him. Just slide a knife in him, and he'll be quiet enough for good.'

'Yes,' Adam said, more quietly.

But he reflected that Philip was a large man. When it came to subduing Jack, Philip should be able to do that with a hand behind his back. And just now, Philip looked as happy to break Adam's neck as Jack's, were Adam to raise any more objections. Soon the pair of them were waiting in the musicians' room. They knew that Jack often slept in there after a light lunch, which seemed only fair since he appeared to spend so much of his evenings and nights out wandering about the place.

'Where *does* he go?' Adam wondered, shifting his leg as it started to go to sleep. Philip wouldn't let him stand or move about in case it warned Jack as he approached the chamber.

'At night, you mean? He says he's got a woman, doesn't he?' Philip said. He was not convinced. 'That man in London said he was spying on the Queen. I think he was telling the truth there. Jack's dangerous.'

'So you do think he's a Despenser man? That evil bastard! Christ alone knows what Despenser will do with anything he can learn about her, poor lady. She is always kind to us.'

'Yes. Now shut up! Do you want him to hear you?'

Adam was silent for a moment. 'Why'd he want us here, though? If he was going to kill Peter to get a place with us, so he was going to be here in any case, why would he need to tell us he was going to spy?'

'Perhaps he's not so stupid as some,' Philip grated. 'Now shut up!'

'Well, it makes little sense to me, that's all I'm saying. Mind you, I never trusted him. Always dodgy, I thought.'

'*Hush!*' Philip had stiffened, and now he stretched his neck, head to one side, listening intently. 'Someone's coming!'

'Oh. Oh, *shit!*' Adam said mournfully. 'I've never—'

'Shut up, or I'll kill you myself!' Philip hissed.

Steps outside in the passageway. Not one pair, though; it was two men. One was familiar, and Philip was convinced that it was Jack – he recognised that pause between each footfall, while the arrogant prickle swaggered like a man-at-arms. The other, though, was unfamiliar. It wasn't Janin or Ricard, he was sure enough of that. But no one else tended to come up here where the musicians had their room. Who on—

The door was thrown wide, and Jack walked in quickly, another man behind him moving to Philip's right as soon as the two men were inside. Neither had knife or sword at the ready, but neither seemed to think they were necessary.

'Ah, Philip. My old friend. I think you have met my companion? He told me you would be here. He's come to help us. I told you the Queen was in danger, and he's heard the same. So there're going to be more of us to keep an eye on things. That'll be nice to know, won't it?'

And he smiled easily at them both. Not that they were looking at him. They were staring at his companion.

The man from the glover's house.

The Queen was in her room when de Bouden tapped on the door. She looked up from her book, and seeing him, she closed it gently as he bent in an elaborate bow.

'There is much sense in books like this, William.'

'My lady?' He peered closely. It was a great book bound in white leather, which he recognised immediately. The Queen was well known to be fascinated with the stories of King Arthur. No man could be in her presence for even a short while without sensing her attraction to the stories of the old English king.

'I have another book. Do you know the story of Aimeri de Narbonne?'

'I fear I have not had the pleasure of hearing it,' he said, hoping that soon she might tell him to stand straight again. His back was beginning to complain.

'Lady Ermengarde, Aimeri's wife, complained when he decided to send his sons out into the world to seek their fame and fortune. She couldn't bear to lose all her children. Yet children have to grow up, don't they, William?'

'Why, yes, Majesty.'

'Even my boys will become men some day. Edward is close to adulthood already.'

'Um. Yes.'

'The thing is, because she complained, Aimeri beat her. And you know what she did? She prayed to God to bless him and his arm for so sensibly bringing her back to reason. Naturally she was only a woman and mustn't question her husband's decision. She even asked him to beat her more so that she could be reminded of her place. What do you think of that, William?'

He had not been her clerk and comptroller for years without seeing the danger of responding. Instead, indicating with an inarticulate mutter that his back was giving him gip, he waited.

'Oh, stand up straight, William. Staying bent like that will break your back. Well, I think that the man who wrote that story was a fool. If he seriously thought that a woman would make a comment like that when her man was beating her, he had no brain whatever. She was being sarcastic. Does a woman have no say in how a man may treat her sons? Even if she is noble-born herself?'

William gave a wary smile. 'Your Majesty, you have to understand that the man has the responsibility for protecting the family and seeing to it that his sons can make their mark in the world. If he did not seek to ensure that the sons would forge their own way, the wife might make them stay at home, and that would not help them to honour God with their great deeds, would it?'

'You think that all women merely want to cosset their little boys? I would endeavour to look after my youngsters, and that is quite right. It is the duty of a woman to be maternal. But to suggest that she would willingly acquiesce when he beat her . . . it is obscene.'

'The Lady Ermengarde would see that her punishment fitted her offence. A woman should not question her man's decisions, after all. A wife should honour and obey her husband.'

'You think so?'

'While he is in his right mind, your highness.'

She gave a short grin, as cynical and unhappy as any he had ever seen on her face. 'Well, as the daughter of a king, married to another king, I would protect my children against any threat I perceived, and would not willy-nilly obey a foolish command. Nor would I submit to being beaten. *Never!*'

William had never seen her quite so discomposed. It was natural for her to be upset on occasion, and he had seen her in tears before, when her husband had snubbed her, ignored her, or simply behaved as though she was no more important than one of the servants in his kitchens. That was normal enough. This, though, this was different.

'Your highness?'

'I wish to meet him again.'

'Who?'

She looked at him very directly. There was no one else in the room, other than her blonde maid, Alicia. 'You know. The Peacock.'

His heart sank. It was days since he had last been told to find Mortimer and deliver a message. 'Your Majesty, that would be rather dangerous now. Have you heard of the man killed out at the front of the castle?'

'Do you think me deaf and stupid? Of course I have heard. It was a man-at-arms, Sir Charles's servant, wasn't it? So what?'

'The man was hunting the Peacock. He and Sir Charles were intending to bring him to bay and capture him so that they could take his head to the King.'

'How foolish. It would take more than two men to do that. The Peacock is a wary fighter. As that man has learned, I suppose.'

'But how can I bring him here to you again? Before, it was easier. Now there will be men all over the place, trying to ensure your safety. If I bring him here, there will be many who will seek to kill him,' William protested. 'The knights are all men who desire money, your highness. They will be keen to catch him and show their devotion to the King by executing him. He is a traitor, after all. And Sir Charles will egg them on. From all I've heard, he is most anxious to have revenge on the man who killed his man-at-arms.'

'You will speak to the Peacock and arrange for him to meet me here this evening as dark falls. Do this for me.'

'Your highness,' he agreed miserably.

Sir Charles had left the chapel a little while before, just as all the servants were making their way to the hall for their lunchtime meal, but he didn't follow them. He was not even remotely hungry. The idea of food did not occur to him. There was nothing he desired. All his attention was fixed upon the one aim: finding the man who had killed his servant and seeing him die.

There was no doubt in his mind who was responsible. Roger Mortimer had realised that Paul was following him, and had killed him. No one else could have wanted him dead. So Sir Charles would see Mortimer sent on his way to hell, and would take his head himself.

Mortimer must have plenty of men of his own in the area, to have been able to catch Paul. Paul had been badly beaten up, and so surely the traitor must have had many fellows at his back. Otherwise, Paul would have been able to defend himself. Sir Charles had little doubt about that. Paul had been an excellent fighter.

Yes, a good fighter. Sir Charles had seen him in one battle defend himself against three men, and he despatched them quickly when he saw that some other scrote was trying to make off with his horse as he fought. Then there was that time in the tavern here in France. A lad had stumbled over Sir Charles's foot, hurting his toe, and as a result they'd been drawn into a fight with a whole group of peasants. It was Paul who killed most of them, another man they only met that day killed one more, and when they left the inn it was Paul who remembered the boy who'd started all the trouble, and went back to kill him too. He would not leave unfinished business, Paul. An excellent man-at-arms. The best squire Sir Charles had ever had.

'Christ's pain, but I miss him!' he moaned. He was in a corridor in the main castle – but he didn't know how he'd reached it. He must have been walking in a dream. Christ's bones, but that was worrying. If he could wander about like that, not even paying attention to his surroundings, then he was in a worse state than he had already thought. He needed to concentrate, to keep his mind set on his purpose. There was no earthly point in his finding Mortimer, only to be slain by the bastard because he was distracted from the task at hand. That way lay death.

'Sir Charles. I was sorry to hear about your man. I know you'd been with him for a long time, eh?'

It was Sir Peter de Lymesey. The tall knight stood nearby, peering over at Sir Charles with his slightly hooded eyes, much like a hawk. He was not a demonstrative man. More a knight who would do anything he needed to protect himself. Someone who might help for money, too, Sir Charles thought suddenly. As was Sir John de Sapy. And both could fight well. They'd proved that over the years.

If he was to attempt to capture and kill Mortimer, he would need men capable of fighting.

'Sir Peter, I have a proposal for you.'

Philip and Adam walked into the bar area with feet that felt like lead.

'There you are,' Janin said cheerily. 'Want some ale?'

'He told me what you were planning,' Ricard said sourly. 'Are you both mad? If we couldn't jump him all together, how in God's name did you think you'd be able to—'

'We weren't going to just jump him. We were going to

knock him on the head once and for all,' Philip admitted.

'So you were going to waylay him and stab him to death? Here in the castle with the whole of the Queen's retinue on hand? Ingenious!' Ricard said witheringly.

'Trouble was, he turned up with some other bastard in tow. The two together made it impossible.'

'How so, Philip? And you so brave!' Janin said lightly.

'He said someone warned them. Who knew? Only *you*!' Philip snarled.

He reached across the table to grasp Janin's shirt, but missed as Janin leaned back, and then, while Philip was still across the table, Janin gripped his outstretched fist and laid the point of his little knife at Philip's throat. 'Don't try to hit me, Philip. I really don't like it.'

'Let go of me!'

Suddenly there was a loud wail. All of them had forgotten Charlie, but now he crouched in the corner of the room, his ball forgotten as he stared at Janin and Philip with eyes full of terror.

'Shite! You bastards cool down,' Ricard said, and went to the lad.

Janin nodded, and held on a moment longer, his eyes fixed on Philip's, but then he pushed the man's hand away.

Ricard took up Charlie, cuddling him close, pressing the lad's head into his shoulder with a face that was torn with grief. 'Are you two mad? Are you all going lunatic? What is all this, eh? We're musicians, not brawlers in a tavern. We're mates, aren't we? We're the *Queen's Men,* in Christ's name! What are you two doing? Look how little Charlie boy reacts when you do that, will you? He's had enough grief, hasn't he?'

'It's partly because of him,' Philip said.

'What are you on about?'

'The man with Jack. It was the man from *his* house in

London,' Philip said with a nod towards the boy. 'Your friend, the man who suggested we should come here with the Queen. He was there, with Jack. Jack is his man.'

'We knew that. He had the mark of the bloody peacock, didn't he?' Ricard snapped. 'What of it?'

'I want to know who he is. But I want to know who told him we'd be looking to get Jack, too. Jack said his friend knew we'd be there. So who told him, eh, Janin?'

'Not me,' Janin declared. 'Did you discuss killing Jack in the street? In a tavern? Where?'

'In the quiet. We're not stupid!'

'Well, I told only Ricard, no one else. Why'd we want to go to the man who got us into this mess? You must have been overheard by someone.'

'Look, I'm sorry, I know you don't want me to say it, but that man is responsible for Peter's death,' Adam said. 'I never liked Jack, but you wouldn't listen to me.'

'Oh, shut up, you prickle! You were the one who demanded that we should take him on, and don't ballock about it now. It's your fault he's here!' Janin said.

'Me? I never—'

'Adam, just belt up or I'll shut you up myself,' Ricard snapped. 'Christ Jesus! I've had enough of this! You lot had best calm yourselves and remind yourselves who it is who pays your upkeep while we're here. Just leave Jack alone, and we can play our music. It's what we're here for.'

'But what if he's here to try to kill the Queen?' Adam said. 'We know he wants to spy on her. What if it's more serious than that?'

'Oh, for God's sake!' Janin said. 'What on earth makes you think that?'

'If he killed the man last night, there's no knowing who else he might kill,' Adam said, wide-eyed and earnest. 'He's a madman, a murderer. For God's sake, if we *don't* tell her, what'll she think if he's caught red-handed? She'll have us all hanged for his crimes. You want that? I certainly don't.'

'Then what do you propose we should do?' Ricard demanded sourly. 'Run away?'

'At least try to tell her. Tell her comptroller, or someone, so we can show we did our best to warn her before the next man dies. All we have to do is say that he's been off walking about the place when someone died. That fellow last night. Jack wasn't in his bed when he was killed. Let's just tell the comptroller. If he doesn't tell the Queen, then it's his fault, not ours.'

Chapter Thirty-Five

Baldwin and Simon returned to the castle a short while after lunch had been served, but Simon managed to find a sergeant-cook and acquire some bread and a small cheese. These he and Baldwin shared out in the court, for the day was growing warm, with a clear sky and the sun shining as though it was summer already.

'Sir Baldwin – I am glad to see you again.'

Baldwin looked up to find himself being studied by Earl Edmund of Kent. The sight was not appealing. The Earl was not the keenest mind in the realm, and had attempted to plot the removal of Despenser earlier in the year. In the event, the Despenser had triumphed, as he tended to. Sir Hugh le Despenser had a sharp mind and a committed, absolute ruthlessness. It was that facet of his nature that made him such a dangerous foe. Earl Edmund detested him for his lackadaisical response when the former had been in charge of the King's men in Guyenne the previous year, and Despenser had been responsible for support and resupply. He still blamed Despenser for the speed with which the Agenais was overrun.

He gathered his thoughts. 'My lord earl, it is good to see you again. What makes you travel all this way?'

'It is always good to be reminded of one's inadequacy. I think that is why I'm here. There were messages to be given to the Lord John Cromwell, and someone had to bring them. I confess, the idea of leaving England's unhappy shores was appealing.'

'I can understand that,' Baldwin said. 'It must be very difficult for you.'

'You can have no idea! Bloody Despenser rules all now.'

Baldwin and Simon exchanged a glance. The man's voice dripped with poison.

'Still, I suppose the truce is holding for the time being?' the cad asked.

'Oh, yes. We hope it will not be too long before we can pack our belongings and set off homewards again.'

'I hope so. The King is keen to have the embassy finished and returned to our shores. I think he is unhappy because of the cost of maintaining this mission. It is an extravagant expense, but then, I told him, the lands we're talking about are worth more than England. It is worth being a little extravagant to win them back.'

'Of course.'

'Not that the idea pleases Despenser, of course. But nothing much does.'

Baldwin said cautiously, 'I suppose he must be careful of not over-stretching the King's budget.'

'More likely he's nervous that the King will be told to hie him over here. If that happens,' he continued, scratching at his nose pensively, 'Despenser will have a fit of the vapours, I think. The idea of being left alone in England with all those nice, gentle barons whom he has insulted, denigrated and downtrodden for the last three or four years would make him anxious as hell, I'd imagine.'

Baldwin and Simon said nothing. This was the sort of dangerous conversation that could cost a man his livelihood, family, lands, wealth and life.

The Earl sniffed absently, gazing about him. 'My sister-in-law – is she about here somewhere? I suppose I ought to make my compliments to her. How has she been?'

'She has her own rooms. Would you like me to show you to her?' Baldwin asked.

'No. For a little I should enjoy a chance to wander about here in wanton idleness. I find that I am good at being idle. There are skills even for men such as me. You didn't say how she was?'

'I am sure she is well enough, but she will be grateful to see a friendly face.'

'Mine? Perhaps. Why, have you heard her say anything about me?'

There was a sudden abrupt sharpness to the question that somewhat surprised Baldwin. He shook his head. 'No, but you are known to be a sensible, rational man, my lord earl. And I know that you and she are on cordial terms. She does not blame you for any of her loss of fortune in the last months, does she?'

'No, thanks to God. She is a good, sensible woman. Always found her so, anyway. Has she had any setbacks?'

'The course of negotiations has been so fast that we have been able to study every cobble in this yard in some detail,' Simon said.

'Ah. So the King is right to be concerned about the length of time spent here and the cost of maintaining this embassy. Anything else giving you trouble here?'

'We have had some incidents. A French comte, Enguerrand de Foix, was killed one night,' Baldwin said slowly. There was no need to mention his own proximity at that death. 'We don't know who did it, but I should think that some outlaw saw him late at night and took a fancy to his purse or something. Then another man was killed, again a Frenchman killed by a countryman. But last night, more seriously, a man-at-arms was murdered just outside the gate there. He was the servant of Sir Charles.'

'In truth? Gracious heaven, you have been enjoying a

small glut of murders in this fair land, then. And now, if you will excuse me, I think I have an urgent need for some ale in my belly. Is the buttery through here?'

'Yes, my lord,'

'There is a man here, a musician called Jack. Tallish, skinny, has an Irish accent. He's gone to deliver my bags to my chamber. If you see him, tell him where to find me, eh? He'll be wearing the Queen's tabard – he's one of her musicians – so shouldn't be hard to see.'

'Of course, my lord,' Baldwin said, and then watched as the brother of the King made his way to the hall's entrance, and ducked inside.

Simon pursed his lips. 'So things improve not at all back at home.'

'So it would seem. I have to admit, Simon, I would give much to have my wife and family here in France with us now. It is a country where a man could make a good life for himself.'

Simon looked at him in surprise. 'You think so? You wouldn't consider finding a lord over here, would you?'

'There are times when the thought of returning to England fills me with sadness, Simon. The idea of going somewhere where—'

'Isn't that one of the musicians?' Simon interrupted. 'Perhaps it's the man Earl Edmund meant?'

Baldwin followed his pointing finger and saw a tall man stalking off towards the Queen's chambers. 'I'm not going to run after him now,' he said. 'We can tell him when he returns.'

Ricard was reluctant to go straight to de Bouden. 'We don't know anything, really. What can we say?'

'Just that Jack is suspicious, and that you suspect not only him, but his friend too. Don't have to say anything about him,' Philip said. 'Only that he is a stranger, and friend to Jack, so probably as dangerous.'

'As dangerous,' Ricard repeated to himself as he made his way on leaden legs to the comptroller's chamber, holding the hand of little Charlie. They were close to the Queen's own rooms, and he glanced towards them with a sense that his whole life was unravelling. He felt really pathetic about being sent to talk to her most senior clerk like this. It was demeaning. He wasn't some magnificent lord or anything, but he had always been in control of his own life, and had known that there was a little place in the world that was perfectly Ricard-shaped. Now, though, he was sensing that his space was growing ever more constricted. There might be room for him for a little longer, but he reckoned that soon he'd be squeezed out. Pop! And there'd be no more Ricard. Not the way things were going just now.

Gloomily he rapped sharply on the door, hoping that there would be no answer, and was relieved when there was no response. De Bouden was always curt and sharp with his 'Come in!' but now there was no sound. More confidently, he knocked again, and was about to turn and leave when he heard something from inside. It sounded like a door closing.

'Master?' he called.

There was silence for a moment, and he was aware of little Charlie looking up at him with those big blue eyes of his. Trusting, always hopeful. And then a quiet voice called 'Yes?'

Grimacing, he turned the great ring to lift the latch inside. 'Hello?' he said.

There was no light in the room, but there was the scent of a recently snuffed candle, and he was sure that there was a figure at the wall, not far from the shuttered window. A tallish, muscular man, from the look of him. Certainly not de Bouden.

'What do you want?'

'I was looking for William de Bouden. I have a message for him.'

'He has gone for a few moments. I think it would be best if you were to go as well. You don't want to be here.'

'Who are you? What are you doing in here?' Ricard said. His confidence was growing. This man shouldn't be here, he felt. The quiet tone, his remaining in darkness, both spoke of his need for secrecy. There was something about the darkness in the room that was intimidating. Not scary, but definitely intimidating, yes. Charlie was tugging backwards, away from the room, and Ricard could hear him moaning quietly. It was enough to break any spell. He took a sharp step backwards, out of the room, and instantly that sly little Irish voice was there behind him.

'Ricard, ah, and I'm glad to see you here. You'll not be wanting to stay, though.'

'Jack,' Ricard spat, startled. He moved further away from the door until he was at the entrance to a narrow, corridor-like alley, which led to the Queen's chamber. Automatically, he moved into it, away from Jack. 'I was sent here because of you.'

'Me? And why would I want to be here, then?'

'We know that you're an enemy of the Queen. You have had something to do with the murders, haven't you?'

'Me? The thought!'

'Not just here, either. You helped kill the glover and his wife in London, didn't you? I dare say you killed Peter too.'

Jack glanced back towards the man in the room as though seeking approval of something. Ricard found himself peering in the same direction, but although the fellow had approached the door, Ricard still couldn't make out his features. He had a niggling suspicion that he ought to recognise him; he was sure that the man was vaguely familiar, but the face stubbornly refused to come to his mind. And then he suddenly felt himself in danger. He had accused a murderer of his crimes, and there was no one else here to protect him except an accomplice.

'Sweet Mother of God,' he muttered to himself. The man in the room was moving towards him now, and when he looked back at Jack he saw that the bodhran player was smiling as he too came nearer. It seemed to him that Jack's face was full of menace. When he smiled, it touched his lips alone. It never even approached his eyes.

Charlie was pulling away. Ricard gripped his hand and retreated down the narrow corridor, never letting his gaze leave the others. He was tempted to turn and fly, but then he saw that Jack's attention was gone from him.

'Musician? What in God's name are you doing here?' de Bouden demanded.

Sir John de Sapy was not the brightest man in the King's household. He had been a loyal supporter of Earl Thomas of Lancaster before the Earl had shown himself to be the King's enemy, and then the King had caught him and had him executed like a common felon, him and hundreds of his supporters from all over the country, barons, knights and commoners. Not Sir John, though.

There were others like him. Peter de Lymesey was another in the same mould. A man who was not noted for his politeness or intellect, yet when he had been found in the camp of the Earl of Lancaster he had been enabled to regain his honour in the King's service.

At times Sir Charles had been happy to denigrate them both, because he had always known himself to be superior. And then, more recently, he had begun to wonder. After all, if they were so stupid, what where they doing in the King's entourage? And then he had realised the simple truth: they were exactly that – dull-witted supporters who were no threat to the King – or his favourite.

Sir Hugh le Despenser was avaricious, yes. And a murderous, thieving devil who'd kill you to steal your teeth if he could see a potential advantage. But he was not an idiot. He liked to have strong men about him and the King, it was true, but he was also very keen that he should be the first among them. So he always sought out those who were less intellectually able than himself.

Sir Charles could smile at that thought, even now. So Despenser viewed Sir Charles as a fool, then? A man in the same mould as Sir John and Sir Peter? He had made an error there.

'This man is worth a fortune to the King, don't forget,' he hissed to them as they all left the castle. 'But it doesn't matter whether he's alive or not.'

Sir John glowered about him. 'How do we find him?'

'I saw him myself before the castle,' Sir Charles said. 'I think there's something keeping him about here. Perhaps he's spying on the Queen with a view to harming her? Or capturing her? It would be a sore blow to the King, were his wife to be taken by his worst foe.'

Sir Peter smiled easily. 'Ah. So you have no idea where he is, then?'

'He is nearby,' Sir Charles said flatly.

'You know for definite that the man who killed Paul was Mortimer?' Sir John said. He had asked that three times so far.

'It was him. I told you: I saw Mortimer here, outside the castle, and he was walking over this way. Paul was trying to find him, and then he was killed. It must have been Mortimer.'

Sir John shrugged. 'Could have been anyone. He was out late after curfew, from what you say. Any man could have seen him as easy prey. There are men who do that sort of thing.'

'It was Mortimer. Paul would have defended himself against any other. He was a capable man-at-arms.'

Sir Peter was more sanguine than Sir John. 'If there's any chance it's Mortimer, we have a duty to find him.'

'That's fine – but where in Christ's name do we start?' Sir John said. 'I've never been to Paris before.'

'Nor I,' Sir Peter admitted. He glanced hopefully at Sir Charles.

'You don't need to know the city,' he said. 'All that matters is we keep to the nearer alleys. The man is here somewhere, and he must have some sort of interest in the castle. Why else would he dump my man's body by the entrance?'

'Very well,' said Sir Peter. 'Then we find a place to wait and watch.'

Roger Mortimer bit at his lower lip as the man scuttled away, up the alley past Jack and into the main yard. He was about to motion to Jack to follow and kill him when wiser counsel persuaded him against it. If it were necessary to do anything about Master Ricard, it could be done later. There was no urgency.

'Your highness,' he said with a bow.

Queen Isabella was radiant even in this dim light. She wore a black tunic and hooded cloak, like a wealthy widow. At her side was de Bouden, as usual, while behind her walked her lady-in-waiting, that blonde girl. Alice? Avice, or something. No threat to him, anyway, which was the most important thing so far as Mortimer was concerned.

Sweet Jesus, what a life! Only a few years ago he had been among the most valued of the King's servants, fêted wherever he went within the realm, and feared abroad as a major general of the King's host. If there was a battle to be fought, the King would send his Mortimer. And now he had to fear meeting people in case he might be sought out and assassinated. He dared not even trust the Queen, a lady who had shown herself to be a friend to him and to his wife.

'Please, Roger, stand.'

'I cannot. You are still my queen,' he murmured.

His eyes were fixed on the floor, but even as he opened his mouth to ask Jack to leave them, he heard the door close softly. Glancing up, he saw that he and the Queen were alone but for the blonde.

'Roger, rise, I beg,' she said, but behind the gentle words was an iron will.

He had been brought up in the culture of courtly love, but her tone showed that this was no time for foolish exhibitions. He nodded and obeyed. 'I am glad indeed to see you again.'

'And I you. Roger, this farce of an embassy has dragged on long enough. It is not likely that I shall be here for much longer.'

'My lady!' he groaned. It was devastating to hear it from her own lips. She was the only true friend he had over here who could influence matters back at home. Isabella was an intelligent woman, and with her support he had been sure that he might have been able to effect a reconciliation with the King. If she was to be called home again, her embassy must have failed, and any possibility of a reconciliation with her husband was effectually closed off. Neither she nor Mortimer could hope to resume their past positions. Communication between them was impossible while the Queen was locked up under the constant watchful eye of those such as Eleanor, Lady Despenser. They needed more time.

'You know it's true, Roger. My brother is a sharp man with a mind like a steel trap. No matter what I do or say, he will demand ever more harsh conditions. It is impossible.'

'You cannot appeal to his brotherly love for you?'

She looked at him very directly. 'He has no heir. If he was still married to that whore Blanche, he might have had children – sons – by now.'

'It was hardly your fault that her crimes were discovered.'

'It would hardly have endeared me to him that it was I who discovered them, nor that it was I who told our father and set in train the destruction of my brothers' marriages.'

Mortimer nodded. 'So he will not assist you?'

'He has indicated as much. And I must obey my husband's instructions. He will demand my return soon.'

'Could you not stall him? Why not discuss with the French king an extension of the truce while you continue to negotiate? That way, at least you remain here and we can hope for something else to come to our aid.'

She smiled. 'Roger, dear Roger. You plan still for a miracle? There can be none, believe me. This whole affair of the invasion of Guyenne has been a ploy. My brother seeks the entirety of the English possessions. He needs England to bow before him.'

'No English king can bend the knee to him. It would be intolerable.'

'No English king can hold lands from him, then,' she said more sharply.

Mortimer bowed his head. He must remember that her loyalties were divided. A large part of her heart was still French. But he needed her help.

He had met her several times now – initially at his own instigation, but recently more often at hers – but he felt as though he was making very little headway. As was she.

What *he* wanted – *needed* – was his wife to be freed so that he could have her back at his side again. She had always been with him until his arrest, and he missed her steadying influence. Always kind, always sweet-natured, it was obscene that she should be held in a dungeon at the King's pleasure.

And he knew that Isabella understood his urgent desire for his companion's return. She had a similar yearning for her own husband to retake his rightful position with her. Not much hope of that, though. The man was besotted with his 'dearest Hugh'. She had to know that. Roger Mortimer could feel sympathy for her . . . no, more than that. They had a deep understanding based on their experiences. Both had been deprived of all they held closest to their hearts: children, spouses, treasure – all that made life worthwhile.

Mortimer had been a contented husband and father, and losing his wife in this manner, knowing that she was incarcerated with only a pittance for her upkeep, was tearing at his heart and soul.

'My poor lady,' he whispered.

'She suffers. As we all do,' Isabella said quietly.

He nodded, and then looked up at her with compassion in his eyes. 'My poor queen, too.'

Because there was no means for her to recover her husband. They both knew that.

'There is hope for your Lady Joan,' Isabella said.

'And you, my lady? My queen?'

'I have to live without hope,' she said bitterly. 'When I return to England, I return to a gaol cell. I am free while I am here, but as soon as I cross the Channel I cease to be a useful ambassador and become the King's prisoner.'

'If only we could cross the seas with a host,' he said, and clenched his teeth. Then: 'It would be good to return with men at my back, ready to fight for the realm and evict Despenser. I would be honoured to install you on your throne again, where you belong, Queen Isabella.'

'I wish it could be so,' she said sadly.

Roger Mortimer nodded, and both were silent a moment, until Roger looked up, his eyes narrowed and thoughtful. He met her own steady gaze, and each recognised the speculation in the other.

'Alicia?' the Queen said after a moment. 'Leave us.'

Chapter Thirty-Six

Ricard scampered away from the confrontation carrying Charlie, his heart pounding so harshly he felt sure that it must explode from his breast. At the corner of the corridor he turned to glance back and make sure that Jack was not following him. He had a fear that the man might chase after him to kill him even as he reached the castle's court. Jack had not hesitated to kill before, after all. Ricard was as sure as he could be that Jack must have murdered poor Peter to get himself in on this embassy with the others.

But no: the man was back there still, bowing to the Queen as she slipped past and entered the room with that man whom Ricard had felt sure he knew. Then the Queen's woman followed her inside, while de Bouden and a guard stood at the doorway with Jack.

He felt sick as he realised that he was safe for now. 'Christ and all his saints,' he muttered, and puffed out his cheeks. There must be an easier way to earn a living, he told himself regretfully. Looking down at Charlie, he saw that the boy's face was smeared with tears and snot, but the lad had stopped his wailing now. Ever since de Bouden appeared Charlie had been making the same low, inconsolable noise, as though one more person coming up behind him was the last shock he could cope with. 'It's all right, lad. We're safe now,' Ricard said.

Other men had nothing like these problems. They could work at their jobs – farming, working in markets, peddling wares of various types – and never get into this kind of mess. But here he was, an innocent in a foreign land, trying to mind his own business, and what happened? He was forced to protect and guard a man who was spying on the Queen.

Casting another look behind him, he frowned. But if the man Jack was actually in the pay of the Despenser, surely the Queen's Comptroller would have nothing to do with him? Everyone knew that the Despenser and the Queen hated each other. You didn't have to be a musician in the palace on Thorney Island for long to see how they loathed each other. So Jack surely wasn't with Despenser.

Shite – perhaps he *was* truly on the side of the Queen. That would be very embarrassing.

Ricard wanted nothing to do with either of them. No. Instead, he made his way along the alleyway to the farther end. What he wanted was a good pot of ale. With that in mind, he hurried down to the hall's bar, over in the buttery, and was about to enter when he saw the other man.

'Christ in chains!' he swore. Charlie looked up, but said nothing. Didn't even hide his face, so he must be over the worst of his shock. Ricard wasn't, though. Ach, he'd be buggered if he'd go in there with the man who'd been in that room in London, the man who Philip and Adam said had been with Jack. Who the hell are you? he wondered, but just then some French guards shoved past him. He saw the man's head turn towards the door, and ducked away before he could be spotted.

Disconsolately, he wandered up the corridor from the buttery to the main door leading to the yard. Here he stood a moment, looking about, wondering where to go and what he could do.

What he really wanted was ale, but the idea of going back in there and drinking under the gaze of the man who'd seen to the murder of the glover and his wife in that little house was enough to make him feel like spewing. Better to go and find a tavern outside somewhere, but even as he had the thought he heard voices behind him, and throwing a look over his shoulder he saw the man walking towards him.

Hurrying out, he was about to run across the yard to escape when he heard a man calling to him. It wasn't the man behind, but someone else in the court itself. Staring about him wildly, he saw the knight, Sir Baldwin, sitting with his companion the bailiff. The two were all but inseparable. At least he'd heard only good reports about them both. They appeared honourable, and they'd not allow some stranger to stab him to death without doing something.

With that reasoning giving him confidence, he crossed to them. 'Sir?'

The knight looked at him, then at Charlie. 'A handsome boy. He is yours?'

'Um. Not really. He's an orphan, and I thought it'd be best to save him from any further pain.'

'Pain?'

'His parents were murdered.'

'Oh . . . Are you well, musician? You look badly flustered, like a man who's been caught in a murder himself!'

That word was enough to send his spirits tumbling again. He remembered the threat the man had made: if the band didn't help him, Ricard would be accused of murder. The two bodies were there . . . but that was ages ago. A month – no, two? – since. The bodies may still be there, but who'd prove he had been? He was surely safe. Except he couldn't be sure.

'I ate some meat that was off, I think,' he said.

'I see,' Baldwin said, and appeared to lose interest, to Ricard's relief. 'Anyway, a man is looking for a musician. I don't know if it was you. Ah, there he is. My lord! Is this the man you meant?'

'Him? No. There is another man, I think his name is Jack. It was he I sought,' the Earl said. He looked at Ricard as though daring him to speak about their last meeting. 'Do you know where Jack is, fellow?'

Ricard licked his lips and nodded. Silently he pointed towards de Bouden's chambers, and watched with relief as the Earl nodded and walked off to see Jack.

'Are you sure you are well?' Simon asked Ricard.

Well! It was hardly the word he'd have used to describe his fluttering heart and empty, roiling belly. 'Yes. Yes, I am well. But that man – do you know who he is?'

Baldwin grinned. 'He is the King's brother. Earl Edmund. Do you not know him?'

Later, when he had found a quiet corner outside a tavern where he could sit and drink from a jug of wine, Ricard looked down at Charlie, playing happily in the dust with some other children, and then rested his head in his hands and closed his eyes. If he had been a little younger, he would have wept for terror. He had no idea what to do. All he knew was that he stood to make an enemy of the Queen or of the King's brother, no matter what he tried.

He must be cautious, else he would find himself like Peter, thrown into a midden with his throat cut.

Jean sat in a doorway and pulled his cloak more tightly about him. The weather was more clement than it had been, but it was still very chill here in the shade of the tall buildings. How he longed for the summer, and long days with the sun high overhead. But perhaps he would be dead before those days arrived.

He ground his teeth as he thought how close he had come to killing Arnaud. And then those interfering fools had got in his way and stopped him from succeeding. The damned sons of—

No. There was no point in getting bitter about them. They saw a man who was about to commit a murder and stopped him. That was all. Ach, but the roaring voice had cut through his bowels like a dagger of ice. He'd felt as though he would die with the shock of it. He'd stood there with his knife in his hand, and hesitated just long enough for the cursed Arnaud to slip aside, and then he'd been forced to flee himself, before those two men could catch up with him. One against a rat like Arnaud was one thing; to stand against Arnaud and two men-at-arms was quite another.

Looking up, he saw that the sky was darkening. Soon dusk would fall, and another day would be over, and his quest for revenge against Arnaud would be deferred for another day.

It was the only thing that lent spice to his life, now, this search for Arnaud. The man deserved to be killed for what he had done. Poisoning the minds of men like le Vieux against him . . . it was so *unjust*! He'd never done anything to Arnaud that he knew of. He'd hated the man – but most who served as executioner were detested. That was hardly to mark him out. What had led Arnaud to seekto hurt him? Presumably just the fact that he had seen the attack on Berengar and knew what Arnaud had done to the other members of the guard at Château Gaillard. Slaying them all, all but himself and le Vieux.

And that was the interesting thing: why did Arnaud do that? At the time, Jean had assumed that it was his evil soul demanding blood. But if that were so, what had *stopped* him killing? There were those who could kill without passion, perhaps, but if a man lost his reason and killed like that for no purpose, he could no longer be considered human. He was no better than a dog with the *rage*. A creature which must be destroyed, because there was nothing else to do with it.

But then a strange, niggling thought began to insidiously work its way into his mind.

What if there had been some motive other than madness which directed Arnaud to kill all the men of the guard?

No. That was impossible. He was just mad, and killed without reason.

Yet there was that strange detail: le Vieux had survived. The two of them had known each other before Jean had met either of them, that much was obvious. They had been prone to talk to each other, and the way that they reacted to each other when they first rescued Jean from gaol had shown a kind of mutual regard. If anything, it had shown that le Vieux was the more senior in rank as well as age.

Le Vieux. A man with all the signs of military service, and Arnaud the executioner. Both taking men like him, like Berengar, like Pons, rescuing them from long terms in gaol and giving them all a chance at a new life, serving the Comte de Foix at Château Gaillard. The Comte, Jean's old master. And yet the château was surely no part of the Comte's territory? It was far from his own *compté*. So why was de Foix arranging for the guards up there?

It was not something which had ever occurred to him before, but now the strange illogicality of his presence in the château seemed important. Just as important, perhaps, as the reason for Arnaud's sudden attack. That, its very irrationality, seemed particularly curious. He had never demonstrated murderous inclinations towards the guards before then. Yes, he was a cruel, vindictive, bestial man, but he had not shown any sign of wishing to harm his companions at the castle. Why should he have suddenly gone berserk just after their prisoner had left the place?

Then there was also the stranger who had been in the room when le Vieux had suddenly attacked him. That man, who had drawn his own sword against Jean, even though they'd never met before. He looked like a noble. Who was he?

* * *

'Come on, Ricard. It can't be all that bad,' Janin said.

'You don't reckon? How much do you want to die?'

Adam grinned, and Philip snorted. Philip said, 'There's nothing so bad we can't—'

'That man, the one you saw today with bloody Jack? The man in London, who killed the glover and his wife? That one? You know who he is?' Their bafflement gave his sarcasm a sharpened edge. He was almost satisfied to see how they shook their heads. 'The King's brother. The Earl of Kent. That's who. Edmund of Kent. So all this time we've been trying to upset and remove the man who's been put here by the King's brother.'

Janin leaned back on his stool and puffed out his cheeks.

They were in their own little chamber in the castle's outbuildings, a draughty room with stone walls on two sides, partitioned with wattle and daub on the other two. The plaster had cracked and fallen away to show the withies in many places, a delightful aspect which gave Charlie plenty of scope to exercise his skills at demolition. He was there now, prying away pieces of plaster and telling himself a story about it as he went, while water seeped in from the courtyard about his feet. Still, at least the musicians had a place of their own where they could sit and talk in peace. Not that there was any comfort in that just now.

Adam was pale. 'So he's the King's own man, this Jack?'

Janin gave a harsh bark of laughter. 'Oh, no, Adam. Not necessarily. The King hates his own wife, and his brothers are not close allies of his, any more than his cousin was.'

'Cousin?'

Ricard shot him a look. Even a lad like Adam should have known that much, damn his heart! 'His bleeding cousin, yes. Earl Thomas of Lancaster, the man who raised an army against the King and was captured and hanged for his pains! Hardly the action of a close relative.'

'Even so, that's a cousin, not a brother . . .'

'Half-brother,' Philip said shortly. 'Different mother from the King. And the King doesn't trust him since the French invaded Guyenne. The Earl was in charge there. He was responsible for the duchy and it was him signed the truce they're trying to renegotiate now.'

'So he's not the flavour of sweetness to the King just now,' Ricard noted with grim satisfaction. 'That's marvellous. He's bitterness incarnate to the King, and it's his man you two tried to jump.'

'We weren't to know,' Adam protested weakly.

'You should have bloody guessed! Now what we've got is a little problem, boys. Is this Earl Edmund working to the King's advantage here, or his own?'

'Surely he'll be here with the King's approval,' Janin said thoughtfully.

'Maybe so,' Ricard agreed. He picked up his citole and strummed pensively.

Philip said, 'But what does that mean to us? So what? He's possibly the King's enemy, so we only have to tell the King's men and we're all right.' He stood as though to make for the door.

'What it means is, we may have made an enemy of Jack, which makes his master think we're his enemies too,' Ricard said scathingly. 'And that is not a position which gives me any great comfort.'

'Did you speak with the Queen or her clerk?' Janin asked.

'No. No time. I was jumped by Jack and this other man before I saw de Bouden.'

'Then the first thing you should do is tell the Queen all about the Earl, Jack, and the other man,' Janin said with certainty. 'That way, at least our own lady knows we're on her side. If anyone tries to lie about us and say we were acting for anyone later, we can show we've told the Queen about this. We did what servants should.'

'Right,' Ricard said, his heart plummeting. He saw again Jack's face, heard the cold voice from de Bouden's chamber, saw the Queen entering . . . 'Wait! She knows the man in de Bouden's room. De Bouden brought her there, and Jack was outside with de Bouden to guard while she was inside.'

'Was it the Earl in there?' Philip asked.

'No. He was in the buttery when I went there. It was someone else.'

Philip nodded, scowling. 'Well, you should tell her anyway. And see if you can learn who the man in the chamber was. It could be worthwhile knowing that.'

'Why?' Ricard asked.

'Why?' He looked nonplussed for a moment or two. 'If the Queen's having funny little meetings with someone, don't you think it'd be worth knowing? I mean, we're the Queen's Men, aren't we? If she's having negotiations on the side with someone, it could be dangerous.'

'What are you talking about?' Janin demanded. 'It's nothing to us who she sees.'

'Oh no? Think on this, Jan. If she's seeing someone and the King himself knows nothing about it, is he going to torture her to find out about it? No. But he may well torture someone else.'

'If we don't know—' Adam began.

'We'll still be tortured. They don't stop because you say you know nothing,' Philip spat. 'Don't you know anything? Look, if Despenser thinks there's something to be found out from you, he'll have the skin cut from your body, the bones broken, the nails ripped away, and he won't stop until you do tell him something. Saying you know nothing just means he'll carry on. Torture isn't about finding out someone's got nothing to tell – it's about making them tell anything. *Everything*. If she's seeing someone, I'd prefer to be able to tell the King, Despenser or whoever, exactly who it was, how long she saw him, and whether they met once or plenty. She's the Queen. She can't just go into a room and meet with men alone.'

Ricard looked towards Janin. Both shook their heads in disgust, but there was little either felt he could say. For Ricard's part, he merely wished he was away from here. The only consolation was that when little Charlie had seen the Earl, it had made not the slightest impact on him. Either he was so young he had not recognised the man who had killed his parents, or maybe he'd forgotten him. It seemed odd to Ricard that the little fellow could have forgotten the man who had so scared him at the time, but perhaps it was natural. The lad was very young, after all. Maybe he didn't think like an adult.

At least it meant the boy wasn't upset and screaming just now, Ricard thought, just in time to see Adam's recorder being used to prise away another chunk of plaster.

'Oi! Charlie, no!'

Chapter Thirty-Seven

Cromwell saw Baldwin and Simon in the main hall when they were all seated for their evening meal. He passed by their mess on his way to the top table, where he took a seat not far from the Queen, his eyes on Baldwin as he sat.

'He is hoping for some good news, I think,' Simon said.

'He can continue to hope, then,' Baldwin said. 'We have learned nothing of any use today.'

'We know *he* was there,' Simon said quietly.

Baldwin nodded. Mortimer was never far from his thoughts just now. 'Yes. And he denied the attack. Which may mean nothing, of course. The man had good reason to defend himself against Paul. The fellow was after a bounty, after all. He would have stabbed first and asked questions later, wouldn't he? Mortimer would have been within his rights to remove such a threat.'

'But you don't think he did?'

'If he had done it, I feel sure he would have told us.' Baldwin shrugged. 'Why hide a justifiable defence? He's a warrior. Surely he'd just say, "Yes. It was me. That fellow was going to kill me and take my head to the King, and I acted in self-defence." It would be understandable, truthful and, over here, he would be acting within the law, I feel sure. Why hide something that was not a crime?'

'Who else could have wanted him dead?'

'Perhaps it was merely a foolish argument in the street? Or perhaps a whore's master, who sought to take more than Paul felt fair? There are so many reasons why men are killed in city streets. And here, of course, we are in a foreign land. He may have offended someone without realising it.'

'Paul? He was always more astute than his master,' Simon said.

Baldwin nodded slowly, his eyes moving about the tables. 'Yes. Paul would always be wary of upsetting people, whereas Sir Charles was far less cautious. Where is he now?'

'Perhaps in his room . . . and perhaps with Sir John and Sir Peter.'

Baldwin grunted. 'He's told them, hasn't he? They're all three trying their luck, hoping to catch Mortimer.'

'It's no surprise, is it?' Simon agreed. 'How much would his head be worth?'

Baldwin admitted to being baffled. 'The man was one of the King's closest friends and advisers, his best general. I should think he'd pay almost anything to have him killed.'

'What, a hundred pounds?'

Baldwin looked at him steadily. 'At least five times that, and he'd still think it a bargain. And if Mortimer ever dared to return to England, he'd find the rewards notified to all the sheriffs in the land. He wouldn't be able to march a step without the bounty hunters aiming their arrows.'

'No more than the man would deserve, either,' Lord John said.

He had approached them as they spoke, and now he rested an elbow on the table at Baldwin's side, peering at both men as he squeezed his arse on to the bench.

'You really think the King would pay five hundred pounds to have him killed?' Simon asked. The thought of so much money was appalling. A daunting sum. 'Just to carry so much would be a challenge. The weight . . .'

'The King would pay a thousand to have the devil removed. All the while he lives, Mortimer is a threat. To the

King, to the realm, to all. Do you think he had a part in Paul's murder, then?'

'I have no means of knowing. All I do know is that Sir Charles apparently thought he saw Mortimer yesterday. Paul was out looking for him when he was killed. Now Sir Charles and your other two knights have missed their meal. I somehow doubt that they are holding vigil over the body, don't you?'

Cromwell looked away, chewing at his inner lip. 'This is mad. They are supposed to be here to help protect the Queen, and they're running off to try to win a prize.'

'If so much money is waved before a man's nose, it is no surprise that he might snatch at it,' Baldwin said.

Cromwell grunted. He did not meet Baldwin's or Simon's eye, but sat staring at the wall, considering. 'Sir Baldwin, I am concerned. I have the charge of the defence of the Queen during these negotiations, but here I have only myself and you whom I can trust. The others are too careless of her safety. They prefer to seek their own rewards. Well, I cannot surrender myself to such greed. If they treat her in such a disrespectful manner, it means I have to be more wary.'

'Would you like us to go and seek out the three knights?' Baldwin asked.

'No. I cannot afford to lose you two as well.' He saw the expression on Baldwin's face and laughed quietly. 'Nay, Sir Baldwin, do not look like that! I do not accuse you of also chasing the reward, I merely say that I can hardly see to her safety all on my own. If you and Simon were to go and seek the others, I would be here alone. I tell you now, I would not feel safe in such a position.' He rose. 'Would you aid me in protecting the Queen, Sir Baldwin?'

'Of course.'

It was enough. Lord Cromwell nodded and returned to his seat near the Queen, and Baldwin and Simon turned back to their food.

'Damn their eyes, what do they all think they're doing?' Simon grumbled.

'Seeking their fortune,' Baldwin said absently. He toyed with some bread. 'But that's not the worst, should news of this sort of reward get out.'

Simon gave a low whistle. 'Oh.'

'We should keep all talk of such money to ourselves, I think. Think what the average man-at-arms would do for five pounds. If some of the men here realised that there was a man nearby with five hundred pounds or more on his head,' Baldwin said quietly, 'just imagine what they might *not* do to win it.'

'What, the men here?' Simon said lightly, but then his smile faded as he glanced about him at the other diners in the hall. Scruffy, hard men, with rough, scarred faces; men whose most fervent desire was for war so that they could loot and pillage.

Baldwin said nothing.

Sir John de Sapy had not taken long to see the flaw in Sir Charles's idea. It was well enough for them to stay together to try to capture and kill Mortimer, but it would undoubtedly be better were they to separate and keep an eye on different streets and lanes. 'That way we may find him. If one of us does see him, we mustn't try to accost the bastard. Just follow him to see where he stays each night.'

'Good idea,' Sir Peter agreed immediately, and Sir John looked at him.

Yes. There was no doubt that both had the same idea in mind. If there was the remotest chance, either would kill Mortimer alone and take his head to the King. A bounty would only remain vast while it remained unshared, and any knight would be pleased to receive the sort of sum which Mortimer's head would bring. It was a simple race to find the man.

Sir John had left them at a corner, and then wandered back

towards the castle, gazing about him at everyone he passed. Mortimer's face was familiar enough to everyone who had spent any time at the court of the King. His features were burned on to Sir John's memory. And Sir John had immense powers of concentration. Others might see a simple wash of faces, none with any distinguishing features, but he knew that here in the streets was his man. Somewhere. All he need do was walk about long enough, and he would find him.

There was a niggling concern at the back of his mind, though, and that was whether he was looking in the right part of town. If he'd been here in hiding, he'd have picked an area that was as far away from the castle as possible. In fact, he would have fled Paris as soon as news of the English queen's arrival had been announced. Yet Mortimer was here. Why was that? Must be a damned fool. Especially now that Sir Charles's man was dead.

He saw a face, but discarded it. No, it was someone he knew, but not Mortimer. He continued on his way, scouring the visages all about, looking hard at any who turned aside as though hiding their features, and staring into any taverns or shops he passed.

'Sir John? I am so pleased to see you.'

He felt the hand at the cloth of his elbow, and shook it free with that indignant anger any knight must feel at being touched by some churl in the street. 'What?'

'It is I, Père Pierre. Do you not remember me?'

Good Friday[1]

Jean woke with a crick in his neck, which felt as if it had locked solid. It was enormously painful to gain any

---

[1] Friday 5 April 1325

movement; the slightest tremor in his skull was enough to send a bolt of anguish straight down into his spine and along his shoulder. He had to sit up slowly, his head turned to the right, tilted, straining to contain his mutters of shock and grief. Only when his upper body was upright did he dare to try to move his head again, and then only extremely gingerly.

The weather was warmer now, praise to Christ! Already he could feel the difference in the air as he snuffed it. This was the best Easter gift God could have given him, he felt.

Already, as he cautiously moved his head about, easing the tension in his muscles, stretching his arms over his head and wincing, he could hear the first stirrings from the houses all about. No bells today. This was the day all men remembered Christ's crucifixion.

He would have liked to join the congregations. It was so long since he had been able to feel comfortable in the presence of the priests amid the flickering candles and slow chanting. All his love of the displays had been eroded as his faith in the Poor of Lyons had grown, and although it was perfectly in order for him to attend church in his village, so as not to draw attention to himself, still he felt uncomfortable. He couldn't tell whether the priest was an honourable, decent man or not, or whether the service was conducted in the words which God had demanded. Instead, all was spoken in that leaden old tongue, Latin, so that all were denied access and understanding.

Still, he did enjoy the peace of the day. The people, driven to remember the hideous death of Christ, would revel in their silence. Men and women who would usually shout and sing would be drawn to silent contemplation. In Jean's old church, a large cross would be taken up and wrapped in plain linen, before being installed in a stone sepulchre over the tomb of a man who had been a successful merchant and had paid for the honour of lying beneath the cross each Easter. There would be no Mass on that Friday. Only a steady murmur and mumble as people remembered Christ's death and Mary's pain and anguish. A terrible day, but somehow reassuring, because all those taking part knew that on Sunday they would be able to celebrate Christ's return from the dead.

More than Berengar or the others could manage, he told himself grimly. They were gone for ever.

Drawing his cloak about him, he set off towards the inn where he had seen Arnaud before. He'd waited outside the place yesterday, but there had been no sign of the man. Possibly he would have better luck today.

He trod the streets carefully, always aware that he could be killed at any moment. Jean was a creature of the wild in many ways, and he felt like a feral animal here in the city. Others walked sublimely unaware of their danger from other men, but not Jean. He had lived too long among the sheep and wolves of the mountains, and for him there were sheep and wolves aplenty here in the city. But the sheep were less self-aware, the wolves more ferocious.

A full street away from the inn, he paused and took stock. There was no obvious danger, no apparent lounger taking a keen interest in him. More important, there was no thin, sallow-featured face staring out at him from a doorway. Jean took care to halt and survey the more obvious places where the executioner could have installed himself, but there was nothing.

He continued onward, his eyes flitting from one window to another, constantly looking for any sign of attention, but there appeared to be no interest in him, and as he approached the inn he began to think that perhaps Arnaud had not realised that Jean knew where he was staying. Of course, it could simply be that Arnaud had seen his danger, and had removed to a different place. That was definitely a risk. But Jean felt sure that it was not so. There was something about the indomitable arrogance of the man who was so used to dealing out death that told Jean that Arnaud would not have thought him a risk. No, Arnaud was probably still here.

So he could catch him.

Baldwin and Simon were up early to join the rest of the castle's guard at the service in the chapel, and then marched into the hall and took up their bread and cups of water. Fasting was apparently serious on this day. Throughout Lent meals had been provided in the evening after a day of moderate abstinence, but today there was literally bread and water.

The two were about to leave when they saw Sir John de Sapy. Baldwin grinned at the sight of him. He was clearly frozen. 'A hard night searching, Sir John?'

'I wonder whether Sir Charles is so besotted with the idea of revenge that he's not seen the immense difficulties. He is determined to stay out there in the city until he kills Mortimer, and yet there's been no sign of the man.'

'Perhaps it was merely a cut-purse, as the French have said,' Baldwin suggested. 'The *sergent* stated as much yesterday.'

'You think so? I reckon it's too much of a coincidence that Sir Charles and Paul saw a man they thought was Mortimer, and then Paul died while trying to find him. To me that sounds as if he succeeded.'

'Perhaps. Except if his search meant that he was wandering the city late at night, it's all the more likely that he was knocked on the head by a common felon.'

Sir John sneered. 'Except he wasn't knocked on the head, was he? He was gutted like a pig. That's more like deliberate murder, I'd say. Not some chance encounter.' He bowed and left them.

'He has a point, Baldwin,' Simon said. 'I've never known

a man killed like that just because he happened to meet a felon in the streets.'

'Nor have I,' Baldwin admitted. 'But did you think that Mortimer was capable of such an act?'

'He is a traitor,' Simon said. There was no accusation in his tone; it was a simple statement of fact, so far as he was concerned.

Baldwin nodded. It was the attitude most men would display. Mortimer was guilty of one crime and thus could be guilty of any number of others.

'Baldwin, don't you think you should keep yourself hidden? After what Mortimer told you about Despenser's allegation, wouldn't it be best for you to be quiet?'

It was something which Baldwin had been considering. His first and most attractive thought was to bolt for the coast, but he had already rejected that. Not only because it would have felt like cowardice, but also because he had agreed to come here to protect the Queen. Were something to happen to her because he had run away, he would never be able to live with the shame. And Mortimer's expression had also affected him. There was such a depth of misery and self-loathing in his eyes.

Baldwin knew that feeling only too well. The self-disgust that came from continuing to live when comrades were dead; from being alive while loved ones, friends and family suffered – and being unable to help them. It was a foul experience. And now others were going to accuse Mortimer of killing Paul as well. And Baldwin felt sure that he was innocent of that.

Suddenly he had a vision in his mind of the day when his Grand Master, Jacques de Molay, had been executed. A frail-looking old man, his mind somewhat disconnected by the horror of the death to come, he had been a tragic figure. But then, under the shadow of the post at which he would die, he had found the courage to denounce the accusations levelled against him and his Order, to accuse the French king and the Pope of corruption, and to call them to account before the throne of God. The injustice of the destruction of the Knights Templar had coloured every decision that Baldwin had taken since that fateful day.

The reflection stiffened his resolve. 'I shall try to remain safe,' he said. 'But I won't allow an injustice. If I can prevent that, I will do so.'

Chapter Thirty-Eight

Jean saw him at last. Christ's balls, but the man had no fear. He could not have realised he was being followed. Sweet Mother of God, how dare he walk the streets like this!

As Arnaud made his way westwards, Jean kept back, his hood up to conceal his face. His hand was already on his dagger's hilt beneath his cloak, and his eyes moved constantly, warily looking for any man who might be watching him, but he saw nothing.

Arnaud was making his way towards the Louvre, and as he left the city beneath the western gate Jean cast a glance up at the massive white walls of the fortress. The towers shone in the brief flashes of sunlight, and the flags moved sluggishly in the still air.

Jean saw that Arnaud was heading towards the northeastern point of the palace. There was a series of houses here in the suburb outside the city itself, and this looked to be a row of merchants' properties. Two-storeyed, for the most part, they had shingled roofs and well-limewashed walls that made them gleam as much as the Louvre's. In the summer, Jean thought, this area must be blinding. Everywhere would shine and sparkle.

It was to the second of the houses that Arnaud went. He knocked on the door, and quickly passed inside. Jean could hear the beam being dropped over the door a moment later, and frowned to himself. He had no idea who lived there. After considering for a few moments, he turned and strolled idly to a shaded area beside another house in an alley that led to a dead end against the city wall. Leaning against the house so that he could watch the door which Arnaud had entered, he gave himself up to a lengthy wait.

Baldwin and Simon met Lord Cromwell at the Queen's chamber.

'She is well enough, Sir Baldwin. But I wish I knew where those devils had got to.'

'We saw Sir John de Sapy just now, but he made it clear enough that he was going to continue to search for Mortimer,' Baldwin said.

'In the hall, was he? I shall go and see whether he will tell me where to find the others.'

'You want us to remain here, then?' Simon asked.

'Yes, in God's name! We must have someone here to protect the Queen.'

When he had hurried off, Simon and Baldwin took stock. There was a bench not far off which Baldwin soon appropriated for his own purposes, dragging it nearer the Queen's door and seating himself. Simon watched him with a smile, leaning against the wall with his arms folded. 'Comfortable?'

Baldwin rested his back against the wall and allowed his eyes to close. 'When you are as experienced in guarding as I, you will know when to take advantage of a comfortable bench.'

'So efficient guarding means having a sleep?'

Baldwin opened an eye and surveyed him glumly. 'No. All too often it means staying awake all night. But when there are two, it is better that one stays alert while the second dozes. You can wake me at lunchtime.'

'Oh, I am so grateful – so that you don't miss your food, I suppose?'

'Correct,' Baldwin said smugly. 'Now be silent. I wish to sleep.'

Simon grinned as the knight closed his eyes once more and settled himself. However, it was only a few moments before the door opened and William de Bouden came from the room. He appeared startled to see the two men on guard, but soon recovered, nodding to Simon and studying Baldwin with some surprise.

A short while after his departure, Alicia appeared in the doorway. She nodded and smiled at Simon. 'My lady would like some music. Could you send for her musicians?'

Simon soon found a servant and instructed him to find Ricard and the others. After only a few minutes, the men arrived and knocked on the door. Simon noticed that one appeared to be missing. 'Isn't there another drummer?'

'If you mean the bodhran player, he's not about just now.'

Simon shrugged. He was there to guard against men going in uninvited, rather than monitor men who were supposed to be there and didn't turn up. He watched the musicians trooping into the room, and resumed the tedious task of observation.

From here he could look straight into the main yard, or to his right along the narrow alleyway that led to William de Bouden's chamber. Of course William had disappeared inside now, and was no doubt already re-counting the gold and coins in his chests to ensure that there would be enough to support the Queen during her lengthy stay here in Paris. It made Simon wonder how much longer they would be here. Of course they now had the Easter celebrations to look forward to. It was the most important period in the Christian calendar, a time of feasting and fun, and that was enough to make Simon sigh. He missed his wife and the children. As soon as he returned, he was sure, Edith, his little girl, would petition him for a day when she might marry her young man. That would be hard enough. But worse, just now, standing here so many miles from home, was the fact that he missed them all. He wanted to be with his wife Meg, he wanted to see his little boy – in God's name, he just wanted to be home again. Enough of this wandering about foreign lands. He wanted to be in Devon.

After Easter, how much longer would it take for them to complete these damned negotiations and turn for home again? Another fortnight? Another month? Dear God, there was no way of telling. And all the while, Baldwin was under the threat of death.

He was shaking his head, feeling an entirely untypical self-pity, when he happened to glance towards de Bouden's door, and saw a figure slipping out. It was the absent drummer, and Simon gave a fleeting frown, wondering whether the man could have been up to no good in de Bouden's room, but then he saw de Bouden at the door, quietly closing it. So he hadn't knocked de Bouden on the head to steal some of the Queen's money, then. But Simon watched the drummer walk away, wondering what the fellow had been talking to de Bouden about.

Sir John de Sapy grunted to himself as he marched along the lanes and streets. The directions he had been given had been perfectly clear, and soon enough he found the place. A pleasant house in a short lane near the river.

He knocked on the door, and soon a man answered. He glowered ferociously, but allowed Sir John inside, and led him along a dark and noisome passageway to a rear door.

'Out there. Second door on the left,' he said, and walked away.

Sir John watched him go with his lip curled. It was disgusting that such a man should dare be so insolent, but it was sadly all too common. Anyway, he had no time just now to teach him manners. He walked out into a broad courtyard. It was cobbled, and the building opposite looked like a stable area, but when he looked along the left he saw the doors. The first and third were closed, but the second was standing ajar, and he walked to it and knocked.

When there was no answer, he pushed gently, and it squeaked softly on its hinges. There was nothing else for him to hear, but something in the atmosphere made his hackles rise. A shiver started in his breast and ran down his spine. 'Someone walking over my grave,' he told himself, but not aloud.

There was no light inside. No candle illuminated the room. He stood at the door for a heartbeat, wondering what to do, and then the stench came rolling out like a barrel of filth. It almost knocked him over.

He kicked at the door, and drew his sword as the door swung wide. And then he grunted with disgust as he took in the sight of the disembowelled figure set atop the table in the corner.

It was some while before the musicians began to leave the Queen's chamber, all looking a little flustered and warm from their exertions. Good for them, thought Simon, who was regretting not wearing his cloak after standing out here for so long.

The last to leave was their leader, who was whistling under his breath and flicking a coin in his hand: spinning it up, catching it, spinning it up, catching it, while his boy watched, transfixed.

Simon shot out his hand and caught the coin in mid-air. The man gaped, while the boy gave a whimper, and darted behind the man, peering up at Simon with anxious, troubled eyes.

'Hey, give that back!' Ricard demanded. He put out his hand protectively to the boy's head.

It was a *livre Parisis*, Simon saw. He tossed it back, winking at the lad. 'Your friend, the other drummer. What's he doing with the Queen's Comptroller?'

Ricard looked away. 'He should have been in there with us.'

'That wasn't what I asked. I saw him leave de Bouden's place a little after you got here. Why was that?'

'I don't know.'

'He won't say because he doesn't want trouble.'

Simon turned to see who had spoken and found himself meeting the gaze of the heavy-set musician. 'Who're you?'

'I'm Philip.'

'Why won't this man tell me the truth?'

Philip sneered. 'He doesn't want anyone to know why we came here in the first place.'

'Philip, just watch your mouth,' Ricard said, worried by the tone of voice. He recognised it from other times. Philip was getting himself into a fierce mood. He did it sometimes when he was drunk, talking himself into aggression, and all too often getting himself beaten later.

'Oh, shut up, Ricard. We've been worrying and worrying about those two. All the way from London to here, and every day since getting here.' He spat contemptuously. 'Well, I've had it up to the throat with all this shit! No more!' He turned to Simon. 'We were forced to come here. A man told us to come or he'd put the blame for two murders on to us.'

'What murders?' Simon shot out. He had taken a half-pace back, giving himself space to draw steel if necessary.

'Philip – think of the boy, in Christ's name!' Ricard blurted.

'A glover and his wife in a little house in London. The woman was all over Ric here the night before, and we went to her house to sleep it off. Next morning there was this man with us, and he told us that the woman and her man were dead and we'd get the blame if we didn't do what he wanted.'

'Which was?'

'Spy on the Queen and report to his man.'

'Who?'

'The very man you say you saw over there at the comptroller's place.'

'Is this all true?' Simon asked Ricard.

What could he say? He was heartily sick of Philip. Truth to tell, he was sick of them all. Jack, Adam's whining . . . the only man he was content with was Janin. At least Jan had a brain and didn't shoot his mouth off in front of law officers. He had a brain all right – he had disappeared. Ricard glanced down at Charlie, apology in every line of his face.

'I asked you . . .'

Ricard nodded sourly. 'It's all true. The wench was dead, her old man beside her.'

'You all saw the bodies?' Simon asked.

'Yes,' Ricard swallowed. The memory of the blood was enough to make the gorge rise all over again.

'Friend, I think you should come and talk to us,' Baldwin said from behind Simon. 'This tale sounds most interesting.'

A little after the middle of the morning, Jean saw Arnaud leave the house with another man, this one cloaked and hooded, but familiar for all that.

What was the priest from Pamiers doing here? Jean was confused now, but he was sure of one thing: if he was to have his revenge on Arnaud, he must follow.

Arnaud and the priest were walking at a fair pace. They hurried along westwards, until they came to a group of houses in a street near the river. Here the priest stopped and pointed, muttering to Arnaud. The executioner nodded twice, and then set off in a hurry in the direction indicated.

Jean settled back in a doorway. They were growing to be his favourite place of concealment, he told himself with a smile. From here he could see Arnaud rapping on a door a little way along the street, and then entering. There was silence for what seemed an age after he went in, but then there was a sudden shriek, the door flew open, and a man rushed out into the street. His face was wild, and he stared up and down the way before choosing his direction and bolting.

It was one of the men from the English entourage. Jean had seen this one before – he was a knight, and from the way he gripped his sword in his hands, he was ready to defend himself. Sure enough, a moment later Arnaud came out, a hand to a small cut above his brow. The priest pointed urgently, and Arnaud gave chase, bellowing and roaring that the man was a murderer. A couple of other men joined in the shouting, and soon there was a veritable mob hurtling along after Arnaud.

As they began to disappear round the bend in the street, the priest appeared to chuckle to himself, and then set off after them all, shaking his head as he went. There was something clearly very entertaining in the sight of the Paris mob in pursuit of a felon.

Jean waited until the priest had himself disappeared, and then went in by the door through which Arnaud and the man had exited.

He had seen plenty of death and horror in his life, but even Jean found this one shocking. Robert de Chatillon's spread body on the table, his belly opened, the blood all over everywhere, spatters on the ceiling, droplets on every surface, and the smell of blood and excrement over all. He covered his face to keep infection away, and hurriedly left.

Once outside again, he leaned against a beam and tried to keep his stomach under control. The sight of that poor man was enough to make him want to throw up everything he had eaten for a week.

But there was one thing he was surprised at. The man had

been killed very recently, and it couldn't have been Arnaud, because Jean knew what he'd been doing, and where, for several hours past.

Yet the man had been murdered, and that most hideously, for some purpose. The very man he had thought to speak to, to learn what he could tell about Arnaud and the Château Gaillard, was as dead as the garrison of the castle.

And that thought was a heavy one. All those who had been selected to guard the prison-castle had died, but for him. And he had lived by the purest chance. The deaths were expected, too, because when he last saw that priest from Pamiers, he had been on the wagon with the *sergent* in Les Andelys.

The priest must hold a clue to what was happening, he reckoned. There had been many deaths already, and he was fearful for his own life, but he must learn what was going on.

Slowly, he began to set off after the hue and cry. However, before he had travelled very far, he started moving more swiftly. Like a boulder, the first few inches were slow, but as the momentum caught him he found himself gathering speed, until at last he was running at full tilt.

He had the impression that today he might learn the truth about all the deaths. He didn't know how, but he was going to try to find out and then avenge them all.

Chapter Thirty-Nine

Ricard sat on the ground near Sir Baldwin, and told his tale. He looked to the others occasionally for verification of the details, but generally even Philip held his tongue. Charlie sat on Ricard's thigh, looking about him with that childish appearance of innocence and wonder that always amused Simon on the face of his own son.

'So this lad is the child of the couple you found dead?' Baldwin asked.

'Yes. And it was Earl Edmund who told us to spy on the Queen for him.'

'Why?'

'He didn't say. We assumed he wanted information about her. Damaging information. So that he could tell the King. Or Despenser.'

'I see,' Baldwin said. 'But why did you think the Earl would want to do that?'

'How were we to know he was an earl? All we knew was, he had men outside, he had two corpses inside, and we were stuffed whichever way we looked at it.'

'The boy,' Simon asked quietly, 'did he see his mother and father—'

'No, I don't think so,' Ricard said hurriedly. 'He was outside. I think he went there himself. Maybe he was told to. He saw nothing, I think.'

'You're a big fellow, aren't you?' Simon said pleasantly.

The boy met his gaze with a serious frown for a while, then

slowly leaned sideways into Ricard's chest for protection. Ricard absent-mindedly put his arm about him. 'He trusts me.'

Baldwin nodded, and then he squatted on the ground in front of Ricard and the boy. He met the lad's eye for a short period, then looked back to Ricard. 'You have done well with him. He trusts you. But are you sure you have never seen him before? He would appear very unconcerned about his sad loss.'

'He's only a boy. Doesn't hardly speak at all,' Ricard said.

'I see. So, Charlie. What is to be done with you? Will you remain with these fine musicians, or are you to find a new home?'

'Stay with Ricard.'

'You will be happy with him, you think?'

Charlie sat a little more upright, watching Baldwin closely. 'Yes. Like Ricard.'

Baldwin nodded. 'Tell me, Ricard. The man who died from your band – was there any reason you can think of which would explain his death? Moneylenders? Gambling? Whores?'

'He was a clean-living fellow compared with others, sir. No, I can't imagine anything like that. He was happy enough with the money we earned playing our music, but his wife wouldn't let him gamble if she had anything to do with it, and he'd not have bothered with whores. His woman, Marg, was more than enough to keep him happy. No, the more I think about it, the more I think he was killed because of our coming here. I don't know why, but I think it must have been Jack who slew him in order to make sure he would get into our group. That was it. Earl Edmund wanted us to come here with the Queen, and he wanted to keep an eye on us, so he had Jack kill Peter so Jack could join in.'

'You told me he had a peacock picture on his bodhran?'

'Yes.'

'But he has been very friendly with Earl Edmund?'

'Yes. Jack and he stood up against Philip and Adam together.'

'But that makes little sense to me,' Baldwin said. 'If the Earl was so keen for you to keep in touch with his man, why would he have your Peter killed? His man would be in touch with you every step in any case. Peter might as well have lived. Then again, why bother to have this Jack installed in your band at all? He could have been a hanger-on of the Queen's cavalcade.'

'I don't know. None of it makes any sense to a simple gittern-player.'

Baldwin rose to his feet. 'Very well. Many thanks for all that. I hope to be able to speak to you again before long. Perhaps I can even explain it all.'

'I hope so. I would be grateful just for a little less fog about everything.'

'I will do what I can,' said Baldwin, looking over to the gate. 'What on earth is all that about?'

'All that' was a sudden roaring from a hundred throats as Sir John de Sapy hurtled through the gates of the castle and demanded that the gates be locked, the portcullis dropped, before the tide of angry Parisians could storm the whole area.

He gazed back in horror, seeing only a sea of enraged faces. They were bellowing for his blood, calling him a murderer and worse, baying like hounds seeing their prey at the far side of a railing, raging at being unable to bring it down. 'Dear Christ, what have I done to deserve all this?'

'Sir John, could you tell me what has happened?' Lord John Cromwell said with an arctic politeness as he arrived, drawn to the court by the howling and bellowing.

'I was at a house where a man was discovered dead. They all blame me for it. I had nothing to do with it!'

Cromwell sighed. It was clear enough that the mob was

here for a while. They would not withdraw just because Sir
John had managed to find his way into a refuge; this was a
more deeply seated hatred than that of men for a murderer.
This was the tribal loathing of a man who was different, who
was a stranger, who was *foreign*. They wanted more than the
chance to arrest him; if these people took hold of Sir John,
they would tear him limb from limb.

'You need to get out of their sight, Sir John. I recommend
that you take yourself off to the chapel. In there you can pray
for a little understanding from your pursuers. But first: you
are sure you had nothing to do with the man's death?'

'Absolutely! I just walked in and there he was, his belly
opened like a gutted fish.'

'Who was it? Did you know him?'

'That man who was with us on the way here. His master
was killed?'

'You mean Robert de Chatillon? The squire?'

'Yes.'

Lord Cromwell glanced back at the angry crowd beyond
the portcullis. 'What were you doing in his house?'

Sir John shrugged. 'A friend asked me to go.'

'Who? What were you to do there?'

Sir John de Sapy cast an eye at the mob. He was reluctant
to speak, but if these people were to be persuaded to leave it
was obvious that he had to talk. 'It was a man I met in
London. He was a priest to the King of France, and I was
introduced to him by Sir Hugh le Despenser. Sir Hugh wanted
me to show him the way to a particular place in London.'

'What did you do?'

'All I did was show him this house. Nothing else, I swear.
Look, I was trying to be accepted back into the King's
household. I needed Sir Hugh to help me; I wouldn't have had
a chance without his aid. So I took the priest to the house he
wanted to see. That was all I did.'

Simon and Baldwin had joined them, and Baldwin was listening intently even as he took in the sight of the men and women shouting and hurling abuse through the stout bars. 'What house was this?'

'Just some place in Lombard Street. Nothing special.'

Baldwin snapped around. 'Lombard Street? When would this have been?'

'When? I don't know. About Ash Wednesday, I suppose. Perhaps the Monday of that week?'

Baldwin almost gaped. Then, 'This priest you say you met. Did you see him again?'

'He and I celebrated Mass shortly afterwards, and he heard my confession. And I saw him yesterday briefly.'

'What did he ask this time?'

'Only that I go to a certain house and deliver a note. But when I got there, the man was already dead. I swear it, Lord John! The man *was* already dead. I did nothing to him!'

'Then why are all these folk here?'

'Another man arrived while I was there. He saw the man and accused me. I didn't know what to say! I just hit him and ran out and back here.'

'It was de Chatillon,' Cromwell said to Baldwin in an undertone. The noise at the gate was beginning to die down, and he felt almost sure that the worst of the crowd's fury was already past. 'Look, you get off to the chapel as I said. I'll see if we can't calm these people down.'

Sir John nodded, and was about to go when there came a bellow from the gates.

'LORD CROMWELL! There's a man here says he's from the French king, wants to talk to you about some murder?'

Jean caught up with the crowd before long, and as he stared about in the broad space before the King's castle in the woods, all he could see was an expanse of heads wearing all kinds of hats. The different colours formed a confusing wash in front of him: scarlets, greens, dull ochres and the occasional yellow or pink. One or two were purple, but they were so rare as to hardly show. Instead he found himself seeking out the bare-headed brown of Arnaud.

There was no sign of him nearby. All about him there were only woollen hats, and even when he stood on tiptoe and strained, he saw no one like Arnaud. But the man wouldn't be here at the back, would he? He'd be up at the front of this mass of people. Jean must get there too. There was no other way to reach him. Jean must force his way through the crowd.

He began elbowing people out of the way. Some grumbled; a few dug their elbows into him, or kneed him as he passed by. One man on his left almost managed to fell him with a deft blow to his leg that all but killed it. The only way he could remain standing was by grasping the jerkin of the nearest man to his right, who turned to spit at him, but then offered him some help when he saw Jean's trouble.

'Make way! This man's hurt!' he roared, and grudgingly people began to part for them both.

It was a slow progress through the reluctant crowd. Nobody wanted to move and let someone else get a better view. Still, Jean's saviour was a large man, for all that he was short, and his stentorian voice ensured that people realised there was someone coming through who needed help. Gradually they made their way towards the castle, where Jean could see the folks roaring and shouting at the portcullis. Behind it was a small guard of men in breastplates and helmets with polearms of different types. Men were gathered nearby, but they appeared to be watching uneasily, and not doing anything that might upset the crowds.

And then he saw him.

Arnaud was at the right of the portcullis, shouting and

pointing, clenching his fist and waving it in the air, bellowing at his neighbours, rousing them to greater effort and noise. Jean saw him turn towards him, and dropped his chin quickly, hoping that he hadn't seen him. Then he heard shouting and noises of a different sort. There were disconcerted calls, and when he risked a glance, he saw that behind him there was a man on a great destrier, a knight with all the pride and haughty contempt of his class. Jean loathed him instantly.

The man was safe even in this mêlée. Jean could see that all about him was a great ring of polearms, their sturdy wooden shafts standing at an angle to guard him. It would take more than a rabble like this to penetrate his defence, Jean could see.

Looking forward again, he stifled a moan of disappointment. Arnaud was gone!

The fool! He thought he could surprise Arnaud, did he? The executioner to the King was not some ignorant cretin to be slain by the knife of a peasant from the Comté de Foix.

Arnaud allowed himself to be drawn back into the crowd by the action of all those who were striving to push forward. He kept his head low, and as he went he took off his scarf, binding it carefully so that he could wrap it about his head like a cap. Soon, he felt comfortable enough to look up. There, a scant five yards or so from him, was Jean. Arnaud ducked his head down once more, and began to make his way at an angle towards the man. It was not easy, but soon he felt he was close enough. That was when he looked up and saw that Jean was staring straight at him.

It was the act of a moment. He drew his knife, holding it good and low, and then, when a man moved, he was in. The executioner never saw it coming. He was there, staring with pure hatred at Jean, and then Jean lunged forward, as much as he could in the press, and felt his knife slide in under Arnaud's jack. At the same time, Arnaud's own dagger slipped in so smoothly that Jean was scarcely aware of its progress until he felt the blade scrape on his lowest rib.

If he was to die, he would make sure that his assailant did too. He jabbed with his fist, shoving up as hard as he could, trying to use the edge of the blade to cut upward into Arnaud's body, but the knife had turned in his grasp. As the pain began to spread from his belly to his chest, he started to panic. His knife wouldn't move. He tried to twist it and turn it, but the thing was hard to shift. It was only when Arnaud started to drop to his knees, dragging clear of the knife, that Jean understood that both of them were dying.

Suddenly there was a shrill scream. Then a series of muttered curses, and the men all about grabbed the pair of them. Arnaud, Jean saw, had a feral, brutal expression fitted to his face, his teeth bared in anger and anguish, and even as he registered the curious ferocity, Jean realised that his own face probably reflected the same emotions.

They were apart. Jean had Arnaud's knife still in his belly, and he looked down at the hilt with near disbelief. Sinking to his knees, he found that breathing was hard. His own dagger clattered to the ground as he opened his hand, and then he let himself fall forward to all fours, breathing shallowly, the stabbing agony spreading all over him. So this was what death felt like, he thought.

There was a liquid drooping sensation, like a lover slipping from his woman's body, and he heard a little metallic rattle as Arnaud's weapon fell from him. The whole of his belly felt like a bladder of boiling water, stinging and heavy. His head was heavy too, like a lump of rock at the end of his neck. Impossible to hold aloft. He must allow it to dangle. The cobbles were smooth under his hands. They looked so comfortable compared to this hideous exhaustion. He let his elbows bend, and closed his eyes as his cheek approached the stone of the roadway.

Pierre d'Artois had ordered his men to force a way through the crowd to the portcullis, and then allowed his mount to walk easily between the lines of polearms to the gate. The guards manning it saw who it was who approached and scrambled to get the great shutter lifted to allow Artois to enter, while behind him his men held their weapons horizontal, trying to clear the space immediately in front of the castle.

He looked about him as he entered the main grounds. 'My Lord Cromwell. I hope I find you well on this fine morning?'

'I am always happy when I meet you, my lord.'

Artois allowed himself a small grin at that. He glanced back at the crowds being shoved and cursed back. 'You have many guests this day.'

'There was a murder, and some mistakenly assumed it was one of my knights who was responsible.'

'I had heard so. And who was the knight so accused?'

'Sir John de Sapy.'

'I see. You are sure of his innocence?'

Cromwell hesitated only a fraction of a second, but it was enough for Artois to raise a corner of his mouth sardonically. 'You are *that* sure?'

Before Cromwell could comment, Baldwin had attracted his attention. 'My Lord John, it would appear that someone is hurt out there.'

Artois stared back over his shoulder. His men were forcing the crowd away from the entrance to the castle, and as the tide of Parisians washed backwards, two bodies were exposed lying on the ground.

'You there! Go and bring those two men in here. Hurry!'

Chapter Forty

Baldwin had not realised who it was who lay on the ground, but as the first men brought in the pale, blue-grey-faced figure of the King's Executioner, he frowned quickly, and then peered out at the second man being brought inside.

'The man from Poissy,' he breathed. 'Simon, this is the man who killed the old fellow and hurt Robert de Chatillon.'

Simon gazed at the two men. 'I wouldn't worry. I doubt that either is likely to last long.'

Artois had heard their words. 'You say this man was at Poissy, Sir Baldwin? Can you be sure?'

'I am certain of it. I saw him walking with the man who was killed there. The other man was being hunted by him. Why would that have been?'

'You must ask them, if they ever recover,' Artois said. 'Now, Lord Cromwell. This man de Sapy. It has been suggested that he was responsible for the death of Chatillon. I have to decide what to do about this allegation.'

'Who says he is guilty?' Cromwell demanded.

'A man of the highest reputation, I fear. A priest from the south, who happens to be a friend of one of the King's own advisers. You may have heard of François de Tours? No? He is held in the very highest regard by the King, and the accuser is his own chaplain, Père Pierre de Pamiers.'

'Would it be permitted to speak to this *père*?' Baldwin asked.

Artois looked at him steadily for a moment. 'I suppose that might be possible.'

'Then I should be grateful if you could arrange it.'

'And what of his accusation?'

Lord Cromwell sighed. 'I swear to you that de Sapy shall not leave this castle until he is shown to be innocent. If he is not, he is still protected by the safe conducts I hold, and I expect them to be honoured. However, I would send him back instantly to England were he discovered to be guilty.'

'That is well.'

'If you will both excuse me,' Baldwin apologised, 'first, my lords, I think I should arrange for these two men to be taken to a place of healing. They will most certainly expire here.'

Both men nodded, and Baldwin began to arrange for men to carry Jean and Arnaud indoors to the little chapel.

De Sapy was already inside, kneeling and praying most assiduously at the altar, when Simon and Baldwin entered, Baldwin directing the men carrying the biers to opposite alcoves from where the injured men could see the cross. 'And please bring wine and water for them,' he urged the men as they deposited their burdens.

Simon and he spent a while checking both men. There was little they could do other than try to cool their brows, but even with such action Baldwin was unsure that either would recover consciousness, let alone revive enough to recover. Still, he and Simon waited until Peter of Oxford arrived.

'Dear God in heaven!'

'I do not think it will be long before they meet Him,' Baldwin said. 'Sadly these two had an altercation in the road outside there.'

'And came to blows?'

'Yes. We saw this one hunting the executioner yesterday

morning, and although he got away that time I think he tried the same assault today, but this Arnaud was able to defend himself.'

'I will do all I may for them,' Peter said, and bent to pray at the side of the nearer, who happened to be Jean.

Baldwin and Simon walked away a short distance as Peter finished his prayers and took up a cloth to begin washing the faces of the dying men. Blood was leaking from their biers on to the floor.

'Sir John,' Baldwin said. 'I could not help but overhear what you told Lord Cromwell earlier. You took this priest to a house in Lombard Street?'

'Yes.'

'Why?'

He rolled his eyes. 'You know how it is. My Lord Despenser asked me to, and I wanted to remain in his favour. I was trying to become rehabilitated.'

'And he told you what he wanted at this house?'

'All he said was that there was a French couple in there. That was all.'

'A couple?'

'Oh, he mentioned a boy as well, I think.'

'What did he do to them?'

'How should I know? He asked me to take him to the house, and I did. Then I waited outside.'

Baldwin remembered the look of horror on Ricard's face. 'He came out with blood over him, didn't he?'

'He might have done.'

'And you heard later of the murders, didn't you?'

Sir John looked at him steadily. 'I was asked by Sir Hugh le Despenser. I didn't trouble myself beyond that. It was his will, and I was helping him.'

'I see,' Baldwin said. He withdrew slightly, then shook his head, spun on his heel and walked back down the nave towards the entrance. On his way, he stopped at Jean's side. 'Peter, I believe this one is dead already.'

Sir John happened to look across as he spoke. His face hardened, and he pointed at Arnaud on the other bier. 'That man! He is the one who came in and accused me in Chatillon's room!'

'Arnaud, the executioner?' Baldwin muttered. 'What was he doing there?'

Ricard was out in front of the hall, playing catch with Charlie. He tossed the ball gently, and the boy, chuckling uncontrollably, holding his hands firmly unmoving in front of his chest, shrieked as the ball landed in his palms and rolled out on to the dirt.

Baldwin smiled to see the lad's delight. As Ricard retrieved the ball again, and returned to attempt to teach him how to catch once more, Baldwin walked to him.

'Master Ricard, I do not know whether my suspicions are correct, but in the name of all that matters to you, keep this boy at your side no matter what. You understand? You must not let him out of your sight, and never allow any man who is French to look after him. Yes?'

'Certainly, Sir Baldwin. But why?'

'I am not sure. But it is possible that this little boy holds the key to all these murders,' Baldwin said.

As he walked away, leaving Ricard looking at the boy with a bemused expression on his face, Simon muttered, 'Baldwin, what do you think is happening here? What secret could that little boy hold?'

'He may know who it was who killed his parents,' Baldwin said. 'And that could itself be dangerous for him. Worse, though, is my concern that he might be the target himself.'

'Who'd want to kill a little boy?'

'There are many who would like to kill the children of

powerful men and women, Simon,' Baldwin said. And then he glanced back at Charlie, who was giggling as he tried to catch again and failed. He scampered through the dust to grab at the ball, and as Ricard watched fondly he swung his arm, and carefully hurled the ball over his head and behind him some six yards. 'And anyone who tries to hurt a lad like that deserves every pain the demons in hell can inflict.'

Arnaud felt the cloth at his brow, but his mouth was so dry, his lips felt gummed together. He tried to speak, but a calm voice told him to be still. Too tired to even think of opening his eyes, he moaned softly. His entire belly felt as though someone had filled it with boiling lead. It was an enormity of anguish, and he was sure that he must soon be dead.

He could remember every thrust of that dagger. It was lucky he got his blow in first. He had been quicker than Jean. His knife had slipped in as easily as a blade spearing a leg from the fire. Soft pressure, smooth and lovely. He'd seen the recognition in Jean's eyes as soon as he'd started to rip upwards, slicing through the man's guts – and then he'd felt it himself. That snagging, parting, wet, foul sensation that meant Jean's own knife was reaching up through his vitals.

'*Père . . . je voudrai mon père . . .*'

'Easy, friend,' Peter said. He recognised enough French to understand the man's demand. 'I am a chaplain. You want me to hear your confession?'

'No, my own . . . my own father. Own priest.'

Peter gave an understanding nod. Sometimes men wanted their own priest. It was natural enough to want the man who'd seen them every day, for every Mass through their lives. 'Who? Where? You haven't much time, my friend.'

Arnaud's eyes opened. He looked down at his belly, and his eyes widened. He had killed often enough to know a deadly wound when he saw one, and the slow pumping of his blood from the great gash meant he had little time indeed.

With a shudder of horror, he closed his eyes and began to make his full confession.

It was the middle of the afternoon when a man came to the Château de Bois, clad in a tunic that bore Artois's insignia, and asked to speak to Baldwin.

'Sir, my lord asked me to fetch you. You wish to meet the Père Pierre Clergue?'

Baldwin shrugged on a cloak. The weather was warm enough, but there were some grey clouds on the horizon that threatened an unpleasant change before long. With Simon at his side, he set off after the man.

Their journey took little time. Soon they were in a broad courtyard, where Artois waited for them. 'Good afternoon,' he said courteously enough, bowing, but there was a reserve in his voice.

'The father?' Baldwin said, looking about them.

'He is not here. He's only a short way away. Come with me,' Artois said, and set off. Baldwin and Simon glanced at each other as they followed him, but both were thinking more of the men behind them than the one in front, because as soon as they started walking twelve men-at-arms took up station immediately behind them.

'I hope Artois has honourable intentions,' Simon muttered.

'If he has not, there is little we can do about it now,' Baldwin responded.

Besides, he thought, what other intention could Artois have? The man had nothing against Baldwin or Simon so far as they knew. And yet the men behind them were a constant reminder that they were a long way from home and any possible aid. The tramping of their boots sounded like the drumbeat of an executioner's escort, and Baldwin could not stifle the grim apprehension that grew in his breast. When he glanced at Simon, he could see that his companion was in the same mood, but neither felt it necessary to speak. They trudged on behind Artois, both dully aware of their danger.

But it wasn't Simon's danger. Baldwin knew that. It was he who had been a Knight Templar, who had not submitted to the Pope and the French king when the Order was disbanded, and who was now legally an outlaw evading justice. If caught, he could expect to be hanged or burned at the stake.

Baldwin could see in his mind's eye his wife and their children. His beautiful little Richalda and his tiny son. Somehow, even as he was thinking of them, the face of Charlie kept intruding. It was irritating at first, seeing that little boy in his mind's eye, but then he welcomed it. Charlie would serve as a happy image of what his own son might look like one day. And if he was to be held in a prison soon, at least that boy's face would be there in his head. No matter what else happened, he would keep Charlie's smile with him. A little picture like that was worth much to a man in gaol, he had heard.

It was a shame to think that after almost ten years in England, living quietly and happily down in Devon, he was to die here. There was something about Artois's silence that assured him that Mortimer had been correct: his secret had become known, and now he was being marched to his doom.

'Simon, I'm sorry,' he said quietly.

'Hmm?'

'Where do you think they're taking us?'

Simon's face showed his bewilderment. 'What, now? To see the priest, aren't they? Do you think they'll offer us something to eat?'

Baldwin found it impossible to say more.

* * *

Sir Charles had encountered Sir Peter twice today, but neither had enjoyed any fortune. 'I will try nearer the river,' Sir Charles said the second time they met.

Sir Peter sucked his teeth. 'Where's Sir John?'

'I suppose he's returned to the castle,' Sir Charles said shortly.

'The idea of food is appealing. Perhaps, Sir Charles, we would be better served to pay someone to keep an eye open for him?'

'And whom exactly would you trust with such a task?'

'I have my own men,' Sir Peter pointed out.

Sir Charles was aware of that. He was also painfully aware that he was without a man-at-arms to support him. If there were a number of men about the place looking for Mortimer, and one of them found him, not Sir Charles, then he would lose all: the chance of revenge for Paul's murder, and the money that Mortimer's head would bring. 'I don't think it's sensible to use hired men instead of ourselves. How much would you want to pay them as their share of the bounty?'

'Let us go and find some food, and then we can discuss it sensibly. I don't know about you, but this weather feels as chill as a Scottish winter to me.'

'You go. I'll wait here until you return.'

'Do you not think we should consider returning to see the Queen is safe? It would be an enormous embarrassment were she to be in any danger while we were engaged on this hunt.'

'My first duty is to my dead man,' Sir Charles said.

'Not to your King?'

The coolness with which the question was uttered was enough to make Sir Charles want to whip out his sword and attack the supercilious bastard right there, but the risk of retribution was enough to stay his hand. Better that he should keep one man on his side, than that he should lose all. 'You go and find some food. I shall wander down towards the river and see whether there's any sign of Mortimer there.'

With an ungracious 'Very well. Do so, then', Sir Peter turned abruptly and marched back the way they had come at daybreak.

Sir Charles gritted his teeth and looked all about him. Apart from a couple of lounging, lazy French sons-of-the-devil up to the north in this road, there was no one in sight. One, a man in a light beige or orange jack, glanced in his direction, but there was nothing to remind Sir Charles of Mortimer in his face.

Paul must have seen the bastard. He had been down this way, Sir Charles knew. It was the same direction in which Sir Charles himself had seen the man. But what was strange was that there were no decent houses down here. A man like him would prefer a decent place. Unless he was concealing himself in a mean hovel.

No. That was impossible. Sir Charles wandered southward to the great river, and stood a while eyeing it gloomily. There had to be somewhere that would appeal more to Mortimer. Looking westward, he watched the small boats and merchant ships that plied their trade along the river here. Their sails concealed much of the view beyond the house of Saint-Lazare. This side of the river there were plenty of decent houses, though. Especially fronting the shoreline. Perhaps Mortimer had taken one of them – perhaps to remind himself of his time in the Tower. That would be ironic.

Sir Charles might be lucky, though. If he were to walk along all the larger riverside houses, he might come across something that indicated Mortimer had been there.

He spat a curse. There was no point. This damned city was too large. The people here were as numerous as ants in a nest. How could he find one man here all on his own?

Paul had.

Well, if Paul could do it, so could Sir Charles. With that

new resolve, he turned and found himself face to face with Roger Mortimer and seven men.

'Good day, Sir Charles. I understand you've been looking for me,' Mortimer said. 'Congratulations. You have succeeded.'

Chapter Forty-One

'Baldwin,' Simon said. 'We're going the wrong way.'

Baldwin said nothing. He was keeping his own watch on the sun. They had gone due east to Artois's house, and from there they had been led south, but now they were walking west, back towards the Château de Bois.

'What are they doing, Baldwin?'

Simon's question was soon to be answered. They followed a new roadway, turning right and immediately left, and found themselves at the city gates again. Passing through, they were confronted with the massive white walls of the Louvre.

'Baldwin!'

It was with a sinking sensation that Baldwin contemplated the beautiful palace. He had ridden past the place many times when he was younger, of course. It was one of those royal châteaux that was a pleasure to behold. He had heard that it had been built in the times of Richard Coeur de Lion, the great English king who had done so much to protect the Holy Land and his estates of Normandy and Aquitaine, but who had died so young in a foolish affray while laying siege to an irrelevant little castle.

This place would have been a more suitable place to attack. It would have taken a master of siegecraft to force the inhabitants to surrender.

Now they were walking to the main gate. Over the moat, their feet tramping hollowly on the timbers of the bridge, and then under the gatehouse itself, where their steps echoed strangely, before entering the main courtyard, where suddenly they were confronted with a loud and raucous blare of noise.

Flags moved gaily overhead, snapping and cracking in the wind, and Baldwin was forced to halt, staring up at the sky, memorising the view, desperate for a last sight of open air to keep with him all the while he was confined. Perhaps the next time he saw the sky, he would be on his way to the scaffold. Would that be Montfaucon, he wondered, or would he be taken to the Temple itself? The Grand Master had been burned on the small isle in the middle of the Seine, the one that lay between the Hermit Brethren's church and the King's garden.

Artois was frowning, casting a long look at him over his shoulder. 'Come along, Sir Baldwin. We can't keep him waiting.'

It was enough to irritate him. There was no need to hurry a man to his death, as though the slow-grinding wheels of bureaucracy mustn't be put to the inconvenience of a moment's delay. A sharp rejoinder sprang to his lips, but he swallowed. There was no point in antagonising people. It would only serve to make Simon's life more difficult. On leaden feet, Baldwin de Furnshill forced himself onward, and climbed the stone steps behind Artois, walking into a large hall. And here, he thought to himself, I shall meet my doom.

'Your royal highness, may I introduce Sir Baldwin de Furnshill, Keeper of the King's Peace in England, and honoured adviser to King Edward II.'

It grated. He was being forced to submit to them, while they paid him every sign of respect, as though they seriously intended to give him some form of honour. Still, as Artois and Simon bowed, he thought he might as well follow suit. He bent at the waist as though his spine was broken, but still watched the King closely.

The King of France was a tall man, slightly taller than

Baldwin himself. Like Edward, he was good-looking, with abundant fair hair and the regular features that were so highly prized among his peers. He was clad in silk and velvet, and as they walked in he was standing discussing a falcon with some other men, who looked as though they could well be his falconers. As Artois introduced Baldwin, and then Simon too, the King looked them both over, and then handed his bird of prey to one of the men and motioned to them to leave.

'So, Sir Baldwin, and Bailiff Simon le Puttock. I am glad to meet you both. You have provided some services to my dear sister. Please, would you accept wine?' He moved from the middle of the hall to a large table, where he already had a large goblet of gold. In moments a servant had filled three more, and brought them to Artois and the friends. At a sign from Artois, Baldwin and Simon stood upright, and Baldwin cast a look over his shoulder. To his astonishment, the other men were all gone. They were alone in this room with the King of France and only a few servants. No one else.

'Artois, have you discussed the matter with them?' the King asked.

'No, my liege. I obeyed you and told them nothing.'

'I see. Good. Sir Baldwin, I am aware that you wish to speak to a delightful gentleman, Père Pierre Clergue. May I ask why that is?'

'I think you know, your highness,' Baldwin said warily.

'Perhaps I do. Could you tell me, though?'

Baldwin took a deeper draught of the wine than was, perhaps, sensible. He was unused to strong wines, and rarely drank much of any alcoholic drink. Today, though, standing in front of the King, he felt the need of courage.

'Your royal highness, the man Pierre Clergue was present at a house in London when a man and woman were slaughtered most hideously. They were, I think, French. A short while later another man was killed. He was murdered in the London ditch. Then, when we came here, we heard of the murder of the garrison of Château Gaillard, all but two or three men. A short while later, Comte Enguerrand de Foix was killed, then another man, who Robert de Chatillon told us was also a guard at the Château Gaillard. Now we hear that Robert is dead, and so are two others: an executioner called Arnaud, and a guard, also from the château, named Jean.'

'So, from what you say, the good Père Pierre was present, perhaps, at a murder in London. Apart from that, he has nothing to do with anything you have mentioned?'

'Except that Sir John de Sapy was asked by the same *père* to visit Robert de Chatillon, and found Robert dead. Immediately men assumed Sir John had murdered him, but he denies it, and I believe him.'

'Ah, you mean you trust one of your countrymen more than some loud-mouthed Frenchman?'

'No. I mean I trust my eyes and ears. Looking at Sir John de Sapy, I felt that he was not acting his horror. And he had no reason to kill de Chatillon.'

'So you would take his word against that of the good *père*?'

Simon thought that the King looked relaxed. But then he grew a little nervous when he saw the man's eyes. He smiled as he spoke, and yet there was a thick layer of ice in his blue eyes.

Baldwin's voice was equally frigid. 'My lord king, I accuse no one. I merely asked to meet him. That is all.'

It was not the words, perhaps, so much as the tone in which they were uttered that made the King's expression harden. Artois moved a little, although whether to remove himself from danger or to give himself space to defend his king, Simon wasn't sure.

'I see that your king's friend was quite right about you, Sir Baldwin.'

'Who? I beg your pardon, your highness, I do not understand.'

'Sir Hugh le Despenser sent me a message about you. I was advised to look at your sword.'

'It is here if you wish it,' Baldwin said, but now with sadness.

Simon shot him a look. It sounded as though Baldwin was about to surrender his sword. 'Baldwin, don't you . . .'

And then he realised. On one side of the blade Baldwin had, in Simon's view rashly, ordered a Templar cross to be engraved just below the cross-guard. Despenser had seen it once, and now clearly he had sent a message to the King of France to show him that this man had Templar sympathies. It was King Charles's father who had commanded the arrest of the Order. His son could scarcely do other than detain a man who displayed such a symbol.

'No, Sir Baldwin – do you not know it would be the height of rudeness to unsheathe a sword in the presence of the French king?' Charles said lightly. And then he smiled. 'I think you and I understand each other well enough.'

Baldwin was feeling light. He did not gape openly, but his hand remained on his hilt. 'You do not wish to . . .'

'No. Leave it where it is. I am a competent judge of people for myself. And I do not like this Hugh le Despenser. He is no more honourable than any other robber pirate from the Cinq Ports, determined to line his own purse at the expense of anyone else. And yet you appear keen to investigate injustice, even when it may affect yourself. I think that is better. I would prefer you as a friend.'

'Your highness,' Baldwin stammered, and bowed again. He felt as though a blow from a feather could knock him over.

'You may speak with Père Pierre . . . I shall consider your request. However, my affairs are my own. If he has overstepped the mark, I will be disappointed, but it is not a matter for you.

You have no powers to arrest him here in my realm, unless I give you the warrant for it. And I do not. So you may question him, but that will be an end to the affair. Is that clear?'

Sir Charles woke again in a dark chamber. There were shutters drawn, because he could see chinks and slits of light from outside, and he was strapped to a bench, arms behind his back, ankles too, so that his whole body could be exposed, were they to rip his tunic and shirt open. Suddenly he had a memory of how Paul's body had been cut from groin to breast, his entrails exposed to the air, and he felt a cold terror infect his bowels.

'Ah. Awake? Glad to see it. So, you are Sir Charles of Lancaster, then? I have heard much about you.'

'And I you, Mortimer.'

'You are angry. I don't know why. Unless it's your man?'

'I will have revenge for that!'

'Sir Charles, let me remind you that you had ordered him to hack off my head and feed my body to the fishes in the Seine! I don't think you could blame me if I'd decided to treat him in a similar fashion. However, more to the point, I didn't. And I don't intend to kill you either.'

'Then why have me trussed like this?' Sir Charles spat. 'You think I'll be more amenable if you hold a knife to my belly?'

Mortimer looked at him blankly a moment. Then, 'Oh! No, but we don't have any chairs here. Strapping you there seemed safer for us. However, you are unarmed. Wait!'

A pair of men threw open the shutters, and then walked to Sir Charles. In a moment or two he had been released, and he could sit up, massaging his wrists and elbows. Looking over at Mortimer, standing comfortably a short distance away, he calculated how easily he could spring upon the man.

'Yes,' Mortimer said. 'I didn't bring you here at some

trouble to myself just to kill you. You are the sort of man who could be very useful to me – once you get over your desire to see my head on a spike in London.'

He paused, eyeing Sir Charles speculatively. 'I am to leave here tomorrow, which is the reason for my urgency. You won't be able to catch me where I am going, so do not bother to try. I swear to you on my wife's life that I had nothing to do with your man's death. We caught him, and yes, we did beat him to learn why he was after me, but apart from that we did nothing. There seemed little point in antagonising the English delegation over him, and I do not wish to upset my host in this country either. No, I prefer to keep friends where I may. I do not have so many that I can afford to lose any more.'

'Then what do you want with me?' Sir Charles demanded.

'I want you to pass on a message to Sir Baldwin de Furnshill. Tell him this: the man and woman in London were originally from Normandy. They were cook's maid and her husband, a leather worker at the Château Gaillard, and I think they took something from there when they left for England.'

'What, a treasure?' Sir Charles asked, this time more politely. A man who could tell him about a rich winning should not be insulted.

Mortimer looked away, through the unshuttered window, out to the Seine. Then he gave a sad little smile. 'You may not think so, but I do. I think Sir Baldwin will too. Tell him, this treasure is one of pride, rather than joy.'

Château de Bois

Jack was in the courtyard when Simon and Baldwin returned to the Château de Bois. He looked at them as Baldwin pointed to him, and then the two strode across the area to him.

'Aha, lordings, I am glad indeed to see you,' he said. 'And there was me thinking I'd be looking for you half the night.'

'Shut up, fool!' Simon grated. He took hold of Jack's shirt

and pushed him back against the hall's wall. 'You have to start answering some questions, I reckon.'

'Happy to do so, Bailiff, but if you strangle me, you may find the answers a little hard to comprehend.'

'You work for Earl Edmund or Mortimer?' Simon demanded.

'Now there's a hard one. I suppose for Mortimer first. But then, a man takes his friends where he finds them, doesn't he?'

Baldwin nodded. 'He had the sign of the peacock, Simon, remember? That was what Ricard said. And the peacock is the sign of Mortimer.'

'Is that true?' Simon asked.

'Oh, yes, sir.' Jack shrugged. 'So I was told to hold it.'

'Why did Earl Edmund get involved in all this?'

'For that, you'll have to ask him. I keep other men's secrets.'

'What are you doing here, then?'

'Now? Packing. You see, I am not popular with the men here. The musicians don't seem to like me, no matter what I do. So I think I may as well be off. I've never done anyone any harm.'

'They think you killed their friend in order to take his place in their band.'

'Did you ever hear anything so silly? Why would I do that? They had already agreed to pass me any information I wanted. I had no need to hurt anyone. No, I did nothing to him. But when the place became free, I thought it'd be a useful berth. And it meant I could keep a close eye on the Queen without too much trouble.'

'Who did kill Peter, then?'

'Aha, now. That's a good question. I don't know for sure. But I do know this: Despenser has a nice property just near the ditch. It's called the Temple. I'm sure you know it.'

'Why would he kill Peter, though?'

'The fellow Peter was not a good companion to his mates. You see, I've heard that he himself went to Despenser with the news that his friends had been blackmailed by Earl Edmund into joining the Queen again. I'd have thought Despenser would be taken with the idea, but perhaps he was out of sorts that night. Or doesn't trust a turncoat.'

'Perhaps,' Baldwin said. But there was a glint in his eye which told Simon that he had worked out something else. 'But who told you that?'

'Earl Edmund himself. There are many in the palace at Westminster who trade in secrets. He had his sources.'

'What of the other deaths?' Simon asked. 'The other musicians reckoned you were always out and about when someone died. Is that true?'

'Yes. And it's true that I was often away when no one was hurt. But you see, my Lord Mortimer sent me to look after the Queen. And that is what I did. I kept an eye open for her every night while I could.'

'Even the night Enguerrand de Foix died?' Baldwin asked sharply.

'Oh, yes. But I can tell you this: I didn't see who was there, but I know who wasn't.'

'Who?'

'The man Robert de Chatillon wasn't, for one. He stayed in his tent. I saw his master leave and walk up the lines to where he died, but no one else came out of his tent.'

'Did anyone come in from outside the camp, do you think?' Baldwin asked.

'I couldn't swear no one did, but there was another man I did see. He was a little, short man, and I think he was a chaplain. Not the English one, but another fellow. Saw him a couple of times. He was travelling with the Queen's Chaplain until we reached Pontoise.'

'Pierre is his name, I think,' Baldwin said.

Chapter Forty-Two

When Sir Charles returned to the château, there was little warmth in his welcome from Lord Cromwell. 'Where have you been?'

'I had thought to bring you a trophy, my lord.'

'You went off on one of your mercenary jaunts, you mean. You thought only of yourself yet again, and sought money from the traitor. At the same time you left Her Majesty all but unprotected. It was unforgivable!'

'You say that? If I had found the King's enemy and brought his body to you, I suppose you would have refused any part of the reward.'

'Do not accuse me of your own vile greed, man! I am a man of honour. I would not have done anything that could have threatened the Queen!'

'Truly. How very honourable of you,' Sir Charles sneered.

'Do not speak to me in that manner!' Cromwell hissed.

'I shall speak to all in any manner I consider suitable, my *Lord*! I am not your vassal. And while I am here with you, I am still the servant of the King himself. I shall do my duty to him as I see fit.'

'It is not your duty to him you seek. It's the filling of your purse. Just like your real master, Sir Hugh le Despenser!' Cromwell called after him.

Sir Charles hesitated, but then continued on his way. The damned fool! Did he really think that he, Sir Charles of Lancaster, was the friend of Sir Hugh? He was only attempting to avenge Paul, nothing more. The idea that he was even remotely similar to Sir Hugh was ridiculous.

He walked to the chapel and peered inside. Where yesterday there had been only his man's body lying under a sheet before the altar, now there were three. He had to go to each, lifting the sheet to peer at the man beneath. Two who looked as though they had died in a brawl, and then poor Paul.

'Old friend, I am sorry,' he said. Suddenly tears filled his eyes, and he had to kneel at his man's side as they streamed down both cheeks. 'I did all I could. I searched for him, but when I found him, it was as it had been for you: he had been following me. And yet he said that you did not die at his hand. He expected me to believe that, Paul. As though I could believe it.'

It was a shaming suggestion. Insulting to think that a man of Sir Charles's intelligence could be persuaded by such a laughable assertion. Although he had not killed Charles himself when Charles was in his control. That was odd. Sir Charles would have slain him at the first opportunity, and he must have known that. Yet he didn't return the favour.

No one else could have wanted to kill Paul, though. He had no enemies. And Mortimer had admitted beating him. Still, it was peculiar that he had done nothing to Sir Charles.

Baldwin and Simon were in their room drinking some spiced French ale when Sir Charles came in upon them.

'I have some news for you, Sir Baldwin.'

'Yes?' Baldwin stood and poured Sir Charles a large cup of ale. 'Please, take your rest here in front of our fire.'

'I cannot deny that it would be pleasant.'

Simon could tell how affected he was by the death of his man. Sir Charles was pale, and his confidence appeared to have taken a knock. His usual ebullience was replaced with a dulled quiet. There was a quality of stillness about him which was entirely abnormal for him. Now he took the drink and sat on Baldwin's stool, staring into the flames.

'Mortimer caught me. Much as he did Paul, I think,' he said after a long while.

'Did he hurt you?'

'Not at all. No. I think he wanted to let me know that he knew what I had been trying to do – to catch and kill him. But he didn't seek to kill me.'

'He would think that the French king has had enough of bloodshed during the Queen's embassy,' Baldwin reasoned.

'And that would threaten his own position, were he to extend the embarrassment himself. But why, then, did he kill Paul? And why deny it? I would be proud of capturing an enemy and destroying him. But he did deny it. He stated that he had nothing to do with Paul's death. I do not understand that.'

'What did he actually say?' Simon asked.

'The main thing he said was that you should look for a treasure.' Sir Charles frowned, trying to recall the precise words Mortimer had used. 'He is leaving the city now, and wanted you to know that. He said that the man and woman in London hailed from Normandy. She was a cook's maid, while her husband was a leather worker. Both were at the Château Gaillard, but they left there and took something with them when they left for London.'

'Did he say what sort of treasure it might have been?' Baldwin wondered.

'He said it was a matter of pride rather than joy,' Sir Charles said.

'*Pride rather than joy*?' Baldwin repeated. Then his face cleared as he remembered the conversation he had held with Mortimer when he had been caught by the traitor. 'A boy?'

Simon eyed him narrowly. 'A boy? Is that what you discussed with Mortimer when you saw him?'

'Yes. We were talking about our sons.'

'That is all he told me to say to you,' Sir Charles said. He stood, tottering a little on legs that were over-tired. 'I can tell you no more. But Sir Baldwin, can you help me with this riddle? Why would he tell me he had not killed Paul when surely no one else could have done so?'

Baldwin eyed him a moment. 'Sir Charles, the way Paul was killed, with his belly opened and his guts brought into the open air. Another man was killed in that same way last night or early today. You remember Robert de Chatillon?'

'Clearly.'

'He too is dead. A man tried to allege that his murderer was Sir John de Sapy, although he denies it. The man who accused Sir John was an executioner called Arnaud.'

'The same Arnaud who had a son with the lady at the Château Gaillard,' Simon breathed. 'Arnaud said that the boy died, though!'

'Perhaps he was lying,' Baldwin said. Suddenly he was in a rush. 'Sir Charles, I am sorry. I do not think that Mortimer killed Paul. Perhaps it was this same Arnaud? He killed for a living, and he had a desire to continue. He was used to hanging and drawing people. And opening their bellies in this manner is much in the way an executioner would work.'

'Why would he do that to Paul?'

'I think he was mad,' Baldwin said simply. 'He probably killed Enguerrand de Foix, and Paul and Chatillon. Someone killed them all, for I doubt that there could be another who suddenly chose to murder one or the other. One murderer is enough. There is no need to invent more.'

'Mad?'

'He met Paul after Paul had been beaten, and saw an easy target. Perhaps he felt in the right. He was, after all, a man who was committed to the upholding of justice. He saw his own job as being just that: to punish those who stepped outside the law.

If he found someone wandering the streets late at night, he may have felt that killing him was justified.'

'Where is this murderer?'

'He is in the chapel now, dead.'

But even as he said it, Baldwin was wondering who the man was who was lying there with him. The man whom Baldwin had prevented from killing Arnaud.

Saturday following Good Friday[1]

Baldwin and Simon were about early, walking in the yard, when they saw Ricard and Charlie. Janin and Philip were nearby, playing idly on their instruments, and Charlie was dancing, crouching low, then springing up to his full height. He clearly thought he was leaping high into the air, but in reality his feet never left the soil. Meanwhile his right arm moved back and forth like Janin's, up and down, up and down.

'Ricard,' Baldwin said as they passed. 'Be very careful of him. There are some, I believe, who may want to hurt or kill him.'

'What, Charlie?' Ricard said with amazement. 'You said that before – but who'd want to hurt him?'

'I think it was he they wanted to kill when his mother and father died,' Baldwin said.

Leaving Ricard staring after them with horror, Simon and Baldwin continued on their way to the Queen's rooms. There was a specific location, to the left of her door, which was perfectly positioned to catch the morning sun. As it crept up over the outer curtain wall, the light first struck the great hall's wall and then slipped past and hit here, and by the time the two

---

[1] Saturday 6 April 1325

friends reached the spot they were in the full glare of the morning sunshine. It was delightful to be able to sit and absorb a little of it.

'You see, Simon, I think that the killings, both those in England and the ones here in France, all have the same root. And I believe that all have been ordered by the same agency.'

'One man killed all of them?'

'Not necessarily – although it is possible. However, one man has, I think, ordered them all killed.'

Baldwin was silent suddenly, peering across the yard, and when Simon looked in the same direction, he saw Earl Edmund strolling about. 'Him?' Simon asked.

'No. I do not think so. There are some aspects which I still find confusing, though. Let us speak to him.'

The Earl was glad to be called. He had spent much of the previous night musing over his actions in the past, wondering what he might achieve in the future. All in all, it was a depressing reflection.

After the farcical war in Saint-Sardos, when he had been summarily ejected from Guyenne by the French forces, he had been treated with contempt and disdain by the King his brother. Despenser had placed him in an impossible position, refusing to respond to his urgent pleas for resupply of men and matériel, until his forces had been destroyed. Since then, the King had made it clear that he was not welcome at court, and he had begun to do all he could to ruin Despenser. Not that he had met with much success.

Coming here to France to bring messages for the Queen had seemed a good idea at first, but since getting here he'd started to wonder whether the Despenser had an ulterior motive in suggesting that he should come. Perhaps it was part of his scheme to remove him from the King's household for a while so that Sir Hugh could plot something else to embarrass him. And then again, maybe it was to make sure that Edmund would have a chance to meet Mortimer.

When dealing with a man like Despenser, it was hard to see where his mind was going. All too often, you only learned what he had planned for you when his plan came to fruition, and you found to your disadvantage that he had succeeded.

It was a welcome interruption to his musings when he saw Sir Baldwin stand and bow in his direction. The invitation was plain enough, and he nodded and made his way to join the pair.

'Good day to you, Sir Baldwin. Bailiff.'

'My lord, would you mind if we asked you some questions?'

'I do not think so. It will distract me.'

'You are troubled?'

'I have matters that concern me.'

'Tell me, you met the musicians in London originally, did you not?'

Earl Edmund shuddered. 'I did.'

'My lord earl, they have told us about that, and I have to advise you that they did not kill the man and woman in Lombard Street. But tell me, what were you doing there yourself?'

'I wanted to persuade them to join the Queen's entourage, but when I got there and found the bodies, I was not sure . . .'

'Who suggested them to you?'

'It was Jack. I knew that he was a member of Mortimer's group, and he told me that he had checked out the men. However, he assured me that they'd not killed . . .'

'They did not,' Baldwin said with certainty.

'I didn't think they had. It was clear that they were appallingly hungover, and when I found them, all were sleeping out in the yard. If they had murdered the people of the house, they wouldn't have gone to sleep in the rain outside, would they? Anyway, just from their reaction it was plain to me that they didn't do it.'

'Who did, then? They all thought it was you.'

'Me? Ha. No, the couple were dead when I got there.'

'Who, then, told you to go there?'

'Sir John de Sapy. He was helping me, and he said that I should meet the musicians there.'

'Sir John?' Simon blurted. 'But he's no friend to you! He's with Despenser.'

'Sir John? But I trusted him!' Earl Edmund's face transformed into a grimace of disgust. 'That prickle has snared John as well? Is there no one immune to his infection? Dear *Jesus*!'

'I thank you for your honesty,' Baldwin said. 'But I fear that there is little you can do to protect yourself against the man. He has an astonishing ability to cause mayhem wherever he goes.'

'You hardly need to tell *me* that.'

Chapter Forty-Three

It was at the middle watch of the day when Père Pierre arrived at the château and asked mildly whether he could see Sir Baldwin.

'Sir Baldwin, the King has asked me to come here and answer your questions.'

The knight was unable to conceal his feelings. His eyes were bright with anger as he took in Pierre's features, but the priest met them without blinking. He had no need to concern himself with this man's feelings. His duty was to a higher master.

'You are Père Pierre from Pamiers?' the knight asked him.

'Well, I originally come from a little way outside. My family name is Clergue. But I became known as "Pamiers" because that is where I worked with my dear bishop, Jacques Fournier. We were there for some years.'

'What were you there?'

'A clerk. I was set the duty of saving the souls of heretics. Have you heard of the Waldensians?'

A second man, whom he recognised as the bailiff, had joined them now, and was leaning against a wall with his arms folded. He shook his head, and Baldwin had to explain.

'They followed a man called Waldes, who came from Lyons, I think. He was a little insane. He wanted the Bible translated into the common tongue so all could understand it. Preachers took up his teaching and began to spread his words.'

'Yes. They were all snared by his foul lies. He wanted to destroy the Church. So the Pope had no choice, and declared all those who followed his teachings to be heretics. Jacques Fournier and I went down to Pamiers to bring men back to their senses.'

'Tell me: how many were fortunate enough to die in the process?' Simon asked nastily.

'Jacques was always a thorough man. He killed only very rarely, when the criminal was obdurate. His patience was exemplary,' Père Pierre said, allowing a trace of asperity to enter his voice.

'I am sure you are right,' Baldwin said soothingly. 'And you were the man who took notes during the interrogations?'

'I was fortunate enough to be able to help him from the time when he first arrived there. I had already been there with Bishop Pelfort de Rabastens, you see, but he had quarrelled with his canons, and all his time was taken up with disputes. It was only when he left – about eight years ago – that Jacques arrived and set up his own inquisitorial office together with the Dominican brother Gaillard de Pomiès. From then I began to take all the records.'

'You were already there?' Simon asked. 'Did you know the man called Jean who tried to kill Arnaud?'

Père Pierre was frankly shocked by that news. 'It cannot be – you mean he has come all the way here?'

'Yes. We know that he was a guard at the Château Gaillard. Did you know him before that?'

'He was in the service of the Comte de Foix.'

'That same man who died on the journey here?' Baldwin said.

'His father, who is dead now, God bless his soul,' Pierre said, rapidly crossing himself. 'Count Robert died at Courtrai, God bless him!'

'Jean was in the garrison, wasn't he? When Berengar went mad.'

'Yes. He had been held in Pamiers because he displayed a wanton disregard for the honour of the bishop. He was held, while his heretical views were examined, and then he was allowed to leave, so long as he wore the star of the heretic.'

'But he didn't stay there?'

'Arnaud had been there at the same time, and Arnaud picked him to help at the château.'

'Were you involved up there too?' Simon asked.

Pierre glanced at him. He remained leaning against the wall, but he was frowning for some reason. 'I was often up there in my capacity as chaplain.'

'To see the Lady Blanche?' Baldwin snapped.

'On occasion. I took messages to her.'

'Did you see her child?'

'Child?' Pierre could not help his voice rising. These fools had learned about her child!

'You know about him, then. Was that the reason you went to London and killed them both?'

'I have not been to London.'

'You were there with Sir John de Sapy. You see he has already told us much.'

'I do not know . . .'

'Her name was Thomassia, wasn't it? That is what the musicians thought, anyway. And her husband was Guy. Both were from the château. I think that they were aware of something about the lady who was installed there. As were the men of the garrison. So you and Arnaud were told to remove all the evidence. You were told to see that all the men there were killed.'

'This is fascinating, but I do not know what you want me to say in response to this nonsense.'

'There was the other old man, too. He and Arnaud were

supposed to kill all the guards, I suppose. And since then, it has been your duty to tidy up all the loose ends. You were to kill the Comte de Foix, weren't you? And it struck you as amusing to do it in such a way that it might incriminate no one; that it would be clever to leave him with an explosion so that it would appear as though he had suffered a terrible accident. So you put that powder beneath him and ignited it.'

'I know nothing of such matters.'

'Really? Yet I saw you at his side when he fired his *gonne*. It scared my horse, and when I turned, there you were, just behind him as he laughed. You must have heard him speak of his weapon.'

'No. Perhaps he was showing someone else, and that person heard all about the *gonne*, but I was thinking of other things.'

'Really?' Baldwin said again. His voice was drooling with sarcasm now, and his disbelief was apparent. It was deeply shaming for a priest to have to hear such doubt.

'Did you hear what happened to Arnaud?' Simon asked.

'Arnaud? He is at the inn near the—'

'No. He got into a fight with Jean yesterday. He is here,' Baldwin said.

'Oh?' Pierre said enquiringly. 'Perhaps I should see him, then.'

'Yes. It would please you to remove yet another embarrassment,' Baldwin said.

'You accuse me of killing him?'

'Let us think of Paul, too, the man you found outside the castle here on the night of last Wednesday,' Baldwin said. He was trying to make the man stumble in his tale, but it was clearly going to be a hard task. 'You found him in a terrible state, badly beaten, and chose to kill him. Was it only because he was already so weakened? Like Robert de Chatillon? Another loose end in your coil of rope. No one likes to leave a loose end lying around where it might trip up the unwary, do they? So you had him slaughtered too, and then sought to put all the blame on your easiest target: an Englishman, who also happened to know what had happened in London. But the plan went awry, because he managed to knock Arnaud to the ground, and then escaped back to the castle.'

'Why should I want to do any of this? To kill this Paul? This Robert?'

'Robert, I believe, knew more than he told me about the garrison. It was through him that you hired all the men for the Château Gaillard, wasn't it? Through him you collected together Jean and the others, so when his usefulness was done it was only right that he should also be silenced for ever. But why you killed Paul, I do not know. Unless it was chance. You happened upon him as you walked the streets of Paris.'

'Why should I kill a man for seeing me?' Pierre said reasonably, his hands outstretched.

'He had been looking for someone,' Baldwin said. 'But perhaps ... perhaps he found another when he had been released. Did he see you leaving some other place where you ought not to have been?'

'I do not know what you are talking about, my friend. And I think I have heard enough wild accusations. I would like to see my old friend Arnaud. Where is he?'

'Let us take you to him,' Simon said with a short grin. 'Follow me, Father.'

Pierre walked along behind the fellow. Really, these English were growing too arrogant for words. He did not like the way that the other man walked behind him, either. It made him feel rather like a prisoner.

They were heading towards a small chapel, he saw, and he frowned quickly, but then shrugged. Perhaps they had some idea that he would tell them more in God's house – but if so they would be disappointed. He had no intention of telling them anything more at all.

His journey had been so long, from those far-off days when he and Arnaud had first arrived in Pamiers ten or more years ago, frustrated and bitter to be dropped in so far-away and wild an area. They had stopped in that little place near a village, where, God help him, he had been so sorely tempted by that woman. And yes, he had taken her. Against her wishes. And killed her afterwards.

It was an act which was uniquely vile in the eyes of many, but for him it was a necessary evacuation of all those humours which sent a man mad. All knew that men must expel the foul liquid every so often, and she had been a useful receptacle. Nothing more. Then her husband returned from the wars, and he had lived in fear for a while that the fellow might come and try to punish him for his aberration. But he hadn't. In fact, although Pierre had ordered him to be followed and spied upon, hoping that he would display the same heretical tendencies as so many others, and that he might be able to have him arrested and tortured, Jean had simply been quiet. It was almost as though he had lived his entire life in the last year or two, and wanted nothing so much as to sit back and endure until his end.

But then one day he opened his mouth in a tavern, and by chance one of Bishop Fournier's men was in the room at the same time. He was reported, arrested, questioned in detail, and gaoled. Only with the help of Arnaud was he released into the Comte's hands, and thence taken up to Normandy.

He entered the dark chapel, and trailed after the bailiff to the altar, where three bodies remained. There was a man there at their side, praying, and Pierre suddenly recognised Peter of Oxford. 'My friend, how are you?' he said with a smile.

But Peter was not so friendly as he had been on their journey here. 'Père Pierre. God save you.'

It was not the fulsome response he had expected, but no matter. Pierre walked to the bodies. 'One of these is Arnaud?'

Peter motioned with his hand. 'He's there.'

Baldwin gestured. 'Please satisfy yourself it is the correct man.'

'Ah. I am sorry to see that it was Arnaud. The poor man.'

'He was an executioner,' Simon pointed out.

'But a good man . . . tormented, but he tried his best. Still, it was a terrible thing he did. Robert de Chatillon, whom John de Sapy found dead in his chamber. This Arnaud was there with John. I do not know which killed Chatillon, but I would be inclined to think that it was Arnaud.'

'What?' Peter said. He was frowning at Pierre.

'I think so. I find it hard to accept that a knight, an English knight, could execute a man in that manner. But a torturer and executioner? It would be natural for him.'

'You blame him for Chatillon's death?'

'I only say what I believe happened.'

'I suppose you blame him for Comte de Foix's death as well?'

'I have to assume that . . .'

'I should warn you, Pierre, that I spoke to Arnaud before his death,' Peter said firmly. His face showed revulsion. 'He confessed his sins. He had time. And he told me all he had done. And for whom.'

'You cannot repeat things told to you under the seal of the confessional,' Pierre said, aghast.

'No. But I can call on all the angels and archangels and all the saints in heaven to witness your words now, Père. For what you say here, in this holy house of God, must be the truth, no matter what. A lie in here would be the same as a lie told barefaced to God Himself. Do you dare perjure yourself in here?'

Père Pierre felt his resolve slipping. 'You seek to accuse me?'

'No. I only listen. Along with all God's Host.'

'I will not remain here to be insulted!'

'You are free to leave,' Baldwin said.

Pierre took one long look at him, then turned on his heel and marched from the chapel. Behind him he heard the knight coming after him, but once he was outside the following steps stopped, and he shot a look over his shoulder to see the knight standing in the doorway, watching.

There was nothing to it. Nothing at all. They could do nothing against him, that much was certain. The King's anger would be fearful, were they to do anything to him. No, he was secure.

He was crossing the yard when he heard bellowing voices, laughter, and then a shriek. Turning, he saw a little boy being up-ended over the shoulder of some man as he ran. On the way, he kicked a ball by accident, and it fell a short distance from Père Pierre. He stooped to it, and picked it up. It was a simple wooden ball, solid and unyielding, chipped and dented where it had been dropped or thrown. He tossed it into the air and caught it, smiling.

Then the boy caught sight of him and his face seemed to constrict, somehow, his eyes widening, and then his mouth opened and he uttered the panicked, mortal shriek of a soul in distress.

And Père Pierre's face changed. He stopped and stared, at first in astonishment, and then disgust. He put his hand to his belt as though to draw a knife, but his action was seen. Ricard held tight to Charlie, and Simon and Baldwin hurried to them.

'The young *bastard* should have died in London,' the good

père declared. He spat at the ground, then spun and marched from the château.

Simon and Baldwin sat down at a table with Peter of Oxford in the main hall with jugs of wine and earthenware cups.

'So, Baldwin, what was that all about?' Peter asked.

'The boy recognised him. It was something of a gamble on my part, but I thought it might work. The lad's apparent calmness in the face of all seemed to me to show that he had not seen the actual death of the woman or her husband, but I felt sure, from all Ricard told us, that he must have been scared. After all, the fellow was found hiding himself in a little hutch in the yard, if Ricard was telling the truth. And yet he went with the men happily enough. So I think he was there when the woman and her man arrived home with all the musicians, and they were left in the yard to sleep off the drinks. Meanwhile, I think that the priest came to the door. The boy was probably woken by all the noise, and heard the priest's arrival. Maybe the woman woke him, though, and sent him to his hiding place.'

'We could ask the lad,' Simon suggested.

'He is three or so, Simon. Would he understand what we were asking?'

'He is a very bright fellow.'

'Perhaps. But to ask him about this would undoubtedly upset him. Better, I am sure, to guess, and to leave him alone. I do not want to upset my witness. So, she woke him, perhaps, and sent him out. He had seen the priest, though, through some hole in a floorboard, let us conjecture, so he recognised the man. And then he fled.'

Peter frowned. 'But Father Pierre was with us all the way from the coast, near enough. Why didn't the boy recognise him before?'

'I saw him once that I remember, on the day I had an

argument with Comte de Foix. I scarcely remember seeing you at all.'

'I was busy. There was a portable altar, and I spent much of my time with it,' Peter said ruefully.

'And I have no doubt that the priest managed to lose himself as well. The boy simply didn't see him then. But he certainly did this morning.'

'So what now?' Simon asked, rubbing his hands together. 'Do you want to walk to the Louvre and explain what this deeply unpleasant little prick has been getting up to?'

Baldwin toyed with his wine cup.

'Baldwin?' Simon said, suddenly anxious.

'I do not think I can, Simon. If I do, I think I shall upset the King. He did not want the truth to come out, and only reluctantly allowed me to question his little priest.'

'You think it could be hazardous?' Simon asked more quietly, thinking about the Templar cross on Baldwin's sword.

'Yes – but not for me!' Baldwin leaned down, beckoning the others to do the same. When their heads were close, he whispered, 'The boy himself is the target. That is what Mortimer told me, Simon, that there is a little treasure. The boy!'

'What makes him so valuable?'

'Think, man! We've heard about how the King's first wife was so cruelly treated. Installed in a cold dungeon and left there for years. And then, in order to provide evidence for the annulment of the marriage, he gave orders that men should be gathered together and told to rape his wife. He wanted her to be shown to be a lewd woman without decency.'

'She was an adulterer,' Peter said.

'How many married men can claim never to have touched another woman in their lives?' Baldwin demanded.

'From the confessions I hear . . .' Peter began, but then he shook his head.

'Precisely,' Baldwin said. What happened was, she was raped several times, but only by this repellent creature Arnaud. Whether he was to her taste or not, I do not know. All I do know is, she fell pregnant. Arnaud was sure that the child was his own, I dare say. So he wanted to see it protected. But others had different ideas. The boy must die, so that there was no possibility later of a supposititious child arriving to confuse the next coronation. But somehow, the woman Thomassia and her husband took the child and fled. Not only the town, but the country. They went all the way to London, and took Master Charlie with them.'

'This is all guesswork,' Simon said.

'No. It is mostly gleaned from the people we have questioned, and some of it is deduced.'

'Then *why*?' Simon asked. 'What would a priest be doing trying to kill all these people?'

'Perhaps he happens to be close to his king?' Baldwin guessed. 'If Charles knows him well, maybe that's why he chose to ask him to help?'

'That horse won't ride,' Peter said with a firm shake of his head. 'No. I think Père Pierre is not of that temper. If a king told a priest to go and commit murder, he would refuse.'

'But we can be sure that this man is guilty of many murders,' Baldwin said. 'Your intervention in the chapel showed that.'

'Yes. Well. I was not going to have a man blaspheme by lying about his offences – especially since he was attempting to have the blame put entirely on the shoulders of a dead man who *had* confessed while in the proximity of his own death. A man in that position doesn't lie.'

'Which crimes did he confess to?' Baldwin asked innocently.

'A good try, Sir Baldwin. I am not so gullible that I can fall for that. His confession is between him and God.'

'If that priest is as guilty as we think,' Simon said, 'is there any way we could bring him to justice?'

'I think that to be able to do that, we'd need the full support of the King. And I have no authority here, as he pointed out. Nor do you!'

'So he escapes? After so many deaths, he just walks away?'

'I fear that may well be the case,' Baldwin said heavily.

'It is not right,' Simon said.

'No. But in a foreign country, there is little else we can do but accept its customs.'

'I still wonder what would lead a man of God into such actions,' Peter said.

'He was staying with you during the journey here – did he give you no indication of what sort of man he is? No clues as to his thinking or anything?'

'The only thing I picked up from him was his hatred of heresy. He does detest those from his old home who profess the Christian faith, and then go and hold their own heretical services afterwards, considering the Catholic religion to be a perverted form of Jesus's. Apparently it's common down in the south.'

'And this Jean came from the south. It is part of the *comté*, too,' Baldwin noted. 'So the Comte was responsible for that area. Perhaps the priest thought that these men were responsible for the heresy? He was eradicating it and doing a service for God.'

'I have known religious madmen, but that would be stretching the point,' Peter said.

'I agree,' Simon said. 'I would think his motive was simpler. He wanted either money or power. If it was money, he would be sure of a reward if he was capable of providing this service to the King; if power, no doubt the King would petition his bishop for his advancement.'

'Advancement . . .' Baldwin wondered. 'Surely a priest would gain all the worldly wealth he could desire as he clambered up the ladder from novice to clerk to deacon and so on. A man like Pierre would have gained all he wanted as he rose through the ranks, and if he were to rise but a little farther, he would command much influence and money.'

'Oh, I shouldn't think he'd ever have enough to justify so many deaths on his conscience,' Peter said.

'There are some men who do not think of other men. Sir Hugh le Despenser is one of them. Perhaps this priest is in the same mould?' Baldwin wondered. Then he stood. 'Simon, come! We have more work to do.'

Chapter Forty-Four

They found Sir John de Sapy sitting disconsolate in the little yard near the Queen's chambers.

'Sir Peter and Sir Charles will have little to do with me since they heard of my efforts,' he said. 'But I swear, all I wanted was to be sure of my post at court.'

'Others are always jealous when someone manages to ingratiate himself with the man they would also like to be close to,' Baldwin said.

'I just don't want to be outlawed again.'

'Tell me, then, the priest. Père Pierre. How did you come to meet him?'

'My brother introduced me in a tavern. He said that if I wanted to get into Sir Hugh's favour, I should help the priest. All I had to do was lead him to that house in London, nothing more, and then keep guard outside. I heard some noises . . . but I didn't think he was going to kill anyone. He was a priest! Later I was taken to Despenser's hall. You know the Temple? He thanked me there. Despenser told me that aiding this little priest had shown I was trustworthy enough for his household. That was when he offered me this embassy.'

'Knowing that all the loose ends would be snipped away,' Baldwin noted. 'He was planning to kill you, Sir John.'

'Sweet Jesus! Does that mean my brother . . . ?'

'I think he will be safe enough. And when you yourself return home, you can tell him what happened over here, which will itself be of use to him.'

'Yes. Yes, I suppose so,' he said, looking anything but confident.

'Now, Sir John, is there anything that could tell us what made the priest want to kill the family?'

'There was one thing he said: that they were guilty of a heresy. He seemed quite warm on the matter.'

'*Heretics*,' Baldwin murmured. And then he gave a little smile. 'I wonder if we could use that against him?'

He left Simon a little while later, wandering off alone into the small orchard area behind the castle, while Simon stood guard outside the Queen's chamber. While he was there, there was a blaring of trumpets at the gate, and when he bent his head that way he saw a great procession arriving. Magnificent horses caparisoned with immensely expensive-looking equipment rode in through the gates, and behind them were more horses. Men-at-arms were everywhere, and then there came a great wagon, obviously the transport of a very wealthy person. The whole entered and formed a sweeping curve in the court, while servants dropped from their horses or the rear of the wagon and ran about, depositing steps by the wagon's door, forming a line, and standing smartly waiting.

Soon the door opened and out stepped two ecclesiastics. From their clothing Simon guessed one was a bishop, the other an archbishop.

'Dear Christ!' he heard behind him.

It was William de Bouden. He looked at the newcomers, cast a glance towards his chamber as though considering bolting for the security of his own desk, and then grimaced and turned to knock on the Queen's door.

'William, who are they?' Simon asked.

'The Bishop of Orange and the Archbishop of Vienne. They are the Pope's envoys, here to seal the peace between France and England. I don't think her Majesty will be happy to see them.'

'Why not?'

'Because we are nowhere near making peace yet. The best you could say is that we are close to extending the truce. No more than that. The whole embassy has been a failure. And those two are probably here to say that their latest discussions have also collapsed.'

'Perhaps they've done well, though?' Simon wondered hopefully.

'Look at their faces,' de Bouden snarled, and as Blaket opened the door he slipped inside.

Simon could see what he meant. If a man ever looked like a thunderstorm, it was the archbishop as he marched towards Simon. Simon stood aside to let him and the bishop pass into the Queen's chamber, and then he relaxed into his comfortable slouch once more. Two guards wandered up and took their own stations nearby, and Simon eyed them as they shared a piece of dried sausage. He saw a servant of the Queen, and asked him to bring wine for the two, who looked parched, and was soon in conversation with the one who spoke reasonable English.

'The peace looks as if it is going to end soon. Yes, the archbishop is sad. He says it is the Queen being difficult, that she never wanted for peace. He says that it is better that the land returns to the French king, but my lord the bishop says it is the French king who has slowed the talks, and that he seeks to prolong the truce.'

'Surely both want the war to end?' Simon said innocently.

The guard translated for his companion, and both chuckled. 'You think so? The French king knows that if it lasts long, your king will lose interest. He will not come to bend his knee to the French king, so the land is lost anyway. No, your queen will soon return to England. That is all there is to it.'

It was a delicious thought. Simon was absorbing this,

thinking of seeing his wife, his children – Christ's ballocks, even seeing Hugh's miserable face again – when Baldwin appeared, walking slowly up from behind the Queen's rooms. He caught a glimpse of the men in the court and stopped, gazing about with surprise.

Simon walked to him and quickly explained all he had heard.

'Well, let us hope that you're right,' Baldwin said.

'What of you?'

'I have been considering what I should do.'

'You were muttering about heresy.'

'You heard me?' Baldwin asked sharply. 'Yes. I was wondering about that. I did think that maybe my heretical past should catch up with me – but that would be very dangerous.'

'I don't understand what you are talking about, you realise?'

Baldwin took a cautious look around them before answering. 'I cannot get out of my mind the fact that the little priest has killed so many, and all at the command of the French king.'

'It happens.'

'It happened to me before. I would not have it happen again,' Baldwin said. 'My Order was destroyed by a lawyerly clerk who invented evil lies to have us arrested and tortured, many of us killed. And this one is worse. He has seen to the murder of the garrison of a castle, not to mention an innocent man and woman in London. And Chatillon, and the Comte de Foix, and Paul . . .'

'So what is in your mind?'

'I was thinking that it would be suitable for me to let him know that I was a heretic. Then, perhaps, he might try to attack me, but this time you and I would be ready for him.'

'What do you mean, let him know you are a heretic?'

'I thought to tell him that I was a Templar. If he is truly so fanatical that he would be party to the killing of any number of heretics in Pamiers after witnessing the torture to which they were put, then maybe he would do anything in his power to harm me too.'

'I may be an innocent abroad, but that strikes me as about the most dangerous, foolhardy idea you have yet had,' Simon said. 'If you tell him you were a Templar, he could call in the secular arm to have you arrested in a moment. What are you thinking of? That he'll come racing pell-mell to kill you? Every other murder he has committed, he has planned carefully to the last detail. We had no idea in most cases that he was even nearby.'

'It was only an idea,' Baldwin admitted.

'And now we are hearing that we're likely to be returning home, it's even more daft than it would be otherwise. It's repellent to have to let him live, but it would be worse to be left mouldering in a gaol here while your wife worried about you back at home.'

Baldwin's face altered subtly. 'Yes. I hadn't thought of Jeanne.'

'That's that, then.'

'I suppose so,' Baldwin agreed softly.

Easter Day[1]

Sainte-Katerine's, Paris

The morning was clear and bright, and Père Pierre sat entranced. After the Mass on Friday, in which all was mournful, desolate and gloomy at the thought of the death of Christ, this morning the whole space was filled with joy.

All about him were scruffy people from Paris, but in many

---

[1] Sunday 7 April 1325

ways that added to his delight. The place was a magnet for all those who wanted to celebrate the magnificent return to life of the Lord. There was nothing better than this. After so many years, he still felt his heart warm to the sights, sounds, and smells. The incense was wafting like a heavenly cloud all about after the procession of the Cross, and the candles appeared like beautiful little stars of golden light in among the fumes. Marvellous! A wonderful service. So much more meaningful than those of so many other churches.

Sainte-Katerine's had always held more meaning for him than the others. Somehow there was a comfort in the plainness and simple symmetry here. There was less opulence than in Notre Dame or the fabulous church at Chartres, although he did like both of them as well. No, for him, this church with its elegant simplicity was the best, and this Mass was the most delightful of the year.

He left the place with a sense of fulfilment and happiness. Stepping into the Grande Rue, he glanced northward before making his way back down towards the river and the Louvre.

'Père? Père Pierre?'

'Who are you?'

'I am called Sir Charles of Lancaster. I wanted to ask your advice, Père.'

'Speak, then, my son. What is troubling you?'

'I am with the Queen's delegation in the Château de Bois. You know of the little boy who is there with the musicians? I know you joined us on a part of the journey from the coast. You were with Peter of Oxford, were you not?'

'Yes. I think I know the boy,' Pierre admitted. He walked not too close to this grim-faced knight. There was a mild thrill of danger about him.

'The boy is to be taken in by the knight Sir Baldwin de Furnshill. You know him?'

'Yes.'

'I am concerned. The boy is my namesake, after all, and it would be wrong to allow him to be put in a position of danger, wouldn't it?'

'Undoubtedly. But what danger can there be with a knight of such reputation as Sir Baldwin?'

Sir Charles bent and whispered, 'What if the knight were a Templar who had never retracted his oaths to the Order?'

Père Pierre was shocked. Disbelievingly, he drew away. 'This is nonsense! How could he be! The Templars have been utterly destroyed. There is no sign of them any more. They are all gone.'

'How many were killed? How many died in the flames compared with the total number of warriors before the arrests? The Germans all escaped, didn't they? The Portuguese and Spanish too. How many survived, Père?'

The priest was a matter of feet away now, and he watched the knight with heavily lidded eyes. 'If what you say is true, why are you telling me? Why not denounce him to your Queen and have him arrested?'

'The Queen? Don't you think she has enough to contend with here? Didn't you hear that the papal envoys were with her all day yesterday? They'll be there again today, too, but they won't get anywhere. There's no chance of peace. Not while Mortimer lives.'

'Why is that?'

'He is holding meetings with her,' Sir Charles said off-handedly. 'He'll try to delay the negotiations, keep them going but have them mired in problems so that the Queen remains here – except she won't stay. The King her husband will demand her return before long. She is terrified of being taken back again, but she must obey her own husband. So no, she has no desire to see Sir Baldwin arrested and put on trial.'

'But you do?'

'He is a Templar. I do not mind that. Even if he is a heretic, he has behaved well enough towards me. But if this boy is given to him, what might he do to him? That is my concern.'

'You must not allow the boy to go with him, then.'

'How can I prevent it?'

'Bring him to me. Let me look after him,' Père Pierre said, and quickly gave him his address near the Louvre.

'I will do that,' Sir Charles said. 'I shall be glad to leave this city.'

'You do not enjoy this place? I find it refreshing. So beautiful, so well regulated and organised. There are few such cities in the world.'

'Alas, all I feel is a malevolence, a violence always near.'

'You must not think of the place in terms of the last few weeks, with all the deaths,' Père Pierre said. 'They were heretics. Men who deserved their end.'

'Even Robert de Chatillon?'

'Oh, yes. He served the Comte de Foix, and Foix was deeply involved in the heresies of his region. He deserved to die, and so did Chatillon.'

'What of the others?'

'If there were any who were innocent, God will know them as His own,' Pierre said easily. 'Ah. My house.'

'I thank you for your help,' Sir Charles said. With a casual look up and down the road, he waited until the priest had opened his door. Then Sir Charles swiftly thrust it wide, drew his sword, and ran Père Pierre's body through three times. Finally, while the priest squirmed on the ground, choking in his own blood, Sir Charles swept his blade along the man's belly.

'There. If God wants *you*, He can have you, and welcome!'

Baldwin was waiting in the château.

'You told him?'

'Yes.'

'Will he come?'

'No. I killed him there.'

Baldwin gaped. 'You did *what*?'

'Did you really expect me to allow Paul's murderer to live?'

'But—'

'How did I know he'd done it? It's the talk of the château. And now, if you do not mind, I shall take my rest and wait for the King of France's men to come and get me.'

'I do mind. You fool! I wanted to make sure that we had him here to confess in front of witnesses. Now what can we do? His body is where?'

'In his house. It's a single building on a road near the river.'

'Were you seen going to it?'

'I don't think so. But many will have seen me leave the church with him, I suppose.'

'I wish I'd never told you what John de Sapy said about his liking that church,' Baldwin muttered.

'You're more worried about that than about telling me you were a Templar?'

Baldwin hesitated, eyeing him contemplatively. 'I think I trust you within your limits. I wouldn't be so sure, were there a lot of money involved.'

'Ha! Well, Mortimer has gone, I think.'

'Perhaps so. Simon? Wait here with Sir Charles a while. I must fetch something.'

He returned a short while later, something bundled in his cloak, and motioned to them to join him as he walked from the castle.

Sir Charles had an excellent memory even for the tiny alleys and lanes of Paris, and before long he had led them to the house where Pierre had lived. There they waited a moment, but there was no sound of alarm, and no apparent interest in them or in the house they were waiting beside.

'Come,' Baldwin said, and hurried inside. 'We do not have much time.'

'Why? There is no urgency,' Simon pointed out.

'Simon, this is Easter Day. There will be people in the streets soon. We must be swift.'

'What do you want us to do?'

Baldwin opened his cloak. Inside was the barrel of black powder which Robert de Chatillon had given him. He stood a moment, peering down at the ruined body of Pierre. Then he withdrew the bung from the barrel and poured a dribble of powder from the body to the door. When that was done, he took one more handful from the barrel, then placed it beside the body. 'Come!'

Outside, he looked up the road again. There was no one in sight. He sprinkled the powder from his hand to make a fine line from the first, leading over the threshold and out to the road.

'No one coming?' he asked.

'No.' Simon said.

Good, Baldwin thought to himself. And he prayed quickly before setting flint to his dagger-blade. There was a spark, then another, and finally one which hit a grain.

'Simon?'

'Yes?'

'RUN!'

Chapter Forty-Five

Monday after Easter[1]

Queen's chamber, Château de Bois

Queen Isabella received the messenger in her front chamber.
As soon as she appeared, the man stood aside in the doorway
to show her brother behind him.

'My lord,' she gasped, curtseying low.

'Get up, woman! In Christ's name, there's no time for this
nonsense.'

'What is it? Is it the papal envoys?'

'Papal envoys be damned! Do you not know what your
people have been doing while you've been here?'

'Your royal highness, I am very confused. Will you please
tell me what the matter is?'

'One of your delegation has killed one of my most trusted
servants.'

'What? Who is dead?'

'A clerk in my service.'

'Who? What is his name?'

'He was called Pierre de Pamiers, and I want to speak to
your Sir Baldwin de Furnshill. I am sure it was he.'

'Why?'

'Why what?'

---

[1] Monday 8 April 1325

'Why are you so sure that it was Sir Baldwin?'

'Because he was asking me about him the day before. Then yesterday Pierre's house went up in smoke, and when we reached it and could put out the flames, there was the body of this priest inside, burned and mangled.'

'No one actually saw him, then?'

'You want me to find someone who saw him there? I will be happy to do so.'

'No. I want somebody who can tell me with their hand on the Gospels that they *did* truly see Sir Baldwin there. Not a feigned witness, a real one.'

'You doubt my words?'

'Brother, who was this man? Why should a foreigner hate him enough to murder him?'

'Baldwin had his reasons.'

'Then I shall speak to him later, if you wish. And when I am convinced I shall decide whether to bring him to you.'

'You will bring him to me immediately, woman! He has murdered in my city.'

'Brother, you will recall that he is one of my honour guard. He has guarantee of safe passage.'

'You wish me to revoke all safe conducts?'

She stared at him, but not in shock or fear. Only coldly. When she spoke, her enunciation was as precise as a bird's song. 'Brother, if you wish to revoke all, you are the King and you may do so. Immediately that happens, I shall advise the Pope and ask the Holy Father to bear in mind that any continuation of this war is now your responsibility and that the English are blameless.'

'Woman!'

'Furthermore, if you demand the arrest of any others, I will resist. I will not have my mission on behalf of my king thrown into jeopardy because of a precipitate action by you.'

'This is all your doing, isn't it? It's all because of you!' he spat suddenly.

She paled. 'I do not know the cause of anything,' she protested.

'Do you not! Well, I shall take pleasure in waving you and all your entourage off.'

'What do you mean?'

'Do you not even know that much yet? It is being bruited about all over – that your *king* has grown bored with waiting for a response to our negotiations, and is to call you home at once. Your mission has failed, my lady. And I do not care. It means I may keep my lands, and I shall not release them back to your husband.'

'What will become of them?'

'It is none of your business, my lady.'

Baldwin and Simon marched behind Blaket as he walked into the Queen's presence.

Simon had thought before that she was beautiful in her majesty, with all her fine clothes and jewels. Today, though, he saw her in her full rage. And though she was still more beautiful, if that was possible, she was also completely terrifying.

She was seated on a small throne in the middle of the room, and while Blaket took his post to the side of Simon and Baldwin, the ladies-in-waiting stood at the side of the Queen, all three on her left, Alicia nearest.

'Sir Baldwin. Do you know who visited me this morning?'

'Your brother, my lady,' he said, bowing low and keeping his eyes on the ground.

'Very observant. And what was he doing here, do you suppose?'

'Discussing the—'

'No. Not the treaty. He was here to accuse you of murdering a man of his. A man called Père Pierre.'

'I did no such thing!' Baldwin stated loudly. 'I am innocent.'

The Queen was quiet a moment. Then she rallied. 'He was convinced.'

'I am afraid I do not care, my lady. I had nothing whatever to do with his death. When was he supposed to have died?'

'I don't know such details!'

'I and my friend here were both at the chapel for the Mass yesterday, and many saw us. We did leave the château briefly later on, but only for a walk about the area. I most certainly did not draw my sword or stab anyone. The idea!'

She seemed about to say something, then hesitated. 'Leave us alone,' she said to the ladies at her side. She waved to Blaket too. 'You wait outside.'

When they were alone, she rested her chin on her knuckles. 'Very well. The truth.'

'I have told you that already.'

'My dear knight, I am no clever inquisitor, but you gave me an alibi for yesterday morning before I told you when he had died.'

'Madam, I was not there when he died, I did not order his death, I did not pay another to kill him, and was not forewarned that he would die. I had no part in it.'

Her eyes moved to Simon.

'No, lady. Nor did he.'

'Then why did my brother suspect you so strongly?'

'Ah. I will need to tell you the full story, then,' Baldwin said, and told her all about Charles's birth, his rescue from the Château Gaillard and his flight to England, where Pierre had attempted to have him killed.

'After that, your brother appears to have desired to remove all those who knew anything about his plot. The garrison, Enguerrand de Foix, Robert de Chatillon, all have died.'

'Why?'

Baldwin took a deep breath and gambled. 'Because no king would wish such news to come to the public. He is to be married to Jeanne d'Evreux in June or July, is he not? How would that lady like to be reminded that her predecessor was gaoled when she was only a child? And worse, how would she like to know that her new husband had ordered that Blanche be given to her gaolers for their sport and pleasure, or that he then commanded that her offspring should be executed for his convenience?'

The Queen studied him with a pale face that was entirely blank.

'You are an astute man, Sir Baldwin. Can no one keep anything secret from you?'

He held her gaze. 'I only seek to restrain those who would hurt others, my lady.'

'The boy. Is he well?'

'You have met him, your highness. He has played in here.'

In a flash she saw pale blue eyes, hair like straw. 'Him? No. Don't tell me. I do not need to know. You may leave. No! Wait a moment. I have heard from my brother that we may soon be recalled to England. The view is that our mission has failed. What do you think?'

Baldwin gave a low grunt. 'I think I miss my wife and children and would return to them as soon as may be. I would escape the mesh of intrigue that surrounds me at every turn here, my lady. But if you are asking whether your embassy has failed and you should abandon it, I would say no. The papal envoys are still here. Surely it will be possible to continue to discuss matters a little longer. There is no agreement so far, but perhaps you can still achieve something.'

She watched him closely. 'Very well. I thank you, Sir Baldwin.'

* * *

Joan of Bar walked slowly back into the room when the two men had left it. 'My queen?'

'You know that the King my brother says that we will be ordered to return to England soon? Sir Baldwin thinks we should remain here a while longer.'

Lady Joan had seen the Queen blossom in the last weeks here in France. She looked exhausted now, still beautiful, but bowed down under the weight of responsibility on her shoulders. The future of the Guyennois territories depended on her: a woman who had little knowledge of diplomacy. She had done her best by her kingdom and her husband. A return home should be a rest.

But to return home meant to return to her husband. Her husband and Despenser.

'My lady . . .'

Her course was clear. The Queen was to be asked to return, so she must do so. It was her duty.

Then she recalled her own husband, and she remembered the years of suffering with him. It had been intolerable, so intolerable that she had persuaded the Pope himself to release her. And now the Queen was asking for *her* advice. It brought a lump to her breast.

'My lady, you should remain here as long as you can. Don't return to him,' she hissed, and hurried from the room.

Chapter Forty-Six

Friday following Easter[1]

Maubisson

Sister Blanche heard the knock and went to the door of her cell.

It was one of those soft, damp days, with a gentle drizzle falling that was a constant delight to her. In the past she would have avoided such weather, complaining that it was uncomfortable, grey, miserable. Now, it was one more of God's pleasures. Never again would she moan and whine about the wet, or the excessive heat, the smells or sensations which He had sent. All were a pleasure to one who had been incarcerated with the fear of death for so long that the soul had grown to long for it.

'My lady?'

She felt her stomach lurch, and almost collapsed. Bile rose in her throat at the sight of the King's signs on the herald's breast. 'Yes?'

'Lady, I have been sent to ask if you are well.'

She swallowed down her terror. 'You may tell him that I am very well. I am dead – to the world and to him.'

The King inclined his head when the messenger approached,

---

[1] Friday 12 April 1325

and listened with a stony countenance as he heard Blanche's message. But when he understood that there was a gift too, a fleeting consternation passed over his face. And then, when he took the little draw-string bag and opened it, he saw the ruby rosary.

'It is a pretty thing,' he murmured to himself. He took it out and admired it for a moment. The messenger was staring with open admiration. 'You like it?'

'My Liege, it is so . . . so beautiful . . .' the man stammered.

'Take it. I gave it once to a whore. It is worthless.'